HARD AS
NAILS

Other Joe Kurtz Novels by Dan Simmons

Hard Case
Hard Freeze

DAN SIMMONS

ST. MARTIN'S MINOTAUR
NEW YORK

www.minotaurbooks.com

Library of Congress Cataloging-in-Publication Data

Simmons, Dan.
    Hard as nails / Dan Simmons.—1st ed.
       p. cm.
    ISBN 0-312-30528-1
    1. Ex-convicts—Fiction.   2. Narcotic addicts—Crimes against—Fiction.
3. Amusement parks—Fiction.   4. Organized crime—Fiction.   5. Buffalo
(N.Y.)—Fiction.   I. Title.

PS3569.I47292H35   2003
813'.54—dc21

                                                                    2003047076

First Edition: October 2003

10   9   8   7   6   5   4   3   2   1

"Hard," replied the Dodger. "As nails," added Charley Bates.
—*Oliver Twist* by Charles Dickens

HARD AS NAILS

CHAPTER ONE

On the day he was shot in the head, things were going strangely well for Joe Kurtz. In fact, things had been going strangely well for weeks. Later, he told himself that he should have known that the universe was getting ready to readjust its balance of pain at his expense.

And at much greater expense to the woman who was standing next to him when the shots were fired.

He had a two P.M. appointment with his parole officer and he was there at the Civic Center on time. Because curb parking around the courthouse was almost impossible at that time of day, Kurtz used the parking garage under the combined civic, justice, and family court complex. The best thing about his parole officer was that she validated.

Actually, Kurtz realized, that wasn't the best thing about her at all. Probation Officer Margaret "Peg" O'Toole, formerly of the Buffalo P.D. narcotics and vice squad, had treated him decently, knew and liked his secretary—Arlene DeMarco—and had once helped Kurtz out of a deep hole when an overzealous detective had tried to send him back to County lock-up on a trumped-up weapons charge. Joe Kurtz had made more than a few enemies during his eleven and a half years serving time for manslaughter in Attica, and odds were poor that he'd last long in general population, even in County. In addition to validating his parking stubs, Peg O'Toole had probably saved his life.

She was waiting for him when he knocked on the door and entered her second-floor office. Come to think of it, O'Toole had never kept him waiting. While many parole officers worked out of cubicles, O'Toole had earned herself a real office with windows overlooking the Erie County Holding

Center on Church Street. Kurtz figured that on a clear day she could watch the winos being dragged into the drunk tank.

"Mr. Kurtz." She gestured him to his usual chair.

"Agent O'Toole." He took his usual chair.

"We have an important date coming up, Mr. Kurtz," said O'Toole, looking at him and then down at his folder.

Kurtz nodded. In a few weeks it would be one year since he left Attica and reported to his parole officer. Since there had been no real problems—or at least none she or the cops had heard about—he should be visiting her once a month soon, rather than weekly. Now she asked her usual questions and Kurtz gave his usual answers.

Peg O'Toole was an attractive woman in her late thirties—overweight by current standards of perfection but all the more attractive in Kurtz's eyes for that, with long, auburn hair, green eyes, a taste for expensive but conservative clothing, and a Sig Pro nine-millimeter semiautomatic pistol in her purse. Kurtz knew the make because he'd seen the weapon.

He liked O'Toole—and not just for helping him out of the frame-up a year ago this coming November—but also because she was as no-nonsense and non-condescending as a parole officer can be with a "client." He'd never had an erotic thought about her, but that wasn't her fault. There was just something about the act of imagining an ex-police officer with her clothes off that worked on Kurtz like a 1,000-cc dose of anti-Viagra.

"Are you still working with Mrs. DeMarco on the Sweetheart Search dot com business?" asked O'Toole. As a felon, Kurtz couldn't be licensed by the state of New York for his former job—P.I.—but he could operate this business of finding old high school flames, first via the Internet—that was his secretary Arlene's part of it—then by a bit of elementary skip-tracing. That was Kurtz's part of it.

"I tracked down a former high school football captain this morning in North Tonawanda," said Kurtz, "to hand him a handwritten letter from his former cheerleader girlfriend."

O'Toole looked up from her notes and removed her tortoise-shell glasses. "Did the football hero still look like a football hero?" she asked, showing only the faintest trace of a smile.

"They were both from Kenmore West's Class of '61," said Kurtz. "The guy was fat, bald, and lived in a trailer that's seen better days. It had a

Confederate flag hung on the side of it and a clapped-out '72 Camaro parked outside."

O'Toole winced. "How about the cheerleader?"

Kurtz shrugged. "If there was a photo, it was in the sealed letter. But I can guess."

"Let's not," said O'Toole. She put her glasses back on and glanced back at her form. "How is the WeddingBells-dot-com business going?"

"Slowly," said Kurtz. "Arlene has the whole Internet thing set up—all the contacts and contracts with dressmakers, cardmakers, cakemakers, musicians, churches and reception halls set in place—and money's coming in, but I'm not sure how much. I really don't have much to do with that side of the business."

"But you're an investor and co-owner?" said the parole officer. There was no hint of sarcasm in her voice.

"Sort of," said Kurtz. He knew that O'Toole had seen the articles of incorporation during a visit the parole officer had made to their new office in June. "I roll over some of my income from SweetheartSearch back into WeddingBells and get a cut in return." Kurtz paused. He wondered how the felons and shankmeisters and Aryan Brotherhood boys in the exercise yard at Attica would react if they heard him say that. The D-Block Mosque guys would probably drop the price on his head from $15,000 to $10,000 out of sheer contempt.

O'Toole took off her glasses again. "I've been thinking of using Mrs. DeMarco's services."

Kurtz had to blink at that. "For WeddingBells? To set up all the details of a wedding online?"

"Yes."

"Ten percent discount to personal acquaintances," said Kurtz. "I mean, you've met Arlene."

"I know what you meant, Mr. Kurtz." O'Toole put her glasses back on. "You still have a room at . . . what is the hotel's name? Harbor Inn?"

"Yes." Kurtz's old flophouse hotel, the Royal Delaware Arms near downtown, had been shut down in July by the city inspectors. Only the bar of the huge old building remained open and the word was that the only customers there were the rats. Kurtz needed an address for the parole board, and the Harbor Inn served as one. He hadn't gotten around to telling O'Toole that the little hotel on the south side was actually boarded up and abandoned or that he'd leased the entire building for less than the price of his room at the old Delaware Arms.

"It's at the intersection of Ohio and Chicago Streets?"

"Right."

"I'd like to drop by and just look at it next week if you don't mind," said the parole officer. "Just to verify your address."

Shit, he thought. "Sure," he said.

O'Toole sat back and Kurtz thought that the short interview was over. The meetings had been getting more and more pro forma in recent months. He wondered if Officer O'Toole was becoming more laid back after the hot summer just past and with the pleasant autumn just winding down—the leaves on the only tree visible outside her window were a brilliant orange but ready to blow off.

"You seem to have recovered completely from your automobile accident last winter," said the parole officer. "I haven't seen even a hint of a limp the last few visits."

"Yeah, pretty much full recovery," said Kurtz. His "automobile accident" the previous February had included being knifed, thrown out of a third story window, and crashing through a plaster portico at the old Buffalo train station, but he hadn't seen any pressing need for the probation office to know the details. The cover story had been a pain for Kurtz, since he'd had to sell his perfectly good twelve-year-old Volvo—he could hardly be seen driving around in the car he was supposed to have wracked up on a lonely stretch of winter highway—and now he was driving a much older red Pinto. He missed the Volvo.

"You grew up around Buffalo, didn't you, Mr. Kurtz?"

He didn't react, but he felt the skin tighten on his face. O'Toole knew his personal history from the dossier on her desktop, and she'd never ventured into his pre-Attica history before. *What'd I do?*

He nodded.

"I'm not asking professionally," said Peg O'Toole. "I just have a minor mystery—very minor—that I need solved, and I think I need someone who grew up here."

"You didn't grow up here?" asked Kurtz. Most people who still lived in Buffalo had.

"I was born here, but we moved away when I was three," she said, opening the bottom right drawer of her desk and moving some things aside.

"I moved back eleven years ago when I joined the Buffalo P.D." She brought out a white envelope. "Now I need the advice of a native and a private investigator."

Kurtz stared flatly at her. "I'm not a private investigator," he said, his voice flatter than his gaze.

"Not licensed," agreed O'Toole, evidently not intimidated by his cold stare or tone. "Not after serving time for manslaughter. But everything I've read or been told suggests you were an excellent P.I."

Kurtz almost reacted to this. *What the hell is she after?*

She removed three photographs from the envelope and slid them across the desk. "I wondered if you might know where this is—or was?"

Kurtz looked at the photos. They were color, standard snapshot size, no borders, no date on the back, so they'd been taken sometime in the last couple of decades. The first photograph showed a broken and battered Ferris wheel, some cars missing, rising above bare trees on a wooded hilltop. Beyond the abandoned Ferris wheel was a distant valley and the hint of what might be a river. The sky was low and gray. The second photo showed a dilapidated bumper-car pavilion in an overgrown meadow. The pavilion's roof had partially collapsed and there were overturned and rusted bumper cars on the pavilion floor and scattered outside among the brittle winter or late-autumn weeds. One of the cars—Number 9 emblazoned on its side in fading gold script—lay upside down in an icy puddle. The final photograph was a close-up of a merry-go-round or carousel horse's head, paint faded, its muzzle and mouth smashed away and showing rotted wood.

Kurtz looked at each of the photographs again and said, "No idea."

O'Toole nodded as if she expected that answer. "Did you used to go to any amusement parks around here when you were a kid?"

Kurtz had to smile at that. His childhood hadn't included any amusement park visits.

O'Toole actually blushed. "I mean, where did people go to amusement parks in Western New York in those days, Mr. Kurtz? I know that Six Flags at Darien Lake wasn't here then."

"How do you know this place is from way back then?" asked Kurtz. "It could have been abandoned a year ago. Vandals work fast."

O'Toole nodded. "But the rust and . . . it just seems old. From the seventies at least. Maybe the sixties."

Kurtz shrugged and handed the photos back. "People used to go up to Crystal Beach, on the Canadian side."

O'Toole nodded again. "But that was right on the lake, right? No hills, no woods?"

"Right," said Kurtz. "And it wasn't abandoned like that. When the time came, they tore it down and sold the rides and concessions."

The parole officer took off her glasses and stood. "Thank you, Mr. Kurtz. I appreciate your help." She held out her hand as she always did. It had startled Kurtz the first time she'd done it. They shook hands as they always did at the end of their weekly interviews. She had a good, strong grip. Then she validated his parking ticket. That was the other half of the weekly ritual.

He was opening the door to leave when she said, "And I may really give Mrs. DeMarco a call about the other thing."

Kurtz assumed that "the other thing" was the parole officer's wedding. "Yeah," he said. "You've got our office number and website address."

L ater, he would think that if he hadn't stopped to take a leak in the first-floor restroom, everything would have been different. But what the hell—he had to take a leak, so he did. It didn't take reading Marcus Aurelius to know that *everything* you did made everything different, and if you dwelt on it, you'd go nuts.

He came down the stairway into the parking garage corridor and there was Peg O'Toole, green dress, high heels, purse and all, just out of the elevator and opening the heavy door to the garage. She paused when she saw Kurtz. He paused. There was no way that a probation officer wanted to walk into an underground parking garage with one of her clients, and Kurtz wasn't keen on the idea either. But there was also no way out of it unless he went back up the stairs or—even more absurdly—stepped into the elevator. *Damn.*

O'Toole broke the frozen minute by smiling and holding the door open for him.

Kurtz nodded and walked past her into the cool semi-darkness. She could let him get a dozen paces in front of her if she wanted. He wouldn't look back. Hell, he'd been in for manslaughter, not rape.

She didn't wait long. He heard the clack of her heels a few paces behind him, heading to his right.

"Wait!" cried Kurtz, turning toward her and raising his right hand.

O'Toole froze, looked startled, and lifted her purse where, he knew, she usually carried the Sig Pro.

The goddamned lights had been broken. When he'd come in less than half an hour earlier, there had been fluorescent lights every twenty-five feet or so, but half of those were out. The pools of darkness between the remaining lights were wide and black.

"Back!" shouted Kurtz, pointing toward the door from which they'd just emerged.

Looking at him as if he were crazy, but not visibly afraid, Peg O'Toole put her hand in her purse and started to pull the Sig Pro.

The shooting started.

CHAPTER
TWO

When Kurtz awoke in the hospital, he knew at once that he'd been shot, but he couldn't remember when or where it happened, or who did it. He had the feeling that someone had been with him but he couldn't bring back any details and any attempt to do so hammered barbed spikes through his brain.

Kurtz knew the varieties and vintages of pain the way some men knew wines, but this pain in his head was already beyond the judging stage and well into the realm where screaming was the only sane response. But he didn't scream. It would hurt too much.

The hospital room was mostly dark but even the dim light from the bedside table hurt his eyes. Everything had a nimbus around it and when he attempted to focus his eyes, nausea rose up through the pain like a shark fin cutting through oily water. He solved that by closing his eyes. Now there were only the inevitable, ambient hospital sounds from beyond the closed door—intercom announcements, the squeak of rubber soles on tile, inaudible conversations in that muffled tone heard only in hospitals and betting parlors—but each and every one of these sounds, including the rasp of his own breathing, was too loud for Joe Kurtz.

He started to raise his hand to rub the right side of his head—the epicenter of this universe of pain—but his hand jarred to a halt next to the metal bedrail.

It took Kurtz two more tries and several groggy seconds of mental effort and the pain of opening his eyes again before he realized why his right arm wouldn't work; he was handcuffed to the metal frame of the hospital bed.

It took him another minute or two before he realized that his left hand

and arm were free. Slowly, laboriously, Kurtz reached that hand across his face—eyes squinted to keep the nausea at bay—and touched the right side of his head, just above his ear, where the pain was broadcasting like the concentric radio-wave ripples in the beginning of one of those old RKO films.

He could feel that the right side of his head was a mass of bandages and tape. But when he saw that there were only two IVs visible punched into his body and only one monitoring machine beeping a few feet away, and no doctors or nurses huddled around with their resuscitation crash cart, he figured he wasn't on the verge of checking out yet. Either that, or they'd already given up on him, issued a Do Not Resuscitate order, and gone off for coffee to leave him to die here in the dark.

"Fuck it," said Kurtz and winced as the pain went from 7.8 to 8.6 on his own private Agony Richter Scale. He was used to pain, but this was . . . silly.

He dropped his hand on his chest, closed his eyes, and allowed himself to float out of the line of fire.

Mr. Kurtz? Mr. Kurtz?"

Kurtz awoke with the same blurred vision, same nausea, but different pain. It was worse. Some fool was pulling his eyelids back and shining a light in his eyes.

"Mr. Kurtz?" The face making the sound was brown, male, middle-aged and mild-looking behind black-rimmed glasses. He was wearing a white coat. "I'm Dr. Singh, Mr. Kurtz. I dealt with your injuries in the ER and just came from surgery on your friend."

Kurtz got the face into focus. He wanted to say "What friend?" but it wasn't worth trying to speak yet. Not yet.

"You were struck in the right side of your head by a bullet, Mr. Kurtz, but it did not penetrate your skull," said Singh in his mild, sing-song voice that sounded like three chainsaws roaring to Kurtz.

Superman, thought Kurtz. *Fucking bullets bounce right off.*

"Why?" he said.

"What, Mr. Kurtz?"

Kurtz had to close his eyes at the thought of speaking again. Forcing himself to articulate, he said, "Why . . . didn't . . . bullet . . . penetrate?"

Singh nodded his understanding. "It was a small caliber bullet, Mr. Kurtz. A twenty-two. Before it struck you, it had passed through the upper arm of . . . of the person with you . . . and ricocheted off the concrete pillar behind you. It was considerably flattened and much of its kinetic energy had been expended. Still, if you had been turning your head to the right rather than to the left when it struck you, we would be extracting it from your brain as we speak—probably during an autopsy."

All in all, thought Kurtz, more information than he had needed at the moment.

"As it is," continued Singh, the soft sing-song voice sawing away through Kurtz's skull, "you have a moderate-to-severe concussion and a subcranial hematoma that does not require trepanning at this time, your left eye will not dilate, blood has drained down beneath your eyes and the whites of your eyes are very bloodshot—but that is not important. We'll assess motor skills and secondary effects in the morning."

"Who . . ." began Kurtz. He wasn't even sure what he was going to ask. *Who shot me? Who was with me? Who's going to pay for this?*

"The police are here, Mr. Kurtz," interrupted Dr. Singh. "It's the reason we haven't administered any painkiller since you regained consciousness. They need to talk to you."

Kurtz didn't turn his head to look, but when the doctor moved aside he could see the two detectives, plainclothes, one male, one female, one black, one white. Kurtz didn't know the black male. He had once been in love with the white female.

The black detective, dressed nattily in tweed, vest, and school tie, stepped closer. "Joseph Kurtz, I'm Detective Paul Kemper. My partner and I are investigating the shooting of you and Parole Officer Margaret O'Toole . . ." began the man in an almost avuncular resonant voice.

Oh, shit, thought Kurtz. He closed his eyes and remembered O'Toole opening a door for him.

". . . can be used against you in a court of law," the man was saying. "If you cannot afford an attorney, one will be appointed for you. Do you understand your rights as I've just explained them to you?"

Kurtz said something through the pain.

"What?" said Detective Kemper. Kurtz changed his mind. The man's voice wasn't nearly as friendly or avuncular-sounding now.

"Didn't shoot her," repeated Kurtz.

"Did you understand your rights as I explained them to you?"

"Yeah."

"And do you wish an attorney at this time?"

I wish some Darvocet or morphine at this time, thought Kurtz. "Yeah . . . I mean, no. No attorney."

"You'll talk to us now?"

How many fucking times are you going to ask me? thought Kurtz. He realized that he'd spoken this aloud only when the male detective got a stern don't-fuck-with-me cop look on his face and the female detective still standing against the far wall chuckled. Kurtz knew that chuckle.

"Why were you in the garage with Officer O'Toole?" asked Kemper. The detective's voice sounded totally un-avuncular this time.

"Coincidence." Kurtz had never noticed how many syllables were in that word before today. All four of them hit him like hot spikes behind the eyes. He needed shorter words.

"Did you fire her weapon?"

"I don't remember," said Kurtz, sounding like every perp he'd ever questioned.

Kemper sighed and shot a glance at his partner. Kurtz also looked at her and watched her look back at him. She obviously recognized him. She must have recognized his name before they started this interview. Is that why she wasn't speaking? She was, Kurtz was startled to realize through the pain in his head, as beautiful as ever. More beautiful.

"Did you see the assailant or assailants?" asked Kemper.

"I don't remember."

"Did you enter the garage as part of a conspiracy to shoot and kill Officer O'Toole?"

Kurtz just looked at him. He knew that he was stupid with pain and concussion at the moment, but nobody was that stupid.

Dr. Singh filled the silence. "Detectives, a concussion of this severity is often accompanied by memory loss of the accident that created it."

"Uh-huh," said Kemper, closing his notebook. "This was no accident, Doctor. And this guy remembers everything he wants to remember."

"Paul," said the female detective, "leave him alone. We have the tapes. Let Kurtz get some painkiller and sleep and we'll talk to him in the morning."

"He'll be all lawyered up in the morning," said Kemper.

The woman shook her head. "No he won't."

It'd been twenty years since Kurtz had last seen Rigby King—what was her married name? Something Arabic, he thought—but she still looked like the Rigby he'd known at Father Baker's and again in Thailand. Brown eyes, full figure, short dark hair, and a smile as quick and radiant as the gymnast she'd been named for.

Kemper left the room and Rigby came to the side of the bed and raised a hand as if she was going to squeeze Kurtz's shoulder. Instead she gripped the metal railing of the hospital bed and shook it slightly, making Kurtz's handcuffed wrist and arm sway.

"Get some sleep, Joe."

"Yeah."

When they were both gone, Singh called in a nurse and they injected something into the IV port.

"Something for the pain and a mild sedative," said the doctor. "We've kept you semi-conscious and under observation long enough to let you sleep now without worrying unduly about the concussion's effects."

"Yeah," said Kurtz.

As soon as the two left, Kurtz reached down, ripped away gauze and tape, and pulled the IV out of his left arm.

Joe Kurtz had seen what could happen to a man doped up and helpless in a hospital bed. Besides, he had a lot of thinking to do through the pain before morning came.

CHAPTER
THREE

The two men came in the night, entering his room sometime after three A.M.

Kurtz had nothing to defend himself with—he would have stolen a knife and hidden it under his pillows if the hospital had provided him with a dinner, but they hadn't fed him, so he was still handcuffed and defenseless. He readied himself the only way he could think of—sliding the long intravenous needle on its flexible tube down into his left hand and focusing his energy to swing it into an attacker's eye if he got close enough. But if one or both of these men pulled a gun, Kurtz's only hope was to throw himself to his left and try to tip the entire hospital bed onto himself while screaming bloody murder.

Squinting through his headache pain at the two shadows in the doorway, Kurtz wasn't sure he'd have the strength to tip the bed over. Besides, mattresses, even hospital mattresses, were notoriously poor armor against bullets.

There was a nurse-call button clipped to his pillow above Kurtz's head, but his right hand couldn't reach it because of the handcuffs and he wasn't about to release or reveal the IV needle in his left hand.

Kurtz could see the two men silhouetted in the doorway in the minute before they entered the room, and then the dim glow from medical monitors illuminated them. One man was tall, very thin, and Asian; his black hair was combed straight back and he was wearing an expensive dark suit. His hands were empty. The closer man was in a wheelchair, wheeling himself toward Kurtz's bed with thrusts of his powerful arms.

Kurtz didn't pretend he was asleep. He watched the man in the wheelchair come on. Any hopes that it was an errant hospital patient out of his bed at three A.M. disappeared as Kurtz saw that this man was also wearing a suit and tie. He was old—Kurtz saw the thinning gray hair cut in a buzz cut and the lines and scars on the man's tanned face, but his eyebrows were jet black, his chin strong, and his expression fierce. The old man's upper body looked large and powerful, his hands huge, but even in the dim light, Kurtz could see that his trousers were covering wasted sticks.

The Asian man's expression was neutral and he stayed two feet behind the big man in the chair.

The wheels of the chair squeaked on tile until the wasted legs bumped into Kurtz's bed. Working to focus, Kurtz stared past his own handcuffed wrist and into the old man's cold, blue eyes. All Kurtz could do now was hope that the visit was a friendly one.

"You miserable low-life useless scumbag piece of shit," hissed the old man. "It should've been you who got the bullet in the brain."

So much for the friendly visit theory.

The big man in the wheelchair raised his huge hand and slapped Kurtz in the side of the head, right where the bandages and tape were massed above the wound.

Riding the pain for the next few seconds was probably a lot like riding the old rollercoaster at Crystal Beach while standing up. Kurtz wanted to throw up and pass out, in that order, but he forced himself to do neither. He opened his eyes and slipped the long IV needle between the third and fourth fingers of his left hand the way he'd learned how to grip a handleless shank-blade in Attica.

"You worthless fuck," said the man in the chair, his voice loud now. "If she dies, I'll kill you with my bare hands." He slapped Kurtz again, a powerful, open-handed smash across the mouth, but this wasn't nearly so painful. Kurtz turned his head back and watched the old man's eyes and the Asian's hands.

"Major," the Asian said softly. The tall man gently put his hands on the grips of the wheelchair and pulled the old man three feet back. "We have to go."

The Major's mad, blue-eyed stare never left Kurtz's face. Kurtz didn't mind this. He'd been hate-stared at by experts. But he had to admit that this old man was a finalist in that contest.

"Major," whispered the tall man and the man in the chair finally broke the gaze, but not before lifting his huge, blunt forefinger and shaking it at Kurtz as if to make a promise. Kurtz saw that the finger was bloody a second before he felt the blood flowing down his right temple.

The Asian wheeled the old man around and pushed him out the door into the dimly lighted hallway. Neither man looked back.

K urtz didn't think he'd go to sleep after that—or, rather, lose consciousness, since real sleep wasn't an option above this baseline of pain—but he must have, because he woke up with James Bond looking down at him in the early morning light.

This wasn't the real James Bond—Sean Connery—but that newest guy: dark hair blowdried and combed back, sardonic smile, impeccable suit from Saville Row or somewhere—Kurtz had no idea what a Saville Row suit looked like—plus a gleaming white shirt with spread collar, tasteful paisley tie sporting a Windsor knot, pocket square ruffled perfectly and not so gauche as to match the tie, tasteful Rolex just visible beneath the perfectly shot starched cuff.

"Mr. Kurtz?" said James Bond, "My name is Kennedy. Brian Kennedy."

Kurtz thought that he did also look a bit like that Kennedy scion who'd flown his plane and passengers upside-down into the sea.

Brian Kennedy started to offer Kurtz a heavy cream business card, noticed the handcuffs, and without interrupting his motion, set the card on the bedside table.

"How are you feeling, Mr. Kurtz?" asked Kennedy.

"Who are you?" managed Kurtz. He thought he must be feeling better. These three syllables had made his vision dance with pain, but hadn't made him want to puke.

The handsome man touched his card. "I own and run Empire State Security and Executive Protection. Our Buffalo branch provided security cameras for the parking garage in which yesterday's shooting took place."

Every other light had been knocked out when we came into the garage, thought Kurtz. *That tipped me.* The memory of the shooting was seeping back into his bruised brain like sludge under a closed door.

He said nothing to Kennedy-Bond. Was the man here because of some lawsuit potential to his company? Kurtz was having trouble working this out through the pain so he stared and let Kennedy keep talking.

"We've given the police the original surveillance tape from the garage," continued Kennedy. "The footage doesn't show the shooters, but it's obvious that your actions—and Officer O'Toole's—are visible and clearly above suspicion."

Then why am I still cuffed? thought Kurtz. Instead, he managed to say, "How is she? O'Toole?"

Brian Kennedy's face was James-Bond cool as he said, "She was hit three times. All twenty-two slugs. One broke a left rib. Another passed through her upper arm, ricocheted, and hit you. But one caught her in the temple and lodged in her brain, left frontal lobe. They got it out after five hours of surgery and had to take some of the damaged brain tissue out as well. She's in a partially induced coma—whatever that means—but it looks as if she has a chance for survival, none for total recovery."

"I want to see the tape," said Kurtz. "You said you gave the cops the original, which means you made a copy."

Kennedy cocked his head. "Why do you . . . oh, you don't remember the attack, do you? You were telling the detectives the truth."

Kurtz waited.

"All right," said Kennedy. "Give me a call at the Buffalo number on the card whenever you're ready to . . ."

"Today," said Kurtz. "This afternoon."

Kennedy paused at the door and smiled that cynical, bemused James Bond smile. "I don't think you'll be . . ." he began and then paused to look at Kurtz. "All right, Mr. Kurtz," he said, "it certainly won't please the investigating officers if they ever discover I've done this, but we'll have the tape ready to show you when you stop by our offices this afternoon. I guess you've earned the right to see it."

Kennedy started through the door but then stopped and turned back again. "Peg and I are engaged," he said softly. "We'd planned to get married in April."

Then he was gone and a nurse was bustling in with a bedpan jug and something that might be breakfast.

It's bloody Grand Central Station here, thought Kurtz. Dr. Singh came in—after Kurtz had ignored everything on the breakfast tray except the knife—to shine a penlight in his eyes, check under the bandages, tut-tut at all the bleeding visible—Kurtz didn't mention the cuff in the head from Mr. Wheelchair—to direct the nurse in replacing the gauze and tape, to tell Kurtz that they'd be keeping him another twenty-four hours for observation, and to order more X-rays of his skull. And finally Singh said that the officer who had been guarding this end of the hall was gone.

"When did he leave?" asked Kurtz. Sitting propped up against the pillows, he found it was easier to focus his eyes this morning. The pain in his head continued like a heavy sleet-storm against a metal roof, but that was better than the steel spikes being driven into his skull the night before. Red and yellow circles of pain from the penlight exercise still danced in his vision.

"I wasn't on duty," said Singh, "but I believe around midnight."

Before Wheelchair and Bruce Lee showed up, thought Kurtz. He said, "Any chance of getting these cuffs off? I wasn't able to eat my breakfast left-handed."

Singh looked physically pained, his brown eyes sad behind the glasses. "I'm truly sorry, Mr. Kurtz. I believe that one of the detectives is already downstairs. I'm sure they will release you."

She was and she did.

Ten minutes after Singh bustled out into the now-busy hospital corridor, Rigby King showed up. She was wearing a blue linen blazer, white t-shirt, new jeans, and running shoes. She carried a 9-mm Glock on her belt on the right side, concealed under the blazer until she leaned forward. She said nothing while she unlocked his cuffs, snapping them onto the back of her belt like the veteran cop she was. Kurtz didn't want to speak first, but he needed information.

"I had visitors during the night," he said. "After you pulled your uniform off hallway guard."

Rigby folded her arms and frowned slightly. "Who?"

"You tell me," said Kurtz. "Old guy in a wheelchair and a tall Asian."

Rigby nodded but said nothing.

"You going to tell me who they are?" asked Kurtz. "The old man in the wheelchair slapped me up the side of the head. Considering the circumstances, I should know who's mad at me."

"The man in the wheelchair must have been Major O'Toole, retired," said Rigby King. "The Vietnamese man is probably his business colleague, Vinh or Trinh or something."

"Major O'Toole," said Kurtz. "The parole officer's father?"

"Uncle. The famous Big John O'Toole's older brother, Michael."

"Big John?" said Kurtz.

"Peg O'Toole's old man was a hero cop in this city, Joe. He died in the line of duty about four years ago, not long before he would've retired. I guess you didn't hear about it up in Attica."

"I guess not."

"You say he hit you?"

"Slapped," said Kurtz.

"He must think you had something to do with his niece getting shot in the head."

"I didn't."

"So you remember things now?"

Her voice still did strange things to him—that mixture of softness and rasp. Or maybe it was the concussion acting on him.

"No," said Kurtz. "I don't remember anything clearly after leaving the P.O.'s office after the interview. But I know that whatever happened to O'Toole in the garage, I didn't make it happen."

"How do you know that?"

Kurtz held up his freed right hand.

Rigby smiled ever so slightly at that and he remembered why they'd nicknamed her Rigby. Her smile was like sunlight.

"Did you have any problems with Agent Peg O'Toole?" she asked.

Kurtz shook his head and then had to hold it with both hands.

"You in a lot of pain, Joe?" Her tone was neutral enough, but seemed to carry a slight subtext of concern.

"Remember that guy you had to use your baton on in Patpong in the alley behind Pussies Galore?" he said.

"Bangkok?" said Rigby. "You mean the guy who stole the sex performer's razor blades and tried to use them on me?"

"Yeah."

He could see her remembering. "I got written up for that by that REMF loot . . . whatshisname, the asshole . . ."

"Sheridan."

"Yeah," said Rigby. "Excessive force. Just because the guy I brought in had a little tiny bit of brains leaking out his ear."

"Well, that guy had nothing on how I feel today," said Kurtz.

"Tough situation," said Rigby. There was no undercurrent of concern audible now. Kurtz knew that the words could be abbreviated 'T.S.' She walked to the door. "If you can remember Lieutenant Sheridan, you can remember yesterday, Joe."

He shrugged.

"When you do, you call us. Kemper or me. Got it?"

"I want to go home and take an aspirin," said Kurtz. Trying to put just a bit of whine in his voice.

"Sorry. The docs want to keep you here another day. Your clothes and wallet have been . . . stored . . . until you're ready to travel." She started to leave.

"Rig?" he said.

She paused, but frowned, as if not pleased to hear him use the diminutive of her old nickname.

"I didn't shoot O'Toole and I don't know who did."

"All right, Joe," she said. "But you know, don't you, that Kemper and I are going on the assumption that she wasn't the target. That someone was trying to kill you in that garage and poor O'Toole just got in the way."

"Yeah," Kurtz said wearily. "I know."

She left without another word. Kurtz waited a few minutes, got laboriously out of bed—hanging onto the metal railing a minute to get his balance—and then padded around the room and bathroom looking for his clothes, even though he knew they wouldn't be there. Since he'd ignored Nurse Ratchet's bedpan jar, he paused in the toilet long enough to take a leak. Even that hurt his head.

Then Kurtz got the IV stand on wheels and pushed it out ahead of him into the hallway. Nothing in the universe looked so pathetic and harmless as a man in a hospital gown, ass showing through the opening in the back, shuffling along shoving an IV stand. One nurse, not his, stopped to ask him where he was going.

"X-ray," said Kurtz. "They said to take the elevator."

"Heavens, you shouldn't be walking," said the nurse, a young blonde. "I'll get an orderly and a gurney. You go back to your room and lie down."

"Sure," said Kurtz.

The first room he looked in had two old ladies in the two beds. The second had a young boy. The father, sitting in a chair next to the bed, obviously awaiting the doctor's early rounds, looked up at Kurtz with the gaze of a deer in a hunter's flashlight beam—alarmed, hopeful, resigned, waiting for the shot.

"Sorry," said Kurtz and shuffled off to the next room.

The old man in the third room was obviously dying. The curtain was pulled as far out as it could be, he was the only occupant of the double room, and the chart on the foot of his bed had a small blue slip of paper with the letters DNR on it. The old man's breathing, even on a respirator, was very close to a Cheyne-Stokes death rattle.

Kurtz found the clothes folded and stored neatly on the bottom shelf of the small closet—an old man's outfit—corded trousers that were only a little too small, plaid shirt, socks, scuffed Florsheims that were slightly too large for Kurtz, and a raincoat that looked like a castoff from Peter Falk's closet. Luckily, the old guy had also brought a hat—a Bogey fedora with authentic sweat stains and the brim already snapped down in a perfect crease. Kurtz wondered what relative would be cleaning this closet out in a day or so and if they'd miss the hat.

He walked to the elevators with much more spring in his stride than he was really capable of, glancing neither left nor right. Rather than stopping at the lobby, he took the elevator all the way to the parking garage and then followed the open ramp up and out into brisk air and sunlight.

There was a cab near the emergency entrance and Kurtz got the door opened before the cabbie saw him coming and then collapsed into the back seat. He gave the driver his home address.

The cabbie turned, squinted, and said around his toothpick. "I was supposed to pick Mr. Goldstein and his daughter."

"I'm Goldstein," said Kurtz. "My daughter's visiting someone else in the hospital for a while. Go on."

"Mr. Goldstein's supposed to be an old man in his eighties. Only one leg."

"The miracles of modern medicine," said Kurtz. He looked the cabbie in the eye. "Drive."

CHAPTER
FOUR

Kurtz's new home, The Harbor Inn, was an abandoned, triangular three-story old bar and bargeman's hotel standing alone amidst weed-filled fields south of downtown Buffalo. To get to it, you had to cross the Buffalo River on a one-lane metal bridge between abandoned grain elevators. The bridge rose vertically as a single unit for barge traffic—almost non-existent now—and a sign on the superstructure informed snowplows: "Raise Plow Before Crossing." Once onto what locals called "the Island," although it wasn't technically an island, the air smelled of burned Cheerios because the only remaining operating structure amidst the abandoned warehouses and silos was the big General Mills plant between the river and Lake Erie.

The main entrance to the Harbor Inn—still boarded over but boarded now with a lock and hinge—was at the apex of the building's triangle where Ohio and Chicago Streets came together. There was a ten-foot-tall metal lighthouse hanging out over that entrance, its blue and white paint and The Harbor Inn logo beneath it so rust-flaked that it looked like someone had machine-gunned it. A fading wooden sign on the boarded door read—FOR LEASE, ELICOTT DEVELOPMENT COMPANY and gave a 716 phone number. Beneath that sign was older, even more faded lettering announcing

Chicken Wings—Chili, Sandwiches—Daily Specials.

Kurtz got the extra key from its hiding place, unpadlocked the front door, pulled the board out of his way, stepped in, and locked it all behind him. Only a few glimmers of sunlight came over and under the boards into this triangular main space—the old lobby and restaurant of the inn. Dust, plaster, and broken boards were scattered everywhere except on the path he'd cleared. The air smelled of mold and rot.

To the left of the hallway behind this space was the narrow staircase leading upstairs. Kurtz checked some small telltales and went up, walking slowly and grabbing the railing when the pain in his head made him dizzy.

He'd fixed up three rooms and one bathroom on the second floor, although there were hidey holes and escape routes out of all nine rooms up here. He'd replaced the windows and cleaned up the big triangular room in front—not as his bedroom, that was a smaller room next to it, but as an exercise room, fitted out with a speed bag, heavy bag, a treadmill he'd scavenged from the junk heap behind the Buffalo Athletic Club and repaired, a padded bench, and various weights. Kurtz had never fallen into the bodybuilding fetish so endemic in Attica during his eleven and a half years there—he'd found that strength was fine, but speed and the ability to react fast were more important—but during the last six months he'd been doing a lot of physical therapy. Two of the windows in here looked out on Chicago and Ohio Streets and the abandoned grain silos and factory complex to the west; the center window looked right into the pock-marked lighthouse sign.

His bedroom was nothing special—a mattress, an old wardrobe that now held his suits and clothes—and wooden blinds over the window. The third room had brick and board bookcases against two walls, shelves filled with paperbacks, a faded red carpet, a single floor lamp that Arlene had planned to throw away, and—amazingly—an Eames chair and ottoman that some idiot out in Williamsville had put out for junk pickup. It looked like some eighty-pound cat had gone at the black leather upholstery with its claws, but Kurtz had fixed that with electrical tape.

Kurtz went to the end of the dark hall, stripped out of the old man's clothes, and took a fast but very hot shower, making sure to keep the spray off his bandages.

After drying off, Kurtz took out his razor, squeezed lather into his palm, and looked at the mirror for the first time.

"Jesus Christ," he said disgustedly.

The face looking back at him was unshaven and not quite human. The bandages looked bloody again and he could see the shaved patch around them. Blood had drained beneath the skin of his temple and forehead down under his eyes until he had a bright purple raccoon mask. The eyes themselves were almost as bright a red as the soaked-through bandages and he had scrapes and road rash on his left cheek and chin where he must have done a face-plant onto the concrete garage floor. His left eye didn't look right—as if it weren't dilating properly.

"Christ," he muttered again. He wouldn't be delivering any love letters for SweetheartSearch.com again anytime soon.

Shaved and showered now, somehow feeling lousier and more exhausted for it, he dressed in clean jeans, a black t-shirt, new running shoes, and a leather A-2 jacket he'd once given to his old wino-addict informant and acquaintance, Pruno, but which Pruno had given back, saying that it wasn't really his style. The jacket was still in pristine condition, obviously never worn by the homeless man.

Kurtz gingerly pulled on the fedora and went into the unfurnished bedroom that adjoined his own. The plaster hadn't been repaired here and part of the ceiling was falling down. Kurtz reached above the woodwork of the adjoining door, clicked open a panel covered with the same mildewed wallpaper as the rest of the wall, and pulled a .38 S&W from the metal box set in the hole there. The gun was wrapped in a clean rag and smelled of oil. There was a wad of cash in the metal box and Kurtz counted out five hundred dollars from it and set the rest back, pulling the weapon free of the oily rag.

Kurtz checked that all six chambers were loaded, spun the cylinder, tucked the revolver in his waistband, grabbed a handful of cartridges from the box, stuck them in his jacket pocket, and put away the metal container and oily rag, carefully clicking the panel back into place.

He walked back to the triangular front room on the second floor and looked in all directions. It was still a beautiful blue-sky autumn day; Ohio and Chicago Streets were empty of traffic. Nothing but weeds stood in the hundreds of yards of fields between him and the abandoned silos and mills to the southwest.

Kurtz flipped on a video monitor that was part of a surveillance system he and Arlene had used in their former office in the basement of an X-rated-video store. The two cameras mounted at the rear of the Harbor Inn building showed the overgrown yards and streets and cracked sidewalks there empty.

Kurtz grabbed his spare cell phone from a shelf by the speed bag and punched in a private number. He talked briefly, said "Fifteen minutes," broke the connection, and then redialed for a cab.

The public basketball courts in Delaware Park showcased some of the finest athletic talent in Western New York, and even though this was a Thursday morning, a schoolday, the courts were busy with black men and boys playing impressive basketball.

Kurtz saw Angelina Farino Ferrara as soon as he stepped out of the cab. She was wearing a tailored sweatsuit, but not so tailored that he could make out the .45 Compact Witness that he guessed she still carried in a quick-release holster under her sweatshirt. The woman looked fit enough to be on the courts herself—but she was too short and too white, even with her dark hair and olive complexion, to be invited by those playing there now.

Kurtz immediately picked out her bodyguards and could have even if they hadn't been the only other white guys in this part of the park. One of the men was ten yards to her left, studiously studying squirrel activity, and the other was strolling fifteen yards to her right, almost to the courts. Her bodyguards from the previous winter had been lumpish and proletarian, from Jersey, but these two were as thin, well-dressed, and blow-dried as California male models. One of them started crossing toward Kurtz as if to intercept and frisk him, but Angelina Farino Ferrara waved the man off.

As he got closer, Kurtz opened his arms as if to hug her, but really to show that his hands and jacket pockets were free of weapons.

"Holy fuck, Kurtz," she said when he got to within four feet and stopped.

"Nice to see you, too."

"You look sort of like *The Spirit*."

"Who?"

"A comic strip character from the 'forties. He wore a fedora and a blue mask, too. He used to have his own comics page in the *Herald Tribune*. My father used to collect them in a big leather scrapbook during the war."

"Uh-huh," said Kurtz. "Interesting." Meaning—can we cut the crap?

Angelina Farino Ferrara shook her head, chuckled, and began walking east toward the zoo. White mothers were herding their preschoolers toward the zoo gates, casting nervous glances toward the oblivious blacks playing basketball. Most of the males on the courts were stripped to shorts even on this chilly autumn day and their flesh looked oiled with sweat.

"So I heard that you and your parole office were shot yesterday," said

Angelina. "Somehow you just took it on your thick skull while she took it in the brain. Congratulations, Kurtz. You always were nine-tenths luck to one-tenth skill or common sense."

Kurtz couldn't argue with that. "How'd you hear about it so fast?"

"Cops on the arm."

Of course, thought Kurtz. The concussion must be making him stupid.

"So who did it?" asked the woman. She had an oval face out of a Donatello sculpture, intelligent brown eyes, shoulder-length black hair cut straight and tied back this morning, and a runner's physique. She was also the first female acting don in the history of the American mafia—a group that hadn't evolved high enough on the political-correctness ladder even to recognize terms like "female acting don." Whenever Kurtz found himself thinking that she was especially attractive, he would remember her telling him that she'd drowned her newborn baby boy—the product of a rape by Emilio Gonzaga, the head of the rival Buffalo mob family—in the Belice River in Sicily. Her voice had sounded calm when she'd told him, almost satisfied.

"I was hoping you could tell *me* who shot me," said Kurtz.

"You didn't see them?" She'd stopped walking. Leaves swirled around her legs. Her two bodyguards kept their distance but they also kept their eyes on Kurtz.

"No."

"Well, let's see," said Angelina. "Do you have any enemies who might want to do you harm?"

Kurtz waited while she had her little laugh.

"D-Block Mosque still has its *fatwa* out on you," she said. "And the Seneca Street Social Club still thinks you had something to do with their fearless leader, whatshisname, Malcolm Kibunte, going over the Falls last winter."

Kurtz waited.

"Plus there's some oversized Indian with a serious limp who's telling everyone who'll listen that he's going to kill you. Big Bore Redhawk. Is that a real name?"

"You should know," said Kurtz. "You hired the idiot."

"Actually, Stevie did." She was referring to her brother.

"How is Little Skag?" said Kurtz.

Angelina shrugged. "He was never returned to general population after that shank job in Attica last spring. Cons don't like Short Eyes. Even scum has to have its scum to look down on. Best bet is that Little Stevie's under federal protection in a country club somewhere."

"His lawyer would know," said Kurtz.

"His lawyer had an unfortunate accident in his home in June. He didn't survive."

Kurtz looked at her carefully but Angelina Farino Ferrara's expression revealed nothing. Her brother had been her only rival to the control of the Farino crime family, and the loss of his lawyer would have cramped Little Skag's ability to operate at least as much as the shanking and beatings had, which had come about because of a pedophile story that Angelina had leaked to the media.

"Who else might want some of me?" said Kurtz. "Anyone I haven't heard about?"

"What would I be getting in return?"

Kurtz shrugged. "What would you want?"

"That jacket," said Angelina Farino Ferrara.

Kurtz looked down. "You want my jacket in exchange for information?"

"No, dipshit. That was one of Sophia's post-fuck presents. She bought them by the gross from Avirex."

Shit, thought Kurtz. He'd forgotten that Angelina's now-dead younger sister had given him this bomber jacket. It was one of the reasons he'd given it to Pruno. And, indeed, it had been a post-fuck going-away present. He wondered now if this concussion had made him too stupid to go out in public. *Right*, said the more cynical part of his bruised brain, *blame it on the concussion.*

"I'll give you the jacket right now if you tell me who else might have been in that parking garage with me yesterday," he said.

"I don't want the jacket," Angelina said. "Nor the sex that made Sophia give you the damn thing. I just want to hire you the way she did. The way Papa did."

Kurtz blinked at this. When he'd gotten out of Attica a year ago, he'd tried out the theory that since he couldn't work as a licensed private investigator any longer, he might find dishonest but steady work doing investigations for shady characters like Don Farino and then the don's daughter, Sophia. It hadn't worked out so well for Kurtz, but even less well for the dead don and his dead daughter.

"Are you nuts?" said Kurtz.

Angelina Farino Ferrara shrugged. "Those are my terms for information."

"Then you *are* nuts. You want to hire me in what capacity? Hairdresser to your boys?" He nodded in the direction of the pretty bodyguards.

"You weren't listening, Kurtz. I want to hire you an investigator."

"At my daily rates?"

"Flat fee for services rendered," said Angelina.

"How flat?"

"Fifteen thousand dollars for a single name and address. Ten thousand for just the name."

Kurtz breathed out and waited. His head felt like someone had displaced it about two feet to the left. Even the color of the leaves blowing around them hurt his eyes. The basketball players shouted at some great rebound under the boards. Somewhere in the zoo, an old lion coughed. The silence stretched.

"You thinking, Kurtz, or just having a Senior Moment?"

"Tell me what I'm supposed to investigate and I'll tell you if I'm in."

The woman folded her arms and watched the basketball game for a minute. One of the younger men playing caught her eye and whistled. The bodyguards glowered. Angelina grinned at the kid with the basketball. She turned back to Kurtz.

"Someone's been killing some of our people. Five, to be exact."

"Someone you don't know."

"Yeah."

"You want me to find out who's doing it."

"Yeah."

"And whack him?"

Angelina Farino Ferrara rolled her eyes. "No, Kurtz, I have people for that. Just identify him beyond any reasonable doubt and give us the name. Five thousand more if you come up with a current location as well."

"Can't your people find him as well as whack him?"

"They're specialists," said Angelina.

Kurtz nodded. "These people close to you getting hit? Button men, that sort of thing?"

"No. Contacts. Connections. Customers. I'll explain later."

Kurtz thought about it. The wad of cash in his pocket was getting close to the last money he had. But what were the ethics of finding someone so these mobsters could kill them? He certainly had an ethical dilemma on his hands.

"Fifteen thousand guaranteed, half now, and I'll find him and locate him," he said. So much for wrestling with ethics.

"A third now," said Angelina Farino Ferraro. She turned around, blocking the view from the basketball court with her body, and slipped him five-g's already bundled into a tight roll.

Kurtz loved being predictable. "I could tell you right now who's doing it," he said.

Angelina stepped back and looked at him. Her eyes were very brown.

"The new Gonzaga," said Kurtz. "Emilio's boy up from Florida."

"No," said Angelina. "It's not Toma."

Kurtz raised his eyebrows at her use of the dead don's son's first name. She'd never been fond of the Gonzagas. Kurtz's well-honed private investigator instincts told him that that might have had something to do with old Emilio raping her and crippling her father years before.

"All right," he said, "I'll start looking into it as soon as I get my own little matter settled. You going to give me the details about the hits?"

"I'll send Colin around to your office on Chippewa this afternoon with the notes." She nodded toward the taller of the two bodyguards.

"Colin?" Kurtz raised his eyebrows again and decided he wouldn't do that anymore. It hurt. "All right. My turn. Who shot me?"

"I don't know who shot you," said Angelina, "but I know who's been looking for you the last few days."

Kurtz had been out of town delivering SweetheartSearch.com letters most of that time. "Who?"

"Toma Gonzaga."

Kurtz felt the air cool around him. "Why?"

"I don't know for sure," said the woman. "But he's had a dozen of his new guys looking—some hanging around that dump you live in by the Cheerios factory. Others staking out your office on Chippewa. A couple hanging around Blues Franklin."

"All right," said Kurtz. "It's not much, but thanks."

Angelina zipped up her sweatshirt. "There's another thing, Kurtz."

"Yeah?"

"There's a rumor . . . just a street rumor so far . . . that Toma's sent for the Dane."

Through the pounding in his skull, Kurtz felt a slight lurch of nausea. The Dane was a legendary assassin from Europe who rarely came to Buffalo on business. Kurtz had seen him in action the last time he'd been here—the day that Don Byron Farino and his daughter, Sophia, and several others, had been shot in the presumed safety of the Farino compound.

"Well . . ." began Kurtz. He couldn't think of anything else to say. He knew, and he presumed that Angelina Farino Ferrara knew, that even if Toma Gonzaga wanted Joe Kurtz dead for some reason, he wouldn't have to bring in the Dane for that. It was far more likely that Gonzaga would hire someone of the Dane's caliber and expense to eliminate his one real rival in Western New York—Angelina Farino Ferrara. "Well," he said again, "I'll look into it when I figure out who did this to me."

The acting female don of the Farino family nodded, zipped her sweat-shirt up the rest of the way, and began jogging, first across the grass with its blowing yellow leaves, then onto the winding inner park road toward the rear of the zoo. The two bodyguards ran to their parked Lincoln Town Car and hurried to catch up.

Kurtz shifted the old man's fedora slightly trying to get the pressure off the bandages and his split skull. It didn't work. He looked around for a park bench, but luckily there was none in sight—he probably would have curled up in a fetal position on it and gone to sleep if there'd been one there.

The basketball players were letting new guys come into the game while the sweaty players leaving the court traded high-fives and clever insults. Kurtz brought his cell phone out of his jacket pocket and called for a cab.

CHAPTER
FIVE

Kurtz knew that Arlene was happy to finally have their office back on Chippewa Street. Their P.I. office before he'd gone to Attica had been on Chippewa, back when it was a rough area. Last year, after he'd been released from Attica, they'd found a cheap space in the basement of the last X-rated-video store in downtown Buffalo. Last spring, after that whole block had been condemned and demolished, Kurtz had considered an office in the Harbor Inn or one of the nearby abandoned grain elevators, but Arlene had come up with the money for Chippewa Street, so Chippewa Street it was.

Their P.I. business here thirteen years ago had consisted of just him, his partner Samantha Fielding, and Arlene as their secretary. The street had been run-down but recovering then—a lot of local coffeeshops, used bookstores, one gunshop—which was handy for Kurtz—and no fewer than four tattoo parlors. In the seventies, when Kurtz was growing up, Chippewa Street had been all x-rated bookstores, prostitutes and drug dealers. Kurtz had spent a lot of time there then.

Now Chippewa Street was the only happening place in the entire rotting corpus that was the greater Buffalo metropolitan area. If one never left this stretch of Chippewa Street, one might be able to imagine that Buffalo, New York, was still a viable entity. For three entire, short city blocks, between Elmwood and Main, there was a heartbeat: lights, wine bars, nightclubs, limousines sliding to the curb, trendy restaurants, and pedestrians on the street after six P.M. After two A.M. as well, when the clubs let out. And a Starbucks. Kurtz thought that the locals were inordinately proud of their Starbucks.

When Arlene had found the money for this office, Kurtz had stipulated only that it not be above a Starbucks. He hated Starbucks. The coffee was all right—Kurtz didn't really pay attention to his coffee as long as it didn't have cockroaches or something worse floating in it—but whenever the Starbucks shops showed up, it meant that the neighborhood had gone to shit—admittedly, upscale to shit—until the area was just a Disney parody of itself.

Arlene had agreed to avoid that particular coffee haven, so here they were a block and a half east of and two stories higher than the Starbucks. But there were rumors that another one was coming in just across the street.

Now, as Kurtz went up the two flights of stairs to the third-floor office and in the door, he saw why Arlene had wanted to locate here. His secretary had first lost her teenage son to a traffic accident and then her husband to a heart attack while Kurtz had been in jail. Both of those males had been computer whizzes and Arlene was the best hacker—or whatever the hell you called them—in the family. She was still using access codes to files and funds for the Erie County District Attorney's office, and she hadn't worked there for five years.

But she worked too hard and smoked too much. Her only hobby was reading detective thrillers. This SweetheartSearch and WeddingBells-dot-com gig brought her into her office—even though she could just as easily access the servers from her suburban Cheektowaga home—at all hours of the day, night, and weekends. Even at two A.M., Kurtz realized, the view out the big south-facing window just beyond her desk was full of life—lights and people below and traffic sounds—just as if they lived in a real city.

He paused in the doorway. He wasn't sure how she'd react to his head wound, bandages, raccoon blood-mask, road rash, and devil's eyes.

"Hey," he said, walking past his cluttered desk to her immaculate one.

"Hey, yourself," said Arlene, tapping the keyboard, her eyes intent on the screen even while a Marlboro dangled from her lip. Smoke curled around her head and then drifted through the small screened window next to the big glass window.

Kurtz perched on the edge of the desk and cleared his throat.

She paused in the typing, flicked ashes, and looked at him from less than three feet away. "You're looking good, Joe. Lose some weight?"

Kurtz sighed. "Gail called you?"

Gail DeMarco, Arlene's sister-in-law and good friend, was a nurse in the pediatric ward of Erie County Medical Center where Kurtz had been handcuffed mere hours earlier.

"Of course she did," said Arlene. "She's only working mornings now because of Rachel and saw your name on the admissions list when she came in at eight. But by the time she got up to see you, you'd flown the coop."

Kurtz nodded.

"Besides," said Arlene, typing again, "the cops have already been here this morning hunting for you."

Kurtz took off the fedora and scratched his head above the bandages. "Kemper?"

"And a female detective named King."

Kurtz looked at her. He and Rigby had been over before he started up the agency with Sam and hired Arlene. And Sam hadn't known about Rigby. So Arlene couldn't know about her. *Could she?*

Suddenly the floor and desk rose like a small boat on a broad swell. Kurtz took a breath and walked to his own desk, dropping into the swivel chair more heavily than he'd planned. He dropped the fedora—blood on the sweatband—onto his desk.

Arlene stubbed out her cigarette and came over to stand next to him. Her fingers began pulling back the tape and bandages. He started to push her away, but his arm felt as if it were handcuffed again.

"Sit still, Joe."

She peeled away the crusted dressings. Kurtz bit his lip but said nothing.

"Oh, Joe," she said. Her fingers hurt him as they probed, but everything hurt him. It was just more noise amidst the jet roar.

"I think I can see the skull itself between these wide stitches," Arlene said calmly. "Looks like somebody took a chunk out of it. No—don't touch. And don't move—just hold this tape here."

She tossed the bandage into his wastepaper basket. Kurtz noticed that the gauze was furred with hair as well as dried blood. She rooted in her lower left drawer and came out with the big first-aid kit that she'd always kept there, just as she'd always kept a .357 Ruger in the top right drawer.

Kurtz closed his eyes for moment while she painted the wound with something that burned like kerosene and then set fresh dressings in place, cutting strips of adhesive off the roll with her teeth.

"So what are we going to do, Joe? Do you know who shot you?"

"I can't remember the shooting."

"You think they were after you or O'Toole? Gail said that the probation officer was in bad shape."

"I don't know which of us they wanted to kill," said Kurtz. "I don't think they came after both of us—we just don't have any common enemies. Odds are it's me they wanted."

"Yeah," said Arlene. She was finished with the re-bandaging. "Don't mess with it for a few minutes." She went back to her desk, brought out a bottle of Jack Daniel's and two glasses, poured for both of them, and handed him his glass.

"To luck," she said and drank hers.

It tasted like medicine to Kurtz, but the warmth helped the headache for a minute.

"I need to get some stuff off a computer," he said, leaning forward to rest his elbows on his desk. SweetheartSearch manilla file folders crinkled under his arms. He stared into the empty glass.

"How much stuff?" Arlene lit another Marlboro.

"Everything that's on it."

"Whose computer?"

"Parole Officer O'Toole's," said Kurtz. He gingerly set the fedora back on, tugging the brim down gently.

Arlene squinted through the smoke. "The cops probably took it already. Searched the hard drive for clues."

"Yeah, I thought of that," said Kurtz. "But the machine's right there in the County offices. It's already County property. There's a chance they just . . . did whatever you have to do to copy the files. Would that leave information still on the hard disk?"

"Sure," said Arlene. "But it's still possible they lifted the hard disk out and took it to some forensic lab to do the searching."

Kurtz shrugged. "But if they looked at it there . . . or haven't got around to it yet . . ."

"We can copy everything in it," said Arlene. "But how do you expect to get into O'Toole's office in the middle of the day? In the same building where they shot you? There are bound to be forensic guys and cops still milling around and her office will be yellow-taped and sealed."

"Tonight," said Kurtz. "Can you give me the stuff I need to copy her files?"

"Sure," said Arlene, "but you'll screw it up. You can barely get online or download a file."

"That's not true."

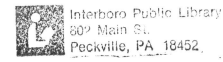

"Well, you'd screw up copying to a backup drive, even though it's simple. I'll go with you tonight."

"The hell you will."

"I'll go with you tonight," said Arlene. "Was there anything else we have to do now?"

"I'd like you to pull up everything you can on Peg O'Toole's old man. Big John O'Toole. He was a . . ."

"Cop," said Arlene. She flicked ashes. "Killed in the line of duty about four years ago. I remember all the fuss in the papers and on TV."

"Yeah," said Kurtz. He told her about his two middle-of-the-night visitors. "Dig up what you can about Big John's brother, Major O'Toole, the guy in the wheelchair. And an Asian man, probably also in his sixties, maybe Vietnamese, Vinh or Trinh. There's a connection between the two. Vinh might work for the Major."

"Vinh or Trinh and a major," said Arlene. "Any first names?"

"You tell me."

"All right. I'll have what I can find by tonight. Anything else you want now?"

"Yeah," said Kurtz.

The list took only a few minutes for Arlene to Google-search and print and a few more minutes for Kurtz to look over. It included one hundred and twenty-three amusement and theme parks in New York's 716 area code and adjacent regions. It began with Aladdins Castle (with no apostrophe) on Alberta Drive in Buffalo and ended with Wackey World for Kidz (with no "s") on Market Street in the town of Niagara Falls, NY.

"So what'd you get out of it?" asked Arlene.

"That these people can't spell for shit."

"Other than that?"

"The abandoned amusement park O'Toole was interested in isn't on this list," said Kurtz. "These are mostly shopping center arcades and water slides."

"And Six Flags out in Darien."

"Yeah."

"Fantasy Island on Grand Island is a real amusement park," said Arlene.

She flicked ashes into her glass ashtray and looked outside as an autumn wind buffeted the big window.

"It's still up and running," said Kurtz. "The photos I saw showed a *very* deserted place. Probably deserted for years, maybe decades."

"So you want me to do serious search—zoning, county building permissions, titles, news articles—going back how far?"

"Nineteen sixties?" said Kurtz.

Arlene nodded, set her cigarette down and made a note on her steno pad. "Just the Buffalo area?"

Kurtz rubbed his temples. The pain throbbed and pulsed now, sometimes worse than others, but never giving him even a few seconds of relief. "I don't even know if the place she was looking for was in New York State. Let's look in Western New York—say from the Finger Lakes to the state lines."

Arlene made a note. "I presume you're going to look again at the photos she showed you tonight when we go in to copy the hard drive."

"I'm going to steal them," said Kurtz.

"But you have no idea if they're important?"

"Not a clue," said Kurtz. "Odds are that they mean nothing at all. But it was weird that she showed them to me."

"Why, Joe? You are . . . were . . . a good P.I."

Kurtz frowned and stood to go.

"You're not driving are you?" asked Arlene.

"Can't. The cops have my Pinto—either impounded or wrapped up in crime-scene tape in the garage."

"Probably improves its looks," said Arlene. She stubbed out her cigarette. "Want a ride?"

"Not yet. I'll grab a cab. I have some people to talk to."

"Pruno's on his October sabbatical, remember?"

"I remember," said Kurtz. One of his best street informants, the old wino, disappeared every October for three weeks. No one knew where he went.

"You should talk to that Ferrara woman," said Arlene. "Anything dirty goes on in this town, she usually knows about it. She's usually *part* of it."

"Yeah," said Kurtz. "Which reminds me, some mobster in Armani is going to drop by here with a folder full of paperwork. Don't shoot him with that cannon you keep under your desk."

"A mob guy in Armani?"

"Colin."

"A mob guy named Colin," said Arlene. "That head injury made you delusional, Joe."

"Pick me up at nine-thirty at the Harbor Inn," said Kurtz. "We'll go to the Civic Center together."

"Nine-thirty. You going to last that long?"

Kurtz touched his hat brim in farewell and went out and down the long stairway. There were thirty-nine steps and every one of them hurt.

CHAPTER
SIX

The Dodger knew their names and where they lived. The Dodger had a picture. The Dodger had a 9mm Beretta Elite II threaded with a silencer in the cargo pocket of his fatigue pants and he could smell the oil. The Dodger had a hard-on.

The guy's address was in the old suburb called Lackawanna and the guy's place was a shithole—a tall, narrow house with gray siding in a long row of tall, narrow houses with gray siding. The guy had a driveway but no garage. Nobody had a garage. The guy had a front stoop four steps up rather than a porch. The whole neighborhood was dreary and gray, even on this sunny day, as if the coal dust from the old mills had painted everything with a coating of dullness.

The Dodger parked his AstroVan, beeped it locked, and strolled jauntily to the front door. His fatigue jacket hid his erection, but the jacket was open so that he could get to the pocket of his pants.

A little girl answered on his third knock. She looked to be five or six or seven . . . Dodger had no idea. He didn't really pay attention to kids.

"Hi," he said happily. "Is Terrence Williams home?"

"Daddy's upstairs in the shower," said the little one. She didn't comment on the Dodger's unusual face, but turned on her heel and walked away from him, back into the house, obviously expecting him to follow.

The Dodger came in, smiling, and closed the door behind him.

A woman came out of the kitchen at the end of the hallway. She was wiping her hands on a dishtowel and her face was slightly flushed, as if she'd been cooking over a hot stove. Unlike the little girl, she did react to the sight of his face, although she tried to hide it.

"Can I help you?" she asked. She was a big woman, broad in the hips. Not the Dodger's type. He liked spinners—the kind of little woman you could sit down, place on your cock, and spin like a top.

"Yes, ma'am," said the Dodger. He was always polite. He'd been taught to be polite as a boy. "I've got a package for Terrence."

The big woman's frown grew deeper. She didn't really have friendly eyes, the Dodger decided. He liked women with friendly eyes. The little girl was running from the dining room through the little living room, past them both in the hallway, and then back around again. The house was tiny. The Dodger decided that the place smelled of mildew and cabbage and that the big woman with the unfriendly eyes probably did, too. But there was a good smell in the air as well, as if she'd been baking.

"Did Bolo send you?" she asked suspiciously.

"Yes, ma'am," said the Dodger. The kid ran past them both again, flapping her arms and making airplane noises. "Bolo sent me."

"Where's the package?"

The Dodger patted the lower right pocket on his fatigue jacket, feeling the steel in the cargo pocket of his pants.

"You'll have to wait," said the woman. She nodded toward the crappy little living room with its sprung couch and uncomfortable La-Z-Boy recliner. "You can sit in there." She frowned at the Dodger's baseball cap as if he should take it off in the house. The Dodger never took off his Dodger cap.

"No problem," he said, smiling and bobbing his head slightly.

He walked into the little living room, removed the Beretta with the supressor, shot the kid when she came buzzing in from the dining room again, shot the wide-hipped woman on the stairway, stepped over her body, and went up to the sound of the water.

The fat man pulled the shower curtain aside and stared at the Dodger as he came in with the gun. The fat man's white, hairy skin and bulges were really repulsive to the Dodger. He hated looking at naked men.

"Hi, Terry," the Dodger said and raised the pistol.

The fat man jerked the shower curtain closed as if that would protect him. The Dodger laughed—that was really funny—and fired five times through the curtain. It had blue, red, and yellow fish on it, and they were swimming in clusters. The Dodger didn't think that blue, red, and yellow fish swam together like that.

The fat man pulled the curtain off its rod as he fell heavily outward. It wasn't even a real shower, just a tub with a rod and curtain and a jerry-rigged sprayer. Now the fat man was sprawled over the edge of the tub. The Dodger didn't understand how people could live this way.

Terry was humped over the edge of the tub, his fat, hairy ass sticking up, his arms and head and upper torso all tangled up in the stupid fish-curtain. Blood was swirling around his toes and running down the drain. The Dodger didn't want to touch that wet, clammy flesh—at least two exit wounds were visible and bubbling in Terry's back—so he patted the curtain until he found the fat man's head, grabbed his hair through the cheap plastic, lifted the head, set the silencer against the man's forehead—the Dodger could see wide, staring eyes through the plastic—and pulled the trigger.

The Dodger picked up his brass, went downstairs again, stepping over the woman, and searched every room, starting from the cellar and working his way back up to the second floor, policing the last two ejected cartridges as he went. He'd fired eight rounds but there were still two live ones left in case there was another kid or invalid aunt or somebody in the house. And he had his survival knife.

There was nobody else. The only sound was the water still running in the shower and the sudden scream of a tea kettle in the kitchen.

The Dodger went to the kitchen and turned off the heat under the kettle. It was an old-fashioned gas-type stove. There were fresh-baked chocolate-chip cookies on the counter. The Dodger ate three of the cookies and then drank from a milk bottle in the fridge. The milk bottle was glass, but he still had his gloves on.

He unscrewed the silencer, slipped the Berretta and silencer back into his trouser cargo pocket, unlocked the kitchen door, then walked to the front of the house and checked the street through the little slivers of window glass in the front door; the street was as empty and gray-looking as when he'd arrived. He went out the front, pulling it locked behind him.

The Dodger went out to his AstroVan and backed it up the narrow driveway. The van filled the drive. Neighbors wouldn't see a damned thing with his van blocking the view like that. The Dodger chose three big mail sacks the right size and went into the house again. He made three trips, dropping each sacked body into the back of the van with an oddly hollow thump from the metal floor. He saved the kid for last, savoring the ease of effort after hauling Mr. and Mrs. Lard-Ass.

Fifteen minutes later, on I-90 headed out of town, he punched in WBFO, 88.7 on his radio. It was Buffalo's coolest jazz station and the Dodger liked jazz. He whistled and patted the steering wheel as he drove.

CHAPTER
SEVEN

Kurtz was listening to jazz at Blues Franklin. He hadn't come to listen to jazz—the place wouldn't be open for another five hours—but when he'd come through the door, one of Daddy Bruce's granddaughters—not Ruby, the waitress, but a little one, perhaps Laticia—had taken one look at Kurtz's face under the hat brim and had run out through the back to fetch Daddy. A young black man was on the low performance platform, noodling at the Steinway that Daddy Bruce kept for the visiting top jazz pianists, so Kurtz found his favorite table against the back wall and tipped his chair back while he listened.

Daddy Bruce came out of the back, wiping his hands off on a white apron. The old man never sat with customers, but he gripped the back of the chair next to Kurtz and shook his head several times, tut-tutting.

"I hope the other guy looks even worse."

"I don't know who the other guy is," said Kurtz. "That's why I came by. Anyone been in here asking for me over the last few days?"

"This very morning," said Daddy Bruce. He scratched his short, white beard. "They so many white people in here this morning asking for you, I considered hanging out a sign saying 'Joe Kurtz ain't here—go away.'"

Kurtz waited for the details.

"First was this woman cop. I remember you in here with her a long, long time ago, Joe, when you was both kids. She identified herself today as Detective King, but you used to call her Rigby. I should've thrown both your asses out back then, being underage and all, but you always loved the music so much and I saw that you were teaching her all about it, plus trying to get in her pants."

"Who else?"

"Three guineas this morning. Button men maybe. Very polite. Said they had some money for you. Uh-huh, uh-huh. Gotta find Joe Kurtz to give him a big bag of money. Lot of that goin' round."

Kurtz didn't have to ask if Daddy Bruce had told them anything. "Were they well-dressed? Blow-dried hair?"

The old man laughed a rich, phlegmy laugh. "Maybe in a *guinea* idea of well-dressed. You know the type—those long, pointy, white collars that don't match their shirts. Off-the-back-of-the-truck suits that they never had tailored. And blow-dried? Those three comb their hair with buttered toast."

Gonzaga's people, thought Kurtz. *Not Farino Ferrara's.*

"Anyone else?"

Daddy Bruce laughed again. "How many people you need after your ass before you feel popular? You want an aspirin?"

"No, thanks. So you haven't heard anything about anyone wanting to cap me?"

"Well, you didn't ask *that*. Sure I do. Last one I heard was about three weeks ago—big halfbreed Indian with a limp. He got real drunk and was telling a couple of A.B. types he was going to do you."

"How'd you know the others were A.B.?"

Daddy Bruce sighed. "You think I don't know Aryan Brotherhood when I smell them?"

"What were they doing in here?" Blues Franklin had never made the mistake of going upscale—despite the Steinway and the occasional headliners—and it still had a largely black clientele.

"How the fuck am I supposed to know why they came in? I just know why and how they went out."

"Lester?"

"And Raphael, his Samoan friend. Your Indian and his pals got real 'noxious about one A.M. We helped them leave through the alley."

"Did Big Bore—the Indian—put up a fight?"

"No one really puts up a fight against Lester. You want me to give you a call if and when Mr. Big Bore come back?"

"Yeah. Thanks, Daddy."

Kurtz stood to leave, swaying only slightly, but the old man said, "You can't go out there lookin' like that, eyes all bloody and with them big bruises under them. You scare the little ones. Stand there. Don't move."

Kurtz stood there while Daddy Bruce hustled into the back room and returned with a pair of oversized sunglasses. Kurtz put them on gingerly. The right stem rubbed against his bandages, but by fiddling, he got them to stay on without hurting.

"Thanks, Daddy. I feel like Ray Charles."

"You *should* feel like Ray Charles," said the old man with a throaty chuckle. "Those be his glasses."

"You stole Ray Charles's sunglasses?"

"Hell, no," said Daddy Bruce. "I don't steal any more than you do. You remember when he come through here about two years ago last December with . . . no, you wouldn't, Joe. You was still up in Attica then. It was a good show. We didn't announce nothing, no warning he was coming, and we had six hundred folks trying to get in."

"And he gave you his sunglasses?"

Daddy shrugged. "Lester and me done him a favor and he give me his pair as a sort of 'mento is all. He travels with extra pairs. But those are the only Ray Charles sunglasses I got, so I'd appreciate them back when you're done with them. Thought I'd use 'em myself when my eyes go bad."

Pruno was on sabbatical, but his homeless roommate, Soul Dad, was at his usual daytime spot—playing chess on the hill above the old switching yards. Soul Dad said that he hadn't heard anything, but promised Kurtz he'd get in touch if he heard anything—the two old men shared a laptop computer in their shack down by the rails and Soul Dad would e-mail in his tip. Kurtz had to smile at that; even the snitches and street informants had gone high-tech.

A cab driver named Enselmo, whom Kurtz had helped with a couple of things, said that he hadn't heard anyone in the back of his cab talking about whacking Kurtz or a parole officer. He had heard rumors though that Toma Gonzaga was looking for Kurtz the last few days. Kurtz thanked Enselmo and paid him two hundred dollars to drive him around the rest of the afternoon.

Mrs. Tuella Dean, a bag lady who favored a grate on the corner of Elmwood and Market—even in the summer—said that she'd heard rumors that some crazy Arab down in Lackawanna had been bragging about planning to shoot someone, but had never heard Kurtz's name mentioned. She didn't know the crazy Arab's name. She couldn't remember where she'd heard the rumor. She thought maybe she was mixing it up with all this al-Qaida news that kept coming over her portable radio.

It wasn't noon yet, but Kurtz began trolling the bars, looking for old contacts and talkative people. He had a couple of hours to kill before heading for Brian Kennedy's security service offices. He welcomed the wait because he wanted his vision to clear a bit before he watched the garage tape.

First he hit the strip bars that catered to the businessman's lunch special—Rick's Tally-Ho on Genessee with its tattered row of recliners, Club Chit Chat on Hertel where, Kurtz had heard, the ass-bruise factor was high and the woody potential was low. His source had been correct, although Kurtz privately judged his current woody potential as negative-five-hundred. On top of that, the music and smell in these places made his head hurt worse.

Kurtz would have liked to check out the higher-class Canadian strip clubs like Pure Platinum just across the river, but cons on probation don't have the option of leaving the country, no matter how close the Peace Bridge might be. So he concentrated on that oxymoron of oxymorons—the greater Buffalo area.

He hit some of the sports bars like Mac's City Bar and Papa Joe's, but the noise was louder there and it just made his headache pound, so he decided to save sports bars for another day. Besides, the kind of snitches or street contacts he was looking for weren't usually the sports-bar types—they preferred dark bars with dubious clientele.

Enselmo was giving him a discount—not charging him for the waiting time—so Kurtz hit some clubs like the Queen City Lounge and the Bradford, just down the street from his office, and the re-opened Cobblestones near the HSBC arena. It was the wrong time of day and the wrong clientele. He was almost certainly wasting his time.

But since he was in the neighborhood, he figured that he might as well check out some of the gay bars. Enselmo obviously didn't approve, based on the number of frowns and glowers he was shooting in the rearview mirror, but Joe Kurtz could care less what Enselmo approved or disapproved of. Buddies on Johnson Park was full of old men who smiled at Kurtz's sunglasses, inspected his bomber jacket, and offered to buy him a drink. None of them seemed to know anything. A sign in the urinal at Cabaret on Allen Street read, "Men who pee on electric fences receive shocking news," and an ad on the wall of the bar offered, "Don't stay home with the same old dildo." But the place was dead.

Kurtz collapsed in the back seat of the cab and said, "KG's. Then we'll call it a day."

"No, no, boss, you don't wanna go to Knob Gobbler's."

"KG's," said Kurtz.

His reaction coming through the door was that he should have followed Enselmo's advice. KG's wasn't all that enthusiastic about straight patrons at the best of times, and they obviously didn't want a bandaged, bruised straight guy in sunglasses there in mid-day during what they advertised as their Wrinkle Club Hour. Kurtz didn't even want to know what a Wrinkle Club was.

The bartender called for the huge bouncer—unimaginatively called "Tiny"—and Tiny flicked a finger the size of a bull pizzle at Kurtz to show him out.

Kurtz nodded passively, pulled the .38, and pressed it into Tiny's face, hammer back, until Tiny's nose mushed flat under the muzzle. It may not have been the best thing to do in the circumstances, but Kurtz wasn't in the best of moods.

The bartender didn't call the cops—Wrinkle Hour was in full wrinkle and he probably didn't want the patrons disturbed by a gunshot—and the man just shifted the toothpick in his mouth, jerked his head, and sent Tiny knuckling back to his grotto.

Kurtz considered this a pretty useless victory since there was nobody to talk to here anyway, unless Kurtz wanted to interrupt something he didn't want to see, much less interrupt. At least in the strip clubs he'd known some of the girls. He was headed out, .38 back in his belt, when a man half again larger than Tiny filled the door. The monster wore a baggy suit and blue shirt with a pointy white collar. It looked like he combed his hair with buttered toast.

"You Kurtz?" grunted the big man.

"Ah, shit," said Kurtz. Gonzaga's people had found him.

The big man jerked his thumb toward the door behind him.

Kurtz stepped backward into the bar. The monster shook his head once, almost sadly, and followed Kurtz into the dark, open space. The Wrinkle Club activities were flailing away in a side room. The goon didn't even glance that way.

"You coming the easy way or the hard way?" asked the big man.

"Hard way's fine," said Kurtz. He took off the sunglasses and set them in his coat pocket.

Gonzaga's man smiled. He obviously preferred the hard way as well. He slipped brass knuckles on and began moving toward Kurtz, arms spread like a gorilla's, eyes on Kurtz's bandages. His strategy was fairly apparent.

"Hey, hey!" shouted the bartender. "Take it outside!"

The ape's gaze shifted for just a fraction of a second at the sound, but it gave Kurtz time to pull the .38 and swing it around full force into the side of the man's head.

Gonzaga's man looked surprised but stayed standing. The bartender was pulling a sawed-off shotgun from under the bar.

"Drop it!" snapped Kurtz, aiming the .38 at the bartender. The bartender dropped it.

"Kick it," said Kurtz. The bartender kicked the weapon away.

The huge man was still standing there, smiling slightly, a quizzical, almost introspective expression on his face. Kurtz kicked him in the balls, waited a minute for the slow neurons to pass the message to the monster's brain, and then kneed him in the face when the mass of flesh slowly bent at the waist.

The man stood straight up, shook his head once, and hit the floor with the sound of a jukebox falling over.

Probably because his head hurt and he was tired, Kurtz kicked the Gonzaga goon in the side of the head and then again in the ribs. It was like kicking a bowling ball and then trying to punt a three-hundred-pound sack of suet.

Kurtz went out the back door, limping slightly, the .38 still in his right hand.

The alley smelled of hops and urine and, without the glasses, the sunlight was way too bright for Kurtz's eyes. He had to blink to clear his vision and by the time he had, it was too late to do anything else. A huge limousine idled fifty feet away on Delaware Street, its black bulk blocking the alley entrance on that side, while a Lincoln Town Car blocked the opposite end.

Two men in dark topcoats totally inappropriate for such a beautiful October afternoon were aiming semiautomatic pistols at Kurtz's chest.

"Drop it," said the shorter of the two. "Two fingers only. Slow."

Kurtz did what he was told.

"In the car, asshole."

Silently agreeing that he was, indeed, an asshole, Kurtz again did what he was told.

CHAPTER EIGHT

You're a hard man to track down, Mr. Kurtz."

The limousine, followed by the Lincoln filled with the other bodyguards, had headed west and was within sight of the lake and river now, moving north along the expressway. They had Kurtz in the jump seat near the liquor cabinet, opposite Toma Gonzaga and one of his smarter-looking bodyguards. The bodyguard held Kurtz's .38 loosely in his left hand and kept his own semiauto braced on his knee and aimed at Kurtz's heart. A second bodyguard sat along the upholstered bench to Kurtz's right, his arms folded.

When Kurtz said nothing, Gonzaga said, "And odd to find you in a place like Knob Gobbler's."

Kurtz shrugged. "I heard that you were hunting for me. I figured I'd find you there."

The bodyguard next to the don thumbed back the hammer on his gun. Toma Gonzaga shook his head, smiled slightly, and set his left hand lightly on the pistol. Eyes never leaving Kurtz, the glowering bodyguard lowered the hammer.

"You're trying to provoke me, Mr. Kurtz," said Gonzaga. "Although in the current circumstances, I have no idea why. I presume you heard that my father exiled me to Florida eight years ago when he found out I was a homosexual."

"I thought all you guys preferred the term 'gay' these days," said Kurtz.

"No, I prefer 'homosexual,' or even 'queer,' " said Gonzaga. " 'Fag' will do in a pinch."

"Truth in advertising?"

"Something like that. Most of my homosexual acquaintances over the years have been anything but gay people, Mr. Kurtz. In the old meaning of the term, I mean."

Kurtz shrugged. There must be some subject that would interest him less—football, perhaps—but he'd be hard-pressed to find it.

Gonzaga's cell phone buzzed and the man answered it without speaking. While he was listening, Kurtz studied his face. His father—Emilio—had been an outstandingly ugly man, looking like some mad scientist had transplanted the head of a carp onto the body of a bull. Toma, who looked to be in his early forties, had the same barrel chest and short legs, but he was rather handsome in an older-Tony-Curtis sort of way. His lips were full and sensuous like his father's, but looked to be curled more from habits of laughter than the way his father's fat lips had curled with cruelty. Gonzaga's eyes were a light blue and his gray hair was cut short. He wore a stylish and expensive gray suit, with brown shoes so leathery soft that it looked as if you could fold them into your pocket after wearing them.

Gonzaga folded the phone instead and slipped it into his pocket. "You'll be relieved to know that Bernard has regained consciousness, more or less, although you may have broken two or three of his ribs."

"Bernard?" said Kurtz, putting the emphasis on the second syllable the way Gonzaga had. *First 'Colin' and now 'Bernard,'* he thought. *What's the underworld coming to?* He'd seen them carry the huge bodyguard out of KG's and fold him into the backseat of the accompanying Lincoln.

"Yes," said Gonazaga. "If I were in Bernard's line of work, I'd change my name as well."

"Isn't Toma a girl's name?" said Kurtz. He wasn't sure why he was provoking a man who might already be planning to kill him. Maybe it was the headache.

"A nickname for Tomas."

Just before they reached the International Bridge, the driver swept them right onto the Scajaquada and the limo headed east toward the Kensington, followed by the Lincoln.

"Did you know my father, Mr. Kurtz?"

This is it, thought Kurtz.

"No."

"Did you ever meet him, Mr. Kurtz?"

"No."

Gonzaga brushed invisible lint off the sharp crease of his gray slacks. "When my father went back to New York for a meeting last winter and was murdered, most of his closest associates here disappeared. It's difficult to discover what really went on during my father's last days here."

Kurtz looked at the bodyguard aiming the Glock-nine at him. The cops had Glocks. Now all the hoods wanted them. They'd turned south on the Kensington and headed back toward downtown. Whatever was going to happen, it wasn't going to happen in Toma Gonzaga's limo.

"Did you ever happen to meet a man named Mickey Kee?" asked Gonzaga.

"No."

"I wouldn't think so. Mr. Kee was my father's toughest . . . associate. They found him dead at the old, abandoned Buffalo train station two days after the big blizzard you people had here in February. It was eighty-two degrees in Miami that week."

"Did you drag me in here at gunpoint to give me a weather report?" asked Kurtz.

Toma squinted at him and Kurtz realized that he was skating now on very thin ice indeed. This man may look like Tony Curtis, he thought, but his genes were all from the murderous Gonzaga line.

"I invited you here to make you an offer you won't want to refuse," said Gonzaga.

Did he really say that? thought Kurtz. These mafia idiots were tiresome enough without having them get self-referential and ironic on you. Kurtz put on an expression that was supposed to look both receptive and neutral.

"Angelina talked to you today about the problem with some people of hers in the drug supply and consumer side of things disappearing," said Toma Gonzaga.

Angelina? thought Kurtz. He wasn't surprised that the gay don knew that Angelina Farino Ferrara had offered him the job—Gonzaga could have people following her, or maybe the two just talked after the offer—but Kurtz couldn't believe the two Buffalo dons were on a first-name basis. *Angelina?* And she had called him "Toma." Very hard to believe—seven months earlier, Angelina Farino Ferrara was doing everything within her power—including the hiring of Joe Kurtz—to get Toma Gonzaga's father whacked.

"Didn't she offer you the job of tracking down the killer?" pressed Gonzaga. "She and I had discussed the idea of her talking to you about this situation."

Kurtz blinked. The concussion was making him fuzz out. "She didn't say anything about drugs," he said, trying to stay noncommittal.

"She told you that the Farino group has lost five people to some crazy person killing them?" said Toma Gonzaga, raising the inflection on the last word just enough to suggest a question.

"She said something about that," said Kurtz. "She didn't give me any details." *Yet.* He wondered if her blow-dried bodyguard had dropped off the information with Arlene yet. *And you'd be my first suspect if I take this job,* thought Kurtz, staring Gonzaga in the eye.

"Well, we've lost seventeen people in the last three weeks," said the don.

Kurtz blinked at this. Even blinking hurt. "Seventeen of your people killed in three weeks?" he said skeptically.

"Not my people," said Gonzaga. "And the people Angelina lost aren't really her people. Not employees. Not directly."

Kurtz didn't understand any of this, so he waited.

"They're the street dealers and users we associate with to move the heavy drugs," said Gonzaga. "Heroin, to be precise."

Kurtz was surprised to hear that the Farinos were moving skag now. It had been the one source of profit that the old don, Byron Farino, had forbidden for his family. His oldest son, David, had wrapped his Ferrari around a tree and killed himself while on coke, and the don had shut down what little drug trade the Farinos had cornered. It had always been Emilio Gonzaga who'd controlled serious drugs in Western New York.

"I've been out of town the last few days," said Kurtz, not believing any of this, "but I would have heard on the national news about twenty-two drug-related murders."

"The cops and press haven't heard about any of them."

"How can that be?" said Kurtz.

"Because the nut-job who whacks them calls us—mostly me, but Angelina twice—to tell us where the murders have taken place. We've been cleaning up after this guy for almost a month."

"I don't get it," said Kurtz. "Why would you help him hide the murders? You're telling me that you didn't kill them."

"*Of course* we didn't kill them, you idiot," snarled Gonzaga. "They're our customers and street-level dealers."

"Which is why you're doing clean-up," said Kurtz. "So the other heroin addicts still able to drive or hold a job don't get wind of this and run down to Cleveland or somewhere to score."

"Yes. The fact that all our street middlemen and dealers are getting murdered wouldn't make these junkies drop their habit—they can't—but it might put them off buying from us. Especially when this psychopath leaves signs behind saying things like 'Score from Gonzaga and die.'"

"He calls you?" mused Kurtz.

"Yes, but we can't tell much about him through that. Voice is all distorted through one of those phone clip-on devices. Probably a white man—he doesn't say 'axe' instead of 'ask' or any of that, or use 'motherfucker' or 'you know' every third word—but we can't identify the voice, or even his age."

"Have you tried tracing . . ."

"Of course we've tried tracing his calls. I had the Buffalo P.D. do it for me—the Family's still got men and women on the arm down there—but this psycho has some way of routing calls through the phone system. My people never get to the pay phone in time."

"Then you go . . . what do you do with the bodies of his victims?" asked Kurtz. He tried not to laugh. "I guess you have your favorite out of the way places for such things. Whole Forest Lawns out there in the woods."

Gonzaga was not amused. "There aren't any bodies."

"What?"

"You heard me. We go and mop up the blood and brains and we plaster over the bullet holes when we have to, but this killer doesn't leave any bodies. He takes them with him."

Kurtz thought about that a minute. It made his head hurt worse. He rubbed his temples. "I already have a client who hired me related to this mess," said Kurtz. "I can't take a second one."

"You're talking like a P.I.," said Gonzaga. "You're not an investigator anymore, Mr. Kurtz. I'm just offering you a private deal, one civilian to another."

The limo came down off the expressway and rolled into the downtown again.

"Angelina's going to pay you ten g's for finding this guy . . ."

"Fifteen," said Kurtz. He didn't usually volunteer information, but his head hurt and he was tired of this conversation. He closed his eyes for a second.

"All right," said Gonzaga. "My offer's better. Today's Thursday. Next Monday's Halloween. You tell us who this asshole is by midnight next Monday, I'll pay you one hundred thousand dollars and I'll let you live."

Kurtz opened his eyes. It took only one look into Toma Gonzaga's eyes to know that the gay don was completely serious. Kurtz realized that whether this man knew that he had been involved in the events that led to Gonzaga's father's death or not, didn't matter. History meant nothing now. Kurtz had just heard his death sentence.

Unless he found the man who was murdering heroin users and dealers.

"One thing," said Gonzaga, smiling slightly as if remembering some amusing detail. "I should tell you that this psychopath hasn't just been whacking the dealers and users—he goes to their homes and shoots their entire families. Kids. Mothers-in-law. Visiting aunts."

"Twenty-two murdered and missing people," said Kurtz.

"Murdered people, bodies missing, but the people aren't really missed," said Toma Gonzaga. "These are all junkies or dealers. Heroin addicts and their families. No one's been reported missing yet."

"But they will be soon," said Kurtz. "You can't keep the lid on twenty-two murdered people.

"Of course," said Gonzaga. "Bobby." He nodded toward the bodyguard on the side bench.

Bobby handed Kurtz a slim leather portfolio.

"Here's what we know, the names of those who've been murdered, dates, addresses, everything we have," said Gonzaga.

"I don't want this job," said Kurtz. "This crap has nothing to do with me." He tried to hand the portfolio back, but the bodyguard folded his arms.

"It has a lot to do with you now," said Gonzaga. "Or it will at midnight on Monday—that's Halloween, I believe—especially if you don't find this man."

Kurtz said nothing.

Gonzaga handed him a cell phone. "This is how you get in touch with us. Hit the only stored number. Somebody'll answer night or day and I'll call you back within twenty minutes."

Kurtz slipped the phone in his pocket and pointed toward the bodyguard who was holding his .38. The bodyguard looked to Gonzaga, who nodded.

The man dumped the cartridges out onto his palm and handed the empty weapon to Kurtz.

"Can we drop you somewhere?" asked Toma Gonzaga.

Kurtz peered out through the tinted windows. They were near the Hyatt and the Convention Center, within a block of the office building where Brian Kennedy had his security company's Buffalo headquarters.

"Here," said Kurtz.

When he was standing on the curb by the open door, Toma Gonzaga said, "One more thing, Mr. Kurtz."

Kurtz waited. The cold air felt good after the stuffy interior of the limousine, filled with the bodyguards' cologne.

"There's word that Angelina has hired a professional killer called the Dane," said Gonzaga. "And paid him one million dollars in advance to settle old scores."

Cute, thought Kurtz. Angelina Farino Ferrara had warned him that Gonzaga was bringing in the Dane. Gonzaga warned him that she had. *But why would either one of them warn me?*

He said, "What's that got to do with me?"

"You might want to work extra hard to earn the hundred thousand dollars I mentioned," said Gonzaga. "Especially since all indications are that you're one of the old scores she wants to settle."

CHAPTER
NINE

Empire State Security and Executive Protection had its offices on the twenty-first floor of one of the few high, modern buildings in downtown Buffalo. The receptionist was an attractive, bright Eurasian woman, impeccably dressed, who politely ignored Kurtz's bandages and bruised eyes; she smiled and buzzed Mr. Kennedy as soon as Kurtz told her his name. She asked if he'd like any coffee, orange juice or bottled water. Kurtz said no, but a light-headedness on top of the pain in his skull reminded him that he hadn't had anything to eat or drink for more than twenty-four hours.

Kennedy came down a carpeted hallway, shook Kurtz's hand as if he was a business client, and led him back through a short maze of corridors and glass-walled rooms in which men and women worked at computer terminals with large flat-display screens.

"Security business seems to be booming," said Kurtz.

"It is," said Brian Kennedy. "Despite the economic hard times. Or perhaps because of them. Those who don't have, are thinking of illegal ways to get it. Those that still have, are willing to pay more to keep what they have."

Kennedy's corner office had solid partitions separating it from the rest of the communal maze, but the two outside walls looking down on Buffalo were floor-to-ceiling glass. His office had a modern but not silly desk, three computer terminals, a comfortable leather couch, and a small oval conference table near the juncture of the glass walls. A professional quality three-quarter-inch tape video machine and monitor were on a cart near the table. Rigby King was already seated across the table.

"Joe."

"Detective King," said Kurtz.

Kennedy smoothly gestured Kurtz to a seat on Rigby's right. He took the opposite end of the oval. "Detective King asked if she could sit in on our meeting, Mr. Kurtz. I didn't think you'd mind."

Kurtz shrugged and took a chair, setting Gonzaga's leather portfolio on the floor next to his chair.

"Can I get you something, Mr. Kurtz? Coffee, bottled water, a beer?" Kennedy looked at Kurtz's eyes when he took off the Ray Charles glasses. "No, a beer probably wouldn't be good now. You must be on a serious amount of pain medication."

"I'm good," said Kurtz.

"You left the hospital rather abruptly this morning, Joe," said Rigby King. Her brown eyes were as attractive, deep, intelligent and guarded as he remembered. "You left your clothes behind."

"I found some others," said Kurtz. "Am I under arrest?"

Rigby shook her head. Her short, slightly spiked hair made her seem younger than she should look; she was, after all, three years older than Kurtz. "Let's watch the tape," she said.

"Peg is still on life-support and unconscious," said Kennedy, as if either one of them had asked. "But the doctors are hoping to upgrade from critical to guarded condition in a couple of days."

"Good," said Rigby. "I called an hour ago to check on her condition."

Kurtz looked at the blank monitor.

"This is the surveillance camera for the door you and Peg came out," said Kennedy.

The video was black and white, or color in such low lighting that there was no color, and it showed only the area of about twenty-five feet by twenty-five feet in front of the doors opening out into the Civic Center garage.

"No cameras aimed at the parked cars area?" asked Kurtz as the tape began to roll, yesterday's date, hour, minute and second in white in the lower right of the frame.

"There is," said Kennedy, "but the city chose the least expensive camera layout, so the next camera is looking the opposite direction, set about seventy-five feet from this coverage area. The shooter or shooters were in a dead area between camera views. No overlap."

On the screen, the door opened and Kurtz watched himself emerge nodding toward the shadow that was Peg O'Toole holding the door. Kurtz watched himself walk in front of the woman, who was staying back.

They had separated ten feet or so and started to go opposite directions when something happened. Kurtz watched himself crouch, fling his arm out, point at the door, and shout something. O'Toole froze, looked at Kurtz as if he was mad, reached for the weapon in her purse, and then her head swung around and looked into the darkness behind the overhead camera. Everything was silent.

He saw sparks as a bullet struck a concrete pillar eight feet behind them. O'Toole drew her 9-mm Sig Pro and swung it in the direction the shooting was coming from. Kurtz watched himself swing around as if he was going to run for the shelter of the pillar, but then O'Toole was struck. Her head snapped back.

Kurtz remembered now. Remembered bits of it. The *phut, phut, phut* and muzzle flare coming from the sixth or seventh dark car down the ramp. Not a silenced weapon, Kurtz realized at the time and remembered now, but almost certainly a .22-caliber pistol, just one, sounding even softer than most .22s, as if the shooter had reduced the powder load.

O'Toole dropped, a black corsage blooming on her pale white forehead in the video. The gun skidded across concrete.

Kurtz dove for the Sig Sauer, came up with it, went to one knee in front of the parole officer, braced the pistol with both hands, and returned fire, the muzzle flare making the video bloom.

There were two figures, remembered Kurtz. *Shadows. The shooter near the trunk of the car, and another man, taller, behind the bulk of the vehicle, just glimpsed through the car's glass. Only the shorter man was shooting.*

Kurtz was firing on the screen. Suddenly he stopped, dragged O'Toole by the arm across the floor, lifted her suddenly, and began carrying her back toward the doors.

I hit the shooter, remembered Kurtz. *He spun and sagged against the car. That's when I tried to get O'Toole out. Then the other man grabbed the gun and kept shooting at us.*

Officer O'Toole's arm seemed to twitch—*a slug going through her upper arm*, Kurtz thought, remembering the doctor's explanation—Kurtz's upper body twisted and his head jerked around to the left as he brought the Sig Pro to bear again, and then he went down hard, dropping the woman.

The two sprawled onto the concrete. Black-looking blood pooled on the floor.

A full minute went by with just the two bodies lying entangled there.

"There was no coverage of the exit ramp," said Rigby. "We didn't see the car leave . . . at least until it got to the ticket station."

"Why didn't he come out to finish us?" said Kurtz. He was looking at his own body sprawled next to O'Toole's and thinking about the second shooter.

"We don't know," said Kennedy. "But a court stenographer comes out through those doors in a minute . . . ah, there she is . . . and she may have spooked the shooter."

Shooters, thought Kurtz. Remembering the adrenaline of those few minutes made his head hurt worse.

On the screen, a woman steps out, claps her hands to her cheeks, screams silently, and runs back in through the doors.

Kennedy stopped the tape. "Another three and a half minutes before she gets someone down there—a security guard. He didn't see anyone else, just you and Peg on the ground. He radioed for the ambulance. Then another ten minutes of people milling until the paramedics arrive. It's lucky Peg survived all that loss of blood."

Why didn't the second shooter finish us? wondered Kurtz. *Whichever one of us he was trying to kill.*

Kennedy pulled the tape and popped another one in. Kurtz looked at Rigby King. "Why was I handcuffed?" His voice wasn't pleasant.

"We hadn't seen this yet," she said.

"Why not?"

"The tapes weren't marked," said Brian Kennedy, answering for her. "There was some confusion. We didn't have this to show Officers Kemper and King until after they visited you yesterday evening."

I was handcuffed the entire fucking night, thought Kurtz, glaring at Rigby King. *You left me helpless and handcuffed in that fucking hospital all night.* She was obviously receiving his unspoken message, but she just returned his stare.

"This is the security camera at the Market Street exit," said Kennedy, thumbing the remote control.

A young black woman was reading the *National Enquirer* in her glass cashier's cubicle. Suddenly an older-make car roared up the ramp and out of the parking garage, snapping the wooden gate off in pieces and skidding a right turn into the empty street before disappearing.

"Freeze frame?" said Kurtz.

Kennedy nodded and backed the video up until the car was frozen in the act of hitting the gate. Only the driver was visible, a man, long hair wild, but his face turned away and his body only a silhouette. The camera was angled to see license tags, but this car's rear tag looked like it had been daubed with mud. Most of the numerals and letters were unreadable.

"Attendant get a good look?" asked Kurtz.

"No," said Kennedy. "She was too startled. Male. Maybe Caucasian. Maybe Hispanic or even black. Very long, dark hair. Light shirt."

"Uh huh," said Kurtz. "There could have been another man on the floor in the back seat."

"Do you remember a second man?" asked Rigby.

Kurtz looked at her. "I don't know," he said. "I was just saying there could have been a second man in the back."

"Yeah," said Rigby. "And the Mormon Tabernacle Choir in the trunk."

"Detective Kemper thinks it's a Pontiac, dark color, maybe late eighties, rust patches in the right rear fender and trunk," said Brian Kennedy.

"That narrows it down," said Kurtz. "Only about thirty thousand of those in Buffalo."

Kennedy gestured toward the frozen image and the license plate. "We've augmented this frame and think that there may be a two there on that tag, perhaps a seven as the last digit."

Kurtz shrugged. "You check Officer O'Toole's computer files? See if she has any pissed-off parolees?"

"Yes, the detectives copied the computer files and went through her filing cabinets, but . . ." began Kennedy.

"We're pursuing the investigation with all diligence," said Rigby, cutting off Kennedy's info-dump.

Kennedy looked at Kurtz and smiled as if to say, man to man, *Women and cops, whattayagonna do?*

"I'm going home," said Kurtz. Everyone stood. Kennedy offered his hand again and said, "Thanks for coming, Mr. Kurtz. I thank you for trying to protect Peg the way you did. As soon as I saw the video, I knew you weren't involved in her shooting. You were a hero."

"Uh huh," said Kurtz, looking at Rigby King. *You left me there handcuffed all night so that an old man in a wheelchair could slap me around. Anybody could've killed me.*

"You want a ride home?" asked Rigby.

"I want my Pinto back."

"We're finished with it. It's still in the Civic Center garage. And I have your clothes and billfold down in my car. Come on, I'll give you a ride to the garage."

Kurtz walked to the elevators with Rigby King, but before the elevator car arrived, Kennedy hustled out. "You forgot your portfolio, Mr. Kurtz."

Kurtz nodded and took the leather folder holding Gonzaga's paperwork listing seventeen murders unknown to the police or media.

CHAPTER
TEN

It wasn't a long ride. Kurtz pulled the little brown-paper package of his clothes and shoes out of the back seat, checked his wallet—everything was there—and settled back, feeling the reloaded .38 against the small of his back.

"You know, Joe," said Rigby King, "if I searched you right now and found a weapon, you'd go in for parole violation."

Kurtz had nothing to say about that. The unmarked detective's car was like every other unmarked police car in the world—ugly paint, rumbling cop engine, radio half hidden below the dashboard, a portable bubble light on the floor ready to be clamped onto the roof, and city-bought blackwall tires that no civilian anywhere would put on his vehicle. Any inner-city kid over the age of three could spot this as a cop car five blocks away on a rainy night.

"But I'm not going to search you," said Rigby. "You wouldn't last a week back in Attica."

"I lasted more than eleven years there."

"I'll never understand how," she said. "Between the Aryan Nation and the black power types, loners aren't supposed to be able to make it a month inside. You never were a joiner, Joe."

Kurtz watched the pedestrians cross in front of them as they stopped at a red light. They were only a few blocks from the civic center. He could have walked it if he wasn't feeling so damned dizzy. Leaving the portfolio on the floor back at Kennedy's office showed Kurtz how much he needed some sleep. And maybe some pain medication. The pedestrians and the street beyond them seemed to shimmer from heat waves, even though it was only about sixty degrees outside today.

"When my husband left me," said Rigby, "I moved back to Buffalo and joined the force. That was about four years ago."

"I heard you had a little boy," said Kurtz.

"I guess you heard wrong," said Rigby, her voice fierce.

Kurtz held up both hands. "Sorry. I heard wrong."

"I never knew my father, did you?" said Rigby.

"You know I didn't," said Kurtz.

"But you told me once that your mother told you that your father was a professional thief or something."

Kurtz shrugged. "My mother was a whore. I didn't see much of her even before the orphanage. Once when she was drunk, she told me that she thought my old man was a thief, some guy with just one name and that not even his own. Not a second-story guy, but a real hardcase who would set up serious jobs with a bunch of other pros and then blow town forever. She said he and she were together for just a week in the late sixties."

"Must have been preparing for some heist," said Rigby.

Kurtz smiled. "She said that he never wanted sex except right *after* a successful job."

"Your old man may have been a professional thief but you never steal anything, Joe," said Rigby King. "At least you never used to. Every other kid at Father Baker's, including me, would lift whatever we could, but you never stole a damned thing."

Kurtz said nothing to that. When he'd first known Rigby—when they'd had sex in the choir loft of the Basilica of Our Lady of Victory—he was fourteen, she was seventeen, and they were both part of the Father Baker Orphanage system. They didn't know their fathers, and Kurtz didn't think either one of them gave a shit.

"You never met your old man either, did you?" he asked now.

"I didn't then," said Rigby, pulling up to the curb by the Civic Center parking lot entrance. "I tracked him down after Thailand. He was already dead. Coronary. But I think he might have been an all right guy. I don't think he ever knew I existed. My mother was a heroin addict."

Kurtz, never the best at social niceties, guessed that there was probably a sensitive and proper response to this bit of news as well, but he had no interest in spending the effort to find it. "Thanks for the ride," he said. "You have my Pinto keys?"

Rigby nodded and took them out of her jeans pocket. But she held onto them. "Do you ever think about those days, Joe?"

"Which days?"

"Father Baker days. The catacombs? That first night in the choir loft? Blues Franklin? Or even the ten months in Thailand?"

"Not much," said Kurtz.

She handed him the keys. "When I came back to Buffalo, I tried to look you up. Found out my second day on the job that you were in Attica."

"Modern place," said Kurtz. "They have visiting hours, mail, everything."

"That same day," continued Rigby, "I found out that you murdered that guy—tossed him onto the roof of a black and white from the sixth floor—the guy who killed your agency partner and girlfriend, Samantha something."

"Fielding," said Kurtz, stepping out of the vehicle.

The passenger window was down halfway, and Rigby leaned over and said, "We'll have to talk again about this shooting. Kemper wanted to brace you today, but I said let the poor bastard get some sleep."

"Kemper has a hard-on for me," said Kurtz. "You could have come and uncuffed me last night. You both knew I didn't shoot O'Toole."

"Kemper's a good cop," said Rigby.

Kurtz let that go. He felt stupid standing there holding his little brown-wrapped bundle of clothes like a con getting sent back out into the world.

But Rigby wasn't done. "He's a good cop and he feels—he *knows*—that you're on the wrong side of the law these days, Joe."

Kurtz should have just walked away—he even turned to do so—but then he turned back. "Do *you* know that, Rigby?"

"I don't know anything, Joe." She set the unmarked car in gear and drove off, leaving him standing there holding his brown-wrapped bundle.

CHAPTER
ELEVEN

Arlene arrived right at nine-thirty. Kurtz was waiting outside the Harbor Inn. The wind blowing in from the lake to the west was cold and smelled like October. Weeds, newspapers, and small debris blew across the empty industrial fields and skittered by Kurtz's feet.

When he got in the blue Buick, Arlene said, "I see you got the Pinto back." It was parked behind the triangular building in its usual spot.

"Yeah," said Kurtz. He'd had some problems with the local project youth the first weeks he'd lived here, until he'd beaten up the biggest of the car-stripper gang and offered to pay the smartest one a hundred bucks a week to protect the vehicle. Since then, there'd been no problem, except that he'd already paid several times what the Pinto was worth.

Making a U-turn and heading back to the lights of the city center, Arlene tapped a sealed manilla envelope on the console between them. "That blow-dried mob guy showed up with the package you said was coming."

"Did you open it?"

"Of course not," said Arlene. She lit a Marlboro and frowned at him.

He opened the envelope. A list of five names and dates and addresses. One guy and two of his family members. A woman. Another guy.

"Angelina Farino Ferrara hired me to look into who's been hitting some of their skag dealers and clients," said Kurtz. "Toma Gonzaga bumped into me this afternoon and offered me the same job, only to see who's been hitting *his* family's clients."

"Someone's been killing both Gonzaga and Farino heroin dealers?" Arlene sounded surprised.

"Evidently."

"I haven't heard about this on the Channel Seven Action News." Kurtz knew that Arlene was old enough to remember and miss Irv Weinstein and his if-it-bleeds-it-leads TV newsreels from long ago. All the day's carnage and corpses wrapped up in forty-five seconds of fast footage. Kurtz missed it, too.

"They've kept it quiet," said Kurtz.

"The *families* have kept it quiet?"

"Yeah."

"How the hell do you keep five murders quiet?"

"It's worse than that," said Kurtz. "Twenty-two murders counting Gonzaga's dealers and addicts."

"Twenty-two murders? In what time period? Ten years? Fifteen?"

"The last month, I think," said Kurtz. He tapped the envelope. "I haven't read their publicity handout here yet."

"Christ," said Arlene. She flicked ashes out the window.

"Yep."

"And you've agreed to dig around for them? As if you have nothing better to do?"

"They made me an offer I couldn't refuse," said Kurtz. "Both Gonzaga and the don's daughter are offering cash and other incentives."

Arlene squinted at him through the cigarette smoke. She knew Kurtz almost never made movie jokes or references, and never Godfather jokes. "Joe," she said softly, "I don't mean to meddle, but I don't think that Angelina Farino has ever had your best interests at heart."

Kurtz had to smile at that. "There's the Civic Center garage," he said. "Do you have an idea how we're going to get in?"

"Did you get any sleep this afternoon?" She pulled up to the curb and parked.

"Some." He'd dozed for about an hour before his headache woke him.

"I brought some Percocet." She rattled the prescription bottle.

Kurtz didn't ask or want to know why she was carrying Percocet. "I took a couple of aspirin," he said, waving away the bottle. "I'm still curious about how we're going to get in. The place is closed up pretty tight at night. Even the parking garage has that metal-mesh screen that has to be raised from the inside."

Arlene held up her big, briefcase-sized purse as if that explained everything. "We're going in through the front door and the metal detectors. If you're carrying a gun, leave it out here."

Help you?" grunted the guard by the metal detectors. One of the front doors had been unlocked, but it led only into this large foyer.

Arlene stepped closer and removed official ID and an official-looking letter on city stationery and handed them to the guard. Kurtz stood back from the overhead lights, keeping his face in shadow and the bandaged side of his head turned away.

"D.A.'s office?" said the guard after he'd read the paper with his lips moving only slightly. "What do you want tonight? Everything's closed. Everyone's gone home."

"You read it," said Arlene. "The D.A. himself has a nine A.M. hearing in front of Judge Garman, of all people, and half the paperwork on this parolee hasn't been sent over."

"Well, Miz . . . uh . . . Johnson . . . I shouldn't really . . ."

"This has to be done *quickly*, Officer Jefferson. The D.A.'s tired of the incompetence here. If he's embarrassed tomorrow by not getting these files *tonight* . . ." Arlene had taken out her cellphone and flipped it open.

"Okay, okay," said Officer Jefferson. "Give me your bag and go through the detectors."

Kurtz went through first and stepped back into the relative shadows. Jefferson was holding a heavy portable disk-drive with dongles hanging out and looking dubious.

"That's a portable hard drive," said Arlene, barely restraining a sigh and eye roll. "You don't think we're going to copy these files by *hand*, do you?"

Jefferson shook his head, set the memory drive back, and lifted out a black rectangular box about twelve inches long with slots in it and an attached cord.

"That's my portable copier for files that *do* have to be copied by hand," said Arlene, glancing at her watch. "The District Attorney needs these files no later than ten-thirty, Mr. Jefferson. He hates staying up late."

Jefferson zipped up her giant purse and handed it back to her. "I didn't get a call about this, Miz Johnson."

Arlene smiled. "Officer, this is the *D.A.'s office*. Have you dealt with us before? The District Attorney is a wonderful man, but he's lucky to remember to zip up his fly."

"Ms. Feldman's on bereavement leave this week," said the officer.

"We know," said Arlene. "But the district attorney still needs her files."

Jefferson smiled. "Yeah." He glanced at Kurtz. "I should show you the way up to Ms. Feldman's parole office, but it'll be a couple of minutes. Leroy's still making his rounds."

Arlene held up a silver key. "Carol's sister gave us her key. This will just take a few minutes." She handed the heavy bag to Kurtz. "Here, Thomas, carry this."

Kurtz followed dutifully as she clacked her way across the lobby and summoned an elevator. Jefferson gave a half-salute as they stepped in.

"This will be on security video," said Kurtz as the doors closed.

Arlene shrugged. "No crime, no need to check the security videos."

"I presume that Ms. Feldman's office is near O'Toole's."

"A few doors away."

"Someday the D.A. will trace all this fun back to his predecessor's former executive secretary," said Kurtz.

"Not in this lifetime," said Arlene.

In another, less obvious pocket of Arlene's bag was the breaking and entering tool kit that Kurtz had always used for black bag jobs. He opened Feldman's office door first, turned on the lights, and then locked it behind them. There were three strands of yellow crime scene tape across O'Toole's doorway, but the door opened inward and they could step through. Kurtz took fifteen seconds to jimmy this lock as well.

They lowered the venetian blinds, took out a pocket-sized low-light, no-flash infrared digital camera and took four photos so they could set everything back exactly the way it was. Then they clicked on halogen penlights. Both had pulled on gloves. Peg O'Toole's computer was still there on the desk extension. Arlene found a power outlet for the backup drive, ran a USB cord to O'Toole's computer, fired up the parole officer's machine and her own, and whispered that they were set to go.

"How long will this take?" whispered Kurtz.

"Depends on how many files she has," whispered Arlene, tapping her gloved fingers on O'Toole's keyboard. "It took me forty-eight minutes to back up the WeddingBells-dot-com files."

"We don't have forty-eight minutes!" hissed Kurtz.

"That's all right," said Arlene. "WeddingBells has three thousand, three hundred and eighty files. Ms. O'Toole has . . . one hundred and six." The backup disk drive blinked a green light and began to whir. "Eight minutes and we're out of here."

"What if they're encrypted or password protected or whatever?" whispered Kurtz.

"I don't think they will be," said Arlene. "But we'll deal with that when we get the drive back to the office. Go do your file thing." She handed him the travel scanner.

The files were locked. He had them open in twenty seconds. He used the penlight to look over several years worth of parolees' thick files. What he needed was a recent list . . . here it was. Peg O'Toole currently had thirty-nine active "clients," including one Joe Kurtz. He made a space, plugged in the digital copier/scanner, and began running pages through the small device. There were smaller scanners—some pen-sized—but this one was reliable and gobbled entire documents quickly, eliminating the need to run the scanner tip over lines of type. Kurtz fed in lists of current clients, addresses, phone numbers.

Arlene looked around the office and found a cassette tape recorder and racked stacks of cassettes. "She must record her notes, Joe," whispered Arlene. "Then transcribe them. And the last three weeks of cassettes are missing."

"Cops," whispered Kurtz. He was digitizing O'Toole's DayMinder, using the slower wand, playing the light over O'Toole's handwritten entries. "We'll just have to hope she had time to type her notes into the computer files." He finished copying the top three pages in each of the active thirty-nine cons' files, including his own, set the originals back, locked the file cabinets and came over to the desk.

The disk drive had already blinked that it was finished. Arlene left it attached and set a CD into the tray on O'Toole's computer. "I want her e-mail," whispered Arlene.

Kurtz shook his head. "That'll be password protected for sure."

Arlene nodded. "The program that I just loaded . . . ah . . . there it is. Will lie hidden in there and if anyone else knows her password and uses this computer, the program will quietly e-mail us a record of all the keystrokes."

"Is that possible?" whispered Kurtz. The idea appalled him and made his headache worse.

"I just did it," whispered Arlene. She unloaded the CD and put it in her bag.

"So all the hard-drive stuff is on the CD now?"

"No. Officer O'Toole didn't have a writable CD drive on this old machine. I just sent the data to the hard drive backup."

"Won't the cops find your keystroke program if they look again?"

Arlene smiled. "It would eat itself first. God, I wish I could smoke in here."

"Don't even *think* about it," whispered Kurtz. "Now move, I need to get into that desk."

"It's locked," whispered Arlene.

"Uh huh," said Kurtz. He used two bent pieces of metal and had the drawers open before Arlene got completely out of his way. The usual desk bric-a-brac in the center drawer—pens, paper clips, a ruler, pencils. Stationery and official stamps in the top right drawer. Old appointment journals in the right center drawer.

O'Toole had pulled the amusement park photographs out of the lower right drawer yesterday.

There were a few personal things there—tampons modestly pushed to the back, toothpaste, a toothbrush in a travel tube, some cosmetics, a small mirror. No photos. No envelope of the kind she'd taken the photos from. Kurtz checked everything again to make sure and then closed the drawers. The photos hadn't been among the loose paperwork or in the recent files he'd checked.

"Police?" whispered Arlene. She knew what he was looking for.

Kurtz shrugged. She could have had the photos in her purse when she was shot. "We done here?"

When Arlene nodded, he relocked everything and checked the infrared digital photos on the LCD screen to make sure everything looked the same. He went back to the desk and adjusted a pencil. They opened the door a crack, made sure the hallway was empty, and stepped out.

Seven minutes twelve seconds.

Kurtz unlocked Ms. Feldman's office and clicked off the lights. Locked the door.

They passed the other guard, Leroy, coming out of the elevator. "Phil told me you folks were here. Done already?"

Arlene held up the thick file of old SweetheartSearch-dot-com papers she'd taken from her briefcase. "We have what the D.A. needs," she said.

Leroy nodded and moved down the hall to check the doors.

Outside, Arlene didn't wait until they got to her Buick. She handed Kurtz the bag and lit a Marlboro. When they got in the car, Kurtz said, "You enjoy that?"

"You bet I did. It's been more than a dozen years since I helped in the field work."

Kurtz thought about that. He didn't remember ever using Arlene in the field.

"Sam," said Arlene. Kurtz was surprised that Samantha had taken Arlene out for fieldwork and never told him. Evidently, a lot had gone on at the agency that he'd been oblivious to.

"Back to the office?" asked Arlene.

"Back to the office," said Kurtz. "But go through a Burger King or something on the way." It had been more than thirty hours since he'd eaten anything.

CHAPTER
TWELVE

They kept the lights low in their office—just two shielded old metal desk lamps—but the neon blaze from the Chippewa Street clubs and restaurants filled the big window and spilled onto Arlene's desk.

Arlene loaded O'Toole's hard drive data into her computer, and then added the digitized scanned material. Kurtz understood just enough to know that essentially she was creating a virtual computer—O'Toole's—inside her own machine, but separated from Arlene's own programs and files by various partitions. The parole officer's computer memory didn't even know it had been hijacked.

"Oh," said Arlene, "I finished the research into Big John O'Toole, his brother the Major, and the amusement park search. I think you'll be pleased with some of the connections. You can read it while I open this stuff."

Kurtz looked on his desk for new files, but there weren't any.

"I e-mailed it to your computer. The files are waiting there," said Arlene. Her cigarette glowed.

"My desk is five feet from yours, and you e-mailed it to me?" Kurtz was finishing the big burger they'd picked up during the drive over.

"It's a new century, Joe," said Arlene.

Kurtz's head hurt too much for him to start expressing his opinion on that happy revelation. He fired up his computer, downloaded the files, and opened them while he ate and sipped a Coke.

Big John O'Toole had been a street cop in Buffalo for almost twenty years and had remained a uniformed cop the entire time. He was a sergeant and three months away from retirement when he'd been shot and killed four years ago, during a drug-bust gone wrong according to the *Buffalo News*. O'Toole had been acting alone—strange for a sergeant with that seniority—investigating a series of car burnings over on Hertel, in a neighborhood famous for torching their cars for insurance, when he'd seen a heroin deal going down and tried to make the arrest by himself. One of the three suspects—all had escaped despite a huge manhunt—had got the drop on O'Toole and shot him in the head.

Weird, thought Kurtz. An experienced cop, even a uniform, trying to bust several drug dealers without calling for backup? It didn't make sense.

There were several related stories, including one covering Sergeant John O'Toole's huge funeral—every cop in Western New York seems to have turned out for it—and Kurtz recognized a slightly younger and somewhat thinner Officer Margaret O'Toole standing in the rain by the crowded graveside. He remembered learning once that she had been a real cop, working Vice at that time.

Kurtz skimmed through the rest of the Big John O'Toole stuff—mostly citations, occasional community related stuff going back more than a decade, and follow-up stories on the fruitless search for his shooters—and then went on to the hero-cop's older brother, Major Michael Francis O'Toole.

Separate photos—the two didn't seem to have been photographed together—showed that the brothers looked vaguely alike in that blunt Irish way, but the Major's face was broader, tougher, and meaner than the cop's. Arlene had somehow gotten into military records—Kurtz never asked her how she did such things—and he printed these pages so as to read them more easily.

Michael Francis O'Toole, born 1936, enlisted in the Army in 1956, a series of American and European base assignments, then his first tour in Vietnam in 1966. This O'Toole had worked his way up through the ranks, been sent to OCS in the early sixties, and was a captain during his first combat tour. There were various citations, medals, and details of heroism under fire—one time running from a landed command helicopter, under fire, to rescue one of his wounded men who had been left behind during a confused evacuation. His specialty had been working with ARVN—Army of the Republic of Vietnam—Kit Carson Scouts, the high-morale, American-trained Vietnamese troops who did scouting, interrogation, and translation for the army and CIA in-country. O'Toole had been shipped Stateside after a minor injury, promoted to Major, promptly volunteered to return to Vietnam, landed at a forward area in the Dan Lat Valley, stepped on an antipersonnel mine, and had lost the use of his legs.

That was the end of Major O'Toole's active military career. After a stint in a Virginia V.A. hospital, O'Toole retired from the Army and returned to his family's hometown of Chappaqua, New York. Then there were some 1972 virtual newspaper clippings about Major O'Toole in Neola, New York, a little town of about twenty thousand people about seventy miles south of Buffalo, along the Pennsylvania border. The Major had opened a major southeast Asian import-export business there along with his Vietnamese partner, Colonel Vin Trinh. They called the little business the South-East Asia Trading Company, SEATCO, which sounded like just another stupid military acronym to Kurtz, who'd had his share of them during his stint as an M.P.

All right, thought Kurtz. The headache was worse and he rubbed his temples. *What the hell does all this mean other than poor, dying Peg O'Toole had had a hero (if not too bright) cop for a father and a Vietnam-hero for an uncle?*

As if reading Kurtz's mind, Arlene stubbed out her cigarette and said, "Read that last file before you go any further with the O'Toole brothers."

"The file marked 'Cloud Nine'?"

"Yeah."

Kurtz dropped the other stuff offscreen and opened 'Cloud Nine.' It was a puff article from *The Neola Sentinel*, dated August 10, 1974, about the wonderful amusement park being opened in the mountains above Neola. It was expected that this new, state-of-the-art amusement park would attract patrons from all over Western New York, Northern Pennsylvania, and North-Central Ohio. The park included a one-third-scale train that would hold up to sixty youngsters and which would follow tracks almost a mile and a half across and around the mountaintop. The park also boasted a huge Ferris wheel, a roller coaster "second only to the Comet at Canada's Crystal Beach," bumper cars, and a host of other amusements.

The park had been built "as a gift to the youth of Neola" by Major Michael Francis O'Toole, president of South-East Asia Trading Company of Neola, New York.

"Ahah," said Kurtz.

Arlene stopped her typing. "I haven't heard you say 'ahah' since the old days, Joe."

"It's a specialized term known only to professional private investigators," said Kurtz.

Arlene smiled.

"Only this time, you're the investigator. I didn't do a damned thing to dig up this information. It's all you and that computer."

Arlene shrugged. "Have you read the file labeled *Neola H.S.* yet?"

"Not yet," said Kurtz. He opened it.

Dateline The Neola Sentinel, The Buffalo News, *and* The New York Times, *October 27, 1977. A high-school senior, Sean Michael O'Toole, 18, entered Neola High School armed with a .30–.06 rifle yesterday and shot two of his classmates, a gym teacher, and the assistant principal, before being wrestled to the ground by four members of the Neola football team. All four of the shooting victims were pronounced dead at the scene. It stated that Sean Michael O'Toole is the son of prominent Neola businessman and owner of the Cloud Nine amusement park, Major Michael O'Toole and the late Eleanor Rains O'Toole. No motive for the shooting has been given.*

Wow, pre-Columbine," said Kurtz.

"Do you remember when that happened?" asked Arlene.

"I was just a kid," said Kurtz. Although it would have been the kind of news item he'd have taken an interest in even then.

"You were already in Father Baker's then," Arlene reminded him. The court sent kids to Father Baker's Orphanage.

Kurtz shrugged. The last thing in that file was the January 27, 1978, court hearing for the Major's kid. Sean O'Toole had been judged by a battery of psychiatrists to be competent to stand trial. He was remanded to a psychiatric institution for the criminally insane in Rochester, New York, for further testing and "continuing evaluation and therapy in secure surroundings." Kurtz knew about the Rochester nuthouse—it was a dungeon for some of New York State's craziest killers.

"Did you read the last bit of the Cloud Nine file?" asked Arlene.

"Not yet."

"It's just a Neola *Sentinel* clipping from May of nineteen seventy-eight," said Arlene, "announcing that the Cloud Nine Amusement Park, already beset by financial difficulties and low attendance, was closing its gates forever."

"So much for the youth of Neola," said Kurtz.

"Evidently."

"But if her uncle was running this business and park in Neola, why wouldn't Peg O'Toole know about it?" Kurtz mused aloud. "Why would she show me those photos of the abandoned park—assuming it's Cloud Nine—and not know it's her uncle's old place?"

Arlene shrugged. "Maybe she knew the photos weren't from her uncle's abandoned park. Or maybe she didn't even know that Cloud Nine existed. Her father, Big John, didn't move to Buffalo and start his cop job here until nineteen eighty-two. Maybe the Major and his cop brother were estranged. I didn't see the Major and his wheelchair in the photos from Big John's funeral four years ago. You'd think the uncle would be right there next to Ms. O'Toole since Peg's mother was dead."

"Still . . ." said Kurtz.

"Remember you telling me that one of the overturned bumper cars in the photo you saw yesterday had the number 'nine' on it?"

"Cloud Nine," said Kurtz. "It's all there. It just doesn't make sense. I'll be right back."

Kurtz got up quickly, hurried to the tiny bathroom back by the purring computer server room, knelt next to the toilet, and vomited several times. When he was done, he rinsed his mouth out and washed his face. His hands were shaking violently. Evidently, the concussion didn't want him to eat yet.

When he came back into the main room, Arlene said, "You okay, Joe?"

"Yeah."

"Do you need any other searches related to this?"

"Yeah," said Kurtz. "I want to find out what happened to this kid, the shooter. Did he stay caged up in Rochester? Is he out now? And I need some details of the Major's specific history in Vietnam—not just his medals, but names, locations, who he worked with, what he was doing when."

"Medical records and military records can be two of the hardest things to hack into," said Arlene. "I'm not sure I can get any of this."

"Do your best," said Kurtz. His cell phone rang. He turned to answer it.

Daddy Bruce's voice said, "You wanted to know when that Big Bore Indian came back to the Blues hunting for you again, Joe."

"Yeah."

"He's here."

CHAPTER
THIRTEEN

Big Bore Redhawk was a born-again Indian. That is, he'd been born Dickie-Bob Tingsley and hadn't really paid attention to the little bit of Native American ancestry his mother had told him he had until he was arrested for fencing jewelry at age twenty-six and discovered—through a sarcastic comment made by the judge at his hearing—that he could have been selling jewelry legally without being taxed because of his reputed Indian blood.

Big Bore Redhawk had chosen his Tuscarora name with care—even though he wasn't a member of the Tuscarora tribe. Always a fan of huge firearms, Dickie-Bob had admired the Ruger Big Bore Redhawk .357 Magnum pistol more than any other heavy-caliber weapon he'd ever owned. He'd killed each of his first two wives with a Big Bore Redhawk—having to toss each weapon away and knock over some liquor stores to earn enough money to replace it each time—and it was while trying to rob a liquor store (with a totally inadequate .22 Beretta) to replace that second beloved weapon, rusting in the Reservation soil not far from his second wife, that he was arrested and sent to Attica.

Big Bore's one legal request before being sent up was to change his name. The judge, amused, had allowed it.

Big Bore had known who Joe Kurtz was in the years they were both in Attica, but he'd stayed away from the smaller man. (Most men were smaller than Big Bore Redhawk.) Big Bore had considered Kurtz a crazy fuck—any man who would kill that Black Muslim mofo Ali in a shower shiv fight and get away with it, fooling the guards but drawing a fifteen-thousand-dollar death price on his head from the D-Block Mosque was a crazy fuck. Big

Bore didn't want any part of him. Big Bore hung out with his A.B. buds and let his lawyer work to get him out early based on the premise that he, Big Bore Redhawk, was a victim of anti-Native American discrimination.

Then, last winter, Little Skag Farino, still serving time for murder in Attica, had sent word to Big Bore through Skag's sister, Angelina Whatsis Whosis, that he'd pay Big Bore ten thousand dollars for whacking Kurtz.

It had sounded good. Little Skag's sexy sister had paid him two thousand dollars in advance and Big Bore had done a week of serious drinking while making his plans. It shouldn't have been too hard to kill Kurtz, since Big Bore had his new Big Bore Redhawk .357, an eight-inch Bowie knife, and Kurtz didn't know he was coming for him.

But somehow Kurtz had found out, driven up to the Tuscarora Reservation just north of Buffalo in a fucking blizzard, surprised Big Bore and challenged him to a fair fight. Kurtz had even tossed his gun aside for the fight. Big Bore had grinned, pulled his giant knife, and said something like, "Okay, let's see what you got, Kurtz." And Kurtz had said something like, "I've got a forty-five," and pulled a second pistol out from under his jacket and shot Big Bore in the knee.

It really hurt.

Because Kurtz had threatened to reveal the bit about where his two wives were buried—Big Bore had done a lot of bragging in stir—the Indian had told the cops he'd blown his own knee off while cleaning a friend's pistol. The cops hadn't been impressed with this story, but they also hadn't really given a damn about Big Bore's ruined knee, so they'd left it alone.

At first, Big Bore had considered leaving it alone as well—Kurtz was a mean little fuck—and the wounded man had planned to just move out west somewhere, Arizona or Nevada or Indiana or one of those states where real Indians lived—and maybe he'd grow his own peyote and live in an air-conditioned tipi somewhere and sell tourists fake rugs or something.

But after several weeks in and out of the hospital while the medics kept futzing with what little cartilage and bone was left in his knee and upper leg, they gave Big Bore a prosthetic hinge—he couldn't call it a knee—of plastic and steel and consigned him to four months of sheer hell called physical therapy. Every time Big Bore whined or cursed from the pain, which was a hundred times a day, he thought of Joe Kurtz. And what he was going to do to Joe Kurtz.

And then, just last month in September, two of Big Bore's good A.B.

buds from Attica got out on parole, and together the three of them began looking for Kurtz. But his two Aryan Brotherhood pals—Moses and Pharaoh—were unreliable, shot up on skag half the time, and now Big Bore was looking for Kurtz on his own. He had his beloved double-action, seven and a half-inch barreled Big Bore Redhawk .357 Magnum. The huge pistol was made even larger by the addition of a big 2X Burris LER pistol scope hooked to the barrel scallops by scope rings.

The assembled weapon with scope was huge. Neither of his two ex-wives could have lifted the thing with one hand, nor could they have pulled the trigger, what with its 6.25-lb. trigger pull. Big Bore couldn't fit the scoped weapon in his custom-made Ruger shoulder holster, so he carried around a little gym bag with the scoped Redhawk and a hundred rounds of Buffalo Bore ammo.

He was carrying the bag when he went back to Blues Franklin this night to apologize to the old nigger who owned the place—Daddy Bruce—and explain that he'd been drunk the last time he'd been in and that the A.B. types with him were no friends of his—and to ask, casually, if Daddy had seen Joe Kurtz recently. Daddy had accepted Big Bore's apology, bought him a drink, and said that if Joe Kurtz didn't show by eleven P.M., he wasn't coming.

Big Bore waited alertly until eleven-thirty and had three more drinks while he waited. Some group was playing music, jazz probably, although all music sounded the same to Big Bore. He sorted through various plans but then decided on the simplest one—when Kurtz came through the door, Big Bore would lift the .357 Magnum, blow a hole in Kurtz wide enough to drop Daddy Bruce's little granddaughter through, and then Big Bore would hop in his Dodge Power Wagon and drive straight out to Arizona or wherever, maybe stop in Ohio to visit his cousin Tami.

Quarter to midnight and Big Bore realized that Kurtz wasn't coming. Just as he was leaving Blues Franklin, Big Bore got the uneasy feeling that he was being set up. What was to keep Daddy Bruce from calling Kurtz. Maybe Kurtz was paying the nigger to be on the lookout.

Franklin Street was dark, everything shut down but the blues club and the coffeehouse three doors down. Big Bore slipped the huge double-action out of the gym bag and carried it muzzle down, pressed against his leg, the massive hammer thumbed back. He moved from shadow to shadow, watching out of the corners of his eyes like they'd taught him in the army before they kicked him out.

No one on the street. No one in the alley. A single other car—a dark and silent Lincoln—was parked half a block up from where his ancient Dodge Power Wagon pickup truck sat high on oversized wheels just across the street. Had he locked it?

Big Bore slipped a flashlight out of the gym bag and shifted the bag under his left arm. Then he moved forward quickly, stabbing the flashlight beam ahead of him toward the cab, the Ruger half-raised.

Both doors were locked. The high cab was empty. Big Bore set the bag down, fished around for his keys, opened the driver's side door, flashed the beam around once more to be sure, looked over his shoulder to check that no one was getting out of the Lincoln, looked up and down the street, and then jumped into the cab, tossing the bag on the seat to his right and laying the huge scoped pistol on top of it.

He felt the breeze on his neck a second before the muzzle of a gun pressed against the back of his head. *Some sonofabitch took the window out of the back of the cab and was hiding in the truck bed.*

"Keep your hands on the top of the wheel, Big Bore," whispered Joe Kurtz. "Don't turn around."

"Joe, I been wanting to talk to you . . ." began the Indian.

"Shut up." Keeping the cocked .38's muzzle deep in the flab at the back of Big Bore's neck, Kurtz reached in, grabbed the Ruger, and dropped it into the bed of the truck.

"Joe, you gotta understand . . ."

"I understand that the next word you say will be your last," hissed Kurtz in Big Bore's ear. "One bullet for each additional word from here on in."

Big Bore managed to keep quiet. His left leg began shaking, but then he remembered *I got the knife on my belt under the vest* and he knew that Kurtz would want to talk, want to threaten him, and that's when Big Bore'd gut him like a fish. He almost smiled.

"Listen," whispered Kurtz. "Start the engine but then put your right hand back on the top of the wheel next to the left one. That's good. Steer with both hands up there."

"I gotta shift . . ." began Big Bore and then winced, shut his eyes, and waited for the bullet. Kurtz pressed the muzzle so deep into his neck that it *felt* like a bullet coming up into his skull.

"No shifting," said Kurtz. "This thing's in second gear, it'll start in second gear—keep it there. Both hands on the wheel. That car in front of you is going to start up and pull out now. Follow it, but not too close. Get within twenty feet of its bumper and I'll blow your head off. Fall more than fifty feet behind it and I'll blow your head off. Go over thirty miles an hour and I'll blow your head off. Nod if all this is clear."

Big Bore nodded.

The Lincoln Town Car ahead of them started up, turned on its headlights, and pulled away from the curb, heading slowly south on Franklin Street.

"Turn left here," said Kurtz. The truck followed the Lincoln as it turned east.

Maybe someone'll see Kurtz in the truck bed behind me reachin' in, thought Big Bore, but the stab of hope faded quickly. It was too dark. The sides of the Power Wagon were too high. Kurtz had the old tarp pulled up over him. The Lincoln was moving slowly, crossing Main into the black ghetto where there were fewer and fewer streetlights.

"You just couldn't leave it alone, could you, Big Bore?" said Kurtz.

The Indian opened his mouth to say something, anything, then remembered Kurtz's threat.

"You can answer this," said Kurtz. "Do you know anything about the parking garage?"

"Parking garage?" repeated Big Bore.

Kurtz could tell from the tone of the man's quavering voice that Big Bore Redhawk had nothing to do with yesterday's shooting.

The Lincoln pulled up in front of an abandoned line of shops in the darkest section of the old black neighborhoods.

"Stop ten feet behind it, put it in neutral, and set the brake," whispered Kurtz. "Do anything else and I kill you here."

Big Bore considered going for the knife then, but the circle of the muzzle pressed into the back of his head was more persuasive than his desperation.

Three men got out of the Lincoln and walked back to the Dodge wagon. Two of them aimed guns at Big Bore, ordered him to step out of the cab, frisked him, took his giant knife, and led him to the Lincoln, where they had him lie down in the trunk. The Town Car's trunk was very well insulated and Big Bore's sobs and entreaties were cut off as soon as the lid came down.

"I understand this is supposed to happen tomorrow, way the hell down by Erie, at ten A.M. exactly," said Colin, Angelina Farino Ferrara's personal bodyguard.

"Yeah," said Kurtz. He held the huge, scoped Ruger up in his gloved hand. "You have any use for this?"

"Are you kidding?" said Colin. "That thing's almost as big as my dick. I like smaller weapons." He hoisted the little .32 he was holding.

Kurtz nodded and dropped the Ruger through the missing window into the driver's seat. He had no doubt that truck and gun would be gone by three A.M.

"Miz Ferrara said I should be getting an envelope," said Colin.

"Tell her I'll send the money to her this weekend," said Kurtz.

The bodyguard gave Kurtz a look but then shrugged. "Why ten A.M.?"

"What?" Kurtz's head was buzzing.

"Why ten A.M. exactly? For the Indian tomorrow."

"It's a sentimental thing," said Kurtz. He hopped down from the Power Wagon bed and began walking toward where his Pinto was parked in front of an abandoned drugstore with broken windows.

When he'd called Angelina on her private line after getting Daddy Bruce's call, the female don had thought he was kidding.

"I'm not," Kurtz had said. "I'll still find this skag basher for you, and you keep your fifteen thousand dollars . . ."

"Ten thousand for finding him," Angelina said. "I already gave you five as an advance."

"Whatever. I send the advance back and you keep the rest in exchange for this little favor now."

"*Little favor*," repeated Angelina, her voice amused. "We do this . . . *little thing* for you now in exchange for your *promise* to do this other thing for us someday?"

"Yeah," said Kurtz. After a minute's silence, he'd said, "You started this Big Bore thing last winter, lady. Look at this as a way to clean it up and save some money at the same time."

There was a brief additional silence on the line and then she'd said, "All right. When tonight? Where?"

Kurtz had told her.

"This isn't your style, Kurtz," she'd said then. "I always thought you took care of your own messes."

"Yeah," Kurtz had said tiredly. "I'm just a little busy right now."

"But no more favors like this," said Angelina Farino Ferrara.

Now Kurtz sat in his Pinto and watched the Lincoln Town Car drive away slowly. The huge Dodge Power Wagon was alone at the dark curb, its heavy brackets for a snowplow blade looking like mandibles, the rest of its hulk looking rusted and desolate and sort of sad so far out of its element here in the inner city.

Kurtz shook his head, wondered if he was getting soft, and drove back to the Harbor Inn to get some sleep. He and Arlene were going to go over the rest of the O'Toole computer stuff in the office at eight the next morning. He'd made another call on the way over to Blues Franklin and had an appointment set for ten A.M.

CHAPTER
FOURTEEN

So why'd you want to meet me here?" asked Detective Rigby King.

"I like the food here," said Kurtz. He glanced at his watch. It was just ten A.M.

They were in the small restaurant area—a long counter and a long, narrow dining area just across the aisle from the counter—set amidst the sprawling, indoor Broadway Market. The market was a tradition in Buffalo, and like most traditions in America, it had seen better days. Once a thriving indoor fresh meat, fruit, flowers, and tchotchke covered market in the old Polish and German section of town, Broadway Market was now surrounded by a black ghetto and really came alive only during Easter time, when the many Polish families who'd fled to Cheektowaga and other suburbs came in to buy their Easter hams. Today, half the market space was empty and there was a half-hearted attempt at some Halloween exhibits and festivities, but only a few black mothers with their costumed kids wandered the aisles.

Kurtz and Rigby sat along the mostly empty counter at the aisle-side restaurant. For some promotional reason, all the waitresses behind the long counter were wearing flannel pajamas. One of them had a sort of sleeping bonnet on. They didn't look all that happy, and Kurtz couldn't blame them.

Kurtz and Rigby were drinking coffee. Kurtz also had ordered a donut, although he nibbled without enthusiasm. Little kids in drugstore Star Wars and Spiderman costumes would glance at him, then look again, and then cringe against their mothers' legs. Kurtz was still wearing the Ray Charles glasses, but evidently the raccoon bruises were turning orange today and creeping out further from beneath the glasses. He was wearing a black baseball cap to cover most of the small bandage he'd left in place.

"Do you remember coming here as a kid?" asked Kurtz, sipping his coffee and watching what little movement there was in the cavernous space. Many of the mothers seemed morose and sullen, their kids hyperactive.

"I remember stealing stuff here as a kid," said Rigby. "The old women would scream at me in Polish."

Kurtz nodded. He knew other kids from Father Baker's who'd come up here to grab and run. He never had.

"Joe," said Rigby, setting down her coffee mug, "you didn't ask to meet to ramble on about old times. Did you have something you wanted to talk about?"

"Do I have to have an agenda to have coffee with an old friend?"

Rigby snorted slightly. "Speaking of old friends and agendas—you know another ex-con named Big Bore Redhawk?"

Kurtz shrugged. "Not really. There was some guy in Attica with that absurd name, but I never had anything to do with him."

"He seems to want to have something to do with you," said Rigby.

Kurtz drank his coffee.

"Word on the street is that this Indian's been hunting for you, telling people in bars that he has a grudge to settle with you. Know anything about this, Joe?"

"No."

Rigby leaned closer. "We're hunting for him. Maybe the grudge he had with you got itself worked out in that parking garage and Peg O'Toole. You think we should question him?"

"Sure," said Kurtz. "But the Indian I remember in Attica didn't look like the twenty-two caliber type. But that's no reason *not* to talk to him."

Rigby sat back. "Why'd you invite me here, Joe?"

"I'm remembering some of the details of the shooting."

Rigby looked skeptical but kept listening.

"There were two men," said Kurtz.

The detective folded her arms across her chest. She was wearing a blue oxford shirt today and a soft, camel-colored jacket with the usual jeans. Her gun was out of sight on her belt on the right. "Two men," she said at last. "You saw their faces?"

"No. Just shapes, silhouettes, about forty feet away. One guy did the shooting until I hit him. Then the other grabbed the twenty-two and started firing."

"How do you know it was a twenty-two?" asked Rigby.

Kurtz frowned. "That's what you and the surgeon told me. That's the slug they pulled out of O'Toole's brain and found next to my skull. What are you talking about, Rigby?"

"But you weren't close enough to make out the type of twenty-two?"

"No. Aren't you listening? But I could tell from the sound—*phut, phut, phut.*"

"Silenced?"

"No. But softer than most twenty-twos would sound in an enclosed, echoing space like that. Sort of like they'd dumped some of the powder in each cartridge. It wouldn't make much difference in muzzle velocity, but it sure cuts down on the noise."

"Says who?" asked Rigby.

"Israel's Mossad for one," said Kurtz. "The assassins they sent out to get payback for the Munich Massacre used reduced loads in twenty-twos."

"You an expert on Mossad assassins now, Joe?"

"No," said Kurtz. He set the remaining half of the donut aside. "I saw it in some movie."

"Some movie," said Rigby and rubbed her cheek. "All right, tell me about the two men."

Kurtz shrugged. "Just like I said—two silhouettes. No details. The guy I hit was shorter than the guy who picked up the pistol and kept firing."

"You're sure you hit one of them?"

"Yeah."

"We didn't find any blood on the garage floor—except yours and O'Toole's."

Kurtz shrugged again. "My guess is that the second shooter crammed the wounded man in the back seat of their car and took off after I went down."

"So they were shooting from behind their own car?"

"How the hell should I know?" said Kurtz. "But wouldn't you?"

Rigby leaned closer, her right elbow on the counter. "I sure as hell wouldn't use a twenty-two to try to kill two people from more than forty feet away."

"No, but I don't think they planned to shoot so soon," said Kurtz. "They were waiting for O'Toole to go to her car just past where they were waiting.

Then the shooter would have stepped out and popped her from a couple of yards away."

Rigby's dark eyebrows went up. "So now you know they were after the parole officer, not you. You're conveniently remembering a lot today, Joe."

Kurtz sighed. "My car was down the ramp to the right. The shooters were on the ramp where O'Toole's car was parked."

"How do you know that?"

"She was walking that direction," said Kurtz. "We both saw it on the tape." He braved another nibble of donut.

"Why two men but only one shooter?" hissed Rigby. They'd been whispering, but they were speaking loudly enough now that one of the waitresses in red polka-dot flannel pajamas looked over at them.

"How the fuck should I know?" Kurtz said in a conversational tone.

Rigby plunked down a five dollar bill for the two coffees and donut. "Do you remember anything else?"

"No. I mean, I remember pretty much what we saw on the security video—trying to drag and carry O'Toole back to the door, or at least behind that pillar, and then getting hit."

Rigby King studied his eyes. "That bit about rescuing O'Toole, risking your life to carry her to safety, didn't strike me as the Joe Kurtz I used to know. You were always the living embodiment of the theory of sociobiology to me, Joe."

Kurtz knew what she was talking about—his wino mentor, Pruno, had given him a long reading list for his years in Attica and Edward O. Wilson had been on the list for year six—but he wasn't going to show her he understood the comment. He gave Rigby the flattest gaze he was capable of and said, "I draped O'Toole over my back like a shield. She's a hefty woman. She would have stopped a twenty-two slug at that range."

"Well, she did," said Rigby. She stood. "If you regain any more memory, Joe, phone it in."

She walked out through the southwest door of Broadway Market.

His phone rang as he was driving the Pinto back to Chippewa Street.

"Errand is all done," came Angelina Farino Ferrara's voice.

"Thanks."

"Fuck thanks," said the female acting-don. "You owe me, Kurtz."

"No. Consider us even when I give you the down payment back, and spend the fifteen wisely. Go buy a new bra for your Boxster."

"I sold the Boxster this spring," said Angelina. "Too slow." She disconnected.

The office smelled of coffee and cigarettes. Kurtz had never picked up the habit for the second and felt too queasy to enjoy more of the first.

O'Toole's computer memory had divulged everything under questioning—password-protected files on her thirty-nine clients, her notes, everything except the password-protected e-mail. Most of what they got was garbage. O'Toole obviously didn't use the company computer for personal stuff—the files were all business.

The files on all the ex-cons, including on Kurtz himself, piled up the usual heap of sad facts and parolee bullshit. Only twenty-one of the thirty-nine were "active clients"—i.e., cons who had to drop in weekly, bi-weekly, or monthly to visit their parole officer. None of O'Toole's notes for the last few weeks' visits started with—"Client so-and-so threatened to kill me today . . ." In fact the level of banality was stunning. All of these guys were losers, many of them were addicts of one or many things, none of them—despite the veil of O'Toole's cool, professional summaries—seemed to show any real signs of wanting to go straight.

And none of them seemed to have a motive for killing his parole officer. (All of O'Toole's clients were male. Perhaps, Kurtz thought, she didn't like ex-cons of the female persuasion.)

Kurtz sighed and rubbed his chin, hearing the stubble there rasp. He'd showered this morning—moving slowly through the haze of pain and queasiness—but he'd decided that the stubble went with the purple and orange raccoon mask and dissolute visage. Besides, it hurt his head to shave.

Arlene had left the office after their meeting this morning—on Fridays she usually went to have coffee with her sister-in-law, Gail, often to discuss Sam's daughter, Rachel, for whom Gail now acted as guardian. So Kurtz had the office to himself. He paced back and forth, feeling the heat from the back room filled with humming servers at one end of his pace and the chill from the long bank of windows at the other end. Yesterday had been brisk and beautiful; today was cold and rainy. Tires hissed on Chippewa Street, but there wasn't much traffic before noon.

He kept shuffling the five pages with their thirty-nine names and capsule summaries and considered ruling himself out as a suspect. *The honed instincts of a trained professional investigator.* No other strategies or conclusions came to mind. Even if he just cut the list to the twenty "active" clients she was seeing weekly or bi-weekly—and there was no logical reason to do that, nor any logical reason to think it was just one of her current clients who did the shooting since it could have been any of the hundreds or thousands who had come before—it would take Kurtz a week or two to get a door-to-door investigation under way.

But something was gnawing like a rodent at Joe Kurtz's bruised brain. One of the names . . .

He shuffled the pages. There it was. Page three. Yasein Goba, 26, naturalized American citizen of Yemeni descent, lives in a part of Lackawanna called "back the Bridge," meaning south of the first all-steel bridge in America, in what was now one of the toughest neighborhoods in America. Goba was on parole after serving eighteen months on an armed robbery conviction.

Kurtz tried to remember what his bag lady informer, Mrs. Tuella Dean, had said—rumors about "some crazy Arab down in Lackawanna talking about wanting to shoot someone."

Pretty thin. Actually, Kurtz realized, thin was too grandiloquent a word for this connection. Invisible, maybe.

Kurtz knew that his search for this Yemeni, if he did it, went straight to the heart of the most pressing question in his world right now—*If the odds are that someone was after Peg O'Toole rather than me, why the hell am I looking into that shooting rather than the heroin killer thing?* After all, Toma Gonzaga was going to kill a guy named Joe Kurtz in—Kurtz glanced at his watch—seventy-eight hours, unless Kurtz solved the mobster's little serial killer problem. Kurtz had only met Toma this one time, but he had the strong feeling that the man meant what he said. Also, Kurtz could use one hundred thousand dollars.

So why am I fucking around investigating my *shooting if O'Toole was the probable target? Get to work on the heroin shooter, Joe.*

Kurtz walked over to the four-foot by five-foot framed map of the Buffalo area set on the north wall of the office. Sam had used the map in their old office, and Arlene had put it up here despite Kurtz's protests that they didn't need the damned thing. This morning, though, he and Arlene had gone through the list of murder sites from both Angelina Farino Ferrara's and Toma Gonzaga's lists and stuck red thumbtacks at each site—fourteen sites for twenty-two missing and presumed murdered people.

The hits had been literally all over the map: three in Lackawanna, four in the black ghetto east of Main, but others in Tonawanda, Cheektowaga, four more in Buffalo proper, and more in relatively upscale—or at least middle-class—suburbs such as Amherst and Kenmore.

Kurtz knew that no investigator in the world, even with police forensic resources behind him or her, could solve these murders in three days if the perpetrator didn't want to be caught. Too many hundreds of square miles to cover, too many hundreds of possible witnesses and potential suspects to interview, too many scores of fingerprints to check out—although Kurtz didn't even own a Boy Detective fingerprint kit—and too many possible local, state, and national killers who'd benefit from putting a crimp in the Gonzaga drug empire in Western New York.

If Kurtz *were* to make a list of suspects in the heroin killings right now, the name *Angelina Farino Ferrara* would fill the first five places on the list. The woman had everything to gain by destroying the Gonzagas' historical claim on the drug scene in the Buffalo area. She was ambitious. My God, was she ambitious. Her life's ambition had been to kill Emilio Gonzaga— which she had done last winter using Joe Kurtz as one of her many pawns— while weakening the Gonzaga crime family's grip on the city and strengthening what was left of the Farino Family power here.

All this "Toma" and "Angelina" first-name crap made sense to Kurtz only if the woman was playing the old game of being friends with her adversary even while plotting his destruction.

But there were the five blue pins on the map—all Farino Family dealers or users who had disappeared with only bloody stains left behind.

Who said they'd been killed?

Angelina Farino Ferrara. Her family, in the first year of her rebuilding, had grabbed just enough peripheral drug action that it would be too suspicious if only Gonzaga people were being murdered. What was the loss of a few dealers and users if it meant gaining Toma Gonzaga's trust? Maybe they'd all been relocated to Miami or Atlantic City while Ms. Farino Ferrara continued to murder Gonzaga junkies.

But Kurtz was sure that Gonzaga didn't trust Angelina. Anyone would be a fool to trust this woman who shot her first husband and kept the pistol out of what she called sentimentality, this woman who married her second elderly husband to be trained in the strategies and tactics of thievery, and who calmly admitted to drowning her only baby because it carried Gonzaga genes.

Kurtz stood at the window and watched the cold rain fall on Chippewa Street. It made sense that Gonzaga "hired" him to find the heroin-connection killer in four days. At the very least, Kurtz's failure would give Gonzaga another reason for whacking him—as if possible collusion in the death of the mobster's father wasn't enough. And Angelina wasn't going to throw a fit when she learned that he'd been whacked—she'd accept Toma's explanation without rancor. The life of one Joe Kurtz wasn't that important in the grander scheme of things for her—especially when that grander scheme included revenge and ambition, which seemed to be the alpha and omega of Angelina Farino Ferrara's emotional spectrum.

Kurtz had to smile. His options were few. At least he'd neutralized the loose cannon that had been Big Bore Redhawk, recording the cell phone conversation with Angelina setting up the hit as he'd done so. Of course, the recording incriminated Joe Kurtz even more than the female don. In truth, they'd both been so circumspect over the phone that the tape was all but useless.

So it came down to the five thousand dollars advance money in an envelope that Kurtz was still carrying around. He'd use that on Tuesday morning—Halloween—when he drove away from Buffalo, New York, forever, buying a different used car before crossing the state line (and violating his parole). Kurtz knew a few people around the country, perhaps the most important right now being a plastic surgeon in Oklahoma City who gave people like Joe Kurtz new faces and identities in exchange for hard cash.

But he'd need quite a bit more hard cash. Kurtz could get fifty thousand dollars in a minute by asking Arlene to buy his theoretical share of WeddingBells-dot-com and SweetheartSearch-dot-com, but he'd never do that. She'd waited for years to start an online business like this, even if the high school sweetheart thing had been his idea in Attica.

Well, he could always get more cash.

Kurtz pulled on his baseball cap, slipped the .38 into his belt, and headed down to the Pinto. He had someone in Lackawanna he wanted to see.

CHAPTER
FIFTEEN

Lackawanna had been one of the great steel centers of the world for almost a century. Raw materials flowed in by ocean freighter coming up the St. Lawrence Seaway and across the Great Lakes, by canal barge, and by locomotive; steel flowed out. Tens of thousands of workers in Lackawanna and Buffalo owed their livelihood to Lackawanna steel for more than fifty years, and it was a good life, with higher wages than those earned at the Chrysler plant or American Standard or any of the other large employers of the blue-collar city called Buffalo. The steel business's medical and pension plans were among the most generous to be found anywhere.

As the market for American steel declined, the heaps of slag near the Lackawanna mills grew higher, the skies grew darker and filthier, the worker housing grew more grim, and the pension plans ate up more and more of the companies' profits, but the *idea* of steel still flourished in Lackawanna. By the late 1960s, the unions had grown too strong, the technologies had lagged behind, corporate accounting practices had become mossbacked and lazy, and the mills themselves were obsolete. The unions still received huge packages. The managers gave themselves raises and bonuses. The companies diverted profits to shareholders rather than reinvest in new technology or pay for managerial changes. Meanwhile, Japanese steel and cheap European steel and Russian steel and Thai steel were running their industries with cheaper labor, newer technologies, and slimmer profit margins. The steel companies in Lackawanna cried foul, cried dumping, diverted money to politicians to get protectionist legislation, and continued with the same pay scales and pension plans and obsolete machinery. They made steel the way their granddaddies had made steel. And they sold it the same way.

By the 1970s, the Lackawanna steel industry was on a gurney and hemorrhaging badly. By the mid-nineties, it was on a cold, stone slab with no mourners waiting around for the wake. Today there were more than a dozen miles of abandoned mills along Lake Erie, a hundred square miles of ghetto where workers' neighborhoods had once been, scores upon scores of empty parking lots that had once been filled with thousands of vehicles, as well as black mountains of slag heaps running back east from the lake for block after block—a cheaper alternative for the defunct mills than cleaning them up—thus insuring that the city of Buffalo, with a third of its population fled seeking work elsewhere, would never spend the money to develop these lakefront properties.

The neighborhoods in the shadow of the huge mills, neighborhoods that once housed German and Italian and some black skilled laborers, now boasted crack houses and abortion clinics and storefront mosques as even poorer blacks and Hispanics and Middle Eastern immigrants flowed into the vacuum created by the fleeing steel workers.

Kurtz knew Lackawanna well. He'd lost his virginity there, lost any illusions about life there, and killed his first man there, not necessarily in that order.

Ridge Road was the main east-west street through the heart of Lackawanna, past Our Lady of Victory Basilica, past Father Baker's Orphanage, past the Holy Cross Cemetery, past the Botanical Gardens and Lackawanna City Hall, then over the narrow steel bridge built more than a century ago, then "back the bridge," south, into the warren of narrow streets that dead-ended against the walls and moats and barriers bordering the mile-wide no-man's land of railroad tracks that ran south to everywhere and north into the grain-mill industrial area near Kurtz's Harbor Inn.

Parolee Yasein Goba's address was south of the old Carnegie Library and the nearby Lackawanna Islamic Mosque. The house was a leaning, filthy gray-shingle affair at the end of a littered cul-de-sac. To the right of and behind the house was the high fence of a salvage yard; to its left was the rusted iron wall and barbed wire fences marking railroad property. Freight trains heaved and clashed in the rainy air.

Kurtz backed the Pinto out of the cul-de-sac, swung it around, drove east a block, and parked it near Odell Playground, the only bit of grass and open space within miles. He made sure the Pinto couldn't be seen from the main north-south street, Wilmuth Avenue, or from Yasein Goba's house.

Black and Middle Eastern faces peered at him from passing cars and from between sooty curtains as he tucked the .38 in his belt, took a long-bladed screwdriver from the glove box, locked the Pinto and walked the two blocks toward Goba's gray house.

Kurtz cut right a block and came at the house along the salvage yard fence, approaching from the north. The smoke and noise from the railyards were almost melodramatic: steel couplers crashing, machines grunting as they hauled heavy loads, men shouting in the distance. More crashes and bangs came from the huge salvage yard beyond the fence.

Kurtz paused when there was nothing but open field between him and the house. Except for one small window on the north side here, all the house's windows looked east up the empty street or west over the railyards. There was no car parked next to the house and no garage, although several abandoned cars, wheels missing, littered the street.

Kurtz pulled the .38, held it loosely against his right leg, and walked behind the house.

The back door wasn't locked. There was dried blood on the steps, the stoop, and the door itself. Standing to one side of the glass, Kurtz opened the door and went in crouched, .38 extended.

The blood trail went up some stairs. A perfect red handprint was in the middle of the half-open door at the top of the inside stairway. Kurtz used the pistol to swing the door open wider. A kitchen. Dirty dishes. Garbage stinking. More blood on the cheap table and chipped tile floor. One of the chairs had been knocked over.

Breathing through his mouth, Kurtz followed the blood trail through a living room—filthy shag carpet with blobs of dried blood, sprung couch covered by a filthy sheet, big color television. The blood trail went up a narrow flight of stairs in the narrow central hall, but Kurtz checked the other two downstairs rooms first. Clear.

Yasein Goba was sprawled half across the grimy tub in the little bathroom at the head of the stairs. The blood trail led there and ended there. Goba had been hit high in the right ribcage—the wound looked consistent with the nine-millimeter slugs O'Toole had loaded in her Sig Pro that Kurtz had been firing—and the man had poured his life's blood half into the tub and half onto the bathroom floor. The bottom of the tub was solid brown with dried blood. There was blood all over the sink and blood on the mirrored door of the medicine chest. Bottles of pills, rubbing alcohol, and Mercurachrome were scattered on the floor and broken in the bloody sink. It looked as if Goba had tried to find something to stop the bleeding, or at least something to dull the pain, before he fainted onto the tub rim and bled out.

O'Toole's file said that Yasein Goba was twenty-six years old and from Yemen. Making sure not to step in the dried pools and rivulets on the floor, Kurtz crouched next to the corpse. The young man may have been an Arab, but the loss of blood added a paleness under the brown skin and tiny black mustache. His lips were white, his mouth and eyes open. Kurtz was no medical examiner, but he'd seen enough corpses to know that rigor mortis had come and gone and that this guy had probably been dead about forty-eight hours—since a few hours after Kurtz and O'Toole had been shot.

Lying in the tub was a Ruger Mark II Standard .22-caliber long-barreled target pistol. The checkered grip was mottled with blood. Kurtz lifted it carefully, letting his gloves touch only the end of the barrel where there was no blood. He held it up into the light, but the serial number had been burned off with acid. He knew it had a ten-shot magazine and he imagined that the mag would be empty, or near so. Kurtz set the gun back in the tub where the grip had been outlined in dried blood.

He stood and walked into Yasein Goba's bedroom. On a high bureau was a sort of altar—black candles, worry beads, and a blown-up photograph of Parole Officer Margaret O'Toole with the words DIE, BITCH written across it in red magic marker.

On a cheap desk by the front window was a spiral notebook. Kurtz flipped the pages, noted the dated entries and the Arabic writing, but some passages were in scrawled English—"*. . . she contenus to prossecute me!!*" and "*purhsed fine pistol today*" and "*the Zionist bitch must die if I am to live!*" The last page had been torn out of the notebook.

Some sense made Kurtz look up, pull open the filthy curtain a bit with the barrel of his .38.

Kemper's and King's unmarked car had stopped half a block away on the next street over. They were approaching Goba's house the same way Kurtz had, and if it hadn't been for the bare trees and the angle on the alley, Kurtz couldn't have seen them even from this high up. Stopping behind the unmarked detectives' car were two black Chevy Suburbans. Eight black-garbed and helmeted SWAT team members carrying automatic weapons boiled out of the Suburbans.

Detectives Kemper and King deployed the SWAT teams, sending them toward the house through alleys, backyards, and along the salvage yard fence. King talked into a hand radio, and Kurtz assumed that there would be more SWAT squads coming from the next block over to the south.

Kurtz folded up the spiral notebook and slipped it into the cargo pocket of his jacket. Then he left the bedroom, went down the stairs, through the kitchen, down more stairs, and out the back door. Because of the slight angle of the backyard and the heavy rain falling, the first of the SWAT guys weren't visible yet.

There was a rusted and abandoned Mercury at the back of this weedy strip, abutting the salvage yard fence and Kurtz ran at it full tilt through the rain and mud. He leaped to the hood, jumped to the roof, heaved himself up and over the fence, and dropped into the salvage yard about five seconds before the first SWAT team loped into sight, the black-vested gunmen covering each other as they ran, automatic weapons trained on the windows of the late Yasein Goba's house.

CHAPTER
SIXTEEN

Kurtz stopped by the Harbor Inn to change out of his muddy, wet clothes and to oil his .38, and then he drove back to the office. It was almost dark now, and colder, and the October rain was coming down hard. The clubs, restaurants, and wine bars along Chippewa Street were beginning to attract patrons and every color of neon reflected on the slick streets.

Arlene was at work, arranging weddings, receptions, wedding dress fittings, and wedding cake designs with happy brides all over the eastern and central United States, but she wiped all that from the screen, lit another Marlboro, and looked at Kurtz when he came in, hung up his leather jacket, and leaned back in his swivel chair. He pulled the pistol out of his belt in the back to keep it from digging into him, and set it in the lower right drawer next to the bottle of Sheep Dip scotch.

"Well?" said Arlene.

Kurtz hesitated. Usually he told Arlene almost nothing of his activities outside the office—much of it was illegal, just as this afternoon's breaking and entering of the dead Arab's house had been, and as far as he knew Arlene had never had so much as a traffic ticket—but she'd already broken the law last night for him, passing herself off as a County D.A.'s assistant, not to mention breaking and entering O'Toole's office and stealing her files. *So what the hell*, thought Kurtz.

He told her about finding Yasein Goba and the Yemeni's little revenge altar, about taking his diary, and about the pistol.

"Jesus, Joe," whispered Arlene. "So do you think it was one of your shots in the parking garage that got him?"

Kurtz nodded. "We won't know for sure until the coroner digs the slug out and they run a ballistics test, but I know that I hit the first shooter."

"So that's the motive," said Arlene. "He was mad at O'Toole for some reason."

"I read just enough of his diary—the parts in bad English—to see that he blamed her for ruining his life, something about not being able to marry his childhood sweetheart because he was treated as a felon by the 'Zionist bitch.' "

" 'Zionist bitch?' " said Arlene. "Didn't this idiot know that O'Toole was Irish?"

Kurtz shrugged.

"Well, that ties it all up in a knot, doesn't it, Joe?"

Kurtz rubbed his cheeks and then his temples. The headache felt like someone tapping, not very gently, on the back of his head with a two-pound hammer wrapped in a thin sock.

"They weren't after you," continued Arlene. "You were just unlucky to get in the way when one of Peg O'Toole's crazy clients came after her."

"Yeah."

"There was nothing in O'Toole's file on Goba that suggests that he was hostile or angry at her—the last several meetings she had with him sound easy, even upbeat. But if he was crazy, I guess it makes sense. Maybe it even ties in to that old Lackawanna Six terrorist thing. There are some crazy people down there in Lackawanna."

"Yeah."

"Now you're free to investigate this other thing." Arlene waved her cigarette toward the map on the north wall with its twenty-two pins, seventeen red, five blue.

"Yeah."

"But you don't buy the Goba thing for a minute, do you, Joe?"

Kurtz closed his eyes. He tried to remember if he'd eaten anything since the half donut with Rigby King at Broadway Market that morning. Evidently not. "No," he said at last. "I don't buy it."

"Because you remember two shooters," said Arlene.

"Yeah. I told Rigby King about the second guy when I saw her this morning."

"If someone other than Goba was driving the car when it busted out of the parking garage, they'll probably find the bloodstains in the backseat," said Arlene.

"The car wasn't there at Goba's," said Kurtz.

"You said it was a rough neighborhood. And Goba had been dead two days. Car thieves were probably just waiting to pounce on a vehicle left unattended for two days."

"Yeah."

"You don't buy that either?"

"I don't know," said Kurtz. "But I know there was a second man in the parking garage Wednesday. And odds are that the second man was driving the car when it crashed out. Goba didn't get home by himself. I don't think he could even have got into the house and up the stairs by himself."

"You said you saw bloodstains and trails everywhere. His handprint on the kitchen door."

"Yeah."

"And you said it looked like he'd rummaged through his medicine chest hunting for bandages or painkillers?" Arlene exhaled smoke and tapped at one fingernail with another.

"Yeah," said Kurtz.

"Any strange footprints in the blood or extra handprints anywhere?"

"No," said Kurtz. "Not that I could see. Whoever dragged him in the house made it look like Goba crawled in under his own power."

"A friend maybe?"

"Maybe," said Kurtz. "But why wouldn't a friend haul Goba to the hospital? He was hurt bad."

"GSW report?" said Arlene.

Kurtz knew that she was right. Doctors and hospitals had to report gunshot wounds to the authorities.

"I bet there are Yemeni doctors in Lackawanna who might've kept it quiet," said Kurtz. "I know for a fact there are medics down there that'll patch you up without reporting it. For a price."

"Goba was poor."

"Yeah," said Kurtz.

"Joe," said Arlene, looking at the map with all the pins, "there's something you're not telling me about this heroin-addict killer situation. About why you agreed to work for Gonzaga and that woman, but why you don't want to do it."

"What do you mean?"

"There's something."

Kurtz shook his head. The action made him dizzy. "Arlene, you want to order from that Chinese place down the street? Get takeout?"

She stubbed out her cigarette. "Have you eaten anything today?"

"Sort of."

She made her snorting noise again. "You stay here, Joe. Catch a couple of minutes rest. I'll go down and order in person, bring something back."

Arlene patted him on the shoulder as she left. The contact made Kurtz jump.

He was half-dozing when the phone rang.

"Joe Kurtz? This is Detective Kemper. I just wanted to let you know that it looks like we've found the man who shot you and Officer O'Toole on Wednesday."

"Who is it?" asked Kurtz.

"You can read about it in the papers tomorrow," said the black cop. "But it looks like the guy was just after Officer O'Toole. If we find any connection between the shooter and you, I'll be the first to let you know."

"I bet you will," said Kurtz.

Kemper disconnected.

Kurtz took Goba's diary out of his jacket pocket and flipped through the pages. The scrawled entries were all dated, although Goba put the day first, then the month, and then the year, in the European manner. Much of it was in Arabic, but the English entries screamed out Goba's hatred of Parole Office "Zionist Bitch" O'Toole, how she was stealing Goba's future, keeping him from getting married, forcing him to return to a life of crime, discriminating against Arabs, part of the Zionist conspiracy, blah, blah.

The entries were made in a hard-tipped ballpoint pen, which was good. Kurtz flipped to the missing page. Only a ragged fringe remained. He found a pencil in his desk and began gently shading the next, empty page. The impressions from the heavily pressed ballpoint came up immediately.

Kurtz was asleep sitting at his desk when Arlene returned with the food, but she woke him gently and made him eat something. She'd brought two cold bottles of iced tea with the Chinese food.

They used chopsticks, sat at Arlene's desk, and ate in silence for a minute. Kurtz slid Goba's spiral notebook across to her. It was opened to the pencil-shaded page. "How does that read to you?" he asked.

Still holding her chopsticks, Arlene pulled the notebook under her desk lamp and squinted for a minute, moving her glasses forward and back. "Letters missing," she said at last. "Lots of misspellings. But it looks like the final sentence reads—'*I can't . . . live with . . .*' something, maybe '*the guilt*,' although he spelled it without a 'u,' and then, *I must also die.*" Arlene looked at Kurtz. "Goba wrote a suicide note."

"Yeah. Convenient isn't it?"

"It doesn't make sense . . ." began Arlene. "Wait a minute. These numbers above the scrawl."

"Yeah."

"It's dated Thursday," said Arlene.

"Uh-huh."

"Didn't you say that there was no sign that he'd crawled into the bedroom, Joe? No blood trail there?"

"That's what I said."

"So his diary ends with the announcement that he can't live with the guilt of shooting O'Toole, and presumably you, too, and that he's going to kill himself. On the day *after* he bled to death."

"A little peculiar, isn't it?" said Kurtz.

"But that page was missing," said Arlene. She pushed the notebook aside and began spearing at her beef and broccoli. "Maybe you shouldn't have taken this notebook, Joe. The cops might have noticed the missing page and shaded in this last entry's imprint just the way you did."

"Maybe," said Kurtz.

"And they'd know that Goba's confession was a fake." She looked at him over the desk lamp and adjusted her glasses. "But you don't want them to know."

"Not yet," said Kurtz. "So far, it's the only advantage I have in this whole mess."

They ate the rest of the meal in silence.

When he was finished and the white cartons were wrapped in plastic and tossed away, Kurtz stood, walked to his own desk, swayed slightly, shook his head, took the .38 out of the Sheep Dip drawer, and lifted his leather jacket off the back of the chair.

"Uh-uh," said Arlene, coming around her desk and taking the pistol out of his hands. "You're not going anywhere tonight, Joe."

"Need to talk to a man in Lackawanna," mumbled Kurtz. "Baby Doc. Have to find . . ."

"Not tonight. Your scalp is bleeding again—sutures are all screwed up. I'm changing the bandages and you can sleep on the couch. You've done it enough times before."

Kurtz shook his head but allowed himself to be led into the little bathroom.

The bandages were blood-encrusted and they pulled scab and scalp when Arlene jerked them off, but Kurtz was too exhausted to react. If the headache was a noise, it was reaching jackhammer and jet-engine levels now. He sat dully on the edge of the sink while she brought out the serious first-aid kit, cleaned and daubed the scalp wound, and set clean bandages in place.

"I have to see a guy," said Kurtz, still sitting, trying to visualize standing and retrieving his .38 and jacket. "Baby Doc will probably be at Curly's. It's Friday night."

"He'll be there tomorrow," said Arlene, leading him into the office and pressing against his shoulders until he sat down and then flopped back on the old couch. "Baby Doc always holds court at Curly's on Saturday mornings."

She turned to grab the old blanket they kept on the arm of the couch. When she turned back, Kurtz was asleep.

CHAPTER

SEVENTEEN

The Dodger liked Saturday mornings. Always had. As a kid, he'd hated school, loved weekends, loved playing hooky. Saturdays were the best, even though none of the other kids in the area would play with him. Still, he'd had his Saturday-morning cartoons and then he'd go out alone into the woods adjoining the town. Sometimes he'd take a pet with him into the woods—a neighbor's cat, say, or Tom Herenson's old Labrador that time, or even that pale girl's, Shelley's, green and yellow parakeet. He'd always enjoyed taking the animals into the woods. Although the parakeet hadn't been that much fun.

Now the Dodger was driving slowly through rural residential roads in Orchard Park, the upscale suburb where the Buffalo Bills played their games out at that huge stadium. The Dodger didn't give the slightest damn about football, but sometimes he pretended he did when befriending some guy in a sports bar. Even the women in Buffalo were ga-ga over football and hockey and assumed everyone else was, too. It was a place to start with people when you were pretending that you were one of them.

Orchard Park was mostly like this street—rural roads masquerading as streets, homes both large and small set back on an acre or less of woods. The house he was looking for was . . . right here. Just as described in the Boss's briefing to him. This rural street ran along a wooded ridgeline and this house, strangely octagonal, was set thirty or forty yards from the road, all but obscured by the trees.

The Dodger drove his van right up the driveway, not hesitating. There was no car parked outside, but the house had a garage so the car might be in there and she might be home. On the lawn, just as described in the briefing, was a stone Buddha.

He parked the van in the driveway turnaround just outside the garage and jumped out, whistling, carrying a clipboard. The van was painted with a common pest control logo and graphic, and the Dodger was wearing coveralls and an orange vest, had a white hard hat over his Dodger cap, and he was carrying a clipboard. The old joke that you could go almost anywhere unchallenged with work coveralls, a hard hat, and a clipboard wasn't really a joke; those cheap props could get you past most people's radar. The Dodger's 9-millimeter Beretta was on his belt, under the orange highway vest, holstered next to a folding seven-inch combat knife.

Still whistling, the Dodger knocked on the front door, taking a half-step back on the stoop as he'd been taught. He'd take another half step back when the door opened, showing how polite he was, how non-aggressive. It was an old door-to-door salesman's trick.

The woman didn't come to the door. The briefing suggested that she'd be home alone on Saturday, unless her boyfriend had slept over. The Dodger was ready for either contingency. He knocked again, pausing in the whistling to look around at the wooded lot and the view from the ridge as if appreciating both even on such a cold and cloudy October day. The air smelled of wet leaves.

When she didn't answer a third knock, he strolled around the house, pretending to inspect the foundation. In the back, there was a cheap deck and sliding glass doors. He knocked loudly on the glass, taking a step back again and arranging a sincere smile on his face, but again there was no answer. The house had that empty feel that he knew well from experience.

The Dodger pulled a multiple-use tool from his coverall pocket and jimmied the doorlock in ten seconds. He let himself in, called "Hello?" a couple of times into the silence, and then strolled through the octagonally shaped ranch house.

The woman—Randi Ginetta—was in her early forties, a high-school English teacher, divorced, living alone since her only child, a son, had gone to college in Ohio the year before. Still getting alimony payments from her former husband, she was now dating another teacher, a nice Italian man. Randi was also a heroin addict. For years Randi—the Dodger wondered what kind of name that was, "Randi," it sounded more like a cocktail waitress's name to him than a teacher's—for years Randi had been into cocaine, explaining her constant runny nose as allergy problems to her co-workers and students, but in the past three years she'd discovered skag and liked it a lot. She always bought from the same source, a black junkie on Gonzaga's payroll in the Allentown section of Buffalo. Randi had gotten to know the junkie-dealer during time she volunteered in an inner-city homeless program. The Dodger hadn't visited the junkie yet, but he was on the list.

He walked from room to room, the combat knife in his hand now, blade still closed. This teacher and skag-addict liked bright colors. All the walls were different colors—blue, red, bright green—and the furniture was heavy oak. There was a giant crystal on the floor near the front door. *New Age-type*, thought the Dodger. *Trips to Sedona to tap into energy sources, commune with Indian spirits, that kind of crap.* The Dodger wasn't guessing. It had all been in the Boss's briefing.

There were a lot of books, a work desk, a Mac computer, stacks of papers to be graded. But Ms. Randi wasn't all that neat—there were jeans and sweaters and bras and other underwear lying around her bedroom and on the bathroom floor. The Dodger knew a lot of perverts who would have lifted that silk, sniffed it maybe, but he wasn't a pervert. He was here to do a job. The Dodger went back across the octagonal living room and into the narrow kitchen.

There was a photo of Randi and her son—he recognized her from the photo he'd been shown—on the fridge, as well as a photo of the teacher and her boyfriend. She was a babe, no doubt about it. He hoped she'd come home soon, and alone, but looking at the photo of the boyfriend—all serious and squinty-eyed—the Dodger changed his mind and hoped the two would come back together. He had plans for both of them.

Pulling on latex gloves, the Dodger turned on the coffeemaker, rooted around in the cupboard until he found the coffee—Starbucks—and made himself a cup. She—or they—would smell the coffee brewing when they came in the door, but that didn't matter. They wouldn't have time to react. He tucked away the knife and laid the Beretta Elite II on the round wooden table as he drank his coffee. He'd rinse the cup well to get rid of any DNA when he was done.

The Dodger decided he'd wait thirty minutes. The neighbors couldn't see his van because of the trees and the size of the lot, but a neighbor driving by might see it and call the cops if he stayed here too long. He rose, found the sugar bowl in the cupboard, and stirred some into his coffee.

The phone rang.

The Dodger let the machine pick it up. He thought Randi's voice was sexy, sort of hoarse and sleepy in a sexy junkie way, as it filled the kitchen silence—"Hi, this is Randi. It's Friday and I'll be gone for the weekend, but leave a message and I'll call you back on Sunday night or Monday. *Thanks!*" The last word was punched with girlish enthusiasm or a heroin-induced high.

Not very smart, Ms. Ginetta, thought the Dodger, *telling every Tom, Dick and Harry who calls that you're out of town and your house is empty. Good way to get robbed, ma'am.*

The caller hung up without leaving a message. It might be a neighbor calling to see what the pest control van was doing there while Randi was gone. But probably not.

The Dodger sighed, rinsed out the coffee cup and coffeemaker, set the sugar and everything else back the way it had been—putting the mug on its proper hook—and then he let himself out the back door, locked it behind him, slipped off the latex gloves, hefted the clipboard, and whistled his way back to the van.

CHAPTER

EIGHTEEN

The restaurant called Curly's was just a few blocks from the Basilica in Lackawanna. Kurtz was at Curly's by nine-thirty on Saturday morning, having slept a fitful nine hours and feeling more surly than ever.

He'd awakened in the office sore and disoriented, looked over the print-outs of O'Toole's case notes for Goba to make sure they hadn't missed anything, left a note for Arlene—who usually came in late on Saturday—and headed back to the Harbor Inn to shower, shave, and change clothes. The headache still buzzed in his skull and if it had let up any, he couldn't notice the change. But his raccoon eyes had improved. If one didn't look carefully, Kurtz thought while he stood in front of the steamy mirror, the dark circles under his eyes only made him look like someone who hadn't slept in a few weeks. The whites of his eyes were pink rather than blood red now, and his vision had cleared.

Kurtz dressed in a denim workshirt and jeans, tugged on faded Red Wing boots and an old peacoat, and pulled a dark navy watchcap low enough over his hair to hide the scalp wound. The .38 went in a small holster on his belt on the left side.

Driving down to Lackawanna, he had to smile at the fact that he'd managed to avoid most of Lackawanna for years, but now he found himself heading that way almost every day.

Curly's was a few blocks east of the Basilica, where Ridge Road became Franklin Street for a few blocks, just west of the old steel bridge. The restaurant—surfaced by brick on the first floor, siding above—had been popular with locals for decades. There were already cars in the small parking lot, although it wasn't officially open for breakfast on Saturdays. On Saturdays, it was court to Baby Doc.

Baby Doc—legally Norv Skrzypczyk—was not officially mobbed up, but he ran most of the action in Lackawanna. His grandfather, Papa Doc, had taken a leave from medical school to help patch up striking steel workers whose heads were being bashed in by Pinkerton operatives. Papa Doc had given up medicine in favor of smuggling guns in to the workers. By the end of the 1920s, Papa Doc's people were selling guns and liquor to civilians as well, keeping the Mafia from muscling in on their territory through the simple strategy of out-violencing them. By the time Papa Doc was gunned down in 1942, his son—Doc—had taken over the family business, negotiated a peace with the mobsters, and retained control of most illegal items moving in Lackawanna. Doc retired in 1992, turning the reins over to Baby Doc and taking an old man's job as a night watchmen in various abandoned steel mills, where he kept his hand in by selling the occasional illegal gun. Joe Kurtz had used Doc as an information source—but not a snitch—before Attica, and had bought weapons from him afterward. Kurtz had never met the son.

Now Kurtz left his holstered .38 under the driver's seat of the Pinto, made sure the car was locked, and went in, ignoring the CLOSED sign on the door.

Baby Doc sat in his regular semicircular booth at the right rear of the restaurant. The booth was raised slightly, unlike the other tables, and gave the sense of a modest throne. There were only half a dozen other men in the room, not counting Baby Doc's three bodyguards and the waiter behind the counter. Kurtz noticed that these bodyguards didn't use blow-driers or wear mafia collars and suits—the two big guys in the booth next to Baby Doc and the other one lounging at the counter could have been stevedores or millworkers except for their watchful eyes and the just-detectable bulges under their union windbreakers.

There was an older man talking to Baby Doc in the rear booth, speaking earnestly, moving his scarred hands as he spoke. Baby Doc would nod in the intervals when the old man stopped talking. This is the first time Kurtz had seen Baby Doc in person and he was surprised how large he was; the older Doc had been a small man.

A waiter came over, poured coffee without being asked, and said, "You here to see the Man?"

"Yeah."

The waiter went back to the counter and whispered to the older body-guard, who approached Baby Doc when the old man had finished his supplication, received some answer that had made him smile, and left the restaurant.

Baby Doc looked at Kurtz a minute and then raised a finger, beckoning Kurtz, and then gesturing to the two guards in the booth next to him.

The huge men intercepted Kurtz in the middle of the room. "Let's visit the restroom," said the one with scar tissue around his eyes.

Kurtz nodded and followed them to the back of Curly's. The men's restroom was big enough to hold all three of them, but one man stood watching out the door while the other gestured for Kurtz to remove his shirt and to lift his undershirt. Then he gestured for Kurtz to drop his pants. Kurtz did all this without protest.

"Okay," said the ex-boxer and stepped out. Kurtz zipped and buttoned up and went out to sit in the booth.

Baby Doc wore horn-rimmed glasses that looked incongruous on such a sharply chiseled face. He was in his late forties, and Kurtz saw that the man wasn't so much bald as he was hairless. His eyes were a startling cold blue. His neck, shoulders, and forearms were heavily muscled. There was a flag and army tattoo on Baby Doc's massive left forearm, and Kurtz remembered that Baby Doc had left Lackawanna and joined the army—over his father's objections—a few years before the first Gulf War and had flown some sort of attack helicopter during the liberation of Kuwait. Doc, his father, had been forced to hold off his own retirement for a few years until Baby Doc returned from the service with a chest covered with combat ribbons which—according to sources available to Kurtz—had been folded away in a trunk with the uniform and never taken out again. Rumor persisted that Baby Doc's chopper had destroyed more than a dozen Iraqi tanks on a single hot day.

"You're Joe Kurtz, aren't you?"

Kurtz nodded.

"I remember you sent flowers to my father's funeral last year," said Baby Doc. "Thank you for that."

Kurtz nodded again.

"I considered having you killed," said Baby Doc.

Kurtz didn't nod this time, but he looked the bigger man in the eye.

Baby Doc put down his fork, took off his glasses, and rubbed his eyes. When he set the glasses back on, he said tiredly, "My father was killed by a rogue homicide detective named Hathaway."

"Yes."

"My sources in the B.P.D. tell me that Hathaway had a hard-on for you and had tapped a call between you and my father. You were meeting him at the old steel mill, a year ago next week, to buy a piece. Hathaway killed my father before you got there."

"That's true," said Kurtz.

"Hathaway didn't have anything against Doc. He just wanted to wait for you in the mill without my father being in the way. If it hadn't been for you, the Old Man might still be alive."

"That's true, too," said Kurtz. He glanced at the two closest bodyguards. They were looking the other way but were close enough to hear everything. Kurtz knew he couldn't take them both even if they weren't armed—he'd seen the bigger man fight professionally years ago—so his only chance might be to crash through the window behind Baby Doc. But he'd never get around front to his car before they did. He'd have to head east through the back-yards, into the railyards. Kurtz had known every tunnel and shack and switch tower in those yards when he was young, but he doubted if he could outrun or hide from these guys there now.

Baby Doc folded his hands. "But they found Hathaway there in the mill, too. Shot in the head."

"I've heard that," Kurtz said quietly.

"My people in the department tell me that the bullet went through his gold detective shield," said Baby Doc. "Like he held it up to stop his assailant from shooting. Maybe while shouting that he was a cop—the slug that went through the shield went into Hathaway's open mouth. Or maybe the stupid shit believed it'd really act like a shield and stop a slug."

Kurtz waited.

"But I guess it didn't work," said Baby Doc. He started eating his scram-bled eggs again.

"I guess not," said Kurtz.

"So what do you want, Joe Kurtz?" He gestured for the waiter to bring Kurtz coffee, and the man at the counter hurried to comply, providing a fresh mug.

Kurtz didn't let out his breath, but he was tempted to. He said, "Yasein Goba."

"That crazy Yemeni who shot the parole officer Wednesday? Today's paper says they found him dead from a gunshot here in Lackawanna. They didn't say whether it was self-inflicted or not." He quit stabbing at his eggs to squint at Kurtz. "The paper said that an unnamed parolee was shot the same time as the female probation officer, but wasn't hurt as bad. You?"

"Yeah."

"That explains the blood that's drained down under your eyes. You're one lucky son of a bitch, Kurtz."

Kurtz had no comment on that. Somewhere outside a generator was chug-chugging and his headache throbbed along with it.

"What about Goba?" said Baby Doc.

"What can you tell me about him?"

"Nothing right now. These Yemenis stick pretty much to themselves. I have some people who can talk to them—them and the other Middle Easterners who've moved into neighborhoods here—but I never heard of this Goba until I read about it in the papers."

"Could you check with your people—see if they had any contact with this guy?"

"I could," said Baby Doc. "And I understand why you're interested in this Goba if he shot you. But it doesn't seem worth my effort to dig into this. All reports—including my people inside the B.P.D.—say that this little guy was mad at his parole officer, shot her, and then killed himself. You just got in the way, Kurtz."

Kurtz sipped his coffee. It wasn't bad. Evidently they brewed fresh for Saturday mornings when Baby Doc was holding court. "Goba didn't kill himself," he said. "He bled out from a wound he received at the Civic Center."

"Did you shoot him?" asked Baby Doc. "Or was it the P.O. who got him before she caught one in the head?"

Kurtz shrugged slightly. "Does it matter?" When Baby Doc said nothing, Kurtz said, "Goba was shooting a twenty-two-caliber target pistol. The serial number had been taken off by acid—not sloppy, the way so many punks do it, but neatly, carefully, the way Doc used to do it on his used stock."

"You think Doc might have sold this Goba the gun sometime last year before . . . you know?"

"No," said Kurtz. "Goba got out of jail after your father was killed. But it's possible that one of your people sold him the weapon in the last couple of months."

About a year and a half earlier, some local black gang members had knocked over an overflow National Guard arsenal near Erie, Pennsylvania, liberating quite a few exotic military weapons. The previous November, bad things had happened to the gang members and the FBI and ATF had recovered some of the proscribed M-16s and other stolen weapons. Some—not all. Word on the street had been that Baby Doc Skrzypczyk had ended up with the bulk of the arms shipment and had been reselling them for a fortune—especially to the Middle Easterners currently moving into Lackawanna in droves.

Baby Doc sipped coffee and looked past Kurtz. The other five civilians in the restaurant were still waiting for their time with him. "I won't ask how you know what Goba was shooting or how you know the serial number had been burned off. Maybe your eyes were real good in that parking garage Wednesday. You happen to notice the make and model?"

"Ruger Mark II Standard," said Kurtz. "Long barrel. I think Goba was shooting diminished loads."

"Why?"

Kurtz shrugged again. "Makes less noise that way."

"Was noise a factor in the parking garage?"

"It could have been."

Baby Doc smiled. "You know why the professional double-tap guys tend to use twenty-twos?"

"Common knowledge says that it's because the point twenty-two slugs rattle around in the skull, causing more damage," said Kurtz. "I never thought that explanation was too convincing."

"Nah, me either. Bigger caliber slugs do just fine in the skull. I heard from an old-timer once it was because the mustaches didn't want to lose their hearing. Most of those old button men were half-deaf anyway."

"Can you find out if some of your men sold Goba the gun?" asked Kurtz. "And see if they have any other information on him?"

Baby Doc glanced at his watch. The Rolex on his wrist was gold and massive, the only thing about him that seemed ostentatious. "Lot of guns in this town that have nothing to do with me," he said. "But if I check, what's in it for me?"

"Gratitude," said Kurtz. "I remember favors. Try to repay them."

Baby Doc's cold blue eyes stared into Kurtz's bloodshot eyes for a minute. "All right, I'll check and get back to you today. Where can I reach you?"

Kurtz handed him a card. He took out a pen and circled his cell phone number.

"What's this SweetheartSearch and WeddingBells stuff?" asked Baby Doc.

"My skip-trace business. We look up old high-school sweethearts for lonely people then help some of them get married using online resources."

Baby Doc laughed loudly. "You're not what I expected, Joe Kurtz."

Kurtz stood to go.

"Just a second," said the man in the booth. He lowered his voice so that even the bodyguards wouldn't hear. "When I saw you here, I thought you'd be asking me about the other thing."

"What other thing?"

"The junkies and skag dealers doing their disappearing act," said Baby Doc. He was watching Kurtz very carefully.

Kurtz shrugged again. "Don't know anything about it."

"Well, I thought since you were so tight with the Farinos and Gonzagas . . ." began Baby Doc and let his voice trail off until it was a question.

Kurtz shook his head.

"Well," said Baby Doc, "word on the street is that one of those guineas brought in a pro called the Dane to settle some old scores."

"Does word on the street say which one of the guineas brought him in?"

"Nope." Baby Doc sipped his coffee. His eyes were colder than blue steel. "It might pay to watch your ass, Joe Kurtz."

H e called Arlene while he was driving north on the Skyway toward the downtown. "You get O'Toole's home address?"

"Yes," said Arlene and gave it to him.

Using the same pen he'd used to write on his business card for Baby Doc, Kurtz scribbled the address on the back of his hand. "Anything else?"

"I called the hospital and asked about Peg O'Toole's condition," said Arlene. He could hear her exhale smoke. "I'm not a family member, so they wouldn't give it to me. So I called Gail. She checked on the intensive-care unit's computer. O'Toole's taken a turn for the worse and is on life-support."

Kurtz resisted telling her that he hadn't asked about the parole officer's condition. "I'll be there soon," he said and disconnected.

The phone rang almost immediately.

"I want to meet with you," said Angelina Farino Ferrara.

"I'm pretty busy today," said Kurtz.

"Where are you? Can you come over to the penthouse?"

Kurtz glanced to his left as he approached the downtown. Her tall marina apartment building was visible less than a mile away. She owned the top two floors—one for business, the top one for herself. "I'm on the road," said Kurtz. "I'll call you back later."

"Look, Kurtz, it's important we . . ."

He cut her off, dropped the phone in his peacoat pocket, and took the exit for downtown Buffalo.

He'd gone less than a mile up Delaware Avenue toward Chippewa Street when the red light began flashing in his mirror. An unmarked car pulled up behind him.

Shit, thought Kurtz. He hadn't been speeding. The holstered .38 was under his driver's seat. That parole violation would send him back to Attica where the long knives were waiting for him. *Shit.*

He pulled to the curb and watched in the mirror as Detective Kemper stayed behind the wheel of the unmarked car. Rigby King got out the passenger door and walked up to Kurtz's driver's side. She was wearing sunglasses. "License and registration, please."

"Fuck you," said Kurtz.

"Maybe later," said Rigby. "If you're a good boy."

She walked around the front of his car and got in the passenger side. Kemper drove off.

"Jesus Christ," Kurtz said to Rigby King, "you smell like Death."

"You say the sweetest things," said Rigby. "You always did know how to chat up a girl, Joe." She motioned him to drive north on Delaware.

"Am I under arrest?"

"Not yet," said Rigby King. She slipped handcuffs off her belt and held them up to catch the October light. "But the day is young. Drive."

CHAPTER
NINETEEN

I got called to a crime scene at three A.M. and I've been there ever since," said Rigby. "Two gay lovers killed each other in a pretty little house in Allentown a week ago—looks like a mutual suicide pact—and nobody found the bodies until last night. Let's go get a drink." She motioned him to keep driving north along Delaware.

"You're kidding," said Kurtz. "It's not even eleven A.M."

"I never kid about drinking," said the cop. "I'm off duty now."

"I don't know where . . ." began Kurtz.

"You know where, Joe."

Blues Franklin wasn't open, but Kurtz parked the Pinto behind the building and Rigby jumped out to knock on the back door. Daddy Bruce's grown granddaughter, Ruby, opened the door and let them in.

Rigby led the way to Kurtz's favorite table at the back of the room. A white piano player named Coe Pierce was noodling on the dark stage and he flicked a salute to Kurtz while his left hand kept the rhythm going.

Daddy Bruce came up from the basement in a plaid shirt and old chinos. "Rigby, don't you know what the hell time this establishment opens yet? And no offense, babe, but you smell like carrion."

Kurtz looked at the woman next to him. During the year he'd been coming to Blues Franklin again since he'd gotten out of Attica, he'd never thought about meeting Rigby King here. At least not after his first few times back at the jazz place. But then, he hadn't known that Rigby was within a thousand miles of Buffalo.

"I know what time it opens," Rigby said to Daddy Bruce. "And I know you've never refused to sell me a drink, even when I was seventeen."

The old black man sighed. "What'll you have?"

"Shot of tequila with a beer back," said Rigby. She looked at Kurtz. "Joe?"

"Coffee," said Kurtz. "You don't have any food back there, do you?"

"I may have me an old moldy biscuit I could slap a sausage or egg into if I had to."

"Both," said Kurtz.

Daddy Bruce started to leave, turned back, and said, "Ray Charles's glasses safe somewhere?"

Kurtz patted his jacket pocket.

When they were alone, Rigby said, "No drink? Coffee and sausage? You getting old, Joe?"

Kurtz resisted the impulse to remind her that she was a couple of years older than he was. "What do you want, Rigby?"

"I have an offer you'll be interested in," she said. "Maybe an offer you won't be able to refuse."

Kurtz didn't roll his eyes, but he was tempted. He thought, not for the first time, that the movie *The Godfather* had a lot to answer for. He didn't think Rigby's offer, whatever it was, would top Toma Gonzaga's "do-my-bidding-or-die" proposal. He focused his attention on Coe Pierce playing a piano-only version of "Autumn Leaves."

"What's the offer?" said Kurtz.

"Just a minute," she said. Big Daddy Bruce had brought her drinks and Kurtz's mug of black coffee. Rigby tossed back the gold tequila, drank some beer, and gestured for another shot.

Daddy sighed and went back behind the bar, returning in a minute to refill her tequila, fill an extra shot glass for her, and top off her glass of beer. He also set a plate brimming over with eggs over easy, patty sausages, toast, and hash browns in front of Kurtz. The old man laid down a napkin and silverware next to it. "Don't expect this service every Saturday," said Daddy. "I'm only doing this 'cause you always tip Ruby and drink the cheapest Scotch."

"Thanks," said Kurtz and laid into the food with a will. Suddenly, even with the continuing throb of the headache, he was starving.

Rigby tossed back the second shot glass of tequila, drank some beer, and said, "What the hell happened to you, Joe?"

"What do you mean?" he said around a mouthful of eggs. "I'm hungry is all."

"No, you dipshit. I mean, what *happened* to you?"

Kurtz ate some hash browns and waited for her to go on. He had no doubt she would.

"I mean," continued Rigby, playing with her tequila glass, "you used to give a shit."

"I still give a shit," said Kurtz, chewing on his toast.

She ignored him. "You were always rough, inside and out, but you used to care about something other than saving your own ass. Even when you were a punk at Father Baker's, you used to get worked up when you thought something wasn't fair or when you saw someone treated like shit."

"Everyone was treated like shit at Father Baker's," said Kurtz. The eggs were good, done just the way he liked them.

She didn't even look at him as she tossed back the third tequila and called to Daddy for another one.

"No more, Rigby," called Daddy from the back room. "You're shitfaced already."

"The fuck I am," said the police detective. "One more or I'll bring the state license people down on your ass. Come on, Daddy—I've had a hard night."

"You look it and smell it," said Daddy Bruce, but he poured the final shot glass of tequila, policing up the empty beer mug and extra shot glass as he left.

"She's going to get you killed," said Rigby, enunciating every word with the care taken by someone who's drunk too much booze in too short a time.

"Who?" said Kurtz, although he knew who she meant.

"Little Angeleyes Fuckarino Ferwhoosis is who," said Rigby. "That Mafia bitch."

"You don't know what you're talking about," said Kurtz.

Rigby King snorted. It wasn't a feminine sound, but she didn't smell all that feminine at the moment. "You fucking her, Joe?"

Kurtz felt his jaw set with anger. Normally he'd say nothing to a question like that—or say something with his fists—but this was Rigby King and she was drunk and tired. "I've never touched her," he said, realizing as he spoke that he *had* touched Angelina, but only to frisk her a couple of times last winter.

Rigby snorted again, but not so explosively this time. She drank the last of the tequila. "Her sister Sophia was a cunt and so is this one," she said. "Word around the precinct house is that you've had both of them."

"Fuck word around the precinct house," said Kurtz. He finished his eggs and went at the last piece of toast.

"Yeah," said Rigby and the syllable sounded tired. "Word around the house this week is that Interpol says a certain Danish guy might be crossing into the States through Canada. Or maybe he already has."

Kurtz looked up. Had he missed something? Were there billboards up with this news? Had it been on the Channel 7 Action News or something? This assassin must have an advance team doing publicity for him.

"Got your attention, huh, Joe? Yeah, why do you think your pal Angelina would call for the Dane?"

"I don't know what you're talking about," said Kurtz. He sipped the last of his coffee. Big Daddy came by, refilled the coffee mug, set down another mug in front of Rigby, filled it with coffee, and went into the back room again.

"Why do you think, Joe?" repeated Rigby. She sounded suddenly sober.

He looked at her. His eyes gave up nothing.

"What if it isn't your female pal or her new friend Gonzaga who called for this particular European, Joe? Ever think of that?"

He was tempted to ask her what she was talking about, but didn't. Not yet.

"You have any enemies out there who want your scalp, Joe Kurtz? I mean, other than Big Bore Redhawk, of course." She sipped coffee, made a face, and put the mug down. "Funny about Big Bore, isn't it?"

"What do you mean?"

She looked surprised. "Oh, that's right, we haven't *told* you yet. The Pennsylvania Highway Patrol called us last night with the news that your Indian friend had been found in the woods behind a Howard Johnson's just off I-90 at the Erie exit. One bullet—nine millimeter—through his left temple. The Erie M.E. says that the shooting took place around ten A.M. yesterday. Ten A.M., Joe."

"What about it?"

"By great good coincidence, that's exactly when you had me meet you for that bullshit meeting at Broadway Market," said Rigby, her face flushing. Her brown eyes were angry.

"You saying that I used you for an alibi, Rigby?"

"I'm saying that you've always been mean, but you didn't used to be so fucking *cute*," snapped the cop. "I really hate cute felons. They really burn my tits."

"And lovely . . ." began Kurtz and stopped when he noted the look in her eyes and the hot coffee in her hand. "What were you going to say about the Danish guy?"

"I was going to ask who has the money and the motive to bring one of Europe's hired assassins into little old Western New York," said Rigby, her voice slurring only slightly from the booze and fatigue. "You want to answer that, Joe?"

"I give up," said Kurtz.

"You should. You should." Rigby held the coffee mug as if for warmth, lowering her face over it and letting the steam touch her cheeks. "They say the Dane's assassinated more than a hundred prime targets, including that politician in Holland not long ago. Never been caught. Hell, never been *identified*."

"What's that got to do with me?" said Kurtz.

Rigby smiled at him. She had a beautiful smile, thought Kurtz, even when it was a mocking one. "Word at the precinct house has you at the Farino estate a year ago when the same Danish guy wasted sister Sophia, Papa Farino, their lawyer—whatever the fuck his name was—and half the old Farino bodyguards. Twenty goombahs protecting Old Man Farino, and the only ones still standing when it was over were the ones the Dane didn't want dead."

Kurtz said nothing. He had a sudden tactile memory of sitting very still, his palms on his thighs, while the tall man in the raincoat and Bavarian-style hat with the feather in it turned the muzzle of his semiautomatic pistol from one target in the room to another, killing each person with a single shot. Kurtz's name hadn't been on the list that day. It had been an oversight of sorts. Little Skag Farino, still in Attica, hadn't thought that Kurtz would be there when the assassin he'd hired came to deal with Little Skag's sister, father, and the others, and he'd been too cheap to pay for Kurtz on spec.

"Little Skag's still a player," whispered Rigby. "He survived the shanking in Attica after you and the Ferrara bitch leaked the word that Skag had raped a minor. Your pal Angelina had his lawyer whacked a few months ago, but Little Skag's still alive—wearing a colostomy bag these days, or so I hear—

and safe in a federal country club where no one can get at him. But he has a new lawyer. And I think he has some unsettled business—with his little sister Angelina, the new, improved, gay Gonzaga, and some mook named Joe Kurtz."

"You're making this up as you go along," said Kurtz. "Bullshitting."

Rigby shrugged. "Can you take the chance to ignore me? Have you become that crazy a gambler, Joe?"

Kurtz rubbed the side of his head. The pain seemed to pulse through his skull, through his hand, and down his arm into his chest. "What do you want?"

"I said that I had an offer for you," she said. "My offer's this . . ." she sipped her coffee and took a breath. "Joe, you're fucking around trying to solve this O'Toole shooting. I know you know about Goba."

"Goba?" said Kurtz in the most innocent voice he could summon through the pain. Kemper hadn't given him the Yemeni's name over the phone last night.

"Fuck you, Joe." She drank her coffee but never took her luminous eyes off his face. "I don't know how you knew about Goba, but I think you were in his house yesterday before we were. I think you probably took some evidence with you. I think you're still acting under the delusion that you're a private detective, Joe Kurtz, ex-con, felon, parolee, and too-cute shithead."

"It was my shooting, too," Kurtz said softly.

"What?"

"You called it the O'Toole shooting," he said. "It was my shooting, too." He raised fingers to his torn scalp. The scab was tender. The wound felt hot and it pulsed under his fingertips.

Rigby shrugged. "She's on life support. You're hanging out with Baby Doc and snarfing eggs. You want to hear my offer?"

"Sure." He conveyed his lack of enthusiasm through flat tone, but he wasn't happy to hear that they knew he'd met with Baby Doc. His parole could be revoked for just speaking to a known felon.

"You keep playing private cop," she said softly, glancing around to make sure that no one could hear. Ruby and Daddy were in the kitchen; Coe Pierce was noodling Miles Davis's little-known "Peace, Peace." "If you insist on playing private cop," she repeated, "I'll give you the information you need to stay one step ahead of the Dane, solve your little shooting case, and maybe survive the Ferrara bitch's attentions."

"Why?" said Kurtz.

"I'll tell you later," said Rigby. "You agree now to help me on something later, and we have a deal. I'll risk my gold shield to feed you information."

Kurtz laughed softly. "Uh huh. Sure. I sign a blank check to help you later on some unspecified crap and you risk your badge to help me now. This is bullshit, Rigby." He stood.

"It's the best deal you'll ever get, Joe." For a second, astoundingly, unbelievably, Rigby King looked as if she was going to cry. She looked away, mopped her nose with the back of her hand, and looked back at Kurtz. The only emotion visible in her eyes now was the anger he'd seen earlier.

"Tell me what I'd have to do," said Kurtz.

She looked up at him across the table. "I help you now," she said so softly that he had to lean forward to hear. "I help you stay alive now, and sometime . . . I don't know when, not soon . . . maybe next summer, maybe later, you help me find Farouz and Kevin Eftakar."

"Who the fuck are Farouz and Kevin Eftakar?" said Kurtz, still standing and leaning his weight on his arms.

"My ex-husband and my son," whispered Rigby.

"Your son?"

"My baby," said the cop. "He was one year old when Farouz stole him."

"Stole him?" said Kurtz. "You're talking about a custody case? If the judge said . . ."

"The judge didn't say a fucking thing," snapped Rigby. "There were no custody hearings. Farouz just *took* him."

Kurtz sat down. "Look, you've got the law on your side, Rigby. The FBI will work the case if your asshole of an ex-husband crossed state lines. You're a good detective yourself and all the other departments will give you a hand . . ."

"He stole my baby from me nine years ago and took him to Iran," said Rigby. "I want Kevin back."

"Ah," said Kurtz. He rubbed his face. "I'd be the wrong person to help you. The last person who could." Kurtz laughed softly. "As you said, Rig, I'm a felon, an ex-con, a parolee. I can't walk across the damned Peace Bridge without ten types of permission I wouldn't get, much less get a passport and go to Iran. You'll just have to . . ."

"I can get the forged documents for you," said Rigby. "I have enough money set aside to get us to Iran."

"I wouldn't know how to find . . ." began Kurtz.

"You don't have to. I'll have located Farouz and Kevin before we leave."

Kurtz looked at her. "If you can find them, you don't need me . . ."

"I need you," said Rigby. She actually reached across and took his hand. "I'll find Farouz. I need you to kill the fucker for me."

CHAPTER
TWENTY

Kurtz insisted on driving Rigby home. They had more to talk about, but Kurtz didn't want to discuss murder in a public place, even in the Blues Franklin, which undoubtedly had been the site for more than one murder being planned.

"Is it a deal, Joe?"

"You're drunk, Rigby."

"Maybe so, but tomorrow I'll be sober and you'll still need my help if you want to find out who shot you and . . . whatshername . . . the parole officer."

"O'Toole."

"Yeah, so is it a deal?"

"I'm not a hired gun."

Rigby barked a laugh that ended in a snort. She rubbed her nose.

"Hire the Dane if you're so hot to take a killer to Iran with you," said Kurtz.

"I can't afford the Dane. Word is that he asks a hundred thousand bucks a pop. Who the hell can afford that? Other than Little Skag and these other Mafia assholes like your girlfriend and the faggot, I mean."

"So you want to hire me because I come cheap."

"Yeah."

Kurtz turned up Delaware Avenue. Rigby had told him she lived in a townhouse up there toward Sheridan. "The problem," said Kurtz, "is that I'm not a killer."

"I know you're not, Joe," said Rigby, tone lower now. "But you *can* kill a man. I've seen you do it."

"Bangkok," said Kurtz. "Bangkok doesn't count."

"No," agreed Rigby, "Bangkok doesn't count. But I know you've killed men here as well. Hell, you went to jail for throwing a mook out a sixth story window. And every black in the projects knows that you took that drug dealer, Malcolm Kibunte, out of the Seneca Street Social Club one night last winter and tossed him over the Falls."

It was Kurtz's turn to snort. He'd never thrown anyone over the Falls. Kibunte had been tied to a rope and dangled over the edge in the icy water while he was asked a few simple questions. The stupid shit had decided to slip out of the rope and swim for it instead of answering. No one can swim upstream at the brink of Niagara Falls in the dark, in winter, at night. It was unusual that the body was found by the Maid of the Mist the next morning—usually the Falls hold the bodies underneath the incredible weight of falling water for years or decades.

Kurtz said, "Nine years is a hell of a long time to wait to get your kid back. He won't remember you. He's probably sporting a mustache and got a harem of his own by now."

"Of *course* he won't remember me," said Rigby, not reacting with the fury Kurtz had expected. She just sounded tired. "And I haven't waited nine years. I followed them over there the month after Farouz kidnapped Kevin."

"What happened?"

"First, I couldn't get a visa from our own State Department. Senator Moynihan—he was our senator then, not this dim-blonde cuckolded bitch we have now—"

"I don't think that a woman can be a cuckold," said Kurtz.

"Do you want to fucking hear this or not?" snapped Rigby. "Moynihan tried to help, but there was nothing he could do, not even get me a visa. So I went through Canada and flew to Iran and found out where Farouz was living with his family in Tehran and went to the police there and made my case—when I found out he'd been cheating on me, Eftakar just *stole* my one-year-old baby—and the cops called some mullah and I was kicked out of the country within twenty-four hours."

"Still . . ." began Kurtz.

"That was the first time," said Rigby.

"You tried again?"

"In *nine years*?" said the cop. She sounded sober. "Of course I've tried again. When I came back after the first attempt, I moved back to Buffalo, joined the B.P.D., and tried to get legal and political help. Nothing. Two years later, I took a short leave of absence and went back to Iran under a false name. That time I actually saw Farouz—confronted him in some sort of coffee and smoking club with his brothers and pals."

"They kick you out of the country again?"

"After three weeks in a Tehran jail this time."

"But you went back again?"

"The next time, I went in overland through Turkey and northern Iraq. It cost me ten thousand bucks to get smuggled through Turkey, another eight thousand to the fucking Kurds to get me across the border, and five grand to smugglers in Iran."

"Where'd you get money like that?" said Kurtz. What he was thinking was *You're lucky they didn't rape and kill you.* But she must have known that.

"This was the 'nineties," said Rigby. "I'd put everything I had into the stock market and did all right. Then blew it all going back to Iran."

"But you didn't find Kevin?"

"This time I didn't get within four hundred kilometers of Tehran. Some religious-police fanatics had my smugglers arrested—and probably shot— and I got questioned for ten days in some provincial cop station before they just drove me to the Iraq border in a Land Cruiser and kicked me out again."

"Did they hurt you?" Kurtz was imagining burns from lighted cigarettes, jolts from car batteries.

"Never touched me," said Rigby. "I think the local chief of police liked Americans."

"So that was it?"

"Not by a long shot. In 1998 I hired a mercenary soldier named Tucker to go get Kevin. I didn't care if he killed Farouz, I just wanted Kevin back. Tucker told me that he used to be Special Forces and had been in Iran dozens of times—had been inserted into Tehran as part of the plan to get the hostages out as part of that fucked-up Jimmy Carter raid in April, 1980 . . ."

"Not the best thing to list on a resume," said Kurtz. He'd reached Sheridan Road and turned left according to Rigby's instructions, then right again into a maze of streets with townhouses and apartments built in the 'sixties. Rigby didn't live far from Peg O'Toole's apartment and he wanted to go there next.

"No," said Rigby. "As it turned out it wasn't a good recommendation for old Tucker."

"He didn't succeed."

"He disappeared," said Rigby King. "I got a cable from him in Cyprus, saying he was ready for 'the last stage of the operation,' whatever the hell that meant, and then he disappeared. Two months later I got a package from Tehran—from Farouz, although there was no return address."

"Let me guess," said Kurtz. "Ears?"

"Eight fingers and a big toe," said Rigby. "I recognized the ring on one of the fingers, big ruby in a sort of class ring that Tucker seemed proud of."

"Why a big toe?" said Kurtz.

"Beats the shit out of me," said Rigby and laughed. She didn't really sound amused.

"So now you're ready to go back again, taking me with you."

"Not quite ready," said the cop. "Next summer maybe."

"Oh boy," said Kurtz. He stopped at the curb in front of the dreary townhouse that Rigby had indicated.

"And I'll help you as much as I can until then," said Rigby, turning to look at him. The smell of death still wafted from her clothes.

"Just trust me to hold up my end of the bargain when the time comes, huh?" said Kurtz.

"Yeah."

"What can you tell me that would help me with this shooting thing?" said Kurtz. He'd made his decision. He wanted her help.

"Kemper thinks that you're right," said Rigby. "That Yasein Goba didn't act alone."

"Why?"

"Several reasons. Kemper doesn't think that Goba had the strength to drag himself up those stairs in his house. The M.E. says that despite all the blood trail and the blood in the bathroom, Goba'd lost two-thirds of his blood supply before he got to the house."

"So someone helped him up the stairs," said Kurtz. "Anything else?"

"The missing car," said Rigby. "Sure, it'd be stolen in that neighborhood, but if Goba'd driven himself from the parking garage, the seat and floor and wheel and everything must've been saturated with blood. Blood everywhere. That might give even the back-the-Bridge Lackawanna thieves pause."

"Unless the blood was all in the back seat," said Kurtz. "Or trunk."

"Yeah."

"Do you trust Kemper's judgment, Rig?"

"I do," said the woman. "He's a good detective. Better than I'll ever be." She rubbed her temples. "Jesus, I'm going to have a headache tomorrow."

"Join the club," said Kurtz. He made a decision. "Anything else on Goba?"

"We're talking to everyone who knew him," said Rigby King. "And the Yemenis are really clannish and close-mouthed—especially after that terrorist thing last year. But they've told us enough to convince us that Goba was a real loner. No friends. No family here. It appears that he's been waiting for his fiancée to be smuggled into the country. We're looking into that. But a couple of neighbors tell us that they'd caught glimpses of Goba being dropped off once or twice by a white guy."

"A white guy dropped him off once or twice," repeated Kurtz. "That's it?"

"So far. We're still questioning neighbors and people who worked with Goba at the car wash."

"Any description on the white guy?"

"Just white," said Rigby. "Oh, yeah—one crackhead said that Goba's pal had long hair—'like a woman's.' "

Like the driver of the car that broke out through the garage barrier, thought Kurtz. "Can you get me some information on Peg O'Toole's uncle?"

"The old man in the wheelchair who slapped you? The Major?" said Rigby. "Yeah, why? We called him and asked how he and his associate, the Vietnamese ex-colonel . . ."

"Trinh."

"Yeah. We asked the Major how they'd heard about Officer O'Toole's shooting. The Major lives in Florida, you know. Trinh in California."

Kurtz waited. He knew where the two lived thanks to Arlene, but he wasn't going to reveal anything to Rigby unless he had to.

"The Major told Kemper that he'd been back in Neola for a shareholders meeting of a company called SEATCO that he and Trinh had started way back in the 'seventies. Import-export stuff. The Major and Trinh are retired, but they still hold honorary positions on the board of directors."

"Which explains why they were in the state," said Kurtz. "Not how he heard about the shooting."

Rigby shrugged. "The Major said that he called Peg O'Toole's house and office Wednesday evening after the shareholders meeting. He said he likes to get together with his niece when he's back in the state. Someone at the parole office told him there'd been a shooting—they didn't have any family member to contact for O'Toole, just the Brian Kennedy guy in Manhattan."

"Was Kennedy in Manhattan when they contacted him?"

"He was in transit," said Rigby. "Flying to Buffalo to see his fiancée." She smiled crookedly. "You suspect the boyfriend? They were engaged, for Christ's sake."

"Gee," said Kurtz, "you're right. He couldn't have been involved if he was engaged to the victim. *That's* never happened before."

Rigby shook her head. "What motive, Joe? Kennedy's rich, successful, handsome . . . his security agency is one of the top three in the state, you know. Plus, we checked—his Lear was in transit."

Kurtz wanted to say *are you sure?* but stopped himself. The headache throbbed and muted flashbulbs were going off behind his eyes. He set his hands firmly on the top of the steering wheel. "The Major had a son who killed some people down in the Neola high school back in the 'seventies . . ." he began.

"Sean Michael O'Toole," said Rigby. "Kemper ran that down. The crazy kid was sent to the big hospital for the criminally insane in Rochester and he died there in 1989 . . ."

"Died?" said Kurtz. Arlene hadn't been able to get into the hospital records. "He would have been young."

"Just turned thirty," said Rigby. For a woman who'd just downed four tequilas and two beers, she was articulating her sentences well enough, but her beautiful brown eyes looked tired. Very tired.

"What happened to him? Suicide?"

"Yeah. Messy, too."

"What do you mean?"

"Young Sean didn't just hang himself or asphyxiate himself with a plastic bag or something . . . uh-uh. He doused himself and several other inmates with gasoline and set fire to his wing of the high-security ward during visiting hours. Three others died as well as Sean and half the wing burned down. The current director says that he still doesn't know where the boy got the gasoline."

Kurtz thought about this. "The Major must have been proud."

"Who knows?" said Rigby. "He wouldn't talk to Kemper or me about his son. He said, and I quote—'Let the dead bury the dead.' Army officers—you gotta love 'em." She opened the door and stepped out onto the grassy curb. Clouds were scuttling and the wind from the northwest was cold. It felt like late October in Buffalo to Kurtz.

"You have tomorrow off?" said Kurtz.

"Yeah." said Rigby King. "I've worked the last five weekends, and now that your and O'Toole's case is officially closed and the dead gay guys have been turned over to the coroner, I get tomorrow off. Why?"

"You want to ride down to Neola with me tomorrow?" Even as he spoke the words, Kurtz was surprised he'd actually suggested this.

Rigby looked equally surprised. "Neola? That little town down near the Pennsylvania border? Why would you . . ." Her expression changed. "Oh, that's where Major O'Toole and the Vietnamese colonel had their homes and business before they retired and moved to warmer climes. What's the deal, Joe? You looking for a little payback for the late-night slap and want some backup while you brace the sixty-something-year-old in his wheelchair?"

"Not quite," said Kurtz. "There's something else I want to check on down there and I thought it might be a pretty ride. We'd be back by night-fall."

"A pretty ride," repeated Rigby, her tone suggesting that Kurtz had begun speaking in a foreign language. "Sure, what the fuck. Why not? What time?"

"Eight A.M.?"

"Yeah, sure. I'll drink some more and pass out early so I'll be in good spirits for our picnic tomorrow." She shook her head as if bemused by her own idiocy, slammed the passenger door, and walked toward her townhouse.

Feeling some of the same bemusement about himself, Kurtz put the Pinto in gear and drove away.

CHAPTER
TWENTY-ONE

Kurtz had just headed east on Sheridan when his phone rang. He fished it out of his peacoat pocket, thumbed it on while trying to avoid an old woman in a Pontiac swerving from lane to lane, and heard only dial tone. A phone rang again in his other pocket.

"Shit." He'd answered the Gonzaga cell phone by mistake. He found his own phone.

"I've got some of the information you wanted," said Baby Doc.

"It didn't take you long," said Kurtz.

"I didn't know you wanted me to take a long time," said Baby Doc. "That would have cost you more. You want to hear this or not?"

"Yeah."

"The guys I chatted with didn't sell Mr. G. the metallic article you were asking about," said Baby Doc.

Kurtz turned left off Sheridan and translated—*Baby Doc's people hadn't sold Yasein Goba the .22 he used in the shooting.*

"But these guys I mentioned have had some contact with our friend."

"Tell me," said Kurtz. He was looking at house numbers on the more upscale neighborhood here south of Sheridan Drive. The trees were larger here than in Rigby's neighborhood, the street quieter. The wind was blowing hard and skittering yellow and red leaves across the pavement ahead of his slowly moving Pinto.

"The guys were asked to do some special paperwork for a friend of his," said Baby Doc.

Forged visa? thought Kurtz. *Passport?*

"What friend?" he asked.

"A lovely girl named Aysha," said Baby Doc. "Our late friend's fiancée. She's coming from the north to visit Sunday night, as it turns out. Evidently her people don't keep abreast of the news up there. Probably because they live on a farm."

Goba's fiance, Aysha, was being smuggled across the Canadian border tomorrow night. Neither she nor the smugglers had heard of Goba's death in Canada where they'd been hiding out and waiting to cross.

"What time tonight? Which place?" said Kurtz.

"You want to know a lot for not much in return," said Baby Doc.

"Add it to my bill." Kurtz knew that his offer to return a favor would be called in sooner or later. He was going into a lot of debt this day. He just hoped that Baby Doc's favor didn't include him having to fly to Iran to shoot someone.

"Midnight Sunday night," said Baby Doc. "Blue 1999 Dodge Intrepid with Ontario plates. The span of many colors. She'll be dropped off just beyond the toll booths at the entrance to the mall."

It took Kurtz only a second to translate this last. They were smuggling her across the Rainbow Bridge, just below the Falls, in two days. The Rainbow Centre Mall was near the first exit after the Customs booths.

"Who's meeting her?" said Kurtz.

"No one's meeting her," said Baby Doc. "All of her friends on this side went on to other things." Translation—*Goba's dead. Any deal we had with him died when he did. We keep the money he paid us and she fends for herself.*

"Why not cancel the delivery?" said Kurtz.

"Too late." Baby Doc didn't elaborate on that, but Kurtz assumed it just meant that no one cared.

"How much did our pal pay for this generosity?" asked Kurtz. Goba worked at a car wash and hadn't been out of jail long enough to save much money.

He heard Baby Doc hesitate. This was a lot of potentially damaging information Kurtz wanted in exchange for nothing more than a promise of future friendship. But then, he knew what Kurtz had done for his father.

"Fifteen bucks," said Baby Doc. "For each side."

Thirty thousand dollars for the paperwork and smuggling, split between Baby Doc's people and the Canadian smugglers.

"Okay, thanks," said Kurtz. "I owe you."

"Yes," said Baby Doc, "you do." He broke the connection.

Peg O'Toole's townhouse was much more handsome than Rigby King's—brick, two-story, large windows with fake six-over-six panes; her unit shared its building with only three other townhouses, a four-door garage was set tucked away in back and mature trees shaded the small yard in front. The clouds were moving grayer and lower now, the wind blew colder, and the last of the leaves were being torn from the trees like the last survivors dropping off the up-ended *Titanic*.

Kurtz found a parking place and crossed the street to look at the townhouse. He had his breaking-and-entering kit in the back seat of the Pinto, but he wanted to think about this first. His concussion headache had grown worse, as it tended to do in the afternoon, and he had to squint to think.

While he was standing there squinting, a man's voice said, "Hey, Mr. Kurtz."

Kurtz whirled, one hand ready to move toward the .38 in its holster under his peacoat.

The security and personal protection guy, Officer O'Toole's fiancé, Brian Kennedy, stepped out of an orangish-red SUV, crossed the street, and held out his hand. Kurtz shook it, wondering what the fuck was up. Had Kennedy tailed him here?

"How do you like it?" said Kennedy, turning slightly with a flourish.

It took Kurtz a second to realize that the handsome young man was talking about his sport utility vehicle. "Yeah," Kurtz said stupidly, following Kennedy back across the residential street toward the big SUV. He'd been wondering if his defensive alertness and powers of observation were suffering because of this stupid concussion, and now he knew. If someone could sneak up on him and park an orange two-and-a-half-ton SUV behind him while he was gathering wool, then perhaps he wasn't quite as alert as he should be.

As if reading his mind, Kennedy said, "I was parked here listening to the end of something interesting on NPR before going in to Peg's apartment when I saw you drive up. Like it?"

Kurtz realized that he was still talking about the truck. "Yeah. What is it?" He wasn't familiar with the badge on the high grill. Kurtz didn't give the slightest goddamn about what make it was, but he wanted to keep Kennedy talking a minute while his aching brain came up with some excuse for him to be standing out in front of the dying Peg O'Toole's townhouse.

"Laforza," said Kennedy. "Limited production out of Escondido. It's not an SUV, it's a PSV."

Pretentious Shithead's Vehicle? thought Kurtz. Aloud, he said, "PSV?"

"Personal Security Vehicle." Kennedy pounded the driver's side door with his knuckles. "Kevlar door inserts. Thirty-two millimeter Spectra Shield bulletproof glass on the windshield, side windows, and sunroof. Hands-free communication and a transponder inside. Supercharged GM Vortec six-oh liter V-8 under the hood that produces four hundred twenty-five horsepower."

"Cool," said Kurtz, trying to make his voice sound like a fourteen-year-old's.

"My personal vehicle is a Porsche 911 Turbo," said Kennedy, "but I drive the Laforza sometimes when I'm around clients. Our agency gets a small kickback from the people in Escondido if we help place an order."

"How much would one of these set me back?" asked Kurtz. He kicked the front left tire. It hurt his foot. He'd just expended his entire cache of car-buying expertise.

"This is a PSV-L4," said Kennedy. "Top of the line. If I get you a discount, oh . . . one hundred and thirty-nine thousand dollars."

Kurtz nodded judiciously. "I'll think about it. I'd have to talk to the missus first."

"So you're married, Mr. Kurtz?" Kennedy was walking back toward the townhouse and Kurtz followed as far as the sidewalk.

"Not really," said Kurtz.

Kennedy blinked and folded his arms. *He may look like the current James Bond*, thought Kurtz, *but he doesn't seem quite as fast on his intellectual feet as the superspy.*

As if responding in delayed reaction, Kennedy laughed twice. He had the kind of loud, easy, unselfconscious laugh that people loved. Kurtz could have happily used a shovel on the man's head at that moment.

"So what brings you to Peg's neighborhood, Mr. Kurtz?" The security man's tone wasn't aggressive, just pleasantly curious.

"I bet you can tell me," said Kurtz. *This guy drives a Porsche 911 Turbo. He's a member of that club that Tom Wolfe called "Masters of the Universe."*

Kennedy nodded, thought a minute, and said, "You still think like a private investigator. You've been working through some things about the shooting and wonder if there's a clue in Peg's house."

Kurtz widened his eyes slightly as if in awe of Kennedy's ratiocination.

"But you weren't thinking about breaking in, were you, Mr. Kurtz?" Kennedy's white smile took the edge off the question. It was a smile, Kurtz thought, that could honestly be called "infectious." Kurtz hated things that infected other things.

Kurtz smiled back, with no fear of his chagrined smirk being thought of as infectious. "Naw. I had enough prison time in Attica. I was just in the neighborhood and was . . . as you say . . . thinking about the shooting."

I always used to stand outside victims' homes and try to pick up on psychic vibes when I was a licensed P.I., thought Kurtz but didn't articulate this coda. It might be gilding the lily a bit, even for someone as self-satisfiedly obtuse as Brian Kennedy.

"Want to come in?" said Kennedy, tossing a ring of keys in the air. "I was just picking up some insurance stuff and legal papers that the hospital wanted. I don't think Peg would have minded if you just step in a minute while I'm here."

Kurtz picked up on the past-tense in that last sentence. Had O'Toole died? The last he'd heard, she was on life support.

"Sure," he said and followed Kennedy into the building.

CHAPTER
TWENTY-TWO

So what did O'Toole's apartment look like?" said Arlene when Kurtz was back in the office later that waning Saturday afternoon. "Any clues lying around?"

"Just clues to her personality," said Kurtz.

"Such as?" said Arlene. She flicked ashes into her ashtray.

Kurtz walked to the window. It had grown colder and darker and begun to rain again. Even though it was an hour from official sunset, the streetlights had come on along Chippewa and the headlights and taillights of passing cars reflected on the wet asphalt.

"Such as the place was neat and clean and filled with art," said Kurtz. "Not a lot of original art—she couldn't have afforded that on her probation officer salary—but tasteful stuff, and more small original oil paintings and sculptures than most people would collect. And books. Lots of books. Mostly paperbacks but all of them looked like they'd been read, not just leather-bound crap to look good on the shelves, but real books. Fiction, non-fiction, classics."

"No real clues then," said Arlene.

Kurtz shook his head, turned back to the room, and sipped some Star-bucks coffee he'd picked up. He'd brought a cup for Arlene, and she was drinking hers between puffs on her Marlboro. "She had a laptop on her desk," said Kurtz. "And two low filing cabinets. But obviously I couldn't look through them with Kennedy there."

"Weird that he let you come in with him," said Arlene. "He must be the most guileless security expert in the world . . ."

"Or too crafty for his own good," said Kurtz. "He made tea for us."

"How nicely domestic," said Arlene. "Made himself right at home in Ms. O'Toole's townhouse, huh?"

Kurtz shrugged. "He told me that he'd been staying there with her when he was in Buffalo every few weeks. I saw some of his suits and blazers in a closet."

"He let you wander into her bedroom?"

"He was grabbing some stuff," said Kurtz. "I just stood in the doorway."

"Fiancés," said Arlene, using the tone that other people did when they said "*Kids. Whaddyagonnado?*" She nodded toward her computer screen where the names of WeddingBells-dot-com clients were stacked like cordwood.

"The question remains, why'd he invite me up?" said Kurtz, turning back to watch the traffic move through the cold October rain. "He asked me what I was doing there, but then he gave the answer—as if he didn't really want to press me on it. Why would he do that? Why wasn't he pissed—or at least suspicious—when he found me hanging around outside O'Toole's townhouse?"

"Good question," said Arlene.

He turned away from the window. "Do you know any Yemeni?"

Arlene stared at him. "Do you mean any Yemeni people?"

"No, I mean the language," said Kurtz.

Arlene smiled and stubbed out her cigarette. "I think Arabic is the language spoken in Yemen. Some of them speak Farsi, I think, but Arabic is the dominant language."

Kurtz rubbed his aching head. "Yeah. All right. Do you speak any Arabic that a Yemeni would understand?"

"*Al-Ghasla*," said Arlene. "*Thowb Al-Zfag, Al-Subhia.*"

"You made that up," said Kurtz.

Arlene shook her head. "Three kinds of wedding dresses—the dress of the eve of the wedding, *Al-Ghasla*, the bridal gown, *Thwob-Al-Zfag*, and the gown of the day following the wedding, *Al-Subhia*. I just helped a client from Utica order all three from a Yemeni dressmaker in Manhattan."

"Well, I guess that'll do," said Kurtz. "I'll bring little Aysha here on Monday night and you two can discuss wedding dresses. She doesn't know she's a widow even before she's married."

Arlene stared at him until he explained about Baby Doc's phone call.

"That's really sad," said Arlene, lighting another Marlboro. "Do you really think that she can tell you anything about what Yasein Goba was doing? She's been in Canada."

Kurtz shrugged. "Maybe we won't even be able to understand each other, but if I don't meet her up in Niagara Falls tomorrow night, no one else is going to. Baby Doc's people have washed their hands of her. She's just going to get picked up by the cops sooner or later and shipped back to Yemen by the INS."

"So you pick her up tomorrow night and try to talk to her," said Arlene. "And can't. What then? Sign language?"

"Any ideas?"

"Yes," said Arlene. "I know some people through my church who take part in a sort of underground railroad helping illegal immigrants get into the States."

"Goba's already had that part arranged," said Kurtz.

Arlene shook her head. "No, I mean I'll get in touch with the guy who helps the immigrants—Nicky—at church tomorrow, he'll call one of the Yemeni people they use to translate, and they can help us talk to the girl."

"All right," said Kurtz. "Get your friend's translator here early Monday morning."

"Can't it wait until later?" asked Arlene. "This woman—Aysha?—can sleep at my place Sunday and we can meet with the translator on Monday."

"Monday's Halloween," said Kurtz, as if that explained anything.

"So?"

He considered telling her about Toma Gonzaga's promise to murder him at midnight on Halloween if he hadn't solved the don's junkie-killer problem. He considered it for about five microseconds. "I have things to do on Halloween," he said.

"All right, early Monday morning," said Arlene. She came over to the window and joined him in looking out at the rain. It was getting dark in earnest now. "Some people just don't get a break, do they, Joe?"

"What do you mean?"

"I mean this Aysha will wake up tomorrow morning thinking she'll be meeting her fiancé in a new country that night, that she'll be a wife and maybe a U.S. citizen, and that everything is working out for her. Instead, she'll hear that her fiancé is dead and that she's a stranger in a strange land."

"Yeah, well . . ." said Kurtz.

"Are you going to tell her that you killed him? Goba?"

Kurtz looked at his secretary. Her eyes were dry—she wasn't going soppy on him—but her gaze was focused on something far away.

"I don't know," Kurtz said irritably. "What the hell's wrong with you?"

"Just that life sucks sometimes," said Arlene. "I'm going home." She stubbed out her cigarette, turned off her computer, tugged her purse out of a drawer, pulled on her coat, and left the office.

Kurtz sat by the window a few minutes, watching the gray twilight and rain and almost wishing that he smoked. During his years in Attica, his non-habit had served him well—the cigarettes he was allowed all went toward barter and bribes. But on days like this, he wondered if smoking would soothe his nerves—or lessen his headache.

His cell phone rang.

"Kurtz? Where are you? What happened to our meeting?"

It was Angelina Farino Ferrara.

"I'm still traveling," said Kurtz.

"You lying sack of shit," said the don's daughter. "You're in your office, looking out the window."

Kurtz looked across Chippewa. There was the ubiquitous black Lincoln Town Car, parked on the other side of the wet street. Kurtz hadn't seen it arrive and park.

"I'm coming up," said Angelina. "I know you have a lock on that outside door, so don't keep me waiting. Buzz me in."

"Come up alone," said Kurtz. He looked at the video monitor next to Arlene's desk. He had no illusions about the lock down there holding out her bodyguards if they really wanted to come up with her. There was a small window in the computer-server room at the back that opened to a seven-foot drop to a lower rooftop, then a ladder back there to not one but two alleys. Kurtz never wanted to be anywhere with just one way out.

"I'll be alone," said Angelina and broke the connection.

Kurt watched the woman cross Chippewa toward him in the rain.

CHAPTER
TWENTY-THREE

The Dodger was frustrated by his morning's failure to take care of the teacher out in Orchard Park, so he was pleased in the early afternoon when a wireless PDA/cell phone connection to the Boss gave him a new and more interesting task.

He knew the target from earlier briefings. In one sense, it didn't make any difference to the Dodger *who* the targets were or *why* they had become his targets—they were all means to the ends of the Resurrection to him. But in another sense, it made everything more interesting when the targets were more difficult. And this one should be more difficult.

He knew the address. It was raining off and on when he drove the extermination van out to the Marina Towers address near the Harbor marina. There was a large public parking lot near the high rise and, as the Boss had promised, a new Mazda sedan was parked there, keys in the tail pipe. A bug van wasn't the best vehicle in which to tail someone.

The Dodger settled in the front seat of the Mazda, tuned some jazz on the radio, and watched the front of Marina Tower through small binoculars. He'd been well briefed on the current struggle over the heroin trade in Buffalo and knew that this apartment building was the headquarters for the Farino daughter; she owned the top two floors and kept the penthouse as her personal address while accountants and others worked and sometimes lived on the floor below. Her personal vehicles were kept in the basement garage and that could only be accessed by internal elevators, locked staircases, or through the underground ramp closed by a steel-mesh gate controlled by the residents' magnetic-strip cards.

The Dodger waited. The cold drizzle fell harder, which was good; passersby in the parking lot or on the nearby marina park road couldn't see him through the rain-mottled windshield. The Dodger turned off the radio to conserve the Mazda's battery and he waited.

Around four P.M., the garage mesh door went up and a black Lincoln slowly emerged. The Dodger watched as the Lincoln came around to the semicircular entrance drive of Marina Towers. The Lincoln's driver got out and walked around the car and a second bodyguard stood watching the street as Angelina Farino Ferrara came out the front door, said something to the liveried doorman, and walked over to the Lincoln.

She didn't get in. She spoke briefly to the two men and then began jogging along the pedestrian path that led out along the shore where Lake Erie narrowed into the Niagara River. The Lincoln pulled around the entrance drive and followed slowly, heading north. The Dodger turned on his wipers and followed several hundred meters behind.

He knew from his briefings that the Farino woman liked to jog early in the morning and again in the afternoon, although usually later than this. Maybe it was the coming storm or increasing drizzle that had brought her out early.

The Dodger also recognized the two men in the Lincoln. The driver was Corso "the Hammer" Figini, serious muscle the female don had brought in from New Jersey the previous spring. The thinner, infinitely more handsome and WASPY-looking man riding shotgun today was Colin Sheffield, a well-dressed, thirties-something London criminal who'd specialized in high-class extortion, drug deals, and security. Sheffield had worked for the second-most-powerful mob boss in England until the day he'd gotten a little too ambitious for his own good—not trying to whack his employer, the story went, just trying to corner some of the action for himself—and ended up leaving the country a few hours ahead of the hit team his own boss had sent.

The Dodger's earlier briefing hadn't included how the Farino woman had ended up hiring Colin Sheffield, but that wasn't all that important.

The Lincoln was moving slowly, essentially keeping pace with the Farino woman's jogging, and the Dodger had to pass it or look suspicious. Drivers were turning on their headlights now, and the view to the west and north was all dark gray clouds coming in with the October twilight. The Dodger didn't turn his head as he passed the Lincoln and the running woman.

He made a large loop, and returned to the parking lot where he'd started, parking next to the exterminator's van. He didn't think that a mob guy's daughter was very smart keeping to a routine like that, and running along the river path every morning and evening. There were several places along the path where the bodyguards couldn't see her if they stayed in their car—which they did—and the Dodger thought the jogging would be a good time and place to take her out.

The briefing had said that Farino ran for forty-five minutes in her river path circuit, and sure enough, she and the Lincoln were back in front of Marina Towers forty-six minutes after they'd left. The Dodger watched through his small binoculars as she spoke to Sheffield and Figini, leaning against the car and lifting her legs as she cooled down, and then went in the front door. The Lincoln idled at the curb. Figini, the driver, was reading a racing form.

Fifteen minutes later, she came out and got in the back seat and the Lincoln pulled away.

It was dark enough and raining hard enough now that the Dodger didn't worry about being spotted as he followed the big, black car over to Elmwood and then north to Chippewa Street. He'd be just another pair of headlights to them in Saturday traffic headed for the one lively spot in Buffalo.

The Lincoln parked on Chippewa and the Dodger paused in a loading zone until he saw the Farino woman cross the street and go in a door. It wasn't a club or a restaurant, so he took note of the address on the PDA, uplinked it through his cell phone, and waited. When a police car trolled by and paused near the loading zone, the Dodger drove around the block, returned, and found a space only three cars behind the idling Lincoln. The patrol car had gone.

He was lucky. In another hour, there wouldn't be public parking within five blocks.

The two bodyguards were watching a lighted third-story window. Sure that he was still unnoticed by the bodyguards in the dark and rain behind them, the Dodger used his binoculars to watch the same window for a second. Angelina Farino Ferrara stepped in front of the window for a second, looking down toward her bodyguards. Then she turned and spoke to someone in the room. The Dodger had learned how to read lips when he was away, but the woman's head was turned just enough that he couldn't make out what she was saying. Then she stepped away, out of sight, and the lights went out in the office up there.

His cell phone chimed softly and the Dodger put away the binoculars.

The two men in the Lincoln Town car were just silhouettes now, the big driver reading and the other staring straight ahead, and the Dodger guessed that the woman's coming to the window was a prearranged sign telling Figini and Sheffield to relax.

Text appeared on the PDA screen—Address confirmed. Execute.

The Dodger wiped the message, removed his 9-millimeter Beretta, and carefully attached the thin suppressor. Then, after pulling on a cheap raincoat that was two sizes too large for him, he switched off the Mazda sedan's overhead light, scooted past the shifter to the passenger side, and stepped out into the rain.

CHAPTER
TWENTY-FOUR

What do you want?" said Kurtz. "Your money?"

"That will do for a start," said Angelina. She moved into the office and watched as Kurtz locked the door behind her. Then she dropped her cashmere coat onto the old leather couch. She was wearing a tight, black dress cut low on top and high on the thighs, expensive leather boots, a single gold necklace, and some subtle gold bracelets. He'd never seen Angelina Farino Ferrara in clothes like that. Come to think of it, thought Kurtz, most of the time he'd seen her, she'd been in gym togs or jogging attire. Her dark hair was swept up and back on the sides, but secured so that it still hung free in back. It looked wet, but he couldn't tell if that was from walking through the rain or some mousse thing.

Kurtz picked an envelope off his desk and handed it to her. The entire five thousand dollars advance was in it. He'd use other money to manage his getaway on Tuesday if he had to run for it. He dropped into his swivel chair and looked up at her. The .38 was in its holster taped to the underside of his desk drawer, inches from his hand.

She took the envelope without comment or counting it, slipped it into the pocket of the coat she'd draped over the arm of the sofa, and walked to the window. The rain was pelting the glass now and the air through the open screen was chill, taking the edge off the heat and stuffiness caused by the servers and other machinery in the back room.

Still looking out at the neon-busy street, she said, "I need your advice, Joe."

"*Joe?*" said Kurtz. She'd never used anything but his last name. The idea of her needing his advice was also bullshit.

She turned, smiled, and sat on the edge of Arlene's desk, switching off the desk light there so that only Kurtz's low lamp and the glow of the two computers and video monitor illuminated her long legs, strong thighs, and shiny boots.

"We've known each other long enough to be on a first-name basis, haven't we, Joe? Remember the ice fishing shack?"

Kurtz did indeed remember the fishing shack out on the ice of Lake Erie the previous February. The body of the man he'd shot barely fit through the ice fishing hole because of the shower curtain and chains wrapped around it. Angelina had been the one to prod it through the round hole with her boot on the corpse's shoulder—less expensive and more practical boots that night than this. *So what?*

"Call me Angelina," she said now. She casually lifted her left foot and set it on Arlene's chair. There were a lot of shadows, but it seemed almost certain that Angelina Farino Ferrara was wearing no underpants above the high shadowed line of her stockings.

"Sure," said Kurtz. "You wearing a wire, Angelina?"

The female don laughed softly. "Me, wearing a wire? Get serious, Joe. Can't you tell I'm not?"

"Informants usually wear their wire microphones *externally*," said Kurtz, speaking softly but never breaking his unblinking stare with the woman.

She blinked first. The flush that rose to her high cheekbones was not unbecoming. She lowered her foot to the floor. "You shithead," she said.

Kurtz nodded. "What do you want?" His head hurt.

"I told you, I need your advice."

"I'm not your *consiglieri*."

"No, but you're the only intermediary I have right now with Toma Gonzaga."

"I'm not your intermediary either," said Kurtz.

"He and I both tried to hire you to find this junkie killer. What did Gonzaga offer you?"

Not to kill me on Tuesday, thought Kurtz. He said, "A hundred thousand dollars."

The angry flush left the woman's cheeks. "Holy fucking Christ," she whispered.

"Amen," said Kurtz.

"He can't be serious," she said. "Why would Gonzaga pay you that much?"

"I thought you two were on a first-name basis," said Kurtz. "Don't you mean, 'Toma?' "

"Fuck you, Kurtz. Answer the question."

Kurtz shrugged. "His family's lost seventeen customers and middlemen. You've only lost five. Maybe it's worth a hundred grand to him to find the people doing this."

"Or maybe he has no intention of ever paying you," said Angelina.

"That's a possibility."

"And why you? It's not like you're Sam Fucking Spade." She looked around the office. "What is this bullshit company you set up? Wedding Bells?"

"Dot com," said Kurtz.

"Is it a front of some sort?"

"Nope." *Was it? Is it who I am now?* Kurtz's head hurt too much to answer epistemological questions like that at the moment.

Angelina stood, hitched her skirt down, and paced around the office. "I need help, Kurtz."

Demoted back to last names so soon, thought Kurtz. He waited.

She paused her pacing next to the couch. Kurtz let his hand slide forward a bit. If she had brought her Compact Witness .45, it would be in the pocket of her coat.

"You know people," Angelina said. "You know the scum of this city, its winos and addicts and street people and thugs."

"Thanks," said Kurtz. "Present company excluded, of course."

She looked at him and reached into the pocket of the draped coat.

Kurtz slid the .38 half out of its holster under the desk.

Angelina removed a pack of cigarettes and a lighter. She lit her cigarette, set the pack and lighter back in the coat pocket, and paced to the window again. She didn't look out but stood exhaling smoke and staring at her own reflection in the glass.

"It's all right," said Kurtz. "You can smoke in here."

"Thank you," she said, voice dripping sarcasm, and tapped ashes into Arlene's ashtray.

"Actually, I'm surprised you smoke," said Kurtz, "what with all the running and jogging and such."

"I don't usually," she said, left hand cradling her right elbow as she stood staring at nothing. "Nasty habit I picked up in all those years in Europe. I just do it now when I'm especially stressed."

"What do you want?" Kurtz asked for the third time.

She turned. "I think maybe Toma Gonzaga and Little Skag are working together to squeeze me out. I need a free agent in my corner."

Kurtz had been called many things in his life, but never a free agent. "Gonzaga being behind this doesn't make any sense," said Kurtz. "He's lost seventeen people."

"Have you *seen* any of these corpses?" said Angelina.

Kurtz shook his head. "But you told me the killer is hauling off the bodies of your connections as well."

"But I *know* my dealers and customers were whacked," she said. "My people went to the addresses, saw the blood and brains, cleaned up after the killer."

"And you think Gonzaga is faking his casualty list just to take out your people?"

Angelina made an expressive, Italian movement with her hands and batted more ashes. "It would be a nice cover, wouldn't it? My family *needs* to get into the serious drug business, Kurtz, or the Gonzagas will have all the real drug money in Western New York wrapped up."

"Gambling and shakedowns and prostitution aren't enough anymore?" asked Kurtz. "What's the world coming to?"

She ignored him and sprawled in Arlene's chair. "Or maybe somebody *is* hitting Gonzaga's people," she said. "There's always been a phantom heroin ring we think is working out of Western Pennsylvania—from Pittsburgh up to the Southern Tier of our state. Some sort of independent group that goes way back—twenty, thirty years. They specialized in heroin and since our family wasn't into that, they never interfered enough with our business to justify a confrontation."

"The Gonzaga Family must have wanted to deal with them," said Kurtz. "Gonzagas have been peddling heroin here since World War Two. I'm surprised old Emilio never dealt with these Pennsylvania people."

"The Gonzagas never identified the Pennsylvania people," said Angelina. "Old Emilio actually asked my father for help once in finding them, if you can believe that. But the Five Families don't know anything about this rogue operation either."

"This phantom skag gang isn't mobbed up?" said Kurtz. "No vowels at the ends of their names?"

She glared at him as if he'd insulted her proud ethnic heritage. Come to think of it, thought Kurtz, he had.

The anger-blush was back in her cheeks when Angelina said, "Can you tell me what you've found out about the murder of Gonzaga's people? Did they really happen?"

"I have no idea," Kurtz slid the .38 all the way back in the holster and rubbed his temples.

"What do you mean? You think Gonzaga may have staged them?"

"I mean I haven't spent five minutes looking into those murders," said Kurtz. "I have my own case to solve."

"You mean finding who shot the probation officer? O'Toole?"

"I mean finding who shot me," said Kurtz. He unzipped the leather portfolio on his desk, removed a file, and handed it across to her. "This might help you decide."

Angelina Farino Ferrara studied Gonzaga's list of seventeen names, ad-dresses, messages left by the killer in each case, and details of cleanup, bul-letholes, blood spatters, and other forensic garbage that Kurtz had glanced over and forgotten. She looked at the map on the wall with its pins—all barely visible in the dark there—and then back at the file. Then she looked at the big Ricoh copy machine next to the couch.

"Can I copy this stuff?"

"Sure," said Kurtz. "Ten cents a page."

"You dumb shit," said Angelina, moving quickly to warm up the machine and set out the file pages. "I would have paid you a thousand bucks a page. I've been asking Toma for these details for the last week, and he's been stonewalling. What do you think he's up to, Kurtz?"

His cell phone rang. He dug it out of his jacket pocket, realized it was the other cell phone ringing, and answered it.

"Toma Gonzaga here," said the familiar, slow voice. "What have you found out, Mr. Kurtz?"

"I thought I was supposed to call you," said Kurtz.

"I was worried that something might have happened to you," said the don. "It's two days to Halloween and you know how crazy the streets can get this time of year. What have you discovered so far? Does any of it lead to Ms. Ferrara?"

"Why don't you ask her?" said Kurtz. He handed the phone to the surprised Angelina and listened to her side of the conversation.

"No . . . I'm here collecting the advance I gave him since he seems to be working for you now . . . no, I don't . . . he hasn't . . . I don't think he's even looked into it . . . no, Toma, believe me, if I thought it was you, I would have acted already . . . How sweet, fuck you, too . . . No, I agree. We should meet . . . Yes, I can do that."

She clicked off, folded the phone, and tossed it back to Kurtz.

Tossing the original file back on his desk, she bundled up the copies, shut off the machine, and slipped into her coat.

"You said something about a thousand bucks a page?" said Kurtz.

"Too late, Kurtz." She went out the door and he heard her high heels tripping down the steps, then watched her on the closed-circuit video monitor as she let herself out the lower door. He leaned closer to the monitor to make sure that the outer door had clicked shut and was locked. It would be embarrassing to relax only to find Angelina's bodyguards kicking down his office door.

When his cell phone rang again, he seriously considered not answering it. Then he did.

"Kurtz," came Angelina's voice. "I think I'm in trouble."

"What happened?"

"Come to the window."

Shutting off his desk lamp and approaching the wide window from the side, Kurtz warily peered out. Angelina was standing on the curb where the Lincoln Town Car had been parked. The spot was empty, but a red Jeep Liberty with five college-age kids in it was trying to park there.

"What's going on?" said Kurtz on the phone.

"My bodyguards and the car are gone."

"I can see that."

"They don't answer their phones or my pages."

Kurtz walked back to his desk, pulled the .38 and holster from beneath the drawer, dumped the used duct tape in the waste basket, went back to the window, and lifted his cell phone. "What are you going to do?"

"I called for help, but it'll be thirty minutes before they get here."

"What do you want me to do about it?"

"Open the door. Let me back in."

He thought about that. "No," he said, "I'll come down there."

CHAPTER
TWENTY-FIVE

In the morning, Kurtz dropped Angelina Farino Ferrara near her Marina Towers and headed toward the expressway to drive to Neola, New York, in search of Major O'Toole's fabled Cloud Nine amusement park. He was sure that Detective Rigby King would be busy today despite her theoretical day off, but every call from his cell phone to hers received only a busy signal. At first he was going to ignore it and drive on to Neola alone, but the thought of standing up an armed Rigby King made him go out of his way to swing by her townhouse. At least he could tell her later that he'd tried.

She was waiting for him at the curb, still talking on her phone. She folded it away when he pulled up and opened the Pinto's battered door to slip into the passenger seat.

"You're coming?" said Kurtz.

"Why so surprised?" said Rigby. She was wearing a tan corduroy blazer, pink Oxford shirt, jeans, and very white running shoes today. Her holster and 9mm were secure on her right hip, only visible if you knew to look. She was carrying a Thermos.

Kurtz shrugged. "Homicide cops, you know," he said. "I thought you might be working after all."

Rigby raised her heavy eyebrows. "Oh, you mean you thought maybe I'd be called in to investigate the murder of your girlfriend, Ms. Purina Ferrari?"

Kurtz gave her nothing but a blank look. He got the Pinto in gear and heading back toward the expressway.

"Not curious, Joe?" said Rigby. She unscrewed the Thermos and poured herself some steaming coffee, taking care not to spill it as the Pinto bounced over expansion joints.

"About what? Are you saying that Farino Ferrara was murdered?"

"We were pretty sure of it," said Rigby, sipping carefully and cradling the plastic Thermos cup in both hands as Kurtz headed up the ramp onto the Youngman Expressway. "Last night we got an anonymous call about an abandoned Lincoln Town Car that the caller said looked like it was filled with blood and gore—which, it turned out, it was—and when the uniformed officers arrived at Hemingway's—you know that café, don't you, Joe? It's only a few blocks from your office isn't it?—they found a locked Town Car registered to your Ms. Farino Ferrara. It was filled with blood and brains, all right, but no bodies. The cops tried to contact the Farino woman at her penthouse out near the lake, but some goombah answering there said she was gone and no one knew where she was."

Kurtz had followed the 290 Youngman around to where it merged into 90 South near the airport. The Pinto rattled and wheezed but managed to keep up with the lighter Sunday morning traffic. It had rained much of the night and the morning was chilly, but the clouds were breaking up now and he could see blue sky to the south. Rigby's coffee smelled good. Kurtz wished he'd had time to grab some this morning. Maybe he'd go through a drive-thru on their way out past East Aurora.

"So is she dead?" said Kurtz at last.

Rigby looked at him. "It looked that way until about thirty minutes ago. We left a black and white at Marina Towers—her lawyer wouldn't let us up in the penthouse and we hadn't found a judge to issue paper yet—and Kemper called me a minute ago to tell me that the Farino woman just walked in. No car, just walked in from that asphalt path that runs along the marina opposite Chinaman's Lighthouse."

"She jogs," said Kurtz.

"Uh huh," said Rigby. "All night? In some sort of mini-skirt and clingy, silk top thing?"

"Sounds like Kemper got lots of detail."

"Part of being a cop," said Rigby.

They rode in silence for a few minutes. Kurtz took the Aurora Expressway exit before 90 became a toll road and they followed the four-lane 400 out east toward East Aurora and Orchard Park.

"Well, aren't you going to ask whose blood and brains it was in her

Town Car?" demanded Rigby. She refilled her plastic mug, poured sugar out of a McDonald's packet, and stirred it with her little finger.

"Whose blood and brains was it in her Town Car?" said Kurtz.

"You tell me," said Rigby.

He looked at her. The expressway was almost empty and the sunlight lit hillsides of autumn orange and yellow on either side. "What are you talking about?" he said.

"I just thought maybe you could tell me, Joe." Rigby smiled sweetly at him. "You want some coffee?"

"Sure."

"Maybe there's a fast food drive-thru place out by the East Aurora exit," she said, "but I don't remember one."

He'd gone downstairs and out the door into the rain the previous night with the .38 in his palm and his eye full of business. If this was some bullshit set-up from Angelina Farino Ferrara, then let it happen.

No ambush came. The woman was really upset, standing there in the rain with her not-so-tiny Compact Witness .45 in her hand while cars were parking and nosing along Chippewa Street and pedestrians ran for the trendy restaurants and coffeehouses and wine bars. So far, no one seemed to have noticed the weapon.

"Where'd they go? Where's the car?" said Angelina, almost gasping the words. It was the first time Kurtz had ever seen the woman at the edge of control.

"How the hell should I know?" said Kurtz. He touched her elbow, guiding her hand into her coat pocket so the Compact Witness was out of sight. "Are these guys reliable?"

She stared at him and it looked as if she was about to laugh, but her eyes were wild. "Is anyone in this fucking business reliable, Kurtz? I pay Figini and Sheffield enough, but that doesn't mean anything."

Not if Gonzaga or your brother Little Skag paid them more, thought Kurtz.

She was squinting at Kurtz and he could read her mind—*What if Gonzaga paid* Joe Kurtz *more?*

"If I wanted you dead, lady, I would have done it upstairs," he said.

She shook her head. Her hair was black and slick with rain. "I have to . . .

we have to . . ." She seemed to be mentally running through her options and rejecting all of them.

"We need to get off the street," said Kurtz. Part of his mind was shouting—*What is this* we *shit, Kemo Sabe?*

He led her across the street and into the alley alongside his building. Neither would go ahead of the other, so they walked side by side, him carrying the .38 in his palm, her with her hand on the Compact Witness in her pocket. If a cat had jumped out at that moment, all three of them would have probably ended up shot full of lead.

The small parking area off the alley where Kurtz and Arlene had reserved spaces held only his Pinto. "Get in," said Kurtz. "I'll take you back to Marina Towers."

"No." She stared at him across the wet, rusted roof of the Pinto. "Not there. Let's look for the Lincoln."

"All right, get in."

They found it within ten minutes, parked in a dark lot near Hemingway's Café. The doors were unlocked and the keys were in the ignition. The overhead light didn't come on when they opened the doors. Both Kurtz and Angelina were wearing gloves. He'd brought his flashlight from the Pinto and now they leaned in from opposite sides as he played the beam over the bloody seats and carpets. Gray matter and tiny, hard white shards glistened in the folds of the dark upholstery.

"Jesus," whispered Angelina. "It looks like a massacre. Even the back seats are bloody."

"I think the shooter just opened the back door, stepped in, and shot both of them in the head," said Kurtz. "Then he dragged the bodies into the back seat, walked around, got behind the wheel, and drove off."

"On *Chippewa Street?*" whispered the female don. She was blinking rapidly. "It was busy there tonight."

"Yeah," said Kurtz. "So far, this guy's been hitting junkies and dealers. Either of your bodyguards fit that description?"

Angelina hesitated a second. "Not really," she said at last. "Well, Sheffield has been coordinating deliveries."

"Sheffield is Colin?" said Kurtz. "The fop I dealt with the night we said good-bye to Big Bore?"

"Yes."

Kurtz ran the flashlight around the interior a final time, let the beam move across the driver's seat where the blood had been smeared, let it dwell on a starred fracture on the blood-spattered windshield for a second, and then flicked off the light. Traffic passed on Pearl Street. They walked away from the Lincoln and paused on the sidewalk. Angelina pulled out her cell phone.

"What are you doing?" said Kurtz.

"Getting in touch with the guys I called, telling them to bring cleanup stuff."

Kurtz reached over and closed the phone. "Why not leave the Lincoln as it is for the cops?"

She wheeled on him. "Are you *crazy*? It's *my* car. It's registered to *me*. I'll have every cop in Western New York on my ass."

Kurtz shrugged. "Look, you and Gonzaga—if you believe Gonzaga— have been doing it the other way for weeks now. This killer whacks your people, you rush out with buckets and mops and clean up after him. You're sitting on twenty-four murders, if Gonzaga is to be believed. Maybe that's just what the killer and whoever's sending the killer wants you to do."

Angelina bit her lip but said nothing.

"I mean, you're so crazy to find him that you're both trying to hire *me*, for Christ's sake," continued Kurtz. "Why not let the Buffalo P.D. deal with this?"

"But the attention . . ." began Angelina.

"Is going to be intense," said Kurtz. "But you won't be a suspect. They're *your* people who were hit. Let the cops do their fingerprint and ballistics stuff and put out an A.P.B. on someone walking around with blood on the seat of their pants."

"The media will go apeshit," said Angelina. "It'll be national news about a gang war."

Kurtz shrugged again. "You keep wondering if Gonzaga *is* behind this. Maybe the attention will smoke him out. Or rule him out."

Angelina turned and looked at the Lincoln in the back of the lot. A Saab pulled off Pearl and parked only two spaces away from it. Three college-age kids got out, laughing, and walked to Hemingway's. When the Saab's headlight beams had moved across the Lincoln, both Kurtz and Angelina had seen the bullet-fractured windshield. It was only a matter of time before someone noticed the gore.

She hesitated another few seconds. Then she brushed strands of wet hair away from her forehead and said, "I think you're right. For once the cops could be some help. At the very least, we won't be playing the murderer's game."

They got back in the Pinto and Kurtz drove down Pearl and cut over to Main. "Where do you want to go if not back to your penthouse?" asked Kurtz.

"Your place."

"Back to the office? Why?"

"Not back to the office," said Angelina Farino Ferrara. "*Your* place. That Harbor Inn hovel that nobody's supposed to know about."

"That's nuts," said Kurtz, shaking his head. "When the cops call, you have to be home with someone there as an alibi so . . ." He turned his head and froze.

Angelina was holding the .45 caliber Compact Witness in her right hand, bracing it on her left forearm, the black circle of the muzzle steady on Kurtz's heart. "Your place," she said. "Not mine."

A penny for your thoughts, Joe," said Rigby King.

"What?" The Rigby King he'd known didn't say things like *A penny for your thoughts*. Not unless she was being *really* sarcastic.

"You've been driving for twenty minutes without saying a word," said Rigby. "And you didn't stop in East Aurora for coffee. You want some from the Thermos? It's still hot."

"No thanks," said Kurtz. He thought, *What are you up to, woman?*

"I didn't mean what I said yesterday," said the cop.

"What's that?"

"About you . . . you know . . . going to Iran with me and killing my ex-husband."

Does she think I'm wearing a wire?

"I'd like the son of a bitch dead," continued Rigby, "but all I really want is my son back."

"Uh-huh," said Kurtz. *She's not going to give me any department information. This ride with her is for nothing.*

They rode in silence again for a few minutes. The sunlight ignited the color in the hills, where about half the trees still showed bright foliage. The grass was still green, the woods very thick. The four-lane highway had ended not far past East Aurora, and now they were headed south on Highway 16, a winding old two-lane road that slowed for such ten-house towns as Holland and Yorkshire and Lime Lake. The hills on either side were getting steeper and clouds covered the southern horizon. A constant wind was blowing from the west, and Kurtz had to concentrate on keeping the Pinto from wandering.

"Do you remember the night in the choir loft?" said Rigby. She wasn't looking at him, but was staring out her window at the passing, empty fruit stands and dilapidated old farms with their broad yards and big satellite dishes.

Kurtz said nothing.

"You were the only boy at Father Baker's who didn't tease me about my big tits when I was seventeen," continued Rigby, still looking away. "So that night I brought the flashlights and walked through the Catacombs over from the Girl's Hall—it was almost two blocks away, you remember?—I knew it was you I was coming to find in the Boy's Hall."

Shadows of clouds were moving across the hills and valley now. Leaves skittered across the road. There was little traffic except for a pest control truck that had been behind them for quite a while.

"You weren't sure you wanted to follow me into the Catacombs," continued Rigby. "You were tough as nails, even when you were . . . what? . . . fifteen that year? But you were nervous that night. They would have beat the hell out of you if you'd been found AWOL from bunk check again."

"Fourteen," said Kurtz.

"Jesus, that makes me even more of a pedophile. But you were a big fourteen." She turned and smiled at that, but Kurtz kept his eyes on the road. It was more shadow than sunlight ahead.

"You liked the Catacombs," said Rigby. "You wanted to keep exploring them, even with the rats and everything. I just wanted to get up into the Basilica. Remember that sort of secret passage in the wall and the narrow, winding staircase that went right up into the sacristy?"

Kurtz nodded and wondered what she was up to with this story.

"We found those other stairs and I took your hand and kept leading you up that other winding staircase, up past the organ loft where Father Majda was practicing on the organ for Saturday's High Mass. Remember how dark it was? It must have been about ten o'clock at night and there was only the light of the votive candles down below, and Father Majda's little lamp above the keyboard as we tiptoed past his loft and kept climbing—I don't know why we were so frightened of being heard, he was playing *Toccata in Fugue in D-minor* and wouldn't have heard us if we'd fired a gun at him."

Kurtz remembered the smells—the heavy incense and the oiled wood scent of the pews and the scent of young Rigby's clean sweat and skin as she pushed him down on the hard pew in the upper choir loft, knelt straddling him, unbuttoned her white blouse, and pulled it off. She'd worn a simple white bra and he'd watched with as much technical interest as teenaged lust as she reached behind her and easily undid the hooks and eyes. He remembered thinking *I have to learn how to do that without looking*.

"Do you know what the odds were against us having a simultaneous orgasm like that on our first try, Joe?"

Kurtz didn't think she really wanted an answer to that, so he concentrated on driving.

"I think that was my first and last time," Rigby said softly.

Kurtz looked over at her.

"For a simultaneous orgasm, I mean," she said hurriedly. "Not for a fuck. I've had a few of those since. Though none in a choir loft since that night."

Kurtz sighed. The pest control truck was falling farther behind, although Kurtz was driving under the speed limit. It was cloudy enough now that cars coming the other way had their headlights on.

"Want some music?" said Rigby.

"Sure."

She turned the radio on. Scratchy jazz matched the buffeting wind and low-hurrying clouds. She poured the last of the Thermos coffee into the red mug and handed him the mug.

Kurtz looked at her, nodded, and sipped.

CHAPTER
TWENTY-SIX

Following the pathetic Pinto south on Highway 16, the Dodger ran through all the reasons he hated this playing-spy bullshit. He wasn't a spy. He wasn't some fucking dork-private eye like this idiot he had watched all night and was tailing now. The Dodger knew very well what he was and what he was good at doing and what his goal was in life right now—the Resurrection—and it had nothing to do with following the clapped-out Pinto with this clapped-out man and the big-tit brunette south toward Neola and the bruised sky down there.

The two goombahs the night before had been no problem at all. Since they were bodyguards, they were arrogant and unobservant, sitting there in their Lincoln Town Car with all the doors unlocked. The Dodger had opened the back door and slipped into the back seat with his 9mm Beretta already raised, the suppressor attached. The Dodger had known that the man named Sheffield in the passenger seat up front would react the fastest—and he had, ducking and reaching for his gun the second the door opened—but the Dodger had put three slugs through the thick seat into the man and, when he reared up in pain, a fourth one through his forehead. The driver had just sat there, mouth open, staring, and the Dodger could have taken time to reload if he'd had to. He didn't have to. The fifth shot caught the driver in the right eye, exited the back of the big man's head, and punched a hole through the windshield. No one on Chippewa Street noticed.

The Dodger had removed the suppressor and slipped the Beretta back in its holster before grabbing first Sheffield and then the driver by their hair and pulling them up and back over the seats. Leaving the bodies sprawled on the floor and upholstery in the back, limbs intertwined, the Dodger had gone around front and driven the Lincoln a block, turning into a dark alley. He walked back, brought up the Mazda, dumped the bodies in the trunk, and then driven the Town Car a few more blocks to park it near a popular restaurant. He'd walked back to the Mazda whistling, gloved hands in his pockets.

The Boss always called Gonzaga or the Farino woman to tell them about the hit and where to find the bodies—using one of his military-intelligence electronic voice distorters and location scramblers—so the Dodger e-mailed him that the job was done. But this night, the Boss had another job for him. He ordered the Dodger to go wait for the private eye whose office the Farino woman was in right then—not at the man's office, but at someplace called The Harbor Inn way over in the mill area on the Island. The Boss e-mailed the address as the intersection of Ohio and Chicago Streets.

The Dodger was not pleased with this assignment. He was tired. It had been a long day, starting with that teacher he'd missed out in Orchard Park. He should be free now to go back to his hidey hole and get a good night's sleep, transporting the corpses to the Resurrection Site the next morning. Now he had to go down past the black projects and spend the night . . . watching. That's what the Boss had said. Just watch. Not even harvest this stupid private eye.

So the Dodger had driven south across the narrow steel bridge onto the Island, past the mills and half-empty projects, had driven by the dark Harbor Inn, checking it out, and then parked a block and a half southeast of the place, walking back to keep vigil in the shadows of an abandoned gas station half a block from the old hotel. The man—the Boss had said his name was Kurtz, as if the Dodger gave the slightest shit—showed up in a rusted-out Pinto about an hour later. There was a woman with him—the Farino woman, the Dodger realized as he stared through the binoculars. She seemed to be holding a .45 semiauto on Kurtz.

The Dodger almost laughed out loud in the shadows. He kills the female don's two bodyguards and steals her car, and what does she do? It looks as if she hijacks the felon ex-private-eye she was visiting on Chippewa Street.

The two went in through the boarded-up front entrance of the abandoned hotel, and the Dodger watched lights come on on the second floor. Driving by twice, he'd cased the place—even noticed the subtle surveillance video cameras on the north and west sides—but he was sure that he could climb one of the rusting fire escapes or a drainpipe and get in one of the darkened windows without being heard or seen. He could even get up to the dark third story—probably empty was the Dodger's guess, this Kurtz seemed like the only resident of the old Harbor Inn—and he could climb *down* to the second floor where three lights now burned behind shades. Whatever the female don and Kurtz were up to in there—and the Dodger could imagine what it was—he could be on them and finished with them and hauling the bodies out to the Mazda before they had a chance to look up.

The Dodger had gone back down the dark, rainy street to the Mazda only to find one black teenager jimmying open the car door and another one using a crowbar on the trunk. The trunk popped up first, the boy stared at the two bodies in it, had time to say, "Mother*fuck*," and the Dodger shot him in the back of the head, not even bothering to use the silencer.

The second boy dropped his tool and ran like hell. Like a lot of these ghetto kids, he was fast. The Dodger—who had always liked to run—was faster. He caught up with the kid on an eyeless side street less than two blocks away.

The boy turned and flicked open a knife. "Jesus fuck man," the kid said, crouching and dodging, "your face . . ."

The Dodger slipped the pistol in its holster, took the knife away from the kid with three moves, kicked his legs out from under him, and crushed the boy's larynx with his boot. He left the body where it was, walked back to the Mazda—no one had responded to the shot—and loaded the first boy's body in the back seat. There was no more room in the trunk.

The Dodger drove the two blocks, found that the second boy was still breathing in a rattling, rasping, twitching sort of way, so he cut his throat with the knife the boy had dropped. He tossed that corpse in the back as well—all the blood would make the Mazda unsalvageable for future use, but the Boss paid for these vehicles and he could afford it—and he drove back to the parking lot near Marina Towers, where he dumped the four bodies in the back of the pest control truck and drove it back to the Harbor Inn area.

The Dodger kept Handi Wipes in the truck, and he had to use eight of them to clean himself up. He had a change of clothes in the truck as well.

Back on surveillance at the empty gas station, the Dodger e-mailed the Boss, described the situation at The Harbor Inn, and asked if he could knock off for the night. There was no need to tell the Boss about the two car thieves; they'd just be extra material for the Resurrection.

The Boss e-mailed back ordering the Dodger to phone on a secure line. It took the Dodger fifteen minutes to find a pay phone that was working. The Boss was curt, pulling rank, and told the Dodger to sleep in the bug van and to keep his eye on The Harbor Inn and to follow Kurtz whenever he left.

"What about the Farino woman?"

"Ignore her. Stay with Kurtz. Call me when he moves and I'll tell you what to do next."

So here he was, the Dodger, exhausted from sleeping in the front seat of the pest control truck, red-eyed from trying to keep watch between naps, still smelling of blood, with four rigor-mortised corpses under tarps in the back, driving south toward Neola, New York.

The Dodger had grown accustomed to taking orders from the Boss, but that was because the Boss had been giving him orders he enjoyed carrying out. He wasn't enjoying this playing-spy shit. If the Boss didn't call him off this joke of an assignment soon, he'd kill Kurtz and this new woman with him and add them to the Resurrection. It was better to apologize to the Boss later, the Dodger had learned decades ago, than to ask permission before doing something you really wanted to do.

And the Dodger really wanted to kill this man who'd kept him awake in the rainy ghetto all night.

But as they approached Neola, he dutifully used his cell phone to call the Boss.

"Sir, I'm not going into Neola with them for Chrissakes," he told him. "Either let me deal with this Kurtz now or let me go about my business."

"Go do what you have to do," said the Boss.

CHAPTER
TWENTY-SEVEN

Neola is about sixty miles south-southeast of Buffalo, but the narrow, two-lane road slowed them enough that they'd been driving almost an hour and a half before they saw signs saying they were close to the little city. The clouds had moved in now, the hills had gotten steeper and the valleys deeper, the October wind had come up stronger and the trees were mostly bare. The few cars that passed going the opposite direction did so with their headlights on and sometimes with their windshield wipers flicking.

Kurtz pulled the Pinto to the side of the road on a cinder apron in front of an abandoned fruit stand and got out of the car.

"What is it, Joe?" said Rigby. "You want me to drive?"

Kurtz shook his head. He watched the traffic going south pass for several silent minutes. Finally, Rigby said, "What is it? You think we're being followed?"

"No," said Kurtz. The pest control truck had fallen back in the gloom and rain some miles ago, and must have turned off somewhere.

Rigby got out of the car and came around, lighting a cigarette. She offered one to Kurtz. He shook his head.

"That's right, you gave up smoking in Bangkok, didn't you? I always thought it was because of that girl's act at *Pussies Galore*."

Kurtz said nothing. It wasn't raining, but the highway was wet and a passing truck set up a hiss and spray.

"What are you going to do about the little girl, Joe?"

He turned a blank stare on her. "What little girl?"

"*Your* little girl," said Rigby. "Yours and Samantha's. The fourteen-year-old who's living with your secretary's sister-in-law. What's your daughter's name? Rachel."

Kurtz stared a second and then took a step toward her. Rigby King's cop instincts reacted to the look in his eyes and her hand came up halfway toward the 9mm Glock on her hip before she froze. She had to lean back over the Pinto's hood to avoid physical contact with Kurtz.

"Get in the car," he said. And turned away from her.

Fifteen miles before they reached the Pennsylvania line, Highway 16 passed under Interstate 86—the Southern Tier Expressway they called it down here—and ran another seven miles into Neola. The town had absurdly wide streets—more like some small place out west where land had been cheap at its settling than in a village in New York State—and it was nestled amid high hills just north of the Allegheny River. Kurtz noticed the variations in spelling—Allegany State Park was a few miles to the west of them, the town of Allegany was just down the road to the west, but the river that marked the southern boundary of Neola was the Allegheny. He didn't think it was worth investigating.

They drove the twelve-block length of Main Street, crossed the broad but shallow river, turned around before the road ran into the hills south into Pennsylvania, and drove back up the length of town again, making two detours to explore the side streets where Highway 305 ran into Highway 16 near the downtown. When he reached the north edge of town again, Kurtz made a U-turn through a gas station and said, "Notice anything?"

"Yeah," said Rigby, still watching Kurtz carefully as if he might get violent at any moment. "There was a Lexus *and* a Mercedes dealership along the main drag. Not bad for a town of . . . what did the sign say?"

"Twenty-one thousand four hundred and twelve," said Kurtz.

"Yeah. And there's something else about the old downtown . . ." She paused.

"No empty stores," said Kurtz. "No boarded-up buildings. No 'for lease' signs. No state employment and unemployment offices in empty buildings." The economy in Buffalo and around Western New York had been hurting long before the recent recession, and residents just got used to defunct businesses, empty buildings, and the omnipresent state unemployment outlets. Downtown Neola had looked prosperous and scrubbed.

"What the hell is the economy here?" said Rigby.

"As far as I know, the Major's South-East Asia Trading Company is the biggest employer with about two thousand people working for them," said Kurtz. "But not only the old Victorian homes off Main here were all spruced up and painted, fresh trim colors, but that trailer park down by the river had new F-150 pickups and Silverados parked by the mobile homes. Even the poor people in Neola seem to be doing all right."

"You don't miss much," said Rigby.

He glanced at her. "You don't either. Did you notice a place we could grab an early lunch or late breakfast?"

"There was that fancy Victorian house called The Library on the hill before the river," said Rigby. "Families in church clothes and ladies in hats going in."

"I was thinking a greasy spoon where people might talk to us," said Kurtz. "Or a bar."

Rigby sighed. "It's Sunday, so the bars are closed. But there was a diner next to the train tracks back there."

The locals didn't rush over to talk to them, or even seem to take notice of them, during their late-breakfast, early-lunch diner meal—except for some kids in a nearby booth who kept staring at Kurtz's bruised eyes and bandaged head and giggling—but the coffee and food helped his headache and Rigby quit looking at him as if worried he was about to strangle her.

"Why did you really want to come to Neola?" the detective said at last. She was eating lunch; Kurtz was eating a big breakfast. "Are you planning to visit Major O'Toole at his home here? You want me along to make sure it doesn't get out of control? He used to be Special Forces in Vietnam, you know. He may be almost seventy and in a wheelchair, but he probably could still kick your ass."

"I don't even know where he lives," said Kurtz. It was true. He hadn't taken time to look it up.

"I do," said Rigby. "But I'm not going to tell you, and I doubt if any of these good people would either." She nodded toward the people eating in the loud diner and others hurrying by outside. The wind was blowing light rain. "Most of them probably get their paychecks from the Major's and Colonel's SEATCO in one way or the other."

Kurtz shrugged. "The Major isn't why I'm here. At least not directly." He told her about Peg O'Toole's question about amusement parks, described the photographs of the abandoned park on a hilltop, and shared Arlene's information about Cloud Nine, and about the Major's kid shooting up the local high school thirty years earlier.

"Yeah, when I learned about the kid dying in the Rochester asylum fire, I had some people look into it," said Rigby. "I thought that might be why you're down here. Do you seriously think the Major might have had someone shoot his own niece?"

Kurtz shrugged again.

"What would the motive be?" asked Rigby. Her brown eyes held a steady gaze on him over her coffee cup. "Drugs? Heroin?"

Kurtz worked hard not to react, even by so much as a blink. "Why do you say that? What do drugs have to do with anything here?"

It was Rigby King's turn to shrug. "Parole Officer O'Toole's old man, the cop, was killed in a drug bust a few years ago, you know."

"Yeah. So?"

"And Major O'Toole's company, SEATCO, has been under suspicion from the Feds for several years as being a Southern New York, western Pennsylvania heroin supplier. The DEA and FBI think that he and his old Vietnamese buddies have been shipping more than Buddha statues and objects of art from Vietnam and Thailand and Cambodia the last twenty-five years or so."

Bingo, thought Kurtz. He couldn't believe he'd found the connection this easily. And he couldn't believe that Gonzaga and Farino Ferrara didn't know about this. He squinted at Rigby. "Why are you telling me this?"

She smiled her Cathy Rigby smile at him. "It's classified information, Joe. Only a handful of us at the department knows anything about it. Kemper and I were briefed by the Feds only last week, because of the O'Toole shooting."

"All the more reason to ask you why you're telling me this," said Kurtz. "You suddenly on my side here, Rigby?"

"Fuck your side," she said and set down the coffee cup. "I'm a cop, remember? Believe it or not, I want to solve Peg O'Toole's shooting as much as you do. Especially if it ties in with rumors we're hearing of junkies and heroin users disappearing in Lackawanna and elsewhere."

Again, Kurtz didn't blink or allow a facial muscle to twitch. He said,

"Well, for now, I just want to find whether this Cloud Nine is real or not. Any suggestions?"

"We could drive through the hills around town," said Rigby. "Look for roller coasters or Ferris wheels or something sticking up above the bare trees."

"I have to be back in Buffalo tonight," said Kurtz. *To meet a woman coming across the Canadian border and ask her why her fiancé shot me.* "Have any smarter suggestions?"

"We could go to the library," said Rigby. "Small town librarians know everything."

"It's Sunday," said Kurtz. "Library's closed."

"Well, I could wander into the Neola Police Department or Sheriff's Office, flash my badge, and say I was following up on a tip and ask them about Cloud Nine," said Rigby.

Kurtz was getting more and more suspicious about all this helpful assistance. He said, "Who will I be? Your partner?"

"You'll be absent," said Rigby. She dug out money for the check. "You go into the local sheriff's office with those raccoon eyes or wearing those sunglasses, with your scalp all carved up like that, they'll throw us both in jail on general principles."

"All right. Shall I meet you back at the car in an hour?"

"Give me ninety minutes," said Rigby. "I have to go find a doughnut place open. You don't go ask local cops for help, even on directions, without bearing gifts."

They'd noticed the green signs for the police station, only a block east of Main, and Rigby decided to walk. She said that she didn't want to lose all credibility by having someone see her being dropped off in that rusted piece of Ford crap Kurtz was driving. Kurtz watched her disappear around the corner, her short hair still being stirred by the strong wind from the west and her corduroy jacket blowing, and then he opened the Pinto's trunk. The .38 was there, hidden under the spare tire, but that wasn't what he wanted. He pulled the still-sealed pint of Jack Daniel's out of its hiding place and slipped it in the pocket of his leather jacket. Then, pulling his collar up against the gusting wind, he headed off down Main Street in search of a park.

Even in an absurdly prosperous town like Neola, there had to be a place where the winos hung out, and Kurtz found it after about fifteen minutes of walking. The two old men and the stoned boy with long, greasy hair were sitting down by the river on a stretch of dirt and grass out of sight of the park's jogging path. The men were working on a bottle of Thunderbird and they squinted suspiciously as Kurtz settled himself on a nearby stump. Their eyes grew a film of greediness over the suspicion when he took out the sealed pint. Only the greediness disappeared when Kurtz said that he wanted to talk and passed the pint over.

The oldest man—and the only one who talked—was named Adam. The other old man, according to Adam, was Jake. The stoned boy—who was focusing on something just below the treetops—evidently didn't deserve an introduction. And although Jake did not speak, at every question and before every answer, old Adam looked to Jake—who made no visible sign but who seemed to pass along permission or denial telepathically—before Adam spoke.

Kurtz shot the shit for fifteen minutes or so. He confirmed Rigby's assumption that everyone in Neola either worked for the Major's South-East Asia Trading Company or benefitted from the money from it or was afraid of someone who did work for it. He also confirmed the details of the 1977 shooting at the high school that had put eighteen-year-old Sean Michael O'Toole in the state asylum.

"That fucking Sean was a crazy fucking kid," said Adam. He wiped the mouth of the bottle and handed the pint to Kurtz, who took a small sip, wiped the mouth, and handed it to Jake.

"Did you know him?"

"Everybody in the fucking town fucking knew him," said Adam, taking the bottle back from Jake. "Fucking Major's fucking kid—like a fucking prince. Little fucking bastard shot and killed my Ellen."

"Ellen?" said Kurtz. Arlene's research had reported that the O'Toole kid had gone to the high school with a .30-.06 one morning and killed two fellow students—both male—a gym teacher, and an assistant principal.

"Fucking Ellen Stevens," slurred the old man. "My fucking girlfriend. She was the fucking girl's gym teacher. Best fucking lay I ever had."

Kurtz nodded, sipped some of the disappearing whiskey, wiped the mouth, and handed it on to Jake. The stoned boy's eyes were glazed and fixed.

"Anybody ever say why he did it? This Sean Michael O'Toole?"

"Because he fucking wanted to," said Adam. "Because he fucking knew that he was the fucking Major's fucking son. Because he'd fucking got away with everything—until Ellen gave him fucking detention that fucking week because the little fuck had drilled a hole in the wall of the girl's locker room and was fucking peeping at Ellen's fucking girls. That fucking old bastard the Major has run Neola since fuck knows when, and his fucking kid didn't know that he couldn't shoot and kill four fucking people and fucking get away with it. You got another fucking pint, Joe?"

"No, sorry."

"That's all right. We got another fucking bottle." Adam showed a smile consisting of three teeth on top and two on the bottom and pulled the Thunderbird wine out from behind his stump.

"Whatever happened to the kid?" said Kurtz. "Sean Michael?"

Adam hesitated and looked to Jake. Jake did not so much as blink. Adam evidently got the message. "Fucking psycho went up to that big fucking nuthouse in Rochester. They say he got fucking burned up a few years later, but we don't fucking believe it."

"No?"

"Fuck no," grinned Adam, checking with Jake before going on. "Little kids in the town've seen him—seen him wandering the woods and backyards at night, all scarred up from his burns, wearing a fucking baseball cap. And Jake here seen him, too."

"No shit?" Kurtz said conversationally. He turned expectantly to Jake, but the other old man just stared unblinkingly, took the Thunderbird from Adam, and helped himself to a swig.

Adam turned his head as if he was listening to Jake, but Jake's expression was as gray and expressionless as the October sky.

"Oh, yeah," added Adam, "Jake reminds me that the kids in town used to see the Artful Dodger's ghost mostly around Halloween. That's when the Dodger would bring Cloud Nine alive again—at least for one night—All Hallow's Eve. I ain't never seen it myself, but kids I knew over the years used to say that the Dodger come back with a bunch of other ghosts from the other side and would ride all them dead rides up Cloud Nine one last time."

"The Dodger?" said Kurtz. "Cloud Nine?"

"When they was all kids, according to my dead Ellen, they used to fucking call that fucking O'Toole kid 'the Artful Dodger.'" replied Adam. "You know, from that fucking Charles Dickens book. Fucking *Oliver Twist*."

"The Artful Dodger," repeated Kurtz.

"Fucking aye," said Adam. "Or sometimes just 'Dodger,' you know, 'cause he was all the time wearing that fucking Dodger cap . . . not the L.A. cap, but the old fucking Brooklyn one."

Kurtz nodded. "What was that you were saying about something called Cloud Nine?"

Adam lowered the bottle and looked at Jake for a long minute. Finally Adam said, not to Kurtz but to the silent old man, "Why the fuck not? Why should we do that fucking Major a favor?"

Jake said nothing, showed nothing.

Adam turned and shrugged. "Jake don't want me to tell you, Joe. Sorry."

"Why not?"

" 'Cause Jake knows that everyone who fucking goes up there in the last twenty fucking years or so to fucking find Cloud Nine gets their ass shot off, and Jake fucking likes you."

"I'll take my chances," said Kurtz. He took two twenties out of his billfold.

"Fucking liquor stores ain't open today," Adam said mournfully.

"But I bet you know somewhere else you could get some good stuff," said Kurtz.

Adam looked at Jake. "Yeah," he said at last.

He told Kurtz about the Major building an amusement park in the hills and gave Kurtz the directions. He warned him to stay away until after Halloween, after the ghost of the Artful Dodger and his pals had their last rides on the abandoned Ferris wheel and little train and dodge-em cars up there. "Wait 'til mid-November," said old Adam. "The Dodger ghost don't come around much in November according to the kids. And the other ghosts only join him on Halloween."

Kurtz stood to go, but then asked. "Do you know why just on Halloween?"

"Fuck yes I know," said Old Adam. "Back when the Major was still running fucking Cloud Nine, Halloween was the last night it was open before shutting down all fucking winter. The last night was fucking free. It was the one time when everyone in the fucking town went up to that fucking amusement park—sometimes it was almost too fucking cold to ride the fucking rides—and the Major always had a big fucking parade with his fucking son on a fucking float—that little weasel, the Artful Dodger, riding up there and waving like the fucking queen of fucking England. Halloween. It was the fucking brat's birthday."

Kurtz looked over to see if the stoned kid was paying any attention, and noticed for the first time that the boy had gone, slipped away into the trees along the river. It was as if he'd never been there.

CHAPTER
TWENTY-EIGHT

Kurtz's plan was to take the Pinto, check out Cloud Nine, and get back to downtown Neola before Rigby King finished her schmoozing with the local sheriff's department. But she was sitting in the car when he walked back to the downtown block where he'd left it.

Shit, he thought. "Hey, Boo," he said. It was an old joke and he'd almost—not quite—forgotten the origin of it back at Father Baker's Friday Movie Night.

"Hey, Boo," she said back. She didn't sound happy. "You find your talkative drunks?"

"Yeah," said Kurtz. "I thought you needed at least ninety minutes to break the ice with your local cops."

"I could've spent ninety days here and they weren't going to tell me anything," said Rigby. "They wouldn't even acknowledge that your goddamned amusement park ever existed. To listen to the Sheriff and his deputies, they never heard of Major O'Toole and barely've heard about his company that seems to rule the roost here."

"Which means that they're all on the Major's payroll," said Kurtz.

Rigby shrugged. "That's hard to believe, but that's what it sounds like. Unless they're all just cretinous smalltown cowturds too stupid and too suspicious of an outside police officer to tell the truth."

"Why would they be suspicious of a B.P.D. detective?"

"Well, no peace officer likes some wiseass coming in from the outside— but I'm not some FBI puke trying to take over some local investigation. I just told them the truth—that we're investigating the shooting of Major

O'Toole's niece up in Buffalo and I came down here on my day off to pick up any loose information."

"But they didn't have any loose information," said Kurtz.

"They were tight as a proctologist's dog's asshole."

Kurtz thought about that for a second.

"So," said Rigby, "you find out where your Cloud Nine is?"

"Yeah," Kurtz said. He was trying to figure out some way he could convince her to stay behind while he went up there. He couldn't. He put the Pinto in gear and headed out of town.

They'd just crossed the Allegheny River marking the south edge of town when Kurtz's phone rang.

"Yeah?"

"Joe," said Arlene, "someone just signed on to Peg O'Toole's account using her computer."

"Just a second," said Kurtz. He pulled the car into a turnout and got out. "Go ahead."

"Someone signed on from her computer at the Justice Center."

"Are you at the office?"

"No, home. But I'd set the software to copy me at both machines."

"Did you get O'Toole's password?"

"Sure. But whoever signed on using her machine did so to delete all of her e-mail."

"Did he have time to do it?"

"No. I copied it all to my hard drive before he deleted it. I think he took time to check what was there first."

"Good," said Kurtz. "Why would whoever this is use *her* machine to sign on for her e-mail if he had the password? Why not do it and erase her mail from his own computer?"

"I don't think whoever it was *had* the password, Joe. I think he—I don't think it's a woman, do you?—I think he used some software to hack it on her machine and signed on immediately."

"It's Sunday," said Kurtz. "The offices would be closed there. It makes sense. What about the e-mails?"

"She only saved a week's worth at a time," said Arlene, "and they're all parole business stuff, except for one letter to her boyfriend."

"Brian Kennedy?"

"Yes. It was e-mailed to his security company e-mail address in New

York, and was time-stamped about ten minutes before your appointment with her."

"What do they say? His *and* hers?"

"She only saved her own mail to file, Joe. Do you want me to fax you a copy?"

"I'm busy now." He had taken several paces away from the Pinto, and now he looked back to where Rigby was frowning at him from the passenger seat. "Just tell me."

"Her e-mail just said, and I quote—'Brian, I understand your reasons for asking me to wait, but I'm going to look into this lead this afternoon. If you come on Friday as usual, I'll tell you all about it then. Love, Peg.' "

"That's it?"

"That's it."

"And she sent it just before I met with her?"

"Ten minutes before, according to the time stamp."

"Then she must have been leaving work early that afternoon for a reason. Nothing else in the mail that we can use?"

"Nothing." There was the hiss and crackle of cell static. Then Arlene said, "Anything else you want me to do today, Joe?"

"Yeah. Track down the home address and phone number of the former director of the Rochester nuthouse. I want to call him or talk to him in person."

"All right. Are you in town now? The connection's lousy."

"No, I'm on the road for a few more hours. I'll call you when I get back to the office. Good work."

He folded the phone and got back in behind the wheel.

"Your stock broker?" said Rigby.

"Yeah. He thinks I should sell when the market opens tomorrow. Dump everything."

"Always a good idea," said the cop.

They drove a mile beyond the river, turned left on a county road for three-fourths of a mile, turned right onto an unmarked gravel road, and then turned left again onto two strips of dirt that ran steeply uphill.

"Are you sure you know where you're going, Joe?"

Kurtz concentrated on keeping the Pinto moving uphill through the trees, around occasional bends that gave them glimpses of the valley, river, and distant town, and then south around the mountain until the dirt track ended at an old wooden roadblock.

"End of the line," said Rigby.

"This is how old Adam described it," said Kurtz.

"Old Adam?"

"Never mind." Kurtz got out of the car, looked uphill toward where the overgrown remnants of the two-rut road continued, and began walking slowly uphill. Various faded signs on the barricade announced private land and warned against trespassing. He went around behind the Pinto, pulled a lumpy old nylon backpack from the trunk, and walked past the barricade.

"You're shitting me," called Rigby from beside the car. "Joe *Kurtz* is going for a hike?"

"Stay in the car if you want," called Kurtz. "I'm just going to walk up here a bit and see if I can see anything."

"Stay here and miss seeing Joe Kurtz go for a hike?" said Rigby, jogging uphill to catch up. "No way in hell."

Shit, thought Kurtz, and not for the first time that day.

They followed the dirt track two hundred yards or so up the hill through the bare and blowing trees until they were stopped by a fence. No old and rotting wood barricade here—the fence was nine feet tall, made of mesh-link steel, and had rows of unrusted concertina razor-wire atop it. Here the yellow no-trespassing signs were new and plastic and warned that the owners were authorized to use deadly force to repel trespassers.

"Authorized by *who*?" said Rigby, panting slightly.

Kurtz took a short-handled pair of wire cutters from the pack.

"Whoa!" said Rigby. "You're *not* going to do this."

Kurtz answered by testing to make sure the fence wasn't electrified and then snipping a three-foot-high line of links. He began working horizontally.

"God *damn* it, Joe. You're going to get us both arrested. Hell, I should arrest you. You're probably packing, too."

He was. He still had the .38 in his belt at the back, under his leather jacket.

"Go on back to the car, Rigby. I'll just be a few minutes. I just want to look at this place. You said yourself that I'm not a thief."

"No," said Rigby. "You're a damned idiot. You didn't meet with the sheriff and his boys back there. This is *not* a friendly town, Joe. We don't want to go to their jail."

"They won't arrest a cop," said Kurtz. He finished with the horizontal cut and bent the little door of heavy wire inward. It didn't want to bend, but eventually it opened wide enough that he could squeeze through if he tossed the pack in first and went in on his knees.

"Arrest me?" said Rigby, crouching behind him as he went through. "I'm worried that they'll *shoot* me." She took the 9mm Sig Sauer from her belt, worked the action, made sure a round was in the chamber, checked that the safety was on, and set the weapon back in its holster. She crouched, duck-walked through the opening as Kurtz held the wire back from the inside, and rose next to him.

"Promise me we'll make it fast."

"I promise," said Kurtz.

Above the fence they headed north along the edge of the woods for fifty yards or so, found the original access road—now overgrown and blocked here and there by fallen trees—and followed it higher into the forest.

Kurtz's headache pounded with every step and even when he paused to rest, the pulse of pain crashed with every heartbeat. The hurt in his skull clouded his vision and literally pressed against the back of his eyes.

"Joe, you okay?"

"What?" He turned and looked at Rigby through the pounding.

"You all right? You look sort of pale."

"I'm fine." He looked around. This damned hill was turning into a mountain. The trees here were some sort of pine that grew too close together, trunks as branchless as telephone poles for their first fifty vertical feet or so, and the mass of them shut out the sky. The clouds were low and dark and seemed to be scuttling by just above the tops of those trees. It couldn't be much later than noon, but it felt like evening.

"There!" cried Rigby.

He had to follow her pointing hand before he saw it.

Above the bare trunks of the deciduous trees up the hill and just visible through the wind-tossed branches, rose the semicircle of a Ferris wheel minus most of its upper cars.

CHAPTER
TWENTY-NINE

The amusement park was much larger than Kurtz had imagined, covering four or five acres of level land—a sort of shelf notched into the steep slope a couple of hundred yards below the brow of the wooded hill. The actual amusement park land had probably been leveled or extended out from the original slope by bulldozers and other heavy equipment, but it was impossible to tell exactly where now that tall trees had grown up over the decades of abandonment.

Kurtz and Rigby approached cautiously, right hands ready to go for their respective weapons, but the place was empty enough; bird and insect sounds—waning but still present on this late October day—suggested that there was no lurking human threat.

From their vantage point at the center of what had once been a sort of midway, Kurtz could see the huge Ferris wheel fifty yards away—rusted, paint missing, lightbulbs mostly gone on the struts and crossmembers, only four cars left on its flimsy wheel—as well as the overgrown bumper car pavilion, some tumbled ticket booths with bushes and small trees grown up inside, a Tilt-a-Whirl with all of its hooded cars ripped off their tracks and scattered in the surrounding weeds, and a line of empty, broken booths that could have housed shooting galleries and other suckers' games.

"Is this it?" asked Rigby. "The place you saw in Peg O'Toole's snapshots?"

Kurtz nodded.

They walked along the overgrown shelf of land between the taller trees, pausing here and there—in front of a tumbledown funhouse with its plywood facade broken, its garish paint faded like some ancient Italian fresco—then next to a beautiful merry-go-round or carousel Kurtz could never remember which went in which direction, although these shattered horses and camels and giraffes had once rotated counter-clockwise.

"What a shame," said Rigby, touching the shattered face of one of the painted horses. They had actually been carved by hand from wood, although the heads were hollow. Vandals had shattered all of the animals' faces, broken their legs, ripped most of them from their poles, and tossed them into the weeds, which had then grown up and around and through them.

They walked past the bumper car pavilion. The flat roof had fallen in and the once-white floor was covered with puddles and plaster. Most of the heavy bumper cars had been dragged out and thrown here and there, some pushed down the hillside, one even wedged in the lower branches of a tree. Kurtz could see the '9' of the Cloud Nine insignia in fading gold paint on some of the rusted cars. He matched up one tumbled car with the memory of the photo Parole Officer O'Toole had shown him. The weeds and trees seemed taller than he remembered from the photograph.

"Well," said Kurtz when they paused by the Ferris wheel, "the old news articles said that the Major had built this place to keep the youth of Neola busy. It looks as if they've been busy enough over the last few decades, although I don't think it was vandalism that the Major had in mind."

Rigby wasn't listening. "Look," she said. "Someone's replaced most of the gas engine that powers the Ferris wheel. And those chains and pulleys are new."

"I noticed that," said Kurtz. "The motor in the center of the carousel has been worked on as well. And did you notice the new bulbs on the wheel?"

Rigby walked around the base of the Ferris wheel. "Weird. Most of them are broken or missing, but it looks like someone is replacing . . . what? . . . one out of ten of the lights?"

"And there are newer electrical cables in the weeds as well," said Kurtz. He pointed to a flat area of battered buildings about a hundred feet up the midway road. "I think they all head that way."

They followed the heavy electrical cable from the Ferris wheel toward the tumbledown funhouse complex. Rigby pointed out several places where the new cable had been covered over with humus or dirt as if for conceal-ment.

To the rear of the rotting funhouse, all but hidden by the peeling facades and trees behind it, someone had fashioned a shack out of new lumber. The sides were still unfinished, but the roof was shingled and plastic kept the weather out. The top of the funhouse facade had bent backwards here, and a huge, inverted clown face hung over the shack and almost touched the small porch. On that porch, covered with plastic wrapped tightly by bungee cords, was an oversized new gasoline-powered electrical generator. Jerry cans of gasoline were lined up nearby.

Rigby checked out the shack and pointed to several covered tool boxes. She lifted a large, yellow power naildriver—the completely portable kind with its massive magazine of nails.

"You think it works?" she asked, holding the heavy thing in both of her pale hands.

"One way to find out," said Kurtz.

Rigby aimed back into the shack and squeezed the trigger.

BWAP. The 5-inch nail ripped through the plastic sheeting and embed-ded itself in the plywood wall ten feet farther in.

"It works," said Rigby.

They spent some time in the shack—found nothing more personal than a moldy cot in the back minus any bedding—and then strolled down the hill to the center of the overgrown midway.

"The newspaper articles Arlene found said that there was a kiddie-locomotive up here somewhere," said Kurtz.

"We'll find it later," said Rigby. She dropped onto a lush patch of grass near the carousel, just where the hill began to rise again, and patted the grass next to her. "Sit down a minute, Joe."

He sat four feet from her and looked out through the trees at the view of the Allegheny River and the town of Neola a mile or so below them to the north. With the remaining fall foliage in the hills surrounding the com-munity and a couple of white church spires visible, Neola looked more like some quaint New England village than a raw, Western New York industrial town.

"Let's talk a minute," said Rigby.

"All right," said Kurtz. "Tell me how it is that the DEA, FBI, AFT and other agencies have suspected the Major and SEATCO of being part of a heroin ring for years and yet the Major's still a free man and Neola still seems to be getting money from the heroin trade? Why haven't the alphabets been all over this place like hair on a gorilla?"

"I didn't mean talk about *that*."

"Answer the question, Rig."

She looked out and down at the town. "I don't know, Joe. Paul didn't tell me everything about the DEA briefing."

"But you think Kemper knows."

"Maybe."

Kurtz shook his head. "What the hell keeps law enforcement off a *heroin* ring, for fuck's sake?" He looked back at Rigby King. "Some sort of national security thing?"

The sun had peeked out and was illuminating their part of the hillside now, making the still-green grass leap out from the dull, autumn background in vibrant color. Rigby took off her corduroy jacket, despite the cold breeze blowing in. The press of her nipples was visible even through the thick, pink material of the Oxford cloth shirt. "I don't know, Joe. I think the feds and feebies have been wise to the Major since long before nine-eleven. Can we talk about what I want to talk about?"

Kurtz looked away from her again, squinting through his Ray Charles sunglasses at Neola now glowing white in the moving shafts of October sunlight. "CIA?" he said. "Some sort of quid pro quo bullshit between them and the Major's network? Arlene's clipped articles said that this SEATCO also traded with Syria and places like that, as well as with Vietnam, Cambodia, Thailand . . ."

"*Joe*," said Rigby. She scooted closer, grabbed his upper arm and squeezed it painfully.

Kurtz looked at her.

"*Listen* to me, Joe. *Please*."

Kurtz removed her fingers from his arm. "What?"

"I don't give a shit about SEATCO or this Major or any of the rest of this. I care about you."

Kurtz looked at her. He was still holding her wrist. He let it go.

"You're lost, Joe." Rigby's large brown eyes seemed darker than usual.

"What are you talking about?"

"I'm talking about *you*. You're lost. Maybe you lost yourself in Attica. Maybe before—but I doubt that, not with Sam in your life. It's probably when she was killed that you . . ."

"Rigby," Kurtz said coldly, "maybe you'd better shut up."

She shook her head. "I know why you're here, Joe." She jerked her head toward the Ferris wheel, weeds, woods, and shifting clouds. The sunlight still fell on them, but the shadows were moving faster up, around and over the hill. "You think that the parole officer—O'Toole—was your client. She showed you the photographs of this place. She asked if you knew where this place was. You're acting like she hired you, Joe. You're not only trying to solve her shooting—and yours—but solve *everything*."

"You don't know what you're talking about." Kurtz shifted another couple of feet away from her on the soft grass. The wind was banging some broken piece of plywood on the funhouse up the hill behind them.

"You know I do, Joe. That's all you have left anymore. The work. The cases you make up for yourself to solve, even if you hire yourself out to some Mafia vermin to get the work. Or to that Farino bitch. It's better than nothing, because that's your only alternative right now . . . work or nothing. No feelings. No past. No love. No hope. Nothing."

Kurtz stood. "Do you bill by the hour?"

Rigby grabbed his wrist and looked up at him. "Lie down here with me, Joe. Make love with me in the sunlight."

Kurtz said nothing, but he remembered the seventeen-year-old Rigby naked above him, straddling him in the dim light of the choir loft, Bach echoing from the huge pipe organ in the darkened basilica. He remembered the exquisite pain in his chest that night and how—only years later—wondering if that strong emotion had been love as well as lust.

"Joe . . ." She tugged. He went to one knee in the grass.

Rigby used her free hand to begin to unbutton her shirt as she lay back. Her short, dark hair was lifted into spikes by the soft grass. "Make love to me," she whispered, "and let it all back in. Me. The world. Your daughter . . ."

Kurtz stood abruptly, jerking his wrist free.

"There's a train track around here somewhere," he said. "I'm going to find it." He stepped past Rigby and began walking up the slope.

———

She caught up to him before he reached the top of the mountain. Neither said anything. Rigby's cheeks were flushed and there was grass on the back of her corduroy jacket.

The miniature train tracks, no more than a yard across, were just below the summit. The trees had been cut back for twenty feet on either side and had never grown back. The gravel under the ties looked fresh.

Kurtz turned north and began following the tracks along the hill.

"The rails aren't rusted," he said. "They're almost polished. Missing spikes have been replaced and the bed built back up. This little line's been used. And recently."

Rigby said nothing. She plodded along ten ties behind him.

They crossed a small trestle that had been built over a stream, then followed the tracks up to the crown of the hill, where they emerged from the woods and continued north-northeast.

A quarter of a mile from where they started, they emerged from the woods. The grasses were high and tan and brittle here, rustling in the stronger breeze as the clouds covered the sun again. The miniature railway's tracks ran down across a ridge and then rose over another treeless hill toward a huge house just visible about a mile away to the northeast.

Kurtz started down the grade.

"Joe, I don't think . . ." began Rigby.

Her voice was drowned out by a deafening THWAP THWAP THWAP and a huge Huey helicopter, Vietnam War-vintage, came swooping just over the trees from which they'd just emerged. Men were visible in both doorways as the big machine side-slipped, its forty-foot-wide rotors filling the mountain top with their bats-wing beat.

Kurtz began to run toward the trees, saw that he would never make it, and dropped to one knee, pulling the small .38 from its holster.

A machine-gun opened up from the side of the Huey and slugs stitched a row between Kurtz and Rigby King.

"DROP YOUR WEAPONS . . . NOW!" boomed an amplified voice from the helicopter.

It swooped low and fast over them, banked hard, and swooped back. A machine gun from the other open door scythed grass not ten feet from Rigby. She threw down her gun.

Kurtz tossed his into the grass.

"ON YOUR KNEES. HANDS BEHIND YOUR HEAD. DO *NOT* MOVE A MUSCLE."

Kurtz and Rigby complied as the huge, black machine hovered over them and then settled heavily onto the grass near the tracks, the wind blowing up straw and dust and dead grass around them in a blinding blast.

CHAPTER
THIRTY

The Dodger stopped at the edge of the woods and then stepped back under the trees when he heard the familiar sound of the Huey's engine and rotors. The goddamned perimeter sensors again.

He'd stalked the man and the woman through the woods, watched as they entered Cloud Nine, attached the suppressor to his Beretta, and begun moving in on them as they sat on the grass talking. Something was weird between the two; it looked as if the woman with the big tits and the short hair wanted to fuck and the man called Kurtz did not. That was new in the Dodger's book, unless Kurtz was all worn out from his night with the Farino woman the night before.

They'd been to the hut. This irritated the Dodger to the point that he planned to take real pleasure in shooting both of them. He would use more bullets than was necessary. It would disturb the aesthetics of his use for them, but that wasn't as important as getting rid of this unaccustomed anger he felt.

I'll put them at the top, he'd thought as he moved stealthily behind the funhouse, into the Beretta's killing range. He carried the weapon with both hands, his palm under the grip as he'd been taught, ready to lift it and aim down his rigid arm—first the man, then the woman. First the body mass to drop them, but not in the heart. Then the arms and legs. It was nice of them to come here.

Then the wind had blown some damned bit of plywood, making a noise near him, and the Dodger had been forced to freeze, bending low, not even breathing. By the time he was ready to move again, so were they, climbing the hill toward his train tracks.

He'd cut over the hilltop, hurrying ahead to the big oak near the edge of the forest. The bulk of it hid him and when they followed the tracks out into the open, he'd have a clear shot of no more than fifteen meters. As his anger faded, he considered a head shot for the man, saving the multiple slugs for the woman. Not because she was a woman or beautiful—the Dodger was indifferent to that—but because he sensed that the man was the more dangerous of the two. Always eliminate the primary danger first, the Boss had taught him. Always. Don't hesitate.

But he'd hesitated, and now it was too late.

The goddamned helicopter. That same, goddamned old Huey the Major had used for more than thirty years.

The Dodger watched the four Vietnamese men flexcuff Kurtz and the woman and load them into the helicopter. Then he faded back into the woods as the Huey lifted off and flew north, its passing flattening the grass for sixty feet around.

He was glad that he'd hidden the bug truck in the thicket where it couldn't be seen from the air. Removing the silencer, the Dodger slipped the Beretta back in its holster, paused only briefly at the hut, and then walked quickly back to the truck.

CHAPTER
THIRTY-ONE

Kurtz watched and noted everything as the Huey hauled them the short mile to the mansion. He and Rigby were unhurt—except for the cutting pressure of the flexcuffs—and surrounded by the four men whom he believed to be Vietnamese or Vietnamese-Americans. There was only one pilot—a Texan judging from his accent when he told everyone to hang on for take-off—and he said nothing for the rest of the flight.

The train tracks came to within a hundred yards of the mansion and then looped in a turnaround. The Cloud Nine kid-sized locomotive and cars were just visible in a long storage shed that straddled the tracks. Evidently the Major had kept the train and tracks maintained all these years.

The Huey landed and the four men half-pushed, half-dragged Rigby and Kurtz out of the open doors. All four were dressed in jeans and field jackets. Two of them carried M-16s that Kurtz was certain were illegally rigged for full auto; the other two carried even more formidable military firepower—M-60 machine guns.

Where are the Alcohol, Tobacco and Firearms pukes in their windbreakers when you need them? thought Kurtz. The man behind him shoved him through doors that a fifth Vietnamese man, this one from inside the house and dressed in a blue blazer, opened for them.

This butler or whatever he was led them through a foyer, down a hallway, through a library, and out onto the rear terrace on the cliff's edge. Kurtz had noted every sideroom and everything else he could see during their short transit through the house, and he knew that Rigby was doing the same. The fact that they hadn't been blindfolded bothered him a bit, since the simplest explanation for that was that they planned to kill both him and Rigby.

The house was large—three stories tall, comprising at least five thousand square feet inside—and it looked as if it had been built in the 1970s, around the time of the Major's retirement to Neola. It was built to fight off Indians. The first story and a half were stone—not only faced with stone, but built of stone. The windows to the rear of the house, nearest the helipad, were all leaded glass, but the leaded parts were actually bars. Thinner, taller windows to either side of the main ones were too narrow to scramble through but would offer perfect firing positions. A five-car garage ran to the north of the house along the same circular driveway, but all five of the wooden doors were down. The house doors they'd come through—the house was situated so that its fancier front was facing the bluff rather than the heliport and driveway—were a thick hardwood reinforced by steel. Enough to stop a Kiowa war lance, that was for sure.

This side of the house facing the cliff was less defensible. The library opened onto the terrace through wide French doors that let in the view and afternoon light to the west. Off the library had been an adjoining bedroom—Kurtz only caught a glimpse but thought it was probably the Major's bedroom, adapted from a huge parlor on the first floor, because of pill bottles and military photos on the burgundy wallpapered walls—and that bedroom also had wide doors opening onto the terrace. Kurtz guessed from oversized drape boxes above the doors that there were steel shutters that could drop down if necessary.

The Major, Colonel Vin Trinh, and three other men were waiting on the terrace. One man wore sheriff's gray, a Colt .45 in a western holster, and a name tag that said "Gerey"—the name of the sheriff that Rigby had talked to little more than an hour earlier; the other two men were younger, white, muscled, and also armed.

That's seven bodyguards so far, counting the servant in the blazer and not counting the chopper pilot and the sheriff, thought Kurtz as he and Rigby were shoved into the sunlight in front of the man in the wheelchair, which was in the shade of a striped canvas awning. *And Trinh, the Major, and this other old guy.*

"Mr. Kurtz, Miss King," said the Major. "How nice of you to drop in."

Ah, Jesus, thought Kurtz. *This old fart gets his material from villains in B movies.*

"I'm a police officer," said Rigby. It was the first full sentence she'd completed since Kurtz had been sitting on the grass with her.

"Yes, Miss King . . . *Detective* King," said the Major. "We know who you are."

"Then you know what a bad idea this is," said Rigby, her voice low but solid. "Get these cuffs off us this minute and we'll let it slide for now. We were trespassing."

The Major smiled again, shook his head almost sadly, and turned toward Kurtz. "I think it was very clever of your masters to send the policewoman along, Mr. Kurtz. If circumstances were different, it might . . . might . . . have been a disincentive to what has to happen next."

Aw, shit, thought Kurtz. He said, "What masters?"

The Major's smile disappeared. "Don't insult my intelligence, Mr. Kurtz. It makes perfect sense that they sent you—with your policewoman chippie here as an escort. From what we can glean, you're one of the few people that both the Gonzaga and Farino families do business with."

"Chippie?" said Rigby. She sounded more amused than insulted.

Colonel Vin Trinh stepped forward and slapped Rigby hard across the mouth. He wiped the blood from his knuckles with a silk handkerchief, took Kurtz's holstered .38 from one of the Vietnamese men, and held his arm at full length, the muzzle inches from Rigby's temple. Kurtz was reminded of a famous photo from the Vietnam era, taken during the Tet Offensive he thought, where a Saigon chief of police had summarily executed a Viet Cong suspect in the street.

Trinh cocked the pistol. "If you say one more word without being told to," he said in almost unaccented English, "I will kill you now."

Rigby looked at the tall man.

"What do you want?" Kurtz said to the Major.

The old man in the wheelchair sighed. The bodyguard in the blazer had moved behind the chair, hands on its grips, obviously ready to move the crippled man back deeper into the shade should the sun encroach or Kurtz or Rigby make any sudden move. *Or to get him out of the path of any arterial sprays,* thought Kurtz.

"We want the obvious, Mr. Kurtz," said the Major. "We want an end to this war. Isn't that what your masters sent you down here to discuss?"

War? thought Kurtz. According to both Toma Gonzaga and Angelina Farino Ferrara, they didn't have a clue as to who was killing their junkies.

They certainly had never talked about fighting back—about any war. Was all that ignorance a ruse to get Kurtz involved? It didn't make much sense.

He said nothing.

"Did they send you with terms?" asked the Major. "Or shall we propose our own?"

Colonel Vin Trinh's arm was still rigid, the hammer on Kurtz's .38 was still cocked. The muzzle ten inches from Rigby's head did not waver by so much as a millimeter.

Kurtz said nothing.

"For instance, what would it be worth to you for us to spare Miss King's life?" said the old man.

Kurtz remained silent.

"She means nothing to you?" said the Major. "But you were fellow orphans together as children. You were in the army together. Surely that must have created some bond, Mr. Kurtz."

Kurtz smiled. "If you've got my military records," he said, "look at them more carefully. This bitch is one of the reasons I was court-martialed."

Major Michael O'Toole nodded. "Yes, that fact is in your records. But you were not, as it turned out, dishonorably discharged, Sergeant Kurtz. The charges appeared to have been dropped. Perhaps you and she have . . . made up?" He showed hard white teeth.

"This isn't about her or me," said Kurtz. "What do you want?"

O'Toole nodded at Trinh, who lowered the hammer, stepped back, and slid Kurtz's pistol into his belt. The man had a stomach flatter than most fences.

"We need to meet, your masters and I," said the Major, speaking in a rapid, clear clip that must have been perfected in a thousand briefings. "This war has become too expensive for both sides."

Rigby glanced over at Kurtz as if seeking to find out if any of this made any sense to him. Kurtz's face revealed nothing.

"When?" said Kurtz.

"Tomorrow. Noon. Both Gonzaga and the Farino daughter must come. They can each bring one bodyguard, but everyone will be disarmed before the meeting."

"Where?"

"This town," said the old man, sweeping his powerful-looking right arm toward Neola visible in the valley to the northwest. With the sunlight gone, all color had faded from the trees and the steeples visible were more a dismal, chimney gray than a New England white. "It has to be in Neola. Sheriff Gerey here . . ." The Major nodded toward the sheriff who never changed his bassett-hound expression or blinked. "Sheriff Gerey will provide security for all of us and offer the meeting space. You still have that secure conference room in the back of the station, Sheriff?"

"Yeah."

"There you have it," said the Major. "Any questions?"

"You're letting both of us go back, right?" said Kurtz.

The Major looked at Colonel Vin Trinh, then at Rigby, then at Kurtz, and smiled. "Wrong, Mr. Kurtz. Detective King stays as our guest until after this conference."

"Why?"

"To insure that you do your absolute best at convincing your principals to be at the Neola Sheriff's office at noon tomorrow, Mr. Kurtz."

"Or what?"

The old man's black eyebrows rose toward his steel-colored crewcut. "Or what? Colonel Trinh? Would you like to demonstrate the 'Or what?' to Mr. Kurtz?"

Without blinking, Trinh pulled the .38 from his belt and shot Rigby in the upper leg. She fell heavily, arms still cuffed behind her, and struck her head on the flagstone. One of the Vietnamese bodyguards dropped to one knee, pulled his belt off, and rigged a makeshift tourniquet.

Kurtz had not moved and he did not move now. He made sure that his face showed no concern.

"Does that explain the 'Or what?' Mr. Kurtz?" said the Major.

"It seems like more trouble for you than it's worth," Kurtz said calmly. "Kill me, nobody much notices. Kill her . . ." He nodded toward Rigby where she lay, face sweaty, eyes wider, but not speaking. "Kill her and you'll have the entire Buffalo Police Department on your ass."

"Oh, no, Mr. Kurtz," said the Major. "We're not going to kill Detective King if you fail in your mission by tomorrow noon. *You're* going to kill her. In Buffalo. Probably in that abandoned flophouse you call a home. A lover's quarrel, perhaps."

Kurtz looked at the .38 still in Trinh's hand. "No GSR with me," he said.

"Gun shot residue?" said the Major. "On your hands and clothing?

There will be, Mr. Kurtz. There will be." The old man in the wheelchair nodded again and two of the young men grabbed Rigby, lifted her—she moaned once—and carried her into the house.

The Major glanced at his heavy and expensive digital watch. "It's after two P.M. You'll be wanting to go. It's a long drive back to Buffalo and it looks as if it might rain."

Colonel Trinh slipped the .38 into his belt but pulled a Glock-nine from a holster behind his back. Two other bodyguards lifted their M-16s.

Kurtz looked toward the driveway to the north of the house.

"No, Mr. Kurtz, the easiest way out for you is down this way." The Major nodded his head toward the almost vertical staircase down the cliff face.

Kurtz took a step closer to the edge, very aware of the two men behind him who could push him over with a shove, and peered down.

It was not so much a staircase as a descending concrete ziggurat. The steps were oversized—each at least twenty-four inches high, maybe thirty inches—and cut into the almost sheer rock cliff face. Far below—two or three hundred feet at least and half as many sheer steps almost straight down—the stairway ended in the black asphalt of the curving driveway.

"You're joking," said Kurtz.

"I never joke," said Major Michael O'Toole.

Kurtz sighed and held his arms up for someone to cut the flexcuffs.

"Perhaps later," said the Major. "Sheriff Gerey will meet you at the bottom." The old man in the chair nodded again and someone behind Kurtz gave him a hard shove.

He almost went over headfirst, staggered, and kept from falling only by jumping from the terrace to the narrow first step. The impact shocked up his spine and almost made him pitch forward again. He teetered there, raising his cuffed arms behind him for balance.

"Tell Mr. Gonzaga and Ms. Ferrara to be there tomorrow at Sheriff Gerey's office precisely at noon," said the Major. "One minute late, and there will be several dire consequences—the demise of Detective King being the least of them."

The man in the blazer pushed the Major's wheelchair through the doors and into the house. Colonel Trinh and four of the other Vietnamese with their rifles at port arms stood at the edge of the terrace and watched Kurtz descend.

———————

At first, Kurtz thought it was going to be easy. That is, if the men above didn't shoot him—which still seemed very possible. Or if he didn't trip and fall with his hands cuffed behind his back—which seemed more probable on every step.

But at first it did seem easy. It was two or three hundred feet—it was hard to tell at this horrible angle—of almost vertical ziggurat slabs, each at least two feet above the other—although it rose to Kurtz's knees, so he guessed more like twenty-eight or thirty inches—with just eight or ten inches of horizontal concrete on each "step"—but if he just balanced easily on the edge of each and sort of hopped down to the next, his hands behind his back but extended for balance—it shouldn't be a problem. Easy as cake, as the Russians might say. A piece of pie.

Except that after nine or ten drops, with only a hundred and fifty or so to go, the impact had jarred his spine, hurt his knees, and pounded red-hot railroad spikes of pain into his aching skull.

Kurtz was glad that they'd pulled everything out of his pockets when they'd cuffed him, and tugged his Ray Charles glasses off his face and taken them as well, because all that junk would be flying out into space right now. It'd be a bitch, Kurtz thought, to have to stop and pick up all that stuff with your teeth. And Daddy Bruce would be mad as hell if he came back without Ray Charles's sunglasses. He stepped to the edge of the tenth or eleventh step and dropped.

The shock ran up through his spine and exploded in fireworks in his head. His vision blurred.

Not yet. Not yet. He'd do a deal with this fucking headache; it could make him throw up, or even faint, once he was all the way down—or even on any of the bottom three steps. But not here. *Not here.*

Another three steps down. He tried just stepping down the mere twenty-eight inches or so. That was better. But the pain still jagged up his back to his skull and exited through the crack in his skull on the right side every time he dropped the other leg and foot. And it was harder to keep his balance that way with his arms behind him. The overly tight flexcuffs had long since cut off circulation to his wrists and hands, and now his forearms were going numb, with a line of pain moving up above the pins and needles of numbness advancing like little forest creatures running from a forest fire.

What? Stay focused, Joe. He paused on the narrow concrete shelf, his toes hanging over, panting, sweat in his eyes—sweat he couldn't blink or rub away—and looked up the near-vertical ziggurat steps at the dark forms looking down at him. The Major wasn't there, but Colonel Trinh was. He wasn't smiling. The other Vietnamese men were. They were enjoying this, probably betting on when he'd fall. Trinh looked like he was enjoying it as well, just too much so to smile.

Stay focused. The cliffside here on either side of the steps was slippery limestone with some granite mixed in—a steep mish-mash of slabs and dirt, with some lichen and low plants and the occasional scrub oak. But getting off the steps would be suicide here; even if his hands were free and circulation flowing, it would take a mountain climber to deal with that slippery slope.

Kurtz hopped down another step, waited for the fireworks to quit going off behind his eyes, and dropped another.

I don't think Dr. Singh would recommend this as therapy for the concussion.

Who was Dr. Singh? Kurtz wondered dully. It was interesting how the headache pain flowed in like breakers along the surf, never stopping, never pausing, just rising and falling and then crashing down.

He dropped to another step, teetered, caught himself, stepped to the edge, and dropped to the next. Was it his imagination or were the horizontal parts of each step getting narrower? The backs of his heels scraped when he tried to put his feet down solidly, even with his toes hanging out over space. Kurtz had started down being glad that he'd worn his sneakers today, but now he wished he had his old combat boots on. His ankles felt splintered. His heels were already bloody.

He dropped again. Again. The sweat stung his eyes and burned in counterpoint to the real pain.

It can't get no worse . . . ran a line from some old army song. Kurtz didn't believe that, of course. If life had taught him one thing, it was that things could *always* get worse.

It started to rain. Hard.

Kurtz's hair immediately matted to his head. He tasted the rain and realized that blood from his scalp wound was mixing in. He couldn't blink away the water in his eyes and on his lashes, so he paused on a step. He didn't know if he was halfway down, two-thirds the way down, or a fourth the way down. His head and neck hurt far too much for him to crane his neck to look up again. And he didn't want to look down anymore.

It can always get worse.

Lightning flashed so close he was blinded. The thunder almost knocked him down. The world was filled with the stink of ozone. Kurtz's wet and bloody hair tried to rise off his head as the hillside around him glowed white from the blast.

Kurtz sat down heavily, his legs flying up. He was panting, disoriented, and so dizzy that he doubted if he could stand again without falling.

The rain pelted him like fists pounding his shoulders and neck. It was cold as hail and hurt his head. *Cold as hail,* he thought again, trying it out with a Texas accent. Everything hurt his head. *Why the fuck didn't that Yemeni kid aim better? Get it over with?* Only it hadn't been the Yemeni kid, had it? He'd already shot the Yemeni kid by then. Then someone else shot him, Kurtz knew. The someone else who had brought the Yemeni kid there to kill . . . who? Peg O'Toole, he thought. Pretty Peg O'Toole, who just one year earlier had risked her job as PO to stand up for him, hell, to save his life, when a detective on the Farino's payroll had ramrodded him into County lockup on a bogus charge in preparation to sending him back to prison where the D-block Mosque and a hundred other guys were waiting to get the bounty on him . . .

Focus, Joe.

Can't get no worse . . .

The rain was coming down in a torrent and the hillside was turning into a thousand rivulets, but the main flood was pouring down this ziggurat stairway. The water struck Kurtz's shoulder blades and butt and threatened to wash him right off the step.

If I stand up, I'm screwed. If I keep sitting here, I'm screwed.

Kurtz stood up. The water flowed around and through his legs, geysering out in an almost comical jet. Kurtz resisted the impulse to laugh.

He stepped down another step. His arms were completely dead to sensation now, just long sticks he was hauling down the hill with him like so much firewood on his back.

He dropped another step. Then another. He resisted the temptation to sit down again and let the waterfall carry him away. Maybe he'd just ride down on it like all the people in all the movies who leap a thousand feet off a cliff and then ride the rapids out of sight of the enemy, who shoot uselessly at them . . .

Focus, Joe.

They're going to kill her anyway. Rigby. No matter what I do or don't do, they're going to kill her with my gun and blame it on me. She may be dead already if that bullet even nicked an artery. Leg wounds that high hurt like hell until you go all cold and numb at the end.

He blinked away water and blood. It was hard to see the edge of each step now. Every step was a mini-Niagara, the concrete invisible under swirling water.

Malcolm Kibunte was the name of the drug dealer and killer he'd dangled over the edge of Niagara Falls one wintry night just under a year ago. He was just asking the gang leader a few questions. Kurtz had a rope on the man—it was Kibunte who'd thought that his best chance was to drop the rope and swim for it right at the brink of North America's mightiest waterfall.

Joke him if he can't take a fuck, thought Kurtz. He stepped over the edge of this waterfall, dropped, fought the pain to stay conscious, teetered on the ever narrower step, found his balance against the flood, and stepped down again.

Again.

Again.

Again.

He finally fell. The step seemed to shift under him and Kurtz fell forward, unable to find the next step or throw himself backward.

So he leaped instead. He leaped out into space, legs as high as he could get them. Leaped away from the waterfall and into the rain. Mouth contorted in a silent scream, Joe Kurtz leaped.

And hit solid ground and crumpled forward, just twisting in time to keep from smashing his face on the wet asphalt. His shoulder struck instead, sending a blinding bolt of pain up the right side of his head.

He blinked, twisted around as he lay prone on the drive, and looked behind him. He'd been on the third or fourth step from the bottom when he'd fallen. The ziggurat stairway was invisible under the waterfall of water. The rain kept coming down hard and the flood washed around his torn sneakers, trying to push his body out along the asphalt.

"Get up," said Sheriff Gerey.

Kurtz tried.

"Grab an arm, Smitty," said the sheriff.

They grabbed Kurtz's unfeeling arms, hauled him to his feet, and half-dragged him to the sheriff's car parked there. The deputy held the rear door open.

"Watch your head," said the sheriff and then pressed Kurtz's head down with that move they'd all learned in cop school but also had seen in too many movies and TV shows. The man's fingers on Kurtz's bloody, battered skull hurt like hell and made him want to vomit, but he resisted the urge. He knew from experience that few things prompted cops to use their batons on your kidneys faster than puking in the back seats of their cars.

"Watch your head," the deputy repeated, and Kurtz finally had to laugh as they shoved him into the back seat of the cruiser.

CHAPTER
THIRTY-TWO

It was still raining hard as Kurtz drove the Pinto north on Highway 16. Only one of his windshield wipers was working, but it was on the driver's side, so he didn't bother worrying about it. He had a lot of phone calls to make and they weren't the kind you wanted to make on a cell phone, but the pay phones were twenty-five miles apart along this two-lane stretch of road, the nearest gas station was forty minutes ahead, he hadn't stopped in Neola to get change, and, basically, to hell with it.

They'd given everything back—except his .38—when Sheriff Gerey had dumped him out at the Pinto where he and Rigby had left it down the hill from Cloud Nine. He even had the Ray Charles sunglasses back in his jacket pocket, which was good. If Kurtz was lucky enough to survive all this other shit, he didn't want Daddy Bruce killing him for losing the Man's sunglasses.

He fumbled, found the cell phone Gonzaga had given him, and keyed the only preset number.

"Yes?" It was Toma Gonzaga himself.

"We need to meet," said Kurtz. "Today."

"Have you finished the task?" asked Gonzaga. *Not "job," but "task." This wasn't your average hoodlum.*

"Yeah," said Kurtz. "More or less."

"More or less?" Kurtz could imagine the handsome mob boss's eyebrow rising.

"I have the information you need," said Kurtz, "but it won't do you any good unless we meet in the next couple of hours."

There was a pause. "I'm busy this afternoon. But later tonight . . ."

"This afternoon or nothing," interrupted Kurtz. "You wait, you lose everything."

A shorter pause. "All right. Come by my estate on Grand Island at . . ."

"No. My office." Kurtz raised his wrist. He'd strapped his watch back on as soon as his fingers had begun working again, but now his head hurt so much that he was having some trouble focusing his eyes. "It's just about three p.m. Be in my office at five."

"Who else will be there?"

"Just me and Angelina Farino Ferrara."

"I want some of my associates . . ."

"Bring an army if you want," said Kurtz. "Just park them outside the door. The meeting will be just the three of us."

There was a long minute of silence, during which Kurtz concentrated on navigating the winding road. The few cars that passed going the opposite way had their headlights on and wipers pumping. Kurtz was driving faster than the rest of the traffic going north.

Kurtz used his phone hand to wipe the moisture out of his eyes again. His fingers and arms still hurt like hell—it had been almost five minutes after they'd dumped him at the Pinto before he regained enough sensation in his hands to be able to drive. The pain of his reawakening arms and hands and fingers had finally been enough to make him throw up in the weeds near the Pinto. Sheriff Gerey and his deputy had been standing by their car, waiting to escort him out of town, and Gerey had said something that had made the deputy chuckle as Kurtz was on his knees in the weeds. Kurtz had put it on the sheriff's bill.

"All right, I'll be there," said Toma Gonzaga and disconnected.

Kurtz threw the phone onto the passenger seat. His hands were still more like gnarled hooks than real hands.

He got his own phone out, managed to punch out Angelina's number, and listened to her voice on an answering machine.

"Pick up, goddammit. Pick up." It was as close to a prayer as Joe Kurtz had come this long day.

She did. "Kurtz, where are you? What's . . ."

"Listen carefully," he said. He explained quickly about the meeting, but told her to get there at 4:45, fifteen minutes before Gonzaga. "It's important you get there on time."

"Kurtz, if this is about last night . . ."

He hung up on her, started to punch in another number, but then set the phone aside for a minute.

The highway had straightened here, but it still seemed to be bobbing up and down slightly, threatening to shift directions at any moment. Kurtz realized that his inner ear had become screwed up again in the last hour or so, probably on the steps. He shook his head—sending water and blood flying—and concentrated on keeping the Pinto on the undulating, quivering highway. Kurtz's shoes were a tattered mess, his jacket was dripping, his pants and shirt and socks and underwear were sodden.

A pickup truck was ahead of him, kicking up spray, but Kurtz passed it without slowing. The pickup had been doing about fifty m.p.h. on the narrow road; Kurtz's whining, vibrating, protesting Pinto was doing at least eighty.

It had taken Rigby and him more than ninety minutes to drive down to Neola from Buffalo that morning. Kurtz wanted to get back to Buffalo in less than an hour. He'd noted the time when the sheriff's car had turned around at the Neola city limits sign—if he kept up this pace, he should make it.

Kurtz punched another phone number in. A bodyguard answered. Kurtz insisted that he talk to Baby Doc himself, and was finally handed over. Kurtz explained to the Lackawanna boss that it was important that they meet today, soon, in the next hour.

"Important to you, maybe," said Baby Doc, "but maybe not to me. You're not on a cell phone, are you, Kurtz?"

"Yeah. I'm coming into Lackawanna from the south in about thirty minutes. Are you at Curly's?"

"It doesn't matter where the fuck I am. What do you want?"

"You know that payment I promised you in return for the favors?"

"Yeah."

"You meet with me in the next hour, and you get a serious payment. I mean, serious. Put me off—nothing."

The silence lasted long enough that Kurtz was sure that the cell phone had lost service here in the hills approaching East Aurora.

"I'm at Curly's," said Baby Doc. "But get here fast. They want to open up for Sunday night dinner in ninety minutes."

———

Highway 16 became four-lanes wide and renamed itself Highway 400 as it turned east toward Buffalo. Kurtz took the East Aurora exit and drove the six miles to and through Orchard Park at high speed, swinging north again on 219 past the Thruway into Lackawanna.

He called Arlene's home number. No answer. He called her cell phone. No answer. He called the office. She picked up on the second ring.

"What are you doing there this late on a Sunday afternoon?" said Kurtz.

"Following up some things," said his secretary. "I finally got the home phone number of the former director of the Rochester Psychiatric Institute. He's retired now and lives in Ontario on the Lake. And I've been trying other ways to get into the military records so . . ."

"Get out of the office," said Kurtz. "I'm going to need it for a few hours and I don't want you anywhere near it. Go home. Now."

"All right, Joe." A pause and he could hear Arlene stubbing out a cigarette. "Are you all right?"

"Yeah, I'm fine. I just want you out of there. And if there are any files or anything on the desks, shove them out of sight somewhere."

"Do you want O'Toole's e-mail printouts in your main drawer?"

"O'Toole's . . ." began Kurtz. Then he remembered the call that morning about someone using Peg O'Toole's computer to log on her e-mail address. Arlene had been able to download the PO's filing cabinet before whoever it was had time to delete it all. "Yeah, fine," said Kurtz. "In the top center drawer is fine."

"And what about Aysha?"

Kurtz had to pause again. Aysha. Yasein Goba's fiance who was being smuggled across the Canadian border tonight at midnight. *Shit.* "Can you pick her up, Arlene? Keep her at your house until tomorrow and . . . no, wait."

Would it be dangerous to pick the girl up? Who knew about her? Would the Major or whoever was killing people for the Major know about Goba's fiance and go after her? Kurtz didn't know.

"No, never mind," he said. "Never mind. Let her get picked up by the Niagara Falls police. They'll take care of her."

"But she may have some important information," said Arlene. "And I got the translator from church, Nicky, all set up to . . ."

"*Just fucking forget about it,*" snapped Kurtz. He took a breath. He never shouted at Arlene. He almost never shouted, period. "Sorry," he said. He was into the industrial wasteland of Lackawanna now, coming at the Basilica and Ridge Road and Curly's Restaurant from the south.

"All right, Joe. But you know I'm going to go pick up that girl tonight."

"Yeah." He thumbed the phone off.

It was the same drill of being taken into the men's room at Curly's and searched head to foot. One of the bodyguards shifted a toothpick in his mouth and said, "Jesus, fuck, man—you're so wet your skin is wrinkly. You been swimming with your clothes on?"

Kurtz ignored him.

When he was seated across from Baby Doc in the same rear booth, he said, "This is private."

Baby Doc looked at his three bodyguards and at the waiters bustling around getting the place ready for the heavy Sunday evening dinner traffic. "They all have my confidence," said the big man with the flag tattoo on his massive forearm.

"It doesn't matter," said Kurtz. "This is *private.*"

Baby Doc snapped his fingers and the bodyguards left, herding the waiters and bartender ahead of them into the backroom.

"For your sake," said Baby Doc, "this had better not be a waste of my time."

"It won't be," said Kurtz.

Speaking as economically as he could, he told Baby Doc about the Major, about the heroin ring, about the "war" that seemed to be claiming only casualties in the Farino and Gonzaga camps, about Rigby being shot and her role in this mess.

"Weird story," said Baby Doc, his hands folded in front of him and his flag tattoo visible under the rolled-back sleeves of his white shirt. "What the hell does it have to do with me?"

Kurtz told him.

Baby Doc sat back in the booth. "You have to be kidding." He looked at Kurtz's face. "No, you're not kidding, are you? What on earth could compel me to take part in this?"

Kurtz told him.

Baby Doc didn't so much as blink for almost a full minute. Finally, he said, "You speak for Gonzaga and the Farino woman?"

"Yes."

"Do they *know* you speak for them?"

"Not yet."

"What are you going to need from me?"

"A helicopter," said Kurtz. "Big enough to haul six or eight people. And you to pilot it."

Baby Doc started to laugh and then stopped. "You're serious."

"As a heart attack," said Kurtz.

"You *look* like you've had a heart attack," said Baby Doc. "You're a fuck-ing mess, Kurtz."

Kurtz waited.

"I don't own a goddamned helicopter," Baby Doc said at last. "And I haven't flown one for more than a dozen years. I'd get us all killed even if there was a reason for me to try this stupid stunt."

"But you know where to get one," said Kurtz.

Baby Doc thought a minute. "There's that big heliport up near the Falls. Hauls tourists around. I know the guy who does charter work up there. They might lease one to me for a day."

Kurtz nodded. He'd hired one of the smaller sightseeing choppers there to fly him over Emilio Gonzaga's Grand Island compound about a year ago. His plan then had been to chart the place before killing Emilio. Kurtz didn't see any compelling reason to share that factoid with Baby Doc.

"They have a Bell Long Ranger there that doesn't get a lot of duty this time of year," continued Baby Doc, speaking more to himself than to Kurtz.

"How many does that carry?" said Kurtz.

Baby Doc shrugged. "Usually seven. You can get eight people in it if you rip out the center jump seats and put a couple on the floor. Nine if you don't bother with a co-pilot."

"We don't need a co-pilot," said Kurtz.

Baby Doc barked a laugh. "I have about twenty minutes logged on a Long Ranger. I don't even qualify to *sit* in the copilot seat."

"Good," said Kurtz, "because we don't need a copilot."

"What else will you be needing?"

"Weapons," said Kurtz.

Baby Doc shook his head. "I'm sure the Gonzagas and Farinos have a few weapons between them."

"I'm talking military-spec here."

The other man looked around. The restaurant was still empty. "What kind?"

Kurtz shrugged. "I don't know. Firepower. Some full-auto weapons, probably."

"M-16s?"

"Maybe smaller. Uzis or Mac-10s. We don't want anyone getting an eye poked out in the slick."

"You don't find Uzis and Mac-10s in a National Guard arsenal," whispered Baby Doc.

Kurtz shrugged again. Truth be told, he'd seen some examples of the old Seneca Street Social Club's little private arsenal—the weapons had been aimed at him—so he knew what was probably available.

"Anything else?" said Baby Doc, sounding bemused now.

"Body armor."

"Cop style or military grade?"

"Kevlar should work."

"Anything else?"

"Night vision goggles," said Kurtz. "I suspect the Major's men have them."

"Would Russian surplus do?" said Baby Doc. "I can get them discount."

"No," said Kurtz. "The good stuff."

"Anything else?"

"Yeah," said Kurtz. "We'll need some light anti-armor stuff. Shoulder launched."

Baby Doc Skrzpczyk leaned back against the back of the booth. "You're not really amusing me any longer, Kurtz."

"I'm not trying to. You didn't see the Major's freehold down there today. I did. The sheriff drove slow to give me a good look at it all. They wanted me to bring the word back to Gonzaga and Farino in case they considered a pre-emptive strike. The house itself is on top of that damned mountain. They have maybe nine, ten men there, and I saw the automatic weapons. But down the hill, they have at least three reinforced gates along the drive—each one of them with steel posts sunk deep into concrete. There are two guardhouses, each with four or five 'security guards,' and each guardhouse has a perfect field of fire down the hill. There are armored SUVs—those Panoz things—parked in defilade sites up and down the hill, and two sheriff's cars that seem to be parked outside the lowest gate on a permanent basis."

"You don't need a shoulder-launched missile," said Baby Doc. "You need a fucking tank."

"If we were trying to fight our way up the drive or along the cliff, yeah," said Kurtz. "But we're not. We just need one or two deterrents to block the drive if anyone tries to drive up it."

Baby Doc leaned forward, folded his hands on the tabletop, and whispered, "Do you have any *idea* how much a shoulder-launched antiaircraft missile costs?"

"Yeah," said Kurtz. "About a hundred grand for cheap shit sold-in-the-bazaar piece of Russian crap. Four or five times that for a Stinger."

Baby Doc stared at him.

"But I'm not talking about buying an antiaircraft missile," said Kurtz. "Just something to stop an SUV if we have to. A cheap RPG should do it."

"Who's paying for this?"

"Guess," said Kurtz.

"But they don't know it yet?"

"Not yet."

"You know you're talking about upwards of three-quarters of a million dollars here, not counting the lease of the Long Ranger."

Kurtz nodded.

"And how soon do you want all this—including me and the Long Ranger, if my terms are agreed upon?" said Baby Doc. "A week? Ten days?"

"Tonight," said Kurtz. "Midnight if we can do it. But departing here no later than two A.M."

Baby Doc opened his mouth as if to laugh but then did not. He closed his mouth and just stared at Joe Kurtz. "You're serious," he said at last.

"As a heart attack."

CHAPTER
THIRTY-THREE

It was only a little after four P.M. and the Dodger didn't have any task assigned to him until midnight, when he was supposed to meet and kill that Aysha woman who was coming across the border from Canada, and he was feeling a little frustrated and at loose ends. Tomorrow was his birthday and the Boss, as he always did, had given him the day off—well, technically, he realized, his birthday began at midnight, and he'd still be working then, killing this foreigner, but that shouldn't take long.

But the day's events had frustrated the Dodger. He didn't like going back to Neola—except on Halloween, of course—and he didn't like being thwarted while stalking someone. It was twice now that he'd decided to kill this ex-P.I., twice that he'd prepared himself to kill a woman with the P.I. as well, and twice he'd been thwarted. The Artful Dodger didn't like to be thwarted—especially when it was by the Major or his men. Even seeing and hearing the old Huey helicopter again had given the Dodger an acid stomach.

So now he had to hang around Buffalo for a full eight hours before he could do his job and get out. And it was raining and cold. It *always* seemed to be rainy and cold in this damned town—when it wasn't *snowy* and cold. The Dodger's joints ached—he was getting older, *would* officially be a year older in a few hours—and his many burn scars always itched when it rained for a long time.

Essentially, he was in a lousy mood. He considered going to a titty bar, but it was the night before his birthday night and he wanted to save the excitement, let it build.

So as the evening began to darken in the rain and the streetlights were coming on and the light Sunday traffic had all but disappeared, the Dodger drove south of downtown, under the elevated interstate, across the narrow bridge onto the island, through the empty area of grain elevators where the air smelled of burned Cheerios, then south to where the triangular intersection of Ohio and Chicago Streets ended with the abandoned Harbor Inn—the P.I.'s hideaway, the little love nest where the Dodger had watched and waited all of last night for Kurtz and the Farino woman.

Odds were that the Major had terminated this minor irritation this afternoon, but if not, if the P.I. and his big-boobed girlfriend were back here, then the Dodger was going to do a little freelancing, and if the Boss didn't like it, well . . . the Boss didn't have to know about it.

The Harbor Inn was dark. The Dodger drove by slowly three times, noting again the almost-but-not-quite-hidden video cameras—one on the rear wall of the triangular building overlooking where Kurtz had parked his Pinto before (the space was empty now), another high above the front door, one under a rain gutter on the Chicago Street side, the last one above the fire escapes on the Ohio Street approach. A lot of security for an abandoned flophouse.

The Dodger parked his truck a block or so from where he'd had to deal with the two black kids. Then he took a small backpack from between the seats, locked the vehicle, and walked back through the rain.

There was a blind spot for the camera covering the front of the Harbor Inn. If he crossed the street from the abandoned gas station just *so*, and didn't walk more than six feet to either side of a certain line, then the front camera would be blocked by the old metal lighthouse on the sign itself.

Once under the overhang—and presumably not yet on any monitor or videotape—the Dodger ignored the front door since the P.I. would certainly have telltales there. Securing the backpack, the Dodger crouched low, jumped straight up, caught the sharp edge of the old hotel sign over him, swung twice back and forth, his legs kicking higher each time—continuing to keep the metal lighthouse between him and the surveillance camera a floor above—and then swung all the way up, doing a complete flip and coming to rest on top of the sign, with his back to the metal lighthouse.

The old sign structure creaked and groaned, but did not collapse. The rusted lighthouse with "Harbor Inn" painted on it was about seven feet tall, was hollow and was made of cheap metal. The Dodger kept his hands on it while he worked his way around it, under the camera's field of view now, and crouched outside one of the three big windows looking out on the intersection of Chicago and Ohio.

It was dark inside, but the glow of monitors in there showed the Dodger that the room was empty.

He propped the backpack by his knee, removed a suction cup and glass cutter on a compass, cut a six-centimeter hole in the glass, carefully laid the circle of glass on the sign base, returned the equipment to his pack, and listened—no audible alarm sounded—and then reached in, unlatched the old window, and shoved it up. The ancient sash groaned and protested, but the window slowly rose.

The Dodger—as agile as Spiderman—swung in and pulled the backpack in after him. He hoisted the pack to his back again, carefully lowered the window, held the silenced nine-millimeter Beretta in his hand, and moved into the darkness to find or wait for Mr. Kurtz, the elusive P.I.

CHAPTER
THIRTY-FOUR

Kurtz wanted nothing so much as to stop by his place, get out of his wet and ruined clothes, take a hot shower, change the bandage on his head, find some clean clothes, pull his only other handgun from its hiding place in the rearmost room of the Harbor Inn, and show up at the meeting with Farino and Gonzaga looking and feeling more like a human being, albeit an armed one.

He had time for none of that.

Traffic was light since it was Sunday evening, but he'd left Curly's Restaurant late and had to head straight for his office on Chippewa if he was going to get there before the others. As it was, he came out of the alley where he'd parked the Pinto and reached the outside door just as Angelina and two new bodyguards pulled up in a black SUV and parked across the street. All three came over at once. The two new personal bodyguards were bigger, heavier, and more the comb-your-hair-with-buttered-toast Sicilian type.

Kurtz paused before unlocking the street door. "Just you," he said.

"We're going to look at the place first," said Angelina.

"You don't trust me?" said Kurtz. "After last night and . . ."

"Just open the fucking door."

They followed him up the steep stairway and waited below him while he unlocked the office door and turned on the lights. The two goombahs brushed past him.

"Be my guest," said Kurtz.

The two quickly searched the office, looking through the warm back room with the servers and checking out the small bathroom. They were efficient, Kurtz had to give them that. On the second quick sweep, one of them looked under Arlene's desk and said, "Mounted holster set-up here, Ms. Ferrara. No gun."

Angelina looked at Kurtz. "My secretary's," he said. "She works here late at night." He thought, *Shit, I was counting on that Magnum being there.*

The don's daughter waved the two bodyguards out and Kurtz closed the door behind them. When he turned around, Angelina had her Compact Witness .45 in her hand. "We going to my place again?" he said.

"Shut up."

"Can I sit down?" He pointed to his chair and desk. Suddenly it was either a case of sit down or fall down.

Angelina nodded and gestured him over to his chair. She sat on Arlene's desk and set the pistol next to her. "What is all this mystery crap, Joe?"

Well, at least I'm back to Joe, thought Kurtz. He glanced at his watch. Gonzaga would be here in a minute or two.

"I'll tell you the whole story when your pal Gonzaga gets here. But I needed to ask you something first."

"Ask."

"Word on the street—hell, word everywhere—is that either you or Gonzaga have brought in the Dane and he's already here. I think it's you that brought him in for a job."

Angelina Farino Ferrara said nothing. Outside, the light was waning. Neon signs glowed through the not-quite-closed blinds. Traffic hissed.

"I want to make a deal . . ." began Kurtz.

"If you're worried that you're on some list," said Angelina, "don't. You're not worth a hundred thousand dollars for a hit."

Kurtz shook his head and had to blink at the pain. "Who is?" he said. "No, I had a different deal in mind." He told her quickly.

It was Angelina Farino Ferrara's turn to blink. "You expecting to die suddenly, Joe?"

Kurtz shrugged.

"And you won't tell me the name?" she said.

"I'm not sure yet."

She set the Compact Witness in her purse. The downstairs door buzzed on Arlene's intercom and Kurtz could see Gonzaga and three of his men on the video monitor.

"You're talking a hundred thousand dollar gift," said Angelina. "Maybe more."

"No, I'm not," said Kurtz. The doorbell buzzed twice more and then stayed on as Gonzaga's man leaned on it. "I'm talking a simple request. Either he'll do it—probably as a gift to you—or he won't. I'm just asking you to ask him."

"And you trust me to?"

"I have to," said Kurtz. The buzzing was hurting his head.

"And you really aren't going to tell Toma and me what this is about tonight unless I agree?"

Kurtz shrugged again.

"All right," said Angelina. "I won't pay for it, but I'll ask him. *If* this big news of yours is worth it to me."

Kurtz walked over and buzzed Gonzaga and his men up.

A fter the obligatory search of the office—Gonzaga's boys also turned up Arlene's empty Magnum holster—the bodyguards were shown out, the door was locked, the lights were turned low except for Kurtz's desklamp, and he told his story. Angelina remained sitting on Arlene's desk. Toma Gonzaga paced near the windows, occasionally pulling down a blind to peer out as Kurtz spoke. At first they each asked some questions, but then they just listened. Kurtz started with him and Rigby arriving in Neola, and wrapped it up with Sheriff Gerey showing him to the city limits.

When Kurtz was done, Gonzaga stepped away from the window. "This Major said that it was a *war*?"

"Yeah," said Kurtz. "As if you've been exchanging casualties for months or years."

Gonzaga scowled at Angelina Farino Ferrara. "You know anything about that?"

"You know I don't. If I'd known that asshole existed, he'd need more than a wheelchair now. He'd be in a coffin."

Gonzaga turned back to Kurtz. "What was he talking about? Is he nuts?"

"I don't think so," said Kurtz. "I think someone's playing two ends against the middle here."

"Who?" said Gonzaga and the woman at the same time.

Kurtz held up his empty hands. "Who the hell knows? If it's not one of you—and I don't see how it would benefit either one of you to play that game—then it's probably someone in the Major's camp."

"Trinh," said Angelina.

"Or the sheriff," said Gonzaga. "Gerey."

"The sheriff's already on the payroll," said Kurtz. "Hell, half the town is. I told you the little burg has a Mercedes and a Lexus dealership."

"Maybe the sheriff got greedy," said Angelina. "Or the Colonel."

Kurtz shrugged. "Either way, the Major's making his move tomorrow. You're supposed to be in the sheriff's office in Neola at high noon."

Gonzaga laughed softly and sat on the arm of the old sofa. "Does the Major think this is a fucking Western?"

Kurtz said nothing.

"They're going to kill us," Angelina said softly. "Us and anyone we bring down there with us."

"Well, sure," said Kurtz. "That goes without saying."

Gonzaga stood again. "Are you two nuts? Knock off the heads of two Families? Would this Major be so crazy to think that he could get away with that? Hell, you can't even hit a made man without the wrath of the Five Families coming down on you. How could he hope to hit . . ."

"Weren't you listening to Kurtz?" interrupted Angelina. "This Major and Colonel and the rest of them have some sort of juice. Federal." She looked at Kurtz. "You think it's FBI? Homeland Security?"

"It's been there for too long for Homeland Security," said Kurtz. "Goes back almost thirty years."

"CIA," said Gonzaga.

"That doesn't make any sense," said Angelina. "Why would the CIA run interference for a heroin ring? Even a pissant operation like this one."

"We don't know how pissant it is," said Gonzaga. "Western New York, North and Western Pennsylvania. Hell, maybe they're that network we keep hearing about in Ohio."

"Still . . ."

"Does it matter right now *why* the CIA or some other secret government agency's been keeping the Feds off them?" asked Kurtz. "Major O'Toole's and Colonel Trinh's network is spread all over the Mideast and Southeast Asia according to what Rigby King told me. During the Vietnam War, the Major set up a Triad to run drugs out of the Golden Triangle. Him for the U.S. connection . . . Colonel Trinh for the Vietnamese end . . . and some unknown Third Man, probably CIA, to provide transport and political cover.

Who the hell knows what favors the Major's doing for who? Who cares? What you two have to decide . . . and soon . . . is what to do before tomorrow."

Gonzaga paced to the window, looked through the blind, and returned to sit on the sofa arm. Angelina ran a lacquered nail over her full lower lip, but didn't bite it.

"We can do nothing," said Gonzaga. "Wait. Offer to negotiate—not in Neola. Hit them at a time of our choosing."

Angelina shook her head. "If we don't go tomorrow, the Major suggested, the war's on, Toma. You know that. *They* know that."

Gonzaga shrugged. "All right. Then the war's on. We fight it. We win it."

"And lose how many more dealers and junkies and button men?" said Kurtz. "You prepared for a *long* war? The Major is. And don't forget that new term we've all learned—*decapitation strike.*"

"What are you talking about?" said Angelina.

"I'm talking about that hit that took place right out there less than twenty-four hours ago." Kurtz jerked his thumb toward the windows, the street beyond. "I don't think whoever took out your two top bodyguards was after them. I think he was after you."

"You're guessing."

"Sure," said Kurtz. "But I think I'm right. You want to bet your life that I'm wrong?"

"We'll bring in more people from New York and New Jersey," Gonzaga said softly, as if speaking to himself. He stood suddenly and looked at Angelina. "Why are we discussing tactics in front of him?"

Angelina smiled. "Because 'him' is the one who found out what's going on after we've been fucking around in the dark for months. And I think 'him' has a plan, don't you, Joe?"

Kurtz nodded.

"Who pays for this 'plan'?" said Toma Gonzaga.

"You do," said Kurtz. "And the price is seven hundred and fifty thousand dollars."

Gonzaga laughed, but the noise carried no hint of amusement. "To you, naturally."

"Not a cent to me," said Kurtz. "Not even the hundred thousand you offered me if I found this perp—which I have, by the way. It just happens to be a small army of perps."

"Seven hundred and fifty thousand dollars is insane," said Gonzaga. "Out of the question."

"Is it, Toma?" Angelina crossed her arms. "You're talking about a long war. You're talking about disrupting *all* our business for weeks or months. You're talking about having to buy off cops and maybe media to keep it quiet, and about bringing in more manpower from New York and New Jersey—*that'll* certainly make the Five Families happy. And do we want Carmine and the others thinking we can't run our own shop out here?"

Gonzaga put his palms flat on Arlene's desk and leaned toward Angelina Farino Ferrara. "Three quarters of a million dollars?" he whispered.

"We haven't heard Joe's plan yet. Maybe it's brilliant."

"Maybe it's fucked," said Gonzaga.

"We won't know if we don't hear it. Joe?"

Speaking slowly and calmly, checking his watch only once, Kurtz told them the plan. When he was finished he stood, walked to the small refrigerator next to the sofa, and took out a bottle of water. "Anyone want one?" he said.

Gonzaga and Angelina only stared at him.

The male don spoke first. "You can't fucking be serious."

Kurtz said nothing.

"He is fucking serious," Angelina said softly. "Christ."

"*Tonight*?" said Gonzaga, pronouncing each syllable as if he'd never heard the word before.

"It would have to be, wouldn't it?" said Angelina. "Kurtz is right. And we don't have much time to decide."

Kurtz looked at his watch again. "You have less than a minute to decide."

"What the *fuck* are you talking about?" snarled Toma Gonzaga.

The downstairs buzzer made its raucous noise.

CHAPTER
THIRTY-FIVE

The conference with Baby Doc Skrzypczyk—whose two men searched longer, harder, and more thoroughly than either Gonzaga's or Angelina's had—lasted longer than Kurtz had imagined it would. There were a lot of details. Evidently Gonzaga and Farino Ferrara wanted their money's worth in exchange for a mere three-quarters of a million dollars.

No one shook hands when Baby Doc's bodyguards left. No one spoke. Kurtz made no introductions. He doubted if the three had ever met, but they knew enough about each other. The powerfully built Lackawanna boss simply took off his expensive, camel hair topcoat, hung it on the coatrack, sat on the sprung couch, looked at Toma Gonzaga and Angelina Farino Ferrara, and said, "Have you decided that it's worth the money to you? Time's wasting here either way."

Angelina looked at Baby Doc, then at Gonzaga, and chewed her lip for a second. "I'm in," she said at last.

"Yeah," said Toma Gonzaga.

"Yeah?" said Baby Doc, sounding like a schoolteacher prompting a student. "What does that mean?"

"That means I'm in for my half. *If* you can provide all that stuff tonight. And *if* you don't have any more demands."

"I do, actually," said Baby Doc. "I want to be able to take over and run the Major's empire if I can."

Well, thought Kurtz, *there goes the old ballgame.*

Angelina shot a glance at Gonzaga where he sat on the far edge of Arlene's desk. "What do you mean?" asked Toma Gonzaga, obviously understanding but stalling for a moment to think.

"I mean what I said. I want you to acknowledge my right to take over the Major's business operations down there. I don't need help . . . I just need your word that if I can do it, you won't try to come in and take it away from me."

Angelina and Gonzaga looked at each other again. "You're going into sale of . . . the product?" said Angelina.

"I will if I can take over the Major's and Colonel's business," said Baby Doc. "It doesn't have to compete with yours. You and I both know that it's small potatoes . . . rural stuff."

"Several million dollars a year worth of small potatoes," said Gonzaga. The don was rubbing his cheek while he thought.

"Yeah," said Baby Doc. And waited.

Angelina shot Gonzaga a final glance, they both nodded as if they were using some sort of special Mafia telepathy, and she said, "All right. You have our word. You manage to take over that network, you can have it. Just don't bring it north of Kissing Bridge."

Kurtz knew that Kissing Bridge was a ski area about halfway between Buffalo and Neola.

"Done," said Baby Doc. "Let's talk about how this gets done."

Kurtz had been working on a sketch of the Major's house and grounds, and now he moved to the photocopier behind Arlene's desk, got the machine warmed up, and made three copies. They all studied the sketch.

"How do you know the guard will be out here in this cupola near the little train tracks?" asked Gonzaga.

"I noticed when they were taking me into the house from the heliport that the cupola had a porta-potty next to it and one of those heavy-duty, gas-powered heaters inside it. It's the logical place for a sentry."

"Where else?" asked Angelina. "Here at this little gatehouse at the top of the driveway before it curls around the back of the house?"

"Yeah," said Kurtz. "One guy there. That little gatehouse doesn't have a gate or barrier. All that stuff is down the hill."

"Anyone on the terrace?" asked Baby Doc.

Kurtz shrugged. "I doubt it. No one's going to be coming up that stairway. Most of their people are down the hill."

They talked for another hour. Finally Baby Doc rose. "Any other details left, speak now . . . I've only got about five hours to fill this order, you know."

"A medic," said Kurtz.

"What?" said Angelina.

"I need someone along who knows how to give some medical treatment," said Kurtz. "If Rigby King is alive down there—and if we can keep her alive during the gunfight at the OK Corral—I want to get her back to Erie County Medical Center. I don't want her to bleed to death on the ride back."

"Why?" said Angelina.

Kurtz looked at her. "Why what?"

"Why do you think she might still be alive? What reason would Major O'Toole and Colonel Trinh have for keeping her alive?"

Kurtz sighed and rubbed his head. He was very tired. Every part of him ached and he realized that he'd managed to screw up his back during his butt-first descent down the ziggurat. "They want me to kill Rigby," he said at last.

"What do you mean?" asked Baby Doc.

"They don't mind taking on the Five Families after they waste Gonzaga and Farino tomorrow in Neola," said Kurtz, "but I don't think their juice necessarily extends to Buffalo P.D. Homicide. Plus, they don't expect me there tomorrow at the sheriff's office, so they'll need to kill me as well. It's tidier if they rig it so it looks like I killed Detective King—probably in my own place up here. Maybe she'll get a shot off to kill me before she dies. They have both of our guns and they used mine to shoot her in the leg."

"M.E.," enunciated Gonzaga—meaning that the Medical Examiner would determine the times of death to within an hour or two, so the Major didn't want King dead days before the hypothetical shoot-out with Kurtz. They had to die at the same time.

"Yeah," said Kurtz.

"How romantic," said Angelina. "A regular Romeo and Juliet."

Kurtz ignored her. "Can you get a medic and some medical supplies on the list?" he asked Baby Doc. "A stretcher, bandages, an IV drip, some morphine? And a doctor?"

The standing man coughed into his fist.

"Is that a yes?" said Kurtz.

"It's a yes," said Baby Doc Skrzypczyk. "But a yes with some irony in it. The only doctor I can get who's guaranteed to take the risk and to keep his mouth shut is a Yemeni, like our mutual friend Yasein Goba. Is that acceptable, Mr. Kurtz?"

"Yeah, that's acceptable." *What the fuck.*

"Midnight then, at Mr. Gonzaga's place," said Baby Doc and barely nodded to Gonzaga and Angelina. He went out the door and down the stairs.

"Who's Yasein Goba?" asked Angelina.

Kurtz shook his head and winced at the motion. He'd never learn. "It doesn't matter," he said through the pain.

A minute later, Toma Gonzaga said, "Midnight then," and went down the long stairs to join his bodyguards. Angelina lingered as Kurtz shut off the lights.

"What?" he said. "You waiting for refreshments?"

"Come home with me," she said softly. "You look like shit."

"What are you talking about, 'Come home with me?' You kidnapping me at gunpoint again?"

"Knock that off, Joe. You really look awful. When's the last time you ate?"

"Lunch," he said. He didn't really remember what he ate with Rigby earlier this endless day, but he clearly remembered throwing up by the Pinto while the sheriff and deputy watched and laughed.

"Do you have food at home?" she said.

"Of *course* I have some food at home." He realized that he'd better stop at Ted's Hot Dogs or somewhere to grab something on the way back to the Harbor Inn.

"Liar. Come on to the Towers. I'll fix us steak. I have one of those good indoor grills, so we can actually grill it."

Kurtz's stomach cramped. It had been cramping, he realized, but he hadn't really paid attention to it because of all the more urgent aches and pains.

"I gotta change clothes," he said dully.

"I have clothes your size at the penthouse. You can shower and shave and brush your teeth while I get the steaks on."

He looked at the don's daughter—the acting don now. He wasn't going to ask why she had men's clothes his size in her closets at Marina Towers. It wasn't his business. "No thanks," he said. "I've got other stuff to do . . ."

"You've got to eat something and get a couple of hours sleep before we go tonight," said Angelina. "In the shape you're in right now, you're going to be more a liability than an asset. Eat, sleep, and I've got some pills that will pep you up for a few hours like you've never been pepped up before."

"I bet you do," said Kurtz.

He followed her out the door and down the stairs. It was still raining out, but the wind had died down and the rain was just a light drizzle. Kurtz looked up to check the cloud cover—Baby Doc had said that would be important—but the neon along Chippewa Street made it impossible to tell what was going on up there.

"Come on, Joe, I'll drive you."

Kurtz shook his head slowly. "I'll drive myself. But I'll follow you." He turned toward the alley but Angelina Farino Ferrara's voice stopped him.

"Kurtz," she said. "This whole thing tonight isn't about saving that female cop, is it? Damsel in distess and all that crap?"

"You have to be kidding," said Kurtz.

"She looks like she might be worth saving," said Angelina. "That cute smile, big eyes, big tits. But that would mean that while you have a hard-on for her, you're going soft on us, and we don't need that right now."

"When did you ever see Rigby King?" asked Kurtz.

"I see lots of things you don't think I see," said Angelina.

"Whatever," said Kurtz and walked down the dark alley to his car.

CHAPTER
THIRTY-SIX

The Dodger didn't mind waiting. He was good at it. He'd done it for years in the bughouse in Rochester—just sitting, reptile-like, not even staring, waiting for nothing and knowing that nothing was coming. It had served him well in the years since, running chores for the Boss, waiting for targets to finish whatever they were doing and to come to him. He didn't mind waiting here for the P.I. who might or might not come, who might or might not still be alive.

He left the lights off, of course. After making sure that his entrance hadn't triggered any alarms, the Dodger took thick, clear tape from his pack and covered the small circle he'd cut from the window. It was already chilly in the abandoned inn, but this Kurtz might feel a draft when he came in downstairs. Ex-cons were always sensitive to changes in their cages.

Using the small, shielded penlight from his pack, the Dodger had gone through the entire three stories and seventeen rooms of the moldering old hotel. He'd found Kurtz's sleeping area and odd little library room, of course, but he'd also found the subtle tripwires and telltales in the triangular room on the first floor, and the two hiding places for weapons on the second—the empty niche over the door molding in the room next to Kurtz's sleeping room, and an even more clever nook under the floor of the coldest, most broken-down back room. Kurtz had hidden a 9mm Colt and ammunition in plastic wrap and oily rags there. The Dodger took the gun and went back to the front upstairs room—staying out of the light of the flickering black-and-white monitors—to wait.

And Kurtz did not come. And Kurtz still did not come. The Dodger began imagining all the ways the Major might have killed the P.I. and his top-heavy cop girlfriend. But he hoped he hadn't. The Dodger wanted Kurtz to come home. But still he did not come.

It was sometime after ten-thirty that the Dodger's phone vibrated against his leg. He answered it with a whispered, "Yeah," his eyes still on the video monitors showing the rain-slicked streets and walls outside.

"Where are you?" It was the Boss.

"At the P.I.'s." The Dodger tried not to lie to the Boss. The Boss had ways of knowing when the Dodger lied.

"Kurtz's?"

"Yeah."

"Is he there?"

"Not yet."

The Dodger heard the Boss expel a breath. He hated it when the Boss grew angry at him. "Never mind the P.I.," said the Boss. "You need to get up to the shopping mall in Niagara Falls. We don't want you to miss our foreign friend."

It took a second for the Dodger to remember that the Boss was talking about the woman coming across the border tonight. "Plenty of time," whispered the Dodger. He didn't need to meet her until midnight. And he didn't want her body lying in his pest control van longer than it had to.

"No, go now," said the Boss. "You can wait up there. Then you're off duty for a whole day and night."

"Yeah," said the Dodger, smiling as he thought about tomorrow.

"Happy Birthday," said the Boss. "I'll have something special for you when I see you on Tuesday."

"Thanks, Boss," said the Dodger. He was always touched by the Boss's gifts. Every year it was something special, something the Dodger would never have thought to get for himself.

"Go on now," said the Boss. "Get going."

"Okay, Boss." The Dodger broke the connection, lifted his pack, slipped the Beretta and its silencer into his specially rigged holster, and left the Harbor Inn by the window and fire escape on the north, where he had dismantled Kurtz's simple alarms.

Twelve miles away, in the mostly Polish and Italian section of the suburb of Cheektowaga, Arlene DeMarco was preparing to head for the closed

Niagara Falls shopping mall to pick up the girl named Aysha. It was only ten minutes after ten P.M., but Arlene believed in arriving early for important things.

She took 190 up and around, over Grand Island, across the toll bridge, and hooked left onto the Moses Expessway past the tower of mist declaring the American Falls and right into the city of Niagara Falls. There was almost no traffic this next-to-last night of October. The rain had stopped but Arlene had to use her Buick's wipers to clear her windshield of the spray from the Falls.

Having grown up in Buffalo, Arlene had seen Niagara Falls, New York, go from being a comfortable, kitschy old place reflecting the roadhouses and dowdy tourist hotels of mid-century America to being a heap of rubble resembling Berlin after WWII—almost everything leveled for urban restoration—before finally becoming the convention-center wasteland it was today. If you wanted to see a pretty and classy and up-to-date city of Niagara Falls, you had to cross the Rainbow Bridge to the Canadian side.

But Arlene didn't care about urban planning this night. She drove down Niagara Street to the Rainbow Centre Mall just a block from the double-wasteland of the Information Center and Convention Center, surrounded by their moats of empty parking lots. The Rainbow Centre Mall had a smaller parking area, with just a sprinkling of vehicles in it this Sunday night—cars belonging to the custodial crews and security people, no doubt. But a retaining wall blocked this part of the lot from the view of the street—from the view of any passing police vehicles late on a Sunday night, she realized—and Joe's instructions had been to wait for the girl, Aysha, to be dropped off near the main, north doors of the mall here.

Arlene patted her large purse, checking for the fifth or sixth time that the big Magnum revolver was in there. It was. She'd felt foolish taking it from the office, but Joe had rarely sent her out on tasks like this, and although she vaguely understood this Yemeni girl's connection to recent events, she wasn't at all clear as to what the other factors might be. Arlene just knew that Joe was doing *something* important tonight if he was sending her to pick up Aysha. So while Arlene wasn't alarmed or unduly nervous, she did have the loaded pistol in her purse, along with a can of Mace, her cell phone, her former and illegally but convincingly updated ID showing her to be a member of the Erie County District Attorney's office—as well as the carry permit for the Magnum. She also had some fresh fruit, two water bottles, a pack of Marlboros, her trusty Bic lighter, a small Yemeni-English dictionary she'd picked up yesterday with some difficulty, a Thermos of coffee, and the better and smaller of the two pairs of binoculars from the office.

Arlene took her time choosing where to wait—she didn't want to be spotted by a mall security patrol and picked up—and finally decided on a spot far back near the Dumpsters, between two old cars that had obviously been parked there all night. She settled in, lowered the window, and lit a Marlboro.

It was about twenty minutes later, just about eleven P.M., when the van entered the parking lot, circled once—Arlene slid low in her seat, out of sight—and then parked near the four workers' cars closer to the front door of the silent mall. Because the vehicle was at right angles to Arlene's Buick, she was able to use the binoculars to check it out.

It was a pest control van. On its side was a cartoon of a long-nosed insect gasping and falling in a cartoon cloud of pesticide. The driver had not emerged. His face was in shadow, but Arlene kept the binoculars trained on his silhouette until he leaned forward over the steering wheel to peer at the shopping mall, and for a moment the tall, mall lights illuminated him clearly.

For an instant, Arlene thought that the man's face was wildly tattooed or covered with white streaks and swirls. Then she realized that it was covered with burn scars. He was wearing a baseball cap, but his eyes caught the sodium vapor lamps and seemed to glow orangely, like a cat's.

As Arlene sat there, transfixed, the binoculars steady, the burned man's head suddenly turned her way—swiveling as smoothly as an owl's—and he stared directly at her.

CHAPTER
THIRTY-SEVEN

Kurtz didn't know why he agreed to follow Angelina Farino Ferrara to her home atop Marina Towers.

He told himself that it was because he knew that Detective Paul Kemper might be hunting for him in the next few hours, almost certainly knowing that Rigby King had started her day with Kurtz and wondering now where the hell she was.

He told himself that it was because he really needed Angelina to agree to do what he'd asked for earlier, and it was not time to offend her. His life might depend on her decision.

He told himself that it was because he was hungry.

In the end, he told himself that he was full of shit.

The dinner—perfectly grilled steak, just rare enough, fresh salad with some sort of mustardy dressing, baked potatoes, fresh and crisply prepared green beans, fresh bread, tall glasses of ice water—was fantastic. It didn't even make Kurtz want to throw up again, which was more than he could say about any food he'd had since the previous Wednesday.

Angelina had insisted, and he hadn't resisted, on Kurtz showering, shaving, brushing his teeth, and getting into clean clothes before dinner. The punishingly hot shower—Angelina had installed no fewer than three pounding nozzles in this huge, glass-enclosed guest room shower—made Kurtz ache all the worse, but he almost fell asleep standing there. When he came out of the bathroom naked, he found his old rags gone and the fresh clothes laid out on the bed: an expensive silk, black turtleneck that seemed to weigh nothing, a butter-soft pair of black tweed pants that fit as if someone had tailored them for him, a new belt, clean socks, and black Mephisto boots in his size. There was also a black, uninsulated windshell-parka on the bed; Kurtz tried it on and found that it was made of some soft fabric that didn't crinkle or make any nylon noise when he moved—a factor that might be important in the next few hours.

Kurtz had tossed the windshell back onto the guest bed and gone out to the main room of the penthouse to eat dinner.

"Normally we'd have wine," said Angelina, lighting a candle, "but we're not going to mix that with the pills I'm going to give you when you wake up."

"Wake up?" said Kurtz, glancing at his watch—the only thing other than his wallet that he'd kept.

"You need to sleep a couple of hours before we leave tonight."

"You're going?" said Kurtz. It had been agreed that the Gonzagas and the Farinos would "each contribute two people" to the night's foray, but Kurtz hadn't heard Angelina or the other don specify that they were going.

Now Angelina just raised an eyebrow at Kurtz. Finally, as she was passing the steak, she said, "It wouldn't be much of that promised bonding experience if Toma and I didn't both go, now would it?"

They ate in silence at the polished rosewood table near the freestanding fireplace. Angelina's penthouse filled the entire top story of Marina Towers and there were few view-blocking walls in the central living and dining areas. Over the woman's shoulder, Kurtz could see the lights of ships out in Lake Erie and entering the Niagara River, and behind him, the electric skyline of Buffalo became brighter as the drizzle ended and the clouds lifted. By the time they were finished with dessert—a flaky apple cobbler—Kurtz could see the stars and crescent moon between the scudding clouds.

She led him to a corner on the Lake side where another gas fireplace burned. The chairs and a broad couch here were in a conversation cluster, but Angelina tossed the couch cushions onto the thick carpet behind the couch, pulled a pillow and two blankets from a cupboard, lay one blanket on the broad couch and set the other on the back. "It's only a little after eight," she said. "You need to get some sleep."

"I don't . . ." began Kurtz.

"Shut up, Kurtz," she said. Then, more softly, "You don't know what a fucking wreck you are. My life may depend on you tonight, and I can't trust a zombie."

Kurtz looked at the couch doubtfully.

"I'll wake you in plenty of time," said Angelina Farino Ferrara. "Right now I have to take the elevator down one floor and decide which of my merry men gets to go with me on our half-assed expedition tonight."

"What are your criteria?" asked Kurtz. A long, lighted ship moved slowly toward the southwest out on the Lake.

"Smart but not too smart," said Angelina. "Able to kill when he has to, but also able to know when not to. Most of all, expendable." She gestured toward the couch as she walked away. "In other words, I'm looking for another Joe Kurtz."

When she was gone, Kurtz thought for a minute, then took off his new Mephisto boots, set the alarm on his watch, and lay down on the couch for a minute. He wouldn't sleep—a couple of hours would just make him more tired—but it felt good just to lie here for a few minutes and let the pounding in his head back off a bit.

Kurtz woke to Angelina shaking his shoulder. His watch was buzzing but he'd slept through it. He looked at the glowing dial—11:10. Kurtz wasn't sure he'd ever felt so groggy. He tried to focus on the woman, but she was now also wearing all black, and all he could see in the dim firelight was her glowing face.

"Here," she said, offering him a glass of water and two blue pills.

"What are they?"

"Don't worry about it. Just take them. I was serious about you needing to be conscious enough to be worth hauling along tonight."

He swallowed the pills, put on his boots, and went into the guest room bathroom to use the facilities and splash water on his face. When he came out, wearing the windbreaker shell with his cell phone in the pocket—he'd left Gonzaga's at the office—Angelina was holding a 9mm Browning semi-auto.

"Here," she said, handing it to him. "Ten in the magazine, one already up the spout." She handed him two extra clips and an expensive belt holster, its leather the smoothest Kurtz had ever felt.

Kurtz slipped the extra magazines into the windbreaker's pocket and attached the holster on the left side of his belt under the unbuttoned wind-shell, the Browning's grip backward where he could reach across his body for it. It was his fastest pull.

They drove to the rendezvous site in two SUVs—Angelina driving one and the goomba she'd chosen, a lean, serious-looking bodyguard named Campbell, following in the other. Kurtz had asked for one van or SUV to use as an ambulance if he got Ridley back alive. *Or as a hearse if he didn't.*

"Shit," said Kurtz. He'd forgotten to call Arlene to tell her to forget the Aysha pickup. Something didn't feel right about that rendezvous, although Kurtz couldn't think what. Whatever it was, it wasn't worth risking Arlene for. He'd figure out this little puzzle without the Yemeni girl.

It was 11:23 when he rang Arlene's cell phone, and he got a busy signal. That wasn't like her. He kept hitting redial until they reached their desti-nation, a large industrial and storage complex near the tracks less than two miles from Erie County Medical Center. Gonzaga owned the complex and Kurtz had asked for the proximity to the hospital. They'd humored him.

Waiting Gonzaga guards opened no fewer than three gates before the two SUVs drove into the center of the complex—a rain-slickened loading area a hundred yards across, flanked on three sides by the dark factory build-ings.

Arlene's line was still busy. "Shit," said Kurtz and put the phone away.

"That's why I like traveling with you, Kurtz," said Angelina. "The con-versation."

Toma Gonzaga rolled in next in a black Suburban. He had three of his men with him, but only one—the heavy-lidded but obviously alert bodyguard Kurtz had seen in the limo with Gonzaga—was going on to-night's raid with the don. Kurtz reached through his headache to find the man's name . . . Bobby. Everyone was wearing black trousers and turtlenecks. It was like some formal event for mafiosa. People began unloading things from the various SUVs when yet another pair of the big vehicles showed up. These were Baby Doc's men and they had the largest number of crates and metal boxes to unload. Everyone was armed, most with automatic weap-ons, and the boxes being unloaded from Baby Doc's vehicles were mostly army-stenciled ammunition and weapons containers.

It's beginning to look like some sport-utility commercial from hell here, thought

Kurtz. He almost chuckled out loud before he realized that his headache had faded about as far as it was going to, most of his early aches and pains were gone, and he felt *great*—alive, alert, eager, ready to fly to Neola under his own power and take on the Major and his men with his bare hands if he had to.

I've got to ask Angelina for the recipe for those blue pills, thought Kurtz.

Then, a few minutes before midnight, Baby Doc himself arrived in a Long Ranger helicopter. The thing buzzed in from the north, circled the enclosed compound twice, and set down next to the gaggle of SUVs. Kurtz was astounded at how large the helicopter was—and at how much noise it made. *We're supposed to sneak up on the Major and his men in this fucking thing?* was his first thought.

Well, this had all been Kurtz's idea. He stepped back with the others as the dark-green Bell Long Ranger settled onto its skids amidst a cyclone of dust and whirling debris. It looked like Baby Doc, in the front right pilot's seat, was the only one aboard. He killed the jet turbines, the howl lowered itself to a whine and became a whisper, the big rotors slowed, and Baby Doc pulled off headphones and a mike, disappeared for a second, and then slid the big side cargo door back and to the side. He gestured impatiently for his men to begin loading some of the boxes.

The interior of the Long Ranger had its six seats pushed aside against the outside bulkheads or fuselage or whatever. The central floor was empty and had been covered with a plastic tarp taped down all around.

I wonder why . . . Kurtz's thoughts began and then ended with an *Oh, yeah*. This chopper was a rental, and Baby Doc certainly didn't want to return it with blood and gore everywhere. *He'll probably lose his damage deposit*, thought Kurtz and had to hold back another snicker.

Baby Doc stood in the doorway and looked at Angelina and Gonzaga. "You folks have anything for me?"

Campbell went back to his SUV and carried a flight bag to the chopper. One of Gonzaga's men did the same thing with a nylon backpack. Baby Doc nodded to one of his men, who opened the bag, counted the three-quarters of a million dollars, nodded to his boss, and carried the bags back to their vehicle. Kurtz wondered idly where even mafia dons found three hundred and seventy-five thousand dollars in cash lying around on a Sunday evening.

"Listen up," said Baby Doc. "Here's what you're getting for your money tonight." The Lackawanna longshoreman and mob boss was wearing his old green Army flight suit—the velcroed-on name badge read *Lt. Skrzypczyk*—and it still fit him after twelve years. He wore a regulation-issue pilot's tan shoulder holster and what looked to be a service .45 tucked in it. Baby Doc began opening the olive green boxes and handing out gear, beginning with canvas shoulder bags to stow the loose crap in.

One of his men pulled automatic weapons from the longest carton—Mp5s Kurtz saw, guessing from the tubular stocks, although his familiarity with Army weaponry started and ended with being qualified on M-16s and sidearms. His weapon of choice as an MP so many years ago was the baton. Baby Doc's man offered one short rifle to each person going on the raid.

"Keep your army toys," said Toma Gonzaga. He and his man, Bobby, held up sawed-off 12-gauge shotguns.

Angelina's bodyguard, Campbell, took an Mp5 for himself and one for his boss, slinging both of them over his shoulder.

"The smaller clips hold thirty rounds, the larger ones a hundred and twenty rounds each," said Baby Doc. "Carry as many as you can stuff into the ditty bag I gave you . . ."

"Holy Mary, Mother of God," whispered Angelina as the larger banana clips were handed out and stowed. "We're really going to war."

"It seems that way," muttered Toma Gonzaga. The handsome don appeared to be amused.

Kurtz waved off the automatic rifle. If the 9mm Browning and two extra magazines didn't prove adequate for the evening, he was in deeper shit than he could imagine.

Baby Doc's men carried the extra Mp5s back to their SUV and opened another olive-green box and began handing out what appeared to be thick, cylindrical grenades.

"Flash bangs," said Baby Doc, still standing in the chopper's doorway. "They're not going to blow anything up, but they'll blind and deafen anyone in a room for a few seconds. Just remember to roll them in *before* you go through the door." He gave quick instructions on how to activate and throw the things.

Kurtz stowed three of the flash-bang grenades in his new little ditty bag.

They opened another container and offered flexcuffs.

"Hey," said Toma Gonzaga. "I'm not going down there to *arrest* these people." Angelina had Campbell grab several. "We'll want someone to talk to us," she said.

Kurtz took several. Baby Doc's men opened another large crate and began handing out black Kevlar vests. Everyone going took one of these.

It's like Christmas morning in downtown Baghdad, thought Kurtz. He set his ditty bag and other gear down, pulled off the windbreaker, and began tugging and velcro-ing the thin but heavy vest in place around him.

"Here, I'll help," said Angelina's bodyguard, Campbell. The man securely adjusted and fastened the side straps for Kurtz.

"Thanks."

"These aren't military spec," Baby Doc was saying. "But they're up to SWAT specifications. In fact, they were stolen from a SWAT supply house."

When everyone was a little bulkier and warmer and less comfortable, Baby Doc himself unlatched the last metal box. He held up a bulky fistful of optics and straps. "State of the art military night vision. Each pair weighs two-point-two pounds, has digital controls and an infrared mode that you won't want to fuck with. They also have five-times magnification that you also won't want to fuck with."

"What *will* we want to fuck with?" asked Gonzaga's man, Bobby.

Baby Doc told them how to get the straps adjusted and to power the things up. The bodyguards tried them on. Gonzaga, Angelina, and Kurtz slipped theirs into their already bulging ditty bags.

"Better be careful," said Baby Doc. "You break 'em, you've bought 'em."

"I thought we'd already bought them," said Gonzaga.

Baby Doc laughed softly. "You're *renting* this stuff, Mr. Gonzaga. For one night. So you don't want to lose it or bruise it."

The men loaded several boxes aboard the Long Ranger and secured them with bungee cords and tie-downs. "Medical stuff," said Baby Doc. He pointed to a small, dark man standing with his bodyguards. The gentleman was wearing a sweater and tie and thick glasses. "This is Dr. Tafer," he said. "He's going with us but he won't get out of the Long Ranger. If you get wounded, you've got to haul your own ass back to the chopper or find someone who will." The little doctor smiled hesitantly and nodded at the cluster of men and Angelina. Everyone just stared back at him.

Baby Doc looked at his oversized wristwatch. "Any questions or second thoughts before we take off?"

"Let's shut up and do it," said Angelina. "I'm beginning to feel like I'm in a Jerry Bruckheimer movie."

Gonzaga's bodyguard, Bobby, barked a laugh at that but shut up quickly when no one else laughed.

"Kurtz," said Baby Doc, "you come sit up front with me."

"Why?" said Kurtz. He hated helicopters—he'd always hated helicopters—and he'd just as soon not sit where he could see better.

"Because," said Baby Doc, "you're the only one who really knows where we're going."

People climbed aboard and the powerful jet turbines fired up again.

CHAPTER
THIRTY-EIGHT

The man with the terribly burned face was staring across the dark parking lot at her.

Arlene didn't know how he could see her without binoculars—and she could see through her own binoculars that he had none—but she was sure that he saw her. She leaned her head back against the Buick's headrest, deeper into the shadows, making sure that there was no glint of the sodium-vapor lamps reflecting off her binocular lenses.

The burned man kept staring at her from the pest control truck. His rapt but blind attention reminded Arlene of something but she couldn't think of what for a moment. When she did remember, it wasn't reassuring.

Like an animal—a predator—that can't see its prey but smells it.

She thumbed her cell phone on and held that thumb over the fifth preset fast-dial button. Earlier in the evening she'd looked up the number for the Niagara Falls precinct house closest to the Rainbow Centre Mall . . . sometimes direct dial brought help faster than 911.

The burned man stared her way for another minute but then pulled his scarred face back into the shadows of the van. Arlene couldn't see even a silhouette.

Is he back in the van? Did he get out the other side? The overhead cab light hadn't gone on in his vehicle, but Arlene was sure that this man had long since broken or removed that bulb. Whatever else he was, he was a stalker. He loved the night.

Arlene licked her lips and considered her options. She assumed that the burned man was also waiting for Aysha, although there was no evidence for that yet. But like her boss, Arlene DeMarco very rarely believed in coincidence.

If the man started across the parking lot on foot toward her—and she was still about eighty yards away from his truck and parked in the shadows here by the Dumpsters—she'd simply start the Buick and drive like hell.

If he pulls a weapon?

She'd get her head down, steer by instinct, and try to run over him.

If he starts that obscene pest control van and drives it my way?

Outrun him. Alan had always kept their Buicks well maintained and Arlene had continued the practice after her husband's death.

But what if he just sits there and waits until Aysha's dropped off?

This was the contingency she didn't have an answer for. The burned man was much closer to the mall doors than Arlene was. The Yemeni girl, Aysha, had been told she'd be picked up by her fiancé—the man Joe had killed—or by someone who'd take her to her fiancé. She'd get in the first vehicle that drove up.

What then?

Let her go. Let them both go. That was the obvious answer. Could this be so important, Arlene thought, that she should risk her life to pick up this strange girl?

Joe asked me to. We don't know how important it might be.

The burned man was still invisible in the darkness of the van's shadowed interior. Arlene had the image of the man pulling a rifle from the back of the van—of him sitting in the darker shadows of the passenger seat, invisible to her binoculars, and sighting through a scope at her this very second.

Stop it. Arlene resisted the urge to sink down out of sight or to start the Buick and drive off at high speed. *He's probably here to pick up his girlfriend who works on the janitorial crew*

"Uh huh," Arlene whispered aloud. "And if you believe that, dearie, I have a bridge in Brooklyn you might want to buy."

She desperately wanted a cigarette, but there was no way that she could light one without showing the burned man that someone was in the dark, silent car out here in the shadows by the Dumpsters.

It might be worth it. Light the Marlboro. Enjoy it. Make him tip his hand.

But Arlene didn't think she wanted to tip the burned man's hand. Not right now. Not yet. Arlene looked at her watch—almost 11:20.

She was peering through the binoculars again, trying to decide if that darkness within the darkness there might be the shapeless silhouette of the man behind the wheel of the van, when her phone rang.

CHAPTER
THIRTY-NINE

They lifted off and flew southeast out of Buffalo, past the few tall downtown buildings, past the twin goddesses atop twin buildings holding their twin shining lamps high toward the last low clouds, south along Highway 90—the Thruway toward Erie, Pennsylvania—then banking east and swooping south again along the four-laned Highway 219. Baby Doc was keeping the Long Ranger at an altitude of about five thousand feet for this first part of the flight to Neola. The remaining clouds were fewer and higher now and the view of the city, the great dark mass of Lake Erie to the west, the hills and villages to the east, was beautiful.

Kurtz hated it. He hated being in a helicopter—even the helicopter pilots he'd known in Thailand and at army bases in the States years ago had admitted, almost gleefully, how treacherous and deadly the stupid machines were. He hated flying at night. He hated being up front in the left seat where he could see more easily—even through bubble windows under his feet in this infernal machine modified for tourists. He hated the bulk of the Kevlar vest under his windshell and the fact that he hadn't shifted the Browning enough on his hip to keep it from digging into his side. Most of all, he hated the sure knowledge that they were going to be shot at in a few minutes.

Other than that, he was in a good mood. The little blue pills were keeping him awake, alert, and happy, even while he was busy hating the hell out of a lot of things. But the problem with pills for Joe Kurtz was that he was always Joe Kurtz there behind whatever curtain of pharmaceutical emotion or relief that was being granted by random molecules, and the Joe Kurtz behind the curtain usually couldn't stand the blue-pill condition of Kurtzness in front of the curtain.

Or at least this was his analysis as the seven of them flew south toward Neola five thousand feet above Highway 219.

Baby Doc had been making cryptic but pilot-sounding comments into his microphone, and now Kurtz shouted at him over the roar of the rotors and turbines—"Are we flying legally?"

Baby Doc looked at him and made arcane motions.

Kurtz repeated the shout.

Baby Doc shook his head, tapped his earphones, covered the microphone in front of mouth with his large fist, and shouted back, "Put on your cans."

It took Kurtz only a blue-pill second to realize that the pilot was talking about the bulky earphones and attached microphone on the console between them. He looked back to where four people sat on the side seats, the little Yemeni doctor sitting alone on the cushioned rear bend that could hold three more, and he realized that Gonzaga and Angelina were already wearing their earphones and mikes.

Kurtz tugged his on. He asked the question again, into the microphone this time.

"You have to click that if you want to be heard on the intercom," came Baby Doc's voice in his earphones. The pilot pointed to a button on the control stick that he'd referred to as the cyclic.

Kurtz clicked the button, touching it only gingerly, and shouted the question again.

"God damn it, Joe," cried Angelina over the intercom.

"Hey!" shouted Gonzaga. "Easy!"

"You don't have to shout now," said Baby Doc, his voice crackly but clear and soft on the intercom. "You're asking if I filed a flight plan? If we're flying legally?"

"Yeah," said Kurtz . . . softly.

"The answer is . . . sort of," said the pilot. "Up until thirty seconds ago, we were a legal Flight for Life charter carrying two kidneys from Buffalo to a hospital in Cincinnati."

"What changed thirty seconds ago?" asked Kurtz, not sure if he wanted the answer.

Baby Doc grinned, pulled his clumsy night-vision goggles down over his eyes, and pushed the cyclic-thing forward, even as he twisted the throttle.

The Long Ranger swooped from an altitude of five thousand feet to an altitude of about two *hundred* feet in fewer seconds than it would take for a roller coaster car to drop the steepest descent of its biggest hill.

Kurtz had always hated roller coasters.

Beneath them, the mostly empty four-lane highway had narrowed to an even emptier two-lane road that wound between ever higher hills. Kurtz knew that they must be south of Boston Hills now, deep into the woods. He couldn't see where they were going—the hills and horizon and sky all blended together into a rushing black on black—but he could *feel* how they were following the ground below. The big chopper banked left and right, then left again, following the valley terrain in a motion that made Kurtz want to roll down the window and throw up. He was fairly certain, however, that these windows didn't roll down with a crank, and he wasn't going to take his hands away from their deathgrips on the side of the co-pilot's seat long enough to hunt for a handle or slide or switch.

Baby Doc said something to him.

"What?" shouted Kurtz, realizing that he'd shouted again only after the volley of epiphets from the back seats.

"I said, do you know what IFR stands for?" Baby Doc said.

"Instrument Flight Rules?" said Kurtz.

"Not tonight," said Baby Doc with another grin. "Tonight it stands for I Follow Roads."

Kurtz didn't really see how, even with those dumb goggles, the big man could see the coming twists and turns and dark hills soon enough and react quickly enough to keep up this swooping, banking game of dodgeball. They passed some lights to the left and Kurtz realized that they must be near the empty Kissing Bridge ski area that Gonzaga had stipulated as Baby Doc's DMZ should he manage to take over the Neola drug trade. More than halfway to Neola. Kurtz decided that he might walk to Buffalo if he survived the next half hour.

Suddenly Angelina's voice in his earphones said, "Skrzypczyk . . ." pronouncing it correctly as *Scrip-zik*, ". . . what happens if there are high tension wires across the valley up ahead?"

"We die," said Baby Doc.

Kurtz closed his eyes and hoped there would be no more questions.

"Do we have our plans clear once we're inside?" said Gonzaga. The mafiosa in the back all had their night vision equipment strapped onto their foreheads. Kurtz hadn't taken his out of the ditty bag yet and he'd be damned if he'd remove his hands from the seat to do so now.

"Campbell and I clear the upstairs," said Angelina. "You and Bobby search the first floor and basement. Kurtz is Rover."

"The doctor . . . whatshisname . . . isn't coming in with us?" asked Kurtz over the intercom.

Baby Doc shook his head. "Dr. Tafer. And no, the deal is that he stays in the chopper. But the folding litter is back there. Take that in with you in case the cop . . . whatshername . . ."

"King," said Kurtz.

"Is still alive," finished Baby Doc. "There's Neola."

They'd come at the town from the west as well as north. There was no highway beneath them now at all, just dark hills. Even without night vision goggles, the little town looked like a blazing metropolis of lights after the blackness south of Boston Hills.

Baby Doc gained more altitude—thank the Lord—so that he flew north to south above the main street at a height that wouldn't wake people from the noise.

"You have to help me find this house," said Baby Doc. "You'd better put your night vision on."

"Maybe I won't need it," said Kurtz. "Just follow Main Street south over the river and bank left . . . there it is."

They'd passed over the starlight-rippled ribbon of the Allegheny River on the south end of Neola—Baby Doc having them gain altitude all the time so they couldn't be heard—and now the county road running east from Highway 16 became visible. Powerful sodium vapor lamps illuminated the base of the ziggurat cliff and there were security lights all along the mile-and-a-half twisting driveway rising through checkpoints to the large house at the summit of the hill. There were no lights visible in the house itself, but more exterior lights illuminated the top of the driveway, the rear of the house, and the terrace.

"Come at it from the south," said Kurtz. He was wondering if Cloud Nine would be visible in the dark.

Baby Doc nodded and made a wide circle, swinging a mile or two to the east, and came at the estate from the south and east, away from the road. Even without night vision goggles, Kurtz could see the starlight gleaming on the rails of the little railroad far below. But rather than land, Baby Doc hovered about a thousand feet off the ground and two-thirds of a mile from the house. He rotated the nose of the Long Ranger until it pointed ninety degrees to the left of its alignment with the estate.

Gonzaga undid his seat belt, lifted a long, bolt-action rifle with a heavy scope from beneath his seat, and went to the side door. His man, Bobby, undogged that door and slid it on interior rails to the left. Gonzaga went to one knee and braced himself against the rear bulkhead, moving the rifle in slow circles as he looked through the scope.

"I see one man at the barrier at the top of the drive," Gonzaga said, still hooked to the intercom circuit, "and another closer, in that little open cupola Kurtz said was heated."

"Do you have a shot?" asked Baby Doc.

"Not on the far guy. But I'll take out the one in the cupola."

Kurtz raised his hands to his ears before he remembered that he was wearing the headphones.

The sniper rifle had some sort of suppressor on it. It spat once, twice . . . a lull . . . then a third time.

"He's down," said Gonzaga. He slipped onto the rear bench next to the doctor and fastened his seatbelt. He was still holding the long gun.

"Did the other guard notice?" asked Angelina.

"No."

"All right everyone," said Baby Doc. "Hang on. I'm going to put it down on that flat, grassy area about forty feet south of where the Huey is tied down. That wind sock is going to help."

"Wait," said Kurtz. "How you going to land this thing without the noise waking everybody."

"I'm going to use a technique called autorotation," said Baby Doc. He was throwing switches.

Kurtz turned to look at him. "Isn't that just sort of a controlled crash, just using the turning rotors without the motor on?"

"Yeah." Baby Doc killed the twin turbines. The night grew silent except for the slowing rush of rotors and the rising sound of the wind.

CHAPTER
FORTY

A rlene? Are you there? Arlene?"
It was her sister-in-law, Gail DeMarco, calling. Arlene answered
in a whisper, although it was doubtful that the burned man could hear from
this distance.

"Is everything all right?" asked Gail. "We were going to talk after the
weather . . ."

The two women spoke almost every night after the Channel 4 weather,
before the sports, before going to bed. Arlene had been looking forward to
tonight's conversation because they were going to talk about Rachel's fif-
teenth birthday later in the week—although Arlene was dreading being asked
if Joe was going to attend. Rachel looked up to and adored the occasional
dinner visitor, Joe Kurtz—the girl's real father, Arlene was absolutely sure—
and Joe seemed oblivious to it all. It had reached the point where Gail almost
couldn't stand Joe—"a jerk" Gail had called him during a recent conversation
with Arlene—but Gail understood the situation, and wanted Rachel to know
the man who was probably her father.

"I'm sorry," said Arlene, still keeping her eye on the dark pest control
truck near the mall. "I'm out running an errand for Joe and just forgot the
time."

"An errand for Joe?" said Gail. "At this hour?" Arlene could hear the
disapproval in her friend's voice. Arlene had been close to her husband's sister
when Alan and her son were alive, but they'd grown even closer in the years
since those deaths.

"Something that had to be done," said Arlene. *I'd kill for a cigarette*, she
thought, and then realized that was an option. Just walk up to Mr. Burned

Face in his bug truck and put two .44 slugs into him. *As he waits for his girlfriend on the night custodial shift to come out for a midnight lunch.* Arlene decided that if she went that way, she'd use the nicotine-withdrawal defense in court. Maybe the jury would be composed mostly of ex-smokers. *Hell, it would only take one.*

She and Gail chatted for a few minutes, Arlene keeping her voice down and the Buick's window up. If the Burned Man was still in the cab of the van, he wasn't showing any movement.

"Well," said Gail, her voice changing slightly, "will Joe Kurtz be coming to dinner on Friday night?"

Arlene chewed her lip. "I haven't asked him yet. He's been . . . busy."

"Yes. Dr. Singh asks me about Joe Kurtz almost every day. I imagine Joe's been in bed a lot, recovering. It must mean extra work for you at the office."

"Not that much," said Arlene, commenting on the first part of Gail's sentence but letting her think she was answering the second part.

"But do you think he'll be up to coming to Rachel's birthday party? It would mean the world to her."

Arlene knew that although Rachel was a sensitive and lovable girl, she had few friends at school. Besides Gail and Arlene—and maybe Joe—there would be only one other teenager besides Rachel at the party, a skinny, bookish girl named Constance.

"I'll ask him tomorrow," said Arlene.

"I mean, he does *remember* it's Rachel's birthday, doesn't he?" asked Gail, voice rising a bit.

"I'll ask him tomorrow whether he feels up to coming," said Arlene. "I'm sure he will if he can. Gail, by any chance do you have Rachel's phone around? The one I gave you in the spring?"

"Rachel's cell phone?" said her sister-in-law. "Yes. She never carries it. I think it's in her room. Why? You want it back?"

"No, but could you go get it right now? And check the battery."

"Now?" said Gail.

"Yes, please," said Arlene. There was movement in the cab of the pest control van. The Burned Man was shifting positions, perhaps getting ready to step out.

Gail sighed, said she'd just be a minute, and set her phone down.

Arlene looked at her options here. They were awkward. She wanted the

Burned Man out of the way so that she could pick up this Aysha person in . . . she looked at her watch . . . twenty-one minutes. Even if the Burned Man wasn't also waiting for the Yemeni girl—although Arlene's instincts told her that he was—it would be better if there were no witnesses. The girl was illegal in more ways than one. What if she didn't want to get into the car with Arlene? Well, to be truthful, that was one reason Arlene had brought the .44 Magnum.

So how to get this guy out of the way? And what to do if he suddenly drove toward her Buick or began walking her way? Arlene had no idea why this scarred man in the bug truck might want to grab Aysha, but she felt that this was precisely what he was going to do in . . . nineteen minutes . . . unless Arlene intervened.

How? She had the Niagara police on speed dial, but even if she got through to someone who actually called a patrol cruiser who actually got here in time, they'd almost certainly still be here when the Canadians dropped Aysha off at the mall door. And if the people-smugglers from the north caught one glimpse of red and blue lights flashing or police cars here in the parking lot, they'd keep going and drop Aysha somewhere else, far from here.

Maybe I could follow their car and . . .

Arlene shook her head. After getting even a glimpse of the police, the already paranoid smugglers would probably be more paranoid. The streets were empty in this wet, botched caricature of a city, and there was little to no chance that Arlene would be able to tail the smugglers without them seeing her. And if she spooked them enough, they might even kill the girl and just dump her out somewhere. Arlene just didn't know the stakes here—for Aysha, for the people smuggling her in, for the Burned Man in that bug truck straight ahead, or even for Joe.

I could just go home. That was certainly the option that made the most sense. In the morning, Joe would probably say, "Oh, that's all right—I just wanted to chat with the girl if possible. No biggee."

Uh-huh, thought Arlene.

"All right, I'm back with the phone," came Gail's voice in her ear. "What next?"

"Ahh . . . just hold onto it for a second," said Arlene, knowing how foolish she sounded. It was like those old practical jokes in high school where some boy would call up pretending to be a telephone repairman and get you to take the cover off the phone—back when phones looked alike and had covers—and then made you do one thing after the other to help "fix" it, until you were swinging a bag of parts over your head and clucking like a chicken.

Joe had talked Arlene into purchasing a cell phone for Rachel a few months earlier. He was always worried that the girl might be in danger, that someone might go after her the way her late stepfather had, and he liked the idea of Rachel carrying around a phone with Arlene's numbers set to speed dial.

Gail had been a little non-plussed at the gift—"If Rachel wanted a phone, I'd buy one for her," she'd said logically enough—but Arlene had convinced her that this was Joe's awkward way of establishing some contact with the girl, of watching over her from afar. "He can establish contact just by coming to dinner and seeing her more frequently," Gail had said sternly. Arlene couldn't argue with that.

She'd thought of the phone right now because although its bills were paid by WeddingBells.com, if someone tried to use reverse-911 on it, the records would show just the WeddingBells PO box number.

Fourteen minutes before midnight. It was quite possible the smugglers could get here a few minutes early with Aysha—any second—and Arlene didn't have a clue what to do. If the Burned Man nabbed Aysha, she could try following the bug truck so at least she could tell Joe where the girl was taken, but the same empty, wet streets in the same empty, wet town here made that no more feasible than following the smugglers themselves.

Arlene didn't like to use obscenities, but she had to admit that her goose was well and truly cooked here.

"Arlene? Are you all *right*?"

"I'm fine. Is the phone charged?"

"Yes."

"Good. Dial nine-one-one."

"What? Is there an emergency?"

"Not yet. But dial nine-one-one. But don't hit the 'call' button yet."

"All right. What do I tell them the emergency is?"

"Tell them that there's a man having a heart attack—in cardiac arrest—just outside the Rainbow Centre Mall."

"Rainbow Centre? That place up in Niagara Falls?"

"Yes."

"Are you there? Is there someone in cardiac arrest? I can talk you through the CPR until the paramedics get there."

"This is just private-eye stuff, Gail. Just tell them that a man's having a heart attack outside the Rainbow Centre Mall. . . . And tell them he's in a van near the south main mall doors and the van has Total Pest Control written on the side."

"Wait . . . wait . . . let me write that down. What was the . . ."

"Total Pest Control. Like in the cereal."

"There's a cereal called Pest Control?"

"Just write it down." Arlene usually enjoyed Gail's odd sense of humor, but there wasn't time tonight.

"Won't they arrest me for false reporting?"

"They won't find you. Trust me. After you make the call . . . *if* you make the call . . . just take a hammer and smash that cellphone and throw the pieces away. I'll provide a new one."

"It looks like a pretty expensive phone. I'm not sure . . ."

"*Gail.*"

"All right. A man undergoing cardiac arrest at the south entrance to the Rainbow Centre Mall—that one near the convention center in Niagara Falls . . . and he's having this heart attack in a van with Total Pest Control written on the side of it."

"Yes." Arlene looked at her watch. Eleven minutes before midnight. It was almost too late to . . .

The van had started up. Arlene could see the oil-rich exhaust in the humid air. She could hear the engine even with her window up.

Oh, thank God. I don't have to . . .

The van made a fast left turn and headed in Arlene's direction. For a second the headlights pinned her like a deer.

She immediately dropped sideways onto the passenger seat and fumbled in her purse for the .44 Magnum. The cell phone fell off her lap and bounced and for a second Arlene was sure that she'd disconnected with Gail.

"Hello? Hello?" Gail and Arlene were both shouting.

The van stopped fifty or sixty feet in front of Arlene's Buick, the head-lights turning her windshield a thick milky white.

"Call nine-one-one," Arlene whispered urgently. "Call nine-one-one. On the cell phone. Keep this line open."

"Oh, my God. Arlene, are you all right? What's . . ."

"*Call nine-one-one!*" shouted Arlene. "Tell them what I said."

Arlene lowered herself to the floor, her back against the passenger-side door. She set the cell phone on the seat, pulled her legs over the console and set her feet on the carpeted floor. She set the heavy Magnum on her knee and cocked it, keeping the muzzle pointing at the ceiling. If the Burned Man came to the passenger side, she might not be visible in the shadow of the footwell here, especially with the headlights making everything else so bright. She aimed the gun at the driver's door.

The van's headlights went off and the van's engine fell silent.

"Arlene!" It was a screech, but not a panicked one. Gail had been a nurse for a long time. The more tense things got, the more calm Gail became, Arlene knew. *On the job.*

"Hussssshhhh," whispered Arlene, leaning left to hiss into the phone. "Don't talk. Don't talk."

There was no further noise. No footsteps. But the van's engine stayed off and the van's headlights stayed dark. Arlene looked across at the driver's door window, aiming the muzzle of her weapon. What seemed like hours passed in the silence, but she knew it must have been just a minute or two.

Oh, dear Lord. Did I lock the doors?

It was too late to lunge across for the locking controls on the far door now. She considered reaching above her head and locking the door on her side—*If he swings it open, I'll fall out backwards like a bag of laundry*—but knew that the power lock driving home would sound like a gunshot. She left it alone.

The van door slammed. Arlene set her finger in the trigger guard. She'd practice-fired this weapon enough to know that it required quite a bit of pressure on the trigger to fire. And the recoil was serious. She propped her head more firmly on the door behind her so that the recoil wouldn't catch her on the chin, cradled the big gun on her knee with her left hand under her right hand to steady it, and thumbed the hammer back until it clicked.

She could hear the footsteps on the concrete now. He was walking toward the driver's side.

CHAPTER
FORTY-ONE

As the big helicoper plummeted, Kurtz banished the blue-pill haze from his mind and body.

He willed away the false good-feeling and tinge of good humor that overlay everything. He willed away the cloud of painlessness and let both his headache and his resolve flow back in like black ink. He willed away the soft pharmaceutical fog and summoned the hard-edged core of Joe Kurtz back to duty.

The big Bell Long Ranger hit hard, jarring Kurtz's spine and sending the old familiar spikes through his skull, slid a few yards across slick grass, and came to a stop. Immediately Gonzaga and his man Bobby were out the side door and running. Angelina and her bodyguard, Campbell, followed a minute later, carrying Mp5s, the ditty bags filled with ammunition rattling at their hips.

Kurtz struggled with the four point straps for a few seconds, slapped them away, grabbed up his bag, set the folded aluminum and web litter over his shoulder on a sling, and went out through the side door just as Baby Doc stepped out his pilot-side door and pulled two long tubes from behind his seat. The pilot hung one of the tubes over his shoulder with a sling and carried the other. They looked like RPGs, the old Russian and Eastern European rocket-propelled grenade launchers.

"What're those?" whispered Kurtz. The two were jogging toward the house now in the dark, passing the dark shape of the Major's Huey.

"RPGs," said Baby Doc and turned in the direction of the driveway.

"Wait!" called Kurtz.

Baby Doc turned but did not stop jogging.

"I thought you were staying with the chopper," whispered Kurtz.

Baby Doc grinned. "I never said I would."

"What if you get killed?"

The grin stayed in place. "You guys will either have to take flying lessons or start walking." He turned his back and ran toward the head of the driveway.

There was a dead man lying in the guardhouse gazebo. Nothing stirred except the six of them jogging toward the house. The external security lights were on in the back, but the house remained dark.

Angelina Farino Ferrara set the C-4 charge on the door, triggered the timed detonator, and stepped back with the other three just as Kurtz came jogging up. The blast wasn't as loud as Kurtz expected, but it was pretty sure to wake everyone in the house. The door flew inward, showing steel reinforcements blown off at the hinges.

Gonzaga went in first. His bodyguard followed a second later. Angelina and her man lunged in a second after that.

This is nuts, thought Kurtz, not for the first time that night. One did not assault a house without knowing the houseplans intimately. He raised the Browning and threw himself through the door.

The foyer and hall lights had come on, which was not good. The layout was as he remembered—the foyer opening on the center hall straight ahead, staircase to the right—Angelina and her man were already pounding up it—a dark, formal living room was visible to his left, closed doors along the hallway to the left and right.

Gonzaga kicked open the first door to the right of the foyer and tossed in a flash-bang. The explosion was very loud. Bobby, the bodyguard, kicked in the second door to the right and dodged back as a hail of automatic weapons fire slashed across the foyer, shattering the chandelier and tearing apart vases and furniture in the living room across the way. Bobby fired his shotgun into the room, pumped it, fired again, pumped it, fired again. The machine gun fire stopped abruptly.

Upstairs, two explosions poured smoke down the stairway.

Kurtz ran across the foyer, scattering crystal as he ran. Plaster was falling from the high ceiling. He could see the glass library doors fifty feet or so straight ahead and anyone in that dark room could see him. There were too many lights in this broad hallway, and they were too recessed to shoot out, so he felt like the target he was as he dodged from one side to the other and paused where the hallway began.

Gonzaga came out of the room behind him and fired up the staircase to Kurtz's right. A black-garbed figure tumbled down the steps and an M-16 fell onto the foyer tiles. *Not one of ours*, thought Kurtz.

"You take the left, Bobby and I'll take the right," shouted Toma Gonzaga.

Kurtz nodded and dodged left just as the library doors exploded shards of glass outward. Toma, Bobby, and Kurtz jumped against doorways. Two shotguns and Kurtz's Browning fired at the same time, smashing the last shards of the glass doors. Kurtz wanted to get to the Major's room, which opened off the left side of the library at the end of the hall, but right now he wasn't going anywhere as someone fired an M-16 again from the darkness of the library.

The second door on the left along that hallway opened and one of the Vietnamese bodyguards peered out, ducked back behind the door, held out an M-16, and sprayed the hallway. Gonzaga and Bobby were out of sight behind Kurtz, in the rooms along the opposite side of the hallway. Shotgun blasts roared and filled the air with cordite stink.

Kurtz pressed into the first doorway on the left—the door was locked—and waited until the spray of plaster and ricochets from the M-16 blast let up. Then he aimed the Browning at the center of the open wooden doorway and fired five slugs into it, about chest high. There was a cry and the sound of a body tumbling down the stairs.

Basement. Kurtz wanted to go down there—it was his job to—but he had to secure the library first. He ran, firing, to the basement doorway. There was no return fire from beyond the shattered glass of the library.

There was a light on downstairs and Kurtz could see the bodyguard's body crumpled at the base of the steps. Kurtz pulled a flash-bang grenade from his bag, flipped the primer, and tossed it down the stairs, stepping back behind the door while it exploded. When he peered around, the basement was full of smoke and the bodyguard's clothing was burning. He hadn't moved.

More explosions from the second floor. The gunfire up there was horrendous. Kurtz wondered if Angelina had survived the Battle of the North Bedroom or whatever the hell it was.

As Kurtz lunged around and crouched on the top step of the basement stairs, still focused on the library doors, Gonzaga and Bobby poked their heads out of their doorways.

"These rooms are clear," shouted Gonzaga. "At least two down here. What about the library?"

Automatic weapons' fire exploded from the dark library again, stitching the walls along the wide hallway and making all three men duck back. Kurtz had caught a glimpse of two splaying muzzle flashes.

"It's not clear," he called from the top step. "Two machine guns at least."

"Throw a flash-bang," called Bobby.

I can do better than that, thought Kurtz. He took a wad of C-4 from his ditty bag, wadded it into a rough sphere, stuck in a primer detonator, and set it for four seconds. He lunged into the hall and threw it like a fastball through the shattered doors, jumping back onto the top step just as both M-16s opened up.

The blast blew the wide doors off their hinges and rolled a cloud of acrid smoke down the hallway.

Kurtz, Gonzaga and Bobby ran into the smoke, firing as they ran.

The last door on the right opened. An Asian woman looked out and screamed. Her hands were empty.

"No!" shouted Kurtz over his shoulder, but too late. Gonzaga fired at her with his shotgun at a range of twenty feet and the woman's upper body flew back into the room as if jerked away on a cable.

Kurtz kicked the hanging library doors open and rolled in among broken glass and splintered doorframe. The carpet was on fire. Smoke rose to the cathedral ceiling and a smoke alarm was screaming, hitting almost the same note the Asian woman had.

Trinh and another Vietnamese had been firing from behind a long, heavy library table they'd turned on its side. The C-4 blast had shattered the table into several chunks and a thousand splinters and thrown it all back over them. The bodyguard had been blown out through the glass terrace doors—a burglar alarm raised its whoop in chorus to the smoke alarm—and that man was obviously dead. Colonel Trinh was lying unconscious on the smoking carpet. His face was bloody and his left arm was visibly broken, but he was breathing. His red slippers had been blown off and one of them sat in a bookshelf ten feet up the high wall of shelves. The colonel's shattered M-16 lay nearby.

Kurtz rolled the colonel on his belly, pulled flexcuffs from his bag, and cuffed the man's wrists behind him. Tightly.

"Take him out to the chopper," he told Bobby, who was swinging his shotgun in short arcs, covering every opening, including the broken doors onto the lighted terrace.

"I don't take orders from you."

"Do it," said Gonzaga, stepping through the broken doors from the hallway.

Bobby grabbed the old Vietnamese man by his hair, pulled him halfway up, tucked a shoulder under him, hoisted him onto his shoulder without releasing his shotgun, and jogged down the hallway with him.

"Strong fucker," said Kurtz.

"Yeah."

The two men had each taken a knee and were covering different doorways. Upstairs, the rock and roll gunfire had resolved itself into the occasional short bursts of full auto.

"That's the Major's bedroom," said Kurtz, jabbing a finger at the closed door on the south wall of the library. "You get him. I'm going to check the basement."

Gonzaga nodded and ran to the right of the bedroom doorway, jamming more shells into his 12-gauge as he did so.

Good idea thought Kurtz as he went back out into the hallway. He pulled another clip from his pocket. He'd kept count of his shots out of old habit— nine fired so far. There should be two bullets left in the Browning, one in the chamber and one in the clip.

The bodyguard's body at the bottom of the steps was still on fire, but the smoke in the basement had dissipated some. Besides the burning carpet and books in the library on the first floor, something on the second floor was also burning—smoke poured down into the foyer. The shooting up there had stopped.

Suddenly there was a double exposion from outside, north of the house, where the driveway came up from the valley.

Well, Baby Doc got to use at least one of his RPGs.

Kurtz went down the steps, pistol extended. A glance at the heaped body at the bottom showed him that he'd managed to put three slugs into the Asian man's chest through the door. Kurtz moved into the basement.

Surprisingly for such a fancy house, the basement wasn't finished. The central part was open and carpeted, there was a big screen TV and some cheap couches near the far wall, a small kitchen and bar area showed a refrigerator and booze, but part of the floor was bare concrete and the place smelled of sweat and cigarettes.. It looked to Kurtz like a place where the bodyguards might hang out. More smoke was roiling down the stairway.

There were three small rooms and a bathroom off the open room, and Kurtz kicked all the doors open.

He found Rigby in the last room.

She was lying half-naked on a bloody mattress set on the concrete floor and she looked dead. Then he saw the crude IV-drip and wad of bandages on her left leg and he went to one knee next to her. She was unconscious and very pale, her skin felt cold and clammy, but when he put fingers to her throat, he could feel the faint pulse. They'd been trying to keep her alive until tomorrow when they could finish the job in Buffalo with Kurtz's gun. Rigby's eyes fluttered but did not open.

He unslung the litter from his back, unfolded it, and then wondered what the hell he was doing. He wasn't going to get anyone else down here to help him carry the stretcher.

"Sorry, Rig," he said, and tucked the Browning in its holster, folded her over his shoulder in a fireman's carry, grabbed the slung IV bottle, and carried her up the steep stairs. She moaned when he moved her but did not regain consciousness.

The house was definitely on fire. There were shots from the library, but Kurtz didn't turn that way. He went down the hall and into the smoky foyer.

Movement on the stairs made him shift the small IV bottle and draw his pistol.

Angelina Farino Ferrara came down the stairs through the smoke, staggering under the load of a man's body on her shoulder. Her face, arms, hands, and sweater were drenched in blood, and she still carried the Mp5 in her right hand.

"Jesus," said Kurtz as they both went out the front door with their burdens. "Your man?"

"Yeah," panted Angelina. "Campbell."

"Alive?"

"I don't know. He took one in the throat." She paused under the *porte cochere* and nodded toward Rigby's pale, bare legs and white underwear. "Your girlfriend? She'd have a nice ass if it wasn't for the cellulite."

Kurtz said nothing. He drank in the fresh air. Flames crackled from the upper stories. A figure moved in the driveway and both he and Angelina swung, weapons coming up.

"Don't shoot," said Baby Doc. He had his own Mp5 slung over his shoulder and was carrying one of the RPGs with its grenade still on the muzzle.

Kurtz looked to where the driveway came up to the last guard barrier and saw an SUV and a sheriff's vehicle burning in a single conflagration. "All that with one RPG?" he said as the three turned and began moving quickly toward the helicopter.

"Yep," said Baby Doc. His face was smudged with soot and there was a burn or cut on his right cheek. He looked at Angelina staggering under the weight of her bodyguard but didn't offer to help. "You two go on," he said as they passed the dark Huey. "I'll be right there."

Halfway to the Long Ranger, Angelina had to pause to shift Campbell's weight on her back, but Kurtz didn't pause with her. Rigby was moaning. Blood poured down her leg and sopped through his sweater and ran down his left arm.

A loud blast made him turn. Baby Doc had fired the remaining RPG into the Huey and the black machine was burning strongly. The Lackawanna boss jogged past him, carrying only his rifle now. "Old Israeli commando rule—don't leave their air force behind," he said as he ran past. "Or something like that."

Baby Doc had already clambered into the chopper and fired up the turbines when Kurtz reached the open door and laid Rigby on the plastic-sheeted floor next to where the Yemeni doctor was working on Colonel Trinh where he lay, still flexcuffed and bleeding. Dr. Tafer moved away from the colonel, leaned over Rigby and shined a flashlight into her eyes and then on her wound.

"How is she?" asked Kurtz, leaning against the open door of the helicopter to catch his breath.

"Barely alive," said Dr. Tafer. "Much blood loss." He pulled the IV needle out and tossed the almost empty bottle out into the grass. "This is saline solution. She needs plasma." He pulled a plastic bag of plasma from his box and slid the needle into Rigby's terribly bruised arm.

Angelina staggered up with her man and dumped him onto the floor next to Rigby. The floor of the Long Ranger was filled with bodies. *"Triage,"* she gasped and sat down on the grass.

Dr. Tafer shone his flashlight into Campbell's open, unblinking eyes and inspected the neck wound. "Dead," said the doctor. "Get him out of way, please."

"We're taking him home," said Angelina from the grass.

Kurtz leaned and shoved the bodyguard's body against the rear bulkhead, tucking him half beneath the bench there.

"It sounds like Napoleon's goddamned retreat from Moscow back there," called Baby Doc from the pilot's seat.

"Shut up," said Angelina over the rotor and turbine roar. She got to her feet, dropped the empty banana clip out of her rifle, and slapped in a new one from her ditty bag. She and Kurtz both began walking back toward the burning house.

CHAPTER
FORTY-TWO

Arlene caught just a glimpse of the Burned Man's ballcap—an old Brooklyn Dodgers' cap, she noticed—before the flashing lights arrived.

It was five minutes before midnight, she noticed, and the man from the pest-control van had spent a few minutes looking at her car and another couple of minutes walking around out there, checking it out, before approaching her driver's side door—still unlocked, she feared—on foot. Then the top of his cap rose above the driver's side doorsill of the Buick. Arlene aimed the Magnum and prepared for the recoil and flying glass.

The red lights flashed first, and then she heard the sirens.

The ball cap disappeared from the window and a few seconds later an engine started up and the van's headlights splayed across her windshield again.

When the headlights turned away, Arlene sat up and peeked over the dashboard.

The ambulance was accompanied by a police cruiser and both vehicles were sweeping around in a turn, away from the mall entrance, toward the pest-control van with its hypothetical cardiac arrest victim.

The van drove away toward the north exit at high speed.

Both the ambulance and police cruiser stopped—as if nonplussed—and then gave chase to what appeared to be the fleeing heart-attack victim. Within a few seconds, the flashing lights had disappeared out onto Niagara Street and the parking lot was quiet again. Arlene had known that Niagara Falls's Memorial Medical Center was only a few blocks north on Walnut Avenue, but this was good time even for that proximity. Evidently midnight on a drizzly Sunday in late October was a slow time for them.

The old Dodge with Ontario plates turned into the mall lot slowly, hesitantly, braking twice, as if the driver and occupants—Arlene could see several heads silhouetted against the street lights along Niagara—were suspicious, ready to bolt at any sign of movement. Arlene shifted to the driver's seat but kept her head low, peering through the Buick's steering wheel.

"*Arlene!*"

It was a good thing, she realized later, that she'd just lowered the hammer on the big Magnum and set it back in her purse, or she probably would have shot herself when Gail's voice erupted from the cell phone. Arlene had forgotten about the phone. Heck, she'd forgotten about Gail.

"*Are you all right!?*"

"Shhh, shhh," Arlene hissed into the phone. "I'm fine."

"Well, *damn* it!" cried her sister-in-law and friend. "You're scaring me to *death*."

The Dodge with the Ontario plates had stopped by the mall doors. Now a small woman carrying an old suitcase was shoved out onto the sidewalk in front of the doors and the Dodge accelerated away toward the Third Street exits.

"Gail, it's quite possible that you just saved my life," Arlene said calmly. "I'll call you tomorrow with the details."

"*Tomorrow!*" squawked the phone. "Don't you dare wait until . . ."

Arlene broke the connection and turned her phone off. She waited only a few seconds, half expecting the bug control van or the police cruiser to reappear at high speed.

Nothing. Just the small woman and the old suitcase and the empty lot.

Arlene started the Buick, turned on the headlights, and drove up to the woman in a wide arc so as not to spook her.

More girl than woman, thought Arlene as she hit the button to roll down the passenger side window. The doors had, as she'd feared, not been locked. "Aysha?" she said.

The young woman did not flinch back. She looked to be a teenager, with a pale face and large eyes above her cheap raincoat. The suitcase she clutched looked like something Arlene's parents might have owned.

"Yes, I am Aysha," said the girl in accented but smooth English. "Who sent you, please?"

Arlene hesitated only a second before saying, "Yasein. Please get in."

The girl got in the front seat. She still clutched her bulky suitcase.

"Toss that in the back," said Arlene and helped her lift it between the seats and drop it on the rear seat. The young woman was smaller than fourteen-year-old Rachel.

Checking her mirrors again, Arlene drove quickly out of the Rainbow Centre's parking lot, took Third up to Ferry, and Ferry to 62. Within minutes they were on the northern extension of Niagara Falls Boulevard, headed toward Buffalo. It was drizzling again and Arlene turned on the Buick's wipers.

"My name is Arlene DeMarco," she said slowly. And then, without planning it, she said, "Welcome to the United States."

"Thank you very much," said the young woman, looking calmly at Arlene. "I am Miss Aysha Mosed, fiancée of Mister Yasein Goba of Lackawanna, New York, United States of America."

Arlene nodded and smiled, while inside she was hurting and thinking, *How am I going to tell her? And how am I going to tell her in a way that will still allow her to talk to Joe tomorrow?*

"Yasein is dead, is he not?" said Aysha.

Arlene looked at her. *Lie to her*, was her thought. Aloud, she said, "Yes, Aysha. Yasein is dead."

CHAPTER
FORTY-THREE

The Artful Dodger lost the ambulance and the cop car in the rainslicked streets of Niagara Falls—all he had to do was get out of sight of them and then duck down an alley between Haeberle Plaza and Oakwood Cemetery—and then he headed back to the Rainbow Centre.

Once there, he parked near the mall doors, watching the street and the Niagara Street entrance for the returning police cruiser.

What the fuck was all that about? He was sure it had something to do with the Buick parked out there. It was gone now, of course. He'd known for half an hour that something had been wrong with that blue Buick—that someone was out there. He should have driven straight out there and shot the shit out of that car as soon as he'd arrived.

But what kind of tough guy drives a blue Buick? That's a granny-lady's car.

Now the Dodger waited fifteen minutes, watching over his shoulder the whole time, before deciding that the package had been dropped off and picked up already. He called the Boss and told him the situation.

"Did you get the tag number on the Buick?"

"Sure I did," said the Dodger, and recited it from memory.

There was a brief pause while the Boss fed it into whatever computer or data bank he had—the Boss had access to everything and anything—before the man on the phone said, "Mrs. Arlene DeMarco," and gave an address out in Cheektowaga.

The name meant nothing to the Dodger.

"The P.I.'s secretary," said the Boss. "Kurtz's secretary."

The Dodger had left the mall and was driving toward the expressway, but he had to blink away red in his vision when the Boss said Kurtz's name.

That motherfucker has to die. "You want me to go out to Cheektowaga now?" said the Dodger. "Get the package back and settle things with Mrs. Arlene DeMarco?" *Maybe Kurtz will be there and we'll get* everything *settled.*

The Boss was silent for a minute, obviously weighing options.

"No, that's all right," said the Boss at last. "It's your birthday and you've got a long drive ahead of you. You go on and take the day off. We'll deal with all of this on Tuesday."

"You sure?" said the Dodger. The Beretta with its silencer was on his lap as he drove. It felt like a blue-steel erection. "Cheektowaga's on my way out of town," he added.

The Boss was silent another few seconds. "No, you go on," said the calm voice. "It might work out better all around if we wait a day."

"All right," said the Dodger, realizing how tired he was. And he *did* have a long drive ahead of him. And much to do when he arrived. "I'll call you Tuesday morning. Want me to go straight to Cheektowaga then?"

"Yes, that would be good," said the Boss. "Phone me when you get near the airport. No later than seven A.M., all right? We want to meet these ladies before Mrs. DeMarco goes in to work."

"Okay," said the Dodger. "Anything else?"

"Just have a good birthday, Sean," said the Boss.

CHAPTER

FORTY-FOUR

'll go in through the door I blew," said Angelina. "You go around by the terrace. I think we'd better wrap this up fast. Baby Doc looks like he's ready to take off without us, and it might be to his advantage to do it. Get Toma and his guy and we'll get the fuck out of here."

Kurtz nodded and they split up.

Kurtz was still carrying his ditty bag, but there was no need for night-vision goggles now. The house was fully engaged, the second floor pouring flames out of its high windows, the roof cedar-shake shingles smoking and more smoke billowing out the first-floor windows on the east and west sides. The flickering light from the flames illuminated everything out to the Bell Long Ranger.

Kurtz paused at the corner of the house and then swung around onto the terrace overlooking the cliff.

Gonzaga's guy, Bobby, swung a shotgun his way.

"Hey!" said Kurtz, holding his hands and the Browning high. "It's me."

Bobby lowered the shotgun. He was watching the open doors to the library and the Major's room, which lay behind two closed, heavy, window-less doors.

"What's the situation?" asked Kurtz. He popped one cartridge out of the Browning's chamber and dropped it in his pocket. Then he racked the next cartridge in, dropped the empty magazine to the terrace, and slapped in another ten-round clip.

"The boss is still in there, gathering up papers and shit and keeping the Major in his room. The whole fucking place is beginning to burn in there, so the boss won't be staying much longer."

This last information was redundant. The flames were pouring out of the second floor windows above the terrace and the heat was significant.

"I think the Major's room connects to Trinh's next to it," said Kurtz over the crackling of the flames. "The old man could get out that way."

Bobby shook his head. "The boss had me shove what was left of that library table up against Trinh's bedroom door and pile up a bunch of shit on it. The Major ain't getting out that way. Not in a wheelchair."

"Anyone else in there with the Major?"

"We don't know. The boss don't think so. We got some handgun fire from the bedroom door right when you left. Then the Major closed and bolted it. The boss thinks he's in there alone."

"C-4?" said Kurtz.

Bobby shrugged. "I guess. Me, I'd let the old fuck burn." He said it loud enough to carry through the outside doors.

"Go help Gonzaga," said Kurtz. "I'll watch out here."

When Bobby had run into the smoking library, Kurtz backed away, then peered over the edge of the cliff to the valley floor far below. There were emergency vehicles down there—he could see a firetruck and at least three sheriff's cars, as well as a gaggle of big SUVs—but no one was coming up the winding drive or climbing the ziggurat staircase.

Kurtz walked off the terrace and stepped around the south corner of the burning house. Inside, something heavy collapsed. There was movement at the opposite end of the house, and Kurtz turned with the Browning before he saw that it was Angelina, Gonzaga, and Bobby, carrying bags of stuff and heading for the helicopter.

"Kurtz!" called the female don. "Come on. We're *leaving*."

Kurtz nodded and waved. And waited where he was.

It was about three minutes later when the barred doors were flung open and the Major came wheeling his chair out onto the terrace. The old man was in pajamas and a robe, a huge service .45 on his lap, both hands busy pushing the manually powered wheelchair away from the smoking doors and the burning house.

The Major got to the edge of the terrace and stopped, coughing heavily and spitting.

"Freeze," said Kurtz, stepping out onto the terrace, Browning aimed and braced with both hands. He walked toward the wheelchair, taking time to glance into the Major's bedroom. It was roiling with heavy smoke. If anyone was left in there, they were out of the game unless they were wearing a respirator. "Keep your hands on the wheels," Kurtz said, stepping to within six feet of the old man.

The Major turned his head and shoulders, keeping his hands on the metal grab-ring of the chair's wheels as instructed. The military man who'd looked so powerful here on this terrace eleven hours earlier looked old and haggard and worn out now. His white crewcut was sweaty and matted, showing an old man's pink scalp. The pajama tops were open, showing the muscled chest but also gray hairs and old scars. Major O'Toole's eyes looked tired and watery. A line of soot under each nostril showed that even old military men couldn't breathe pure smoke for long.

"Turn around," said Kurtz.

The Major swung the chair around. Both men were obviously aware of the .45 on the old man's lap, but there was no way to get rid of it unless Kurtz allowed the Major to lift his hands or Kurtz stepped closer to grab it. The old cripple couldn't kick it away from him.

Kurtz decided to leave it alone for now.

"Mr. Kurtz," said the Major and then began coughing again. He started to lift a fist to his mouth, saw Kurtz thumb the hammer back on the Browning, and finished the coughing fit with his big hands firmly clamped on the wheels. When he was finished, he raised his soot-streaked face and said, "You win, Mr. Kurtz. What do you want?"

"Did you order Peg O'Toole killed?"

The old gray eyes widened. "Order my niece killed? Are you crazy?"

"Who did?"

"I have no idea. I presume it was one of your Mafia friends."

Kurtz shook his head. "You killed your brother, John. Why not his daughter, too?"

The Major flinched as if Kurtz had slapped him in the face. His powerful arms and huge hands flexed.

"Why'd you kill your brother?" said Kurtz. "He was a cop, but close to retirement. No, wait . . . it was because he found out you were trying to move your heroin ring into Lackawanna and Buffalo, wasn't it?"

The Major snarled—he literally snarled.

"So did you sic your crazy son on Peg O'Toole as well?" pressed Kurtz.

"My son . . ." said the Major. The old man's chiseled face seemed to shift, like some morphing special effect in a movie. The strong bones seemed to sag. "My son is dead. Sean Michael is dead. He died fifteen years ago in a fire."

"Your fucking son, the Artful Dodger, dodged that fire, too, didn't he, Major? Who'd you send to be a corpse in his place? One of your Vietnamese lackeys? No, it'd have to be someone who looked more like a crazy Irish bastard, even after he was burned up, wouldn't it? And then you supplied the dental records, didn't you?"

"My son is *dead*!" snarled the Major. He grabbed for the .45.

Instead of firing, Kurtz lunged closer and kicked the wheelchair, wedging his boot between the old man's withered knees and pushing hard.

The Major let out a cry and dropped the .45, grabbing the steel rims of the wheels with both of his powerful hands, leaning forward to brake the sliding chair just as it slid back to the edge of the rain-slicked terrace. The gun bounced on the flagstones.

"I'll kill you, I'll kill you, I'll kill you," panted the Major. He obviously wanted to grab Kurtz's leg, get both hands on Kurtz's throat, to choke the life out of him. But to do that, the Major would have to release the wheels.

Kurtz hopped on one leg, Browning still aimed, and kicked again, pushing hard with all of his weight. The wheelchair, wheels locked, slid and screeched another yard, until it teetered right on the edge of the near-vertical ziggurat staircase.

"Who shot me?" gasped Kurtz, leaning closer. "Who shot Peg O'Toole? Who did you send?"

"I'll fucking kill you," panted the old man. Sweat flew from his straining forehead and pelted Kurtz's face. The Major's breath smelled of smoke and death. "Fucking kill you. *Kill you*." His upper body strength was tremendous. Kurtz was being pushed back, his right leg folding back as the wheelchair moved forward six inches . . . then another six inches.

"Send your crazy, fucked-up son to do it," panted Kurtz. His right leg was cramping wildly, but his boot remained firmly planted on the chair between the Major's knees.

"Aarrrrgggghhh!" screamed the Major and lifted both of his huge hands to grab Kurtz's throat, to choke the life out of him, to drag him over the edge with him.

Kurtz threw his upper body back, avoiding the lurching hands as he'd avoid a cobra strike, throwing himself almost horizontally backward. He landed heavily on one elbow, the Major's huge hands still grasping air above him. Kurtz gathered his legs like springs and kicked the wheelchair and the Major's withered knees with both boots.

The wheelchair and the flailing old man flew backwards off the terrace and over the cliff.

By the time Kurtz stood and stepped to the edge, the broken chair and flying, screaming figure had already pinwheeled off thirty steps and were picking up speed as they tumbled into darkness.

CHAPTER
FORTY-FIVE

Rigby came to when they were somewhere near Kissing Bridge.

The take-off had been interesting. Coming down from Buffalo, the interior of the Long Ranger had been neat enough, even with all the ordnance. Everyone had been strapped in. Taking off, it was pure confusion—most of the people crouching on the floor, the little Yemeni doctor jumping back and forth as he worked on Rigby King and Colonel Trinh, the interior of the chopper smelling of smoke and sweat and blood and cordite and shit—Kurtz guessed that Campbell had voided his bowels when he died.

"We're too fucking heavy," Baby Doc cried from the pilot's seat. "Throw someone out."

"Campbell goes home with us," yelled Angelina. She was mopping blood off her face with her sleeve, but the sleeve was so bloody that it just moved the gore around in swirls.

"Don't blame me if we end up in the side of some goddamned hill," shouted Baby Doc Skrzypczyk. But the turbines screamed, the rotors blurred, they bounced once on skids, and the overladen chopper lifted off.

No one closed the side door. Kurtz hung on and looked below as they rose, banked left away from the burning house, and flew down the valley toward Neola.

The road below was still filled with vehicles and lights, but except for the two burning vehicles at the top of the hill, the driveway was empty. No one had tried to assault the guardpost from where Baby Doc had fired his first RPG and then rained automatic rifle fire on the fleeing rescuers. Just as they banked and dropped over the edge, the Huey's gas tank exploded behind them, sending a second ball of flame into the air. The whole top of the hill seemed to be on fire.

No one from the valley shot at them. Or at least Kurtz saw no muzzle flashes. Maybe, he thought, they believed the Long Ranger was the Major's private Huey.

When Rigby awoke a few minutes later, they were flying a thousand feet or so over the dark hills, the air rushing in the open rear door. Dr. Tafer had covered her with a blanket, and now Kurtz tucked it in. She was shaking.

"Joe?"

"Yeah." He put a hand on her shoulder.

"I knew you'd come for me."

He had nothing to say to that. "Rigby," he shouted over the wind and turbine roar, "you need some morphine?"

The woman's teeth were chattering, but not from the cold, Kurtz guessed. He suspected that she was on the verge of going into shock because of the pain and blood loss. "Oh, yeah, that'd be good," she said. "They didn't give me anything for the pain all day. Just that goddamned IV. And they couldn't get the bleeding to stop."

"Did they do anything else to you?"

She shook her head. "Just asked stupid questions. About you. About who we were working for. If I'd known the answers, I would've told 'em, Joe. But I didn't know anything, so I couldn't."

He squeezed her shoulder again. Dr. Tafer leaned closer, but Kurtz pushed him back. "Rigby, the doc's going to give you a shot, but you have to listen to me a minute. Can you hear me?"

"Yeah." Her teeth were chattering wildly now.

"You're going to be out of it," said Kurtz. "Probably wake up in the hospital. But it's important you don't tell them who shot you. Don't tell anyone—not even Kemper. Do you understand that?"

She shook her head 'no' but said, "Yeah."

"It's important, Rigby. Don't tell anyone about coming down to Neola, the Major . . . none of that. You don't *remember* what happened. You don't remember where you were or who shot you or why. Tell them that. Can you do that?"

"I don't . . . remember," gasped Rigby, gritting her teeth against the waves of pain.

"Good," said Kurtz. "I'll see you later." He nodded to the doctor, who scooted forward on his knees and gave the woman a shot of morphine.

The helicopter bucked and pitched. "We're too heavy!" called Baby Doc. "The Ranger's supposed to haul no more than seven people. We've got *nine* in here. At least come up front again, Kurtz. Help trim it."

"In a minute," shouted Kurtz. He crawled farther back, to where Gonzaga and Angelina were grilling Colonel Trinh near the open door.

The older Vietnamese man's visibly broken arm was twisted behind him, his wrists still flexcuffed. Gonzaga had also cuffed the man's ankles and he was propped precariously against the frame of the open door. The air roared past at over a hundred and thirty miles an hour.

"Tell us what we want to know," shouted Toma Gonzaga, "or out you go."

Trinh looked out at the darkness rushing by and smiled. "Yes," he said so softly that his voice was barely audible over the noise. "It is very familiar."

"I bet," said Angelina. Her face and hair were a mask of blood. "Why did you kill our junkies and dealers?"

Trinh shrugged and then winced from his arm and wounds. "It was a war."

"It's no goddamned war," shouted Gonzaga. "We didn't even know you existed until today. We never touched you. Why kill our people?"

The old colonel looked Gonzaga in the eye and shook his head.

"What's the connection?" shouted Kurtz. He was on his knees, straddling Campbell's sprawled legs. Blood sloshed back and forth on the plastic that covered the floor as the overladen chopper banked and rose and fell. "Who's been protecting your operation all these years, Trinh? CIA? FBI? Why?"

"There were three of us in Vietnam," said the old man. "We worked together very well. We have worked together very well since."

"Three?" said Gonzaga. He looked at Kurtz.

"The Major for the army," shouted Kurtz over the wind roar. "Trinh for the Vietnamese. And somebody in U.S. intelligence. Probably CIA. Right, Colonel?"

Trinh shrugged again.

"But why cover for you?" shouted Angelina. "Why would some federal agency keep your heroin ring a secret?"

"We brought in much more than heroin," said Trinh. He leaned back against the pitching door frame almost casually, as if he were in his own living room. "Our people in Syria, the Bekkah Valley, Afghanistan, Turkey . . . all very useful."

"To who?" shouted Gonzaga.

"What are you going to do with me?" asked the Colonel. He had to repeat the question because of the noise. His voice was calm.

"We're going to throw you out the goddamned door if you don't answer our questions better," shouted Gonzaga.

"We'll take you to a hospital with Rigby," said Kurtz. "Just tell us who the federal connections were and why they . . ."

"Do you know the irony?" interrupted Colonel Trinh, smiling suddenly. "The irony was that Major O'Toole and I are retired . . . we only came back to New York because of the SEATCO stockholder's meeting and because Michael wanted to see his niece."

The colonel shook his head, still smiling, and then deliberately pitched over to his left.

Gonzaga and Angelina grabbed at the man's legs and boots, but before they could get a grip, he was gone, out the black door, whipped away and down by wind and gravity.

"Oh, fuck," said Angelina Farino Ferrara.

"That's better!" shouted Baby Doc from the front. "Now someone get up here in the co-pilot's seat and help me trim this pig."

CHAPTER

FORTY-SIX

Angelina drove Kurtz and Rigby to the hospital.

They took the extra SUV that Campbell had driven to Gonzaga's compound and tossed his body in the back. Dr. Tafer and Kurtz carried Rigby to it on a litter, sliding her onto the flat floor left after all the seats were folded away. Then Tafer drove off with Baby Doc's men, Gonzaga had driven away with Bobby and his crew, and Baby Doc himself had lifted the Long Ranger off with a roar of turbines amidst a hurricane of litter.

Kurtz had grabbed the keys and gone around to the SUV's driver's door, but Angelina had swung up first. "I'll drive," she said. "You stay in the back with Ms. Cellulite. I'll send somebody for the other vehicle."

He had jumped in the back, propping Rigby's head on his leg. Tafer had put her on a second unit of plasma and she was unconscious from the morphine. The Yemeni doctor had warned that she was in shock and in bad shape from loss of blood.

They were only a couple of miles from the Erie County Medical Center. For once, Kurtz thought, he'd planned ahead.

"We can't carry her in, you know," called Angelina from the front. She was driving carefully, staying under the speed limit and stopping for lights even when the intersection was dark and empty. Kurtz smiled to himself when he thought of what a haul it would be for the policeman who pulled them over for speeding—a wounded cop, a dead thug, a cache of stolen night-vision gear and automatic weapons, with a bloody, female Mafia don driving.

"I know," said Kurtz. "We'll drop her at emergency. I trust this truck isn't registered and the plates are bogus."

"Totally," said Angelina. "This thing will be in a chop shop before sunrise."

They drove in silence for a block or two. It was about two-forty-five in the morning. The time, Kurtz knew from experience, when human beings held their least firm grip on life. Rigby was cold to the touch and she looked dead. Kurtz used three fingers to find the pulse in her neck—it was hard to find.

"Well," said Angelina, "you sure provided Toma and me with a bonding experience, just like you promised."

Kurtz had nothing to say to that. He looked out at the dark buildings going by—they'd just crossed Delavan and were within a couple of blocks of the hospital.

"This third party that Trinh was talking about before he took a header," said Angelina. "Did you ever consider that it might be Baby Doc? That he's been working both sides against the middle?"

"Yeah."

"If it is, we just paid the son of a bitch three quarters of a million dollars to help him take over a drug ring he's been trying to take over for years."

"Yeah," said Kurtz. "But it's not Baby Doc."

"How do you know?"

"I just know," said Kurtz.

They pulled up the emergency room drive. Kurtz kicked the back doors of the SUV open, pulled the IV needle, lifted Rigby out, and laid her on the wet concrete. Angelina laid on the truck's horn. Kurtz was inside and they were driving off at high speed just as the first nurses and orderlies came out the automatic doors.

"Think she'll make it?" asked Angelina. She swung the truck up onto the Kensington Expressway. No one was giving chase.

"How the fuck do I know?"

The bodyguard's body rolled against Kurtz as the SUV took the turn toward downtown. Kurtz crawled up into the passenger seat. "Where does Campbell go? Another chop shop?"

"More or less."

"Then why bring him back?"

"Leave no man behind or somesuch macho shit, right?" Angelina looked at him. "You in love with the cop, Joe?"

Kurtz rubbed his temples. "You going back to the Towers?"

"Where else?"

"Good. My Pinto's there."

"You're not going back to your Harbor Inn dump, are you?"

"Where else?"

"Do you have any idea what's going to happen when they ID your girl-friend back there?"

"Yeah," Kurtz said tiredly. "Buffalo P.D.'s going to go apeshit. And Rigby's partner, a hard-on named Kemper, is going to go more apeshit than the rest. I'm pretty sure Rigby told him that she was going to be with me yesterday, so he'll send black-and-whites out to pick me up as soon as he hears."

"And you're still going back to your place?"

Kurtz shrugged. "I think we've got a few hours. There was no ID on Rigby and she'll either be unconscious for hours or . . ."

"Dead," said Angelina.

". . . or she'll wake but keep her mouth shut for a while."

"But it's a gunshot wound," said Angelina, meaning that the police would be informed straight from the emergency room and that a cop would be sent over to check it out.

"Yeah."

"Come spend the night in the penthouse," said Angelina. "I won't rape you."

"Another time," said Kurtz. He looked at the don's daughter. "Although I have to say, you do look ravishing."

Angelina Farino Ferrara laughed unselfconsciously and pushed her sweaty and gore-matted hair off her bloody forehead.

K urtz knew as soon as he went through the front door of the Harbor Inn that someone had been there—perhaps was still there. He pulled the Browning. Then he went to one knee, laid the ditty bag on the floor, tugged on the night-vision goggles that he'd conveniently forgotten to give back to Baby Doc in the confusion, and clicked on the power. The glasses whined up and the dark foyer-restaurant glowed bright green and white in his vision.

The telltales were in place by the stairs and in the center of the main room, but that meant nothing. Kurtz could sense a movement of air that shouldn't be there—air that smelled of piss.

He searched all the ground floor rooms before going up the stairs with the Browning extended.

He found the taped circle of missing glass in the front window. Someone had destroyed all three of his video monitors, firing a slug into each of the CRTs. In his bedroom, someone had urinated on his mattress and pillows and thrown his clothing around the room. In his reading room, the same someone had used a knife on his repaired Eames chair, slashing the cushions beyond salvage. Most of the books had been thrown off the shelves and the bookcases had been tumbled over. His visitor had defecated on the Persian carpet.

Kurtz didn't have to wonder who it'd been—this wasn't quite the style of the local kids. He searched the rest of the building and discovered his backup pistol missing. The window to the fire escape was still partially open. He pushed it shut and reset the lock.

"Hope you had a good time, Artful Dodger," muttered Kurtz. He found some clean, dark clothes that hadn't been peed on, went in and took a shower—checking carefully for booby traps before turning on the water. He threw the borrowed clothes into a laundry bag along with the stuff his night visitor had urinated on. Then he cleaned up the poop in the library—feeling like one of those idiots whom he saw walking their big dogs in the park along the river, pooper scooper at the ready—dropped the whole mess— filthy clothes, baggy of feces, mattress, bed clothes, pillows, and Eames chair—into the Dumpster below the rear window. Then Kurtz washed his hands again and, fully dressed except for the Mephisto boots he'd decided to keep, curled up on his weight-press bench in the front second-floor room, set his mental alarm clock for seven A.M., and went instantly to sleep.

CHAPTER
FORTY-SEVEN

My Yasein was working for the CIA."

Kurtz was at the breakfast table in Arlene's kitchen. The girl named Aysha was speaking. Arlene had explained in a whisper when she'd come to the door that she told the girl the truth—mostly—explaining to her that her fiancé had been killed in a shootout at the Civic Center, probably while trying to assassinate a parole officer. But Arlene had let Aysha think that it had been Peg O'Toole who had returned fire with deadly effect.

"How do you know he was working for the CIA?" said Kurtz.

"He wrote to me about it. Yasein wrote to me every day."

"While you were in Canada?"

"Yes. I have been in Toronto for more than two months, waiting until Yasein could bring me into the United States of America."

"What did he tell you about working for the CIA?"

The girl sipped her tea. She seemed very calm, her large, brown eyes dry, her voice steady. "What do you want to know, Mr. Kurtz?"

"Did he give you any names? Tell you who approached him about working for the CIA?"

"Yes. His controller was code-named Jericho."

"Did he give Jericho's real name?"

"No. I am sure that Yasein did not know it. He wrote me that everyone in the CIA used code names only. Yasein's code name was 'Sparrow.' "

Kurtz looked at Arlene, who was on her third Marlboro. "How did Jericho first contact Yasein?"

"He came into an . . . how do you say the word? Room in police headquarters where people are questioned?"

"Interrogation room?"

"Yes," said Aysha in her pleasant accent. "Interrogation room. Mr. Jericho came to see Yasein in the interrogation room when Yasein was arrested as an illegal immigrant and possible terrorist." She sipped her tea and looked at Arlene. "My Yasein was not a terrorist, Mrs. DeMarco."

"I know," said Arlene and patted the girl's arm.

Kurtz rubbed his aching head and raised his coffee cup, letting the steam from the coffee touch his face. He'd wakened at five with the mother of all headaches and gotten out of the Harbor Inn before the cops showed up. An anonymous call to Erie Medical Center hadn't even told him if Rigby was alive—they'd asked him repeatedly if he was family and tried to keep him on the line; Kurtz had left the pay phone quickly.

"So Yasein was taken into the Buffalo police headquarters?" asked Kurtz. "Or the federal building?"

"It was, as you say, federal," Aysha said carefully. "He wrote that it was Homeland Security people who detained him."

"FBI?"

The pretty young woman frowned. "I think not. But my Yasein was not proud of being detained, and he did not share all details."

"But this Jericho CIA guy first talked to him while he was in detention either at the Justice Center or FBI headquarters here in Buffalo?"

"I believe, yes. Yasein did write to say that he had been terrified—they arrested him on his way home from work, four men, put a black bag over his head, and drove him to the center where he was interrogated. He wrote that it had smelled like a large building—parking garage in the basement, a . . . what do you call a very quick and direct lift?"

"Express elevator?" said Arlene.

"Yes, thank you. They took an express elevator from basement. My Yasein's hands were handcuffed behind him and he had black bag over his head, but he could hear. And smell. It was a tall building, at least twenty stories tall, with many offices and computers. Several men from Homeland Security questioned him for two days and two nights."

"Was Yasein kept in a holding cell?" asked Kurtz. "With other detainees or prisoners?"

"No. He wrote me that they kept him in a small room with a cot. It had a sink but no toilet. He was very embarrassed that he had to . . . how do you say it? Urinate?"

"Yes," said Arlene.

"That he had to urinate in a sink when they came for him late on the third morning. That is when he met the CIA man. Mr. Jericho."

"But no description of this Jericho?" said Kurtz.

"No." The girl ventured a small smile. "Are CIA spies allowed then to send descriptions of their fellow agents in letters?"

Kurtz had to smile back. "I don't think CIA agents are allowed to write letters to their fiancées about any of this stuff. But who knows?"

"Indeed," said Aysha. "If your CIA is like our State Security Service in Yemen. Who does know?"

Kurtz rubbed his head again. "But it was this Mr. Jericho and the CIA who provided Yasein with the money to bring you in?"

"Yes."

"But you had to wait almost ten weeks in Canada after they flew you from Yemen to Toronto."

"Yes. I wait while Yasein earn the rest of the money to pay men to bring me across the border."

"It if was the CIA, why didn't they just bring you straight into the States?"

"That would be illegal, Yasein tell me in letter."

Kurtz looked at Arlene and resisted the urge to sigh. "But they were training Yasein to kill a parole officer," he said.

"So you tell me. Yasein never wrote about the name or nature of the . . . is 'operation' the right word, Mrs. DeMarco? For secret CIA plan to assassinate someone?"

"Yes," said Arlene.

"My Yasein was no killer, Mr. Kurtz. He was trained as a mechanic. Does that wound hurt you?"

"What?" said Kurtz. He'd been thinking.

"The head wound. It was not stitched correctly and has not healed properly and the bandage is all bad. May I look at it?"

"Aysha was trained as a nurse," said Arlene, rising to get more coffee and tea for them all.

Kurtz shook his head. "No, thanks. It's fine. Did Yasein say anything else about the CIA or about Jericho?"

"Just that two weeks after he agreed to work for them, they brought him to CIA headquarters, where they trained him."

"In Langley, Virginia?" said Kurtz, surprised.

"I do not know. My Yasein said it was on a . . . what do you call a farm for horses? Expensive horses, such as the kind they race in Derby of Kentucky?"

"Thoroughbreds? A sort of ranch?"

"Not ranch," said Aysha, frowning as she hunted for the right word. "Where they do the breeding of expensive horses?"

Kurtz had no idea what she was talking about. He drank more coffee and closed his eyes against the headache.

"Stud farm," said Arlene.

"Yes. They trained my Yasein how to fire guns and do other CIA things at stud farm in the country. Several men, all with code names, taught him over three-day Labor Day weekend. He had to pass test before being allowed to return to Buffalo and go back to work."

"How'd he get to this stud farm?" asked Kurtz. "Did he tell you in his letters?"

"Oh, yes. He said that they flew in a private CIA jet. Yasein was very impressed."

"So am I," said Kurtz.

A ysha had gone to her room while Kurtz and Arlene spoke in the small, neat living room.

"I want you to take the girl and go to Gail's place this afternoon when I leave," Kurtz said.

"Is someone after us, Joe?"

"Maybe."

"Is it the Burned Man?"

"Probably," said Kurtz. "But I have a hunch he won't show up today. But stay at Gail's tomorrow until I call or show up."

Arlene nodded. "What do you think of Aysha's whole CIA story?"

"Well, it's absurd," said Kurtz. "But it fits, in a weird sort of way."

"How so?"

He shook his head. He didn't want to tell Arlene about last night. Not yet. With luck, never. He'd read her copy of the *Buffalo News*, even turned on the local TV news when he'd arrived, but there was no mention of the bloodletting, fire, and mayhem in Neola the night before.

Incredible, he'd thought, *if they can keep that covered up. It must be the CIA or Homeland Security or some serious federal agency involved. Either that or the local authorities kept it all hushed up.*

But why train an illegal Yemeni immigrant, trained as a mechanic, to kill a parole officer? If the feds were covering up for the Major's drug-and-spy operation down there, why draw attention by shooting Peg O'Toole? None of it made any sense.

"None of this makes any sense," said Arlene. She batted ashes into an old beanbag ashtray.

Kurtz just sighed. He expected the front door to be kicked in with a hydraulic ram any moment and for Paul Kemper to lead a SWAT team in.

As if reading his mind again, Arlene said, "Gail will call from the hospital as soon as she hears about Detective King."

Kurtz had told her about Rigby. Arlene's sister-in-law was a pediatric nurse at Erie County, and it was the only way he was going to find out whether Rigby King was dead or alive.

"Were you going to call the ex-director today?" asked Arlene.

"Who?" Kurtz had no idea what she was talking about. His head seemed to be full of bees. *I don't know why. I got a full two hours sleep.*

"The ex-director of the Rochester Psychiatric Hospital," Arlene said patiently. "You asked me to get his home phone, remember? He's living in Ontario on the Lake." She handed him a slip of paper with the number on it.

"All right," said Kurtz. "Can I use your kitchen phone?"

CHAPTER
FORTY-EIGHT

It was cold and windy again when Kurtz headed south out of Buffalo just after dark. Driving through residential neighborhoods near the park from Gail's home, he saw kids in costumes and carrying plastic pumpkins going from door to door.

It's Halloween. As if he had to be reminded. It was raining off and on and the air smelled like the rain wanted to turn to snow. It was almost cold enough.

Kurtz was wearing another dark outfit, black jeans, the Mephistos, and dark sweater, all under his peacoat. He'd tugged a navy watch cap down gingerly over his aching scalp. He'd borrowed Arlene's Buick, leaving her and Aysha the Pinto. But they wouldn't be using it tonight. Gail DeMarco's second-floor apartment on Colvin north of the park was small—one small bedroom for Gail and a tinier one for Rachel, but they didn't seem to mind sharing tonight. Arlene said that she was going to bunk with Gail, Aysha was going to get the fold-out couch, and they were all going to make some popcorn tonight and watch videos of "The Thing from Another World" and "The Day the Earth Stood Still" in honor of Halloween. Rachel would love the company, Gail had said.

Kurtz's mind wanted to linger on Rachel, but he skittered away from that topic, recalling his conversation with Dr. Charles from the psychiatric hospital instead.

"Yes, of course I remember the fire," the old gentleman had said. "A terrible thing. We never did find out how it started. Several people died."

"Including Sean Michael O'Toole?" said Kurtz.

"Yes." A pause. "Did you say you worked for the *Buffalo Evening News*, Mr. Kurtz?"

"No, I'm a freelancer. Doing a magazine article. School shootings are hot these days and Sean Michael O'Toole was an early school-shooter."

"Yes," Dr. Charles said sadly. "Columbine still seems fresh, even after all these years."

"Did you ever hear your patient—Sean—referred to as the Dodger?" asked Kurtz. "Or the Artful Dodger?"

"The Artful Dodger?" said the old man with a chuckle. "As in Dickens? No. I'm sure I would have remembered that."

"You say he had visitors the day of the fire," prompted Kurtz. "In fact, the fire broke out in the visitor's wing while they were there."

"Yes."

"Do you remember who the visitors were?"

"Well, one I certainly remember," said Dr. Charles. "It was Sean Michael's younger brother."

"His younger brother," repeated Kurtz, pausing as if he was writing this down. Arlene's kitchen looked out onto a tiny backyard. *Sean Michael O'Toole had no siblings.* "A year or two younger than Sean?" said Kurtz. "Redheaded?"

"Oh, no," said Dr. Charles. "I met him and his friend when they signed in to see Sean. Michael Junior was much younger than our patient—he was only about twenty. Sean had just turned thirty that week. And Sean's younger brother didn't look at all like Sean—much darker, much more handsome."

"I see," said Kurtz, although he didn't see at all. "And who was the other man visiting?"

"I don't remember. He didn't speak at all during the time I was chatting with Sean's younger brother. He seemed—distracted. Almost drugged."

"Was he, by any chance, about Sean's height and age and weight?" said Kurtz.

The doctor was silent for a moment while he tried to recall. "Yes, I believe he was. It's been fifteen years, you know, and—as I said—the other visitor didn't speak when I was talking to Sean's brother."

"But both the brother and other man got out of the burning building all right?"

"Oh, yes." Dr. Charles sounded distressed by memories of the fire even after all these years. "There was much confusion, of course—fire engines arriving, patients and attendants screaming and running to and fro, but we made sure that all our visitors were safe."

"Did you see Sean's brother—Michael Junior—and this other man after the fire?"

"Very briefly. Sean's brother was fine and the other man was receiving oxygen."

"Did he go to the hospital?" asked Kurtz.

"I don't believe so, no. What are you driving at, Mr. Kurtz?"

"Absolutely nothing, Dr. Charles. Just curious about the details. You say that no visitors were seriously hurt in the fire. Nor attendants. Just the three inmates?"

"We preferred to call them *patients*," Dr. Charles had said coolly.

"Of course. Just the three patients died. Including Sean Michael O'Toole."

"That is correct."

"And did you carry out the identification, Dr. Charles?"

"Of two of them I did, Mr. Kurtz. With Sean Michael, we had to resort to remnants of clothing, a class ring he was wearing, and dental records."

"Provided by his father?" said Kurtz. "By Major O'Toole of Neola?"

"I believe so, yes." The ex-director's friendly voice was no longer friendly. "What are you getting at, Mr. Kurtz? This is no idle curiosity."

"One never knows what one's readers will find interesting, Dr. Charles," Kurtz had said in his most pedantic voice. "Thank you for your help, sir." And he had hung up.

Kurtz drove the Buick east and then south on the four-lane 400, following it into the dark hills when it became Highway 16. The little towns passed one after the other. There was almost no traffic. In the tiny town of Chaffee, Kurtz could see late-night trick-or-treaters going from one large, white house to the other down a treelined street. Dead leaves skittered across the highway. Clouds ran ahead of the wind across a cold, quarter moon. It looked, felt, and *smelled* like Halloween.

Kurtz had watched the evening and late-night local news at Gail's place—he sensed that Gail didn't like him and was nervous when he was around, but he didn't know why—and there had been no mention of the

Neola massacre. There had been a fifteen-second piece about a Buffalo police detective being shot—the officer had been in surgery that day and there were no details or leads at this time. She was expected to recover.

Gail had kept Arlene posted during the day on Rigby's condition—which had been upgraded from critical to serious by the end of the day. The ICU nurses had told Gail only that Detective King had a twenty-four-hour police guard outside the unit and that a black police detective had been there much of the day waiting for the patient to regain consciousness.

Kurtz listened to his favorite Buffalo jazz station until the signal faded as he got into the deeper valleys near Neola. He realized that he was half-dozing at the wheel when he passed under the Interstate and found himself on the four-lane road for the last seven miles into Neola.

The city was asleep, the over-wide Main Street empty and mostly dark. It had rained hard here from the looks of it and the orange-and-black crepe paper decorations on some of the shop fronts were wilted and wind-torn.

Kurtz drove through town slowly, confident that the Neola Sheriff's Department wouldn't be on the lookout for a late-model blue Buick. *Although one person here has seen this car—up at the Rainbow Centre Mall.*

He crossed the bridge over the Allegheny, turned left on the county road, and killed the headlights as soon as he turned off the paved road. Kurtz tugged down the military-spec night vision goggles and powered them up, easily following the gravel road and then dirt ruts up the hill the way he had come before.

Parking at the barricade, he got the gear he needed out of the back seat, tugging some on, then pulling on the peacoat again and filling the pockets with extra clips for the Browning and two flash-bangs, then tossing the empty ditty bag onto the back seat.

He went up the hill, crawled through the same cut in the fence he'd made the day before, but then made a wide loop around the forested hill, planning to come over the top and then down into Cloud Nine. The night vision goggles made the weak moonlight and occasional starlight as bright as daylight.

He was following the rails of the kiddie railroad near the top of the hill, Browning still in its holster, when he heard the noises and saw the moving lights.

Music. Organ-grinder, calliope-type music. Coming from where the midway had once been. And lights moving there. A partially illuminated Ferris wheel turning.

But another light and a louder noise loomed closer, higher up the hill, here where Kurtz lay waiting.

The train was coming.

CHAPTER
FORTY-NINE

The train's single headlight blinded him from fifty yards away as it turned around the curve of the hill and chugged toward him down the gleaming green-white tracks.

Kurtz tugged off his night-vision goggles and let them dangle around his neck as he climbed fifteen yards up the hill and hid in some thick shrubs. He racked a slug into the Browning's chamber and propped his elbow on his knee, holding his aim steady as the train racketed closer. Avoiding looking into the single, bobbing headlight, Kurtz pulled the goggles up and into place.

Then the amusement-park mini-train was chugging past him, filling the air with its two-stroke lawnmower engine chug and exhaust stink. And then it was past, rattling and rocking around the curve of the hill and into the woods to the south.

"Jesus," whispered Kurtz.

There had been no driver; the engine car was empty. But the following three cars, each styled like a passenger or freight car in miniature, but each also open to the air and just big enough for two children to sit in comfort or a single adult in discomfort, butt on a low cushion and knees high, had been carrying passengers. Kurtz had counted eight corpses propped up in the passenger cars—four dead men, two dead women, and two dead children.

"Jesus," Kurtz whispered again. The train was audible on the other side of the hill through the bare trees and rustling leaves now, heading back toward the burned mansion and then around again in its closed loop. There must have been a line switch thrown somewhere to keep the train looping around this hill, its metal throttle lever taped in the open position.

No dead man lever, thought Kurtz and resisted the urge to laugh.

He crossed the tracks and headed downhill toward the lighted midway, pistol at his side, trying not to break branches or step on more leaves than he had to. But any sound that he made was lost under the tinny carnival music that grew louder as he grew nearer. Right now, speakers were blaring with an organ version of "Pop Goes the Weasel."

The sight of the midway when he arrived was too surreal through the night vision goggles, so he took them off again. The images remained surreal in moonlight and midway glow.

Somewhere nearby a generator popped and sputtered. The broken, rusted Ferris wheel moved creakingly, in spurts and fits, but it turned. There were a dozen or so working lights on its frame, where scores had once burned when Cloud Nine was new. But those few were enough to illuminate the half dozen adult corpses riding in the four remaining passenger benches on the creaking wheel. Two had slumped forward against the rusted restraining bars.

The merry-go-round was turning ponderously. The music came from there, from a boom box set up in the center of the creaking, groaning circle. The broken horses and shattered zebras and headless lions were not going up and down, but five of them had riders—a dead woman with a bullet hole in her blue forehead slumped forward against the vertical pole rising out of the golden palomino; a male corpse with three black holes in his Eddie Izzard t-shirt lay sprawled stiffly across the lion with the missing lower jaw; a little girl no older than five, part of her skull missing between braids, slumped against a giraffe's long, splintered neck.

The merry-go-round turned round and round to the music in the rustling woods.

Kurtz tried to move from shadow to shadow, his finger clammy against the trigger. He could smell popcorn. Popcorn and something sticky-smelling—either fresh blood or cotton candy. The lawnmower exhaust stink of the train wafted down as the locomotive rumbled by just up the hill again.

The bumper car pavilion was still shattered and flooded, dead leaves blowing across the rubber-streaked floor, but a single floodlight illuminated the pavilion, showing where a man and a woman—long dead from the looks of the sunken eyes and gums pulled back from the teeth—sat in one of the upright cars. The male corpse had his arm around the female corpse and the brittle bone-fingers seemed to be pawing at her shrunken breast under the tattered rags of what had been a pink sweater.

"Holy Christ," Kurtz whispered to himself, mouthing the words but making no noise. He raised the Browning in both hands and proceeded stealthily uphill, past the patch of grass where he had almost made love to Rigby King less than thirty-six hours earlier, past the fallen plywood front facade of the funhouse where a faded clown's face looked up from the grass, past the funhouse ticket booth where a male corpse had been propped up behind the wiremesh of the ticket cage. This corpse had had a clown's face painted on it and was wearing a red rubber nose. Its white shirt had a row of bloody holes across the chest.

Kurtz approached the shack he and Rigby had peered into. This new building was the epicenter of the night's madness. The big gasoline generator was running just beyond the shack, somehow powering the various lights and motors turning the Ferris wheel and merry-go-round.

Kurtz moved from tree to tree approaching the shack, his gun extended. He tried to breathe shallowly through his mouth, tried to listen. The porch of the little shack creaked slightly as he stepped onto it. He moved to one side of the doorway and peered in. There was a lantern glowing in there and a figure lying on the cot in the corner. Kurtz pulled the goggles down out of the way, the better to use his peripheral vision. His mouth was dry.

The wind came up then, blowing leaves across the moldy midway, rattling branches in the bare trees. Because of that noise—as well as the repetitive, tinny carousel music from the boom box, as well as the creaking and groaning of the Ferris wheel and the putt-putt of the train making yet another round uphill—Kurtz didn't hear or see the dead clown in the ticket booth sit up, turn its white face, and step outside.

Because of the glow of the lantern light inside the shack and because of his own rapt attention on the corpse under the blanket, because he was watching and waiting for anything to move in or around the shack, Kurtz didn't see or hear the clown with the bloody white shirt step lightly and carefully around the edge of the funhouse twenty-five paces behind him.

Kurtz's instincts had served him well through almost twelve years in Attica's prison yards and showers and halls, but they failed him now in this strange place as the clown raised its silenced 9mm Beretta and fired three times from less than fifteen yards away, all three slugs striking Kurtz high up in the back, two between his shoulder blades and the third just beside his neck.

Kurtz pitched face forward into the shack, landing hard and lifelessly on his face, the dropped Browning bouncing away across the plywood floor.

The dead clown that was the Dodger approached cautiously, Beretta raised and unwavering. He never blinked, but he was grinning so widely that his great, horse's teeth glowed yellow against the flat, white makeup of his face.

He stepped up onto the small porch and paused at the doorway, Beretta aimed at the back of Kurtz's head.

Kurtz had fallen with one arm flung out and one pinned under his body. The detective's pistol was six feet away on the floor. Three holes in the back of the peacoat showed where all three bullets had struck and a small pool of blood was beginning to pool near the fallen man's face.

The Dodger lowered his gun and laughed. "I've saved the last car of the Ferris wheel for you, Kurtz, you . . ."

Kurtz rolled onto his back and fired the big, yellow nail gun with a pneumatic *whoomp*. The nail drove into the Dodger's belly and knocked him back into the doorframe, but the Beretta still came up.

Dazed, working more from instinct than cognition, still holding the heavy cordless nail gun he'd fallen on, Kurtz lurched up and crashed into the Dodger, shoulder-slamming him against the doorframe again and then pushing him out across the porch. Kurtz used his free left hand to grab the Dodger's right wrist as the two plunged off the porch and rolled across the grass and down the hill, through the leaves, onto the scattered plywood of the fallen funhouse facade.

"Goddamn you, goddamn you," grunted the Dodger, flailing and biting at Kurtz's right wrist even as he tried to wrench his own gun hand free.

Kurtz hit the clown face with the wide barrel of the heavy nail gun. White makeup turned to a bloody streak and the rubber nose flew off. The Beretta fired twice, the second slug burning past Kurtz's left ear and ripping through the collar of his peacoat.

The Dodger was very strong, but Kurtz was heavier and came out on top as they rolled onto the fallen plywood clown face. He smashed the screaming man's face with the heavy butt-magazine of the industrial nail gun and tried to knock the Beretta free again. Even with a four-inch galvanized nail in his belly, the Dodger wouldn't let go of the gun. He flailed his left hand free and grabbed his own wrist, trying to force the muzzle of the Beretta upward toward Kurtz's face.

On his knees now, straddling the bloody-shirted figure, Kurtz drove the big yellow nail gun down against the Dodger's right wrist and fired again. Twice.

The nails slammed through the burned man's wrist between the radius and ulna, pinning it to plywood. The Dodger screamed at the top of his lungs.

Kurtz stood and kicked the Beretta and silencer into the woods.

The Dodger kicked and writhed and flopped on the wooden clown-face board. Kurtz pinned down the flailing left arm with his boot, aimed, and fired a nail through the man's left hand.

The Dodger ripped his palm free with a scream and a gout of blood that splattered Kurtz's black vest.

Kurtz stepped on his hand again and fired the nail gun three more times, two of the nails hammering home through the palm and wrist.

Panting, weaving back and forth, only half conscious himself because of the terrible impact through his Kevlar armor, Kurtz stood astride the frenzied figure. "Lie still, goddamn you," he gasped.

The Dodger kicked upward, kneeing at Kurtz's legs, boots clattering on the rotted wood.

Kurtz shook his head, laid the wide muzzle of the yellow nail gun against the Dodger's crotch, and said, "Lie *still*, you crazy fuck."

The Dodger laughed and screamed and writhed, trying to rip his wrists and palm free.

Kurtz fired twice through the twisting man's testicles, nailing his center deep to the wood.

Now the Dodger lay still, his clown mouth open wide, red lips gaping, teeth very yellow and eyes very white as he stared up at Kurtz. Much of the white paint had come off, showing the old burns that covered Sean Michael O'Toole's ravaged face and ran up into the hairline like cords of white rope.

"I want. . . . to know . . ." panted Kurtz. "Did you . . . shoot . . . Peg O'Toole? Were you part of that?"

The Dodger's mouth stayed open and silent as he strained up against the nails. It seemed like he was trying to breathe.

"Who do you take your orders from?" said Kurtz. "I know it wasn't the Major."

The Dodger's clown mouth opened and closed like a fish's. He was trying to speak.

Kurtz leaned over, listening.

"I . . . learned . . . something," gasped the Dodger, voice almost inaudible, tone almost conversational. The merry-go-round music switched from "Farmer in the Dell" to "Three Blind Mice."

Kurtz leaned and listened. Blood and sweat from his chin and torn neck dripped onto the white face.

"Always . . . go . . . for . . . the . . . head . . . shot," said the Dodger and started laughing and screaming. The noise came up out of the open, straining mouth like a black stink from hell. And it kept coming. The Dodger was laughing hysterically, his screams and laughs echoing back from the hillside and funhouse.

Kurtz was suddenly very, very tired.

"Yeah," he said softly. "You're right." He leaned forward again, into the geyser of screams and laughter and stench, lifted the heavy nail gun, aimed the muzzle into that dark, braying maw, and fired three times.

CHAPTER
FIFTY

When Kurtz knocked softly on Gail DeMarco's outside door a little after three A.M., he expected the wait and then the slowly opening door, Gail's concerned face over the security chain, but the .44 Magnum aimed at his face was a surprise.

"Joe!" said Arlene and lowered the gun. She and Gail opened the door and Kurtz staggered inside. He tried to remove his shredded peacoat, but it took the women's help to get it off.

"Oh, Joe," said Arlene.

"I couldn't get the damned vest off," said Kurtz, sagging against the counter.

Arlene and Gail undid the straps and Velcro connections. The thick SWAT vest that had saved his life fell heavily to the tile floor.

"Come near the sink light," said Gail. "Lift your head."

Kurtz did the best he could. The girl, Aysha, came into the kitchen. She was wearing one of Arlene's old bathrobes. It was much too large for her and made her look even more like a child.

"Please stand to one side," said Aysha. It was a nurse's tone of command.

"I'll get a first aid kit," said Gail. She hurried out of the kitchen and Kurtz could hear her telling Rachel to go back to bed and to keep the door to her room closed.

"I think I'd better sit down," said Kurtz. He collapsed into one of the chairs at the Formica table.

The next few minutes were a blur—Gail and Aysha both doing nurse things to him, swabbing the cut on his upper shoulder and neck, cutting off his sweater. *I'm going through sweaters like Kleenex*, he thought dully as they poked and prodded him.

The ride back from Neola had seemed longer than usual. Three times he'd had to pull over to the side of the road to throw up. His back had hurt so much that he couldn't put his weight back against the plush seat of the Buick, so he'd driven like an old man, hunched forward over the wheel. His throat and shoulder had kept dripping blood, but never so violently that he was worried.

"The bullet must have hit the upper edge of your vest and careened upward, nicking your neck and catching the skin of your cheek," said Gail. "Another millimeter to the right and it would have taken out your jugular. You would have bled out in seconds."

"Huh," said Kurtz. He kept hearing the goddamned carnival music echoing in his skull. That and the chug-chug of the train. And the laughter. He'd shut off the generator near the shack, which had stopped the Ferris wheel and merry-go-round and shut off the lights. But he hadn't had the energy to climb the hill, jump aboard the train, and untape the throttle lever.

Leave that to the Neola cleanup crew, he thought. *They'll be busy the next few days.*

"Joe, did you hear me?" said Arlene.

"What?"

"We need to get you in the shower to get the caked blood off so we can see the bruises and cuts better."

"All right."

The next few minutes were as surreal as the rest of his week—three women pushing him, undressing him, half holding him up, turning him as he stood naked in the shower spray. And this Aysha was pretty cute. *No erections allowed*, thought Kurtz. *Not now.* Everyone was in the little bathroom except Rachel.

There was no fear of an erection when the hot shower spray hit the bruises on his back.

"Oh," said Kurtz, coming fully awake. "Ouch."

He caught sight of his back in the steamy mirror—a solid line of bruises connecting both shoulder blades and a bloody slash up near his collarbone. *New scar.*

"We need to sew this shoulder up," said Gail DeMarco. "Actually, we should drive you to the hospital."

"No hospital," he said firmly, but he thought, *I don't know why not. Everyone I know is in the hospital.*

They had him sit on the closed toilet while Aysha sewed him up. There'd been a quick consultation, and evidently they decided she had the most experience. Kurtz felt the needle slide in and out, but it was no big deal. He looked at the fuzzy pink toilet cover and tried to concentrate.

"Did the police call tonight?" he asked. "Kemper?"

"No," said Arlene. "Not yet."

"They will. They'll hunt for me, then for you . . . then somebody'll find out that Gail's your sister and call here."

"Not tonight," said Gail as Aysha finished the sewing. The two nurses applied a bandage and taped it in place.

"No," agreed Kurtz. "Not tonight." He realized that he was still naked. The fuzzy toilet cover felt soft under his butt.

Gail came in with a pair of men's pajamas, still in a wrapper. "These should fit," she said. "It was a Christmas present I never got to give Alan, and he was about your size."

The three women wandered off to the living room while Kurtz struggled into the pajamas. He knew he had more he had to do tonight, but he couldn't quite remember what it was. Every time he closed his eyes, he saw the Dodger's face and open mouth. The trick, he discovered, was to button the pajamas without letting the cotton touch his back or neck. He couldn't quite master it.

He felt better by the time he joined the three in the little living room. Aysha gestured toward the opened sleeper sofa and its tangle of pillows and blankets. "You sleep here, Mr. Kurtz. I sleep with your daughter."

Kurtz could only stare at the woman.

"Gail leaves around seven-thirty," said Arlene. "What time do you want to get going, Joe?"

Kurtz looked at his watch. He couldn't quite focus on the dial.

"Seven?" he said. That would give him a full three and a half hours.

"Go to sleep, Joe," said Arlene, leading him to the opened bed.

For the second time that night, Kurtz fell face forward. This time he did not rise.

Kurtz drove the Pinto behind Gail DeMarco's little Toyota in the morning and, thanks to her intercession, was in the ICU when Rigby King woke up.

"Joe. What's up?"

"Not much," said Kurtz. "What's new with you?"

"Can't think of anything," said Rigby. "Except I *love* this Darvocet morphiney stuff they put in the IV drip. And I don't think that I can pretend to be asleep much longer today—Paul Kemper won't buy it. And he wants your ass."

"Why?" said Kurtz. "Didn't you tell them you couldn't remember who shot you?"

"Yeah," sighed Rigby. "But the problem with saying that you don't remember who did something is that you can't say that you *do* remember who *didn't* do something. If you follow my drift."

"More or less," said Kurtz. He had to sit forward on the upright hospital chair next to her bed, making sure the back of it didn't touch his back. He'd slept on his stomach during the time he did sleep. "Feeling the drugs, Rig?"

"Yeah. Li'l bit. I'm going to doze for just a few minutes if you don't mind. You going to be here when I wake up, Joe?"

"Yeah."

Her eyes fluttered and then opened. "The doctor told me that another hour, they would've had to amp . . . ampa . . . cut off my leg."

"It's okay," said Kurtz, touching her arm. "We'll talk when you wake up."

With her eyes closed, Rigby said, "You don't know who shot me yet, Joe?"

"Not yet."

" 'Kay. Tell me when you do." She started snoring softly.

The blue steel muzzle touched the back of Kurtz's scarred neck. He jerked awake. He'd fallen asleep in the chair, still leaning forward so his back didn't touch.

"Don't move a muscle," said Paul Kemper. "Put your hands behind your head. Slowly."

Kurtz did so slowly because it hurt too much to do it quickly.

"Stand up."

Kurtz did that slowly as well. Kemper patted him down expertly, not noticing when Kurtz drew in his breath sharply when his back and shoulders were touched. He wasn't armed.

Kurtz had run out of luck this morning as far as his streak of being around women who happened to have fresh clothes ready for him; he couldn't wear the sweater and peacoat, but none of the ladies had happened to stock a supply of shirts. In the end, he'd pulled on an oversized sweatshirt of Gail's that said HAMILTON COLLEGE on the front. Since he didn't think it would be a good idea to wear the peacoat with three bullet holes in it, Kurtz had just gone without a jacket this brisk but sunny first-of-November morning. He'd left the Browning with Arlene at Gail's apartment. When Arlene had said, "Can I go home yet, Joe?" he'd answered, "Not yet."

"Sit down," said Kemper. "Keep your hands clasped behind the chair."

Kurtz did as he was told. Kemper walked over to the hospital table by Rigby's bed and set a steaming, Styrofoam cup of coffee on it. He held his Glock on Kurtz as he opened the coffee one-handed and took a careful sip from it.

"You didn't cuff me," said Kurtz. "You haven't read me my rights. You're not arresting me. Yet."

"Shut the fuck up," said Kemper. He lowered the Glock when the nurse bustled in and changed one of Rigby's IV bags, but he kept it in his hand when she left.

They sat there for a while. Kurtz wished he had some coffee.

"I know you're involved in this, Kurtz. I just haven't figured out how."

"I'm just visiting a sick friend, Detective."

"My ass," said Kemper. "Where did you and Detective King go Sunday? She says she can't remember."

"We just took a ride in the country. Talked over old times."

"Uh huh," said Kemper. The black cop looked as if he was trying to decide whether to pistol-whip Kurtz or not. "Where'd you go?"

"Just out in the country," said Kurtz. "Just riding and talking. You know how it is."

"When'd you get back?"

Kurtz shrugged and barely succeeded in not wincing. His shoulders didn't like this posture with his hands clasped behind his back. "Late morning," he said. "I don't know."

"Where'd you drop her off?"

"At her townhouse."

"You want to make this easy, Kurtz? And come down to the station to make a statement?"

"I don't have any statement to make," said Kurtz. He met the cop's glare watt for watt.

"Paul," said Rigby. It was a very weak syllable. She'd just opened one eye.

Kemper slid his Glock back into its holster. "Yeah, babe."

"Leave Joe alone. He didn't do anything."

"You sure of that, Rig?"

"He didn't do anything." She closed her eye. "Paul, can you get the nurse. My leg really hurts."

"Yeah, babe," said Kemper. He motioned Kurtz out of the room ahead of him.

Outside the glass wall, Kemper told the nurse on duty at the central station that Detective King needed her eight A.M. pain medication. The nurse said she'd get to it soon. Kemper grabbed Kurtz by the shoulder and pulled him into the short hallway to the lavatories. "I'm going to find out what happened Sunday, Kurtz. You can count on it."

"Good," said Kurtz. "Let me know when you do."

"Oh, yeah," said Kemper. "You can count on that, too."

Kurtz let him have the last word. He turned and walked slowly and stiffly to the elevator.

The goddamned Pinto wouldn't start. Kurtz tried four times—didn't get as much as a click—and then got out of the car and flipped the hood up. It was a simple little engine and a simple little battery, but after checking the leads to the battery and trying the starter again to no avail, Kurtz had used up his complete stock of automotive know-how.

He looked around. The Medical Center parking lot was busy this time of the morning, but no one was paying attention to his little problem. Kurtz fumbled in his pocket for his cell phone, but remembered that he'd left it at Gail DeMarco's place.

"Need some help?"

Kurtz turned and blinked. A huge, orange, and strangely familiar SUV had stopped. Kurtz didn't recognize the driver or the man in the front passenger seat, nor the one in the far rear seat, but the smiling man leaning out the near window was familiar enough. Brian Kennedy. Peg O'Toole's handsome fiancé. The security service man got out of the . . . what had he called the armored SUV? Lalapalooza? *Laforza* . . . and so did the well-dressed young man in the back with him. Kurtz looked at the two fine suits and realized that he'd have to sell his grandmother to the Arabs to afford clothes like that . . . and he didn't even have a grandmother.

"Get in," said Brian Kennedy. "Turn it over again, old sport. Tom here will fiddle with it."

Tom fiddled, obviously trying to keep his white, starched cuffs from getting greasy. Kurtz turned the key. Nothing happened. Both Kennedy and Tom fiddled some more. People walked by briskly, hardly glancing at the men in the three thousand dollars suits fiddling with a clapped-out Pinto.

"There," said Kennedy, brushing off his hands the way manly men did after fixing something.

Kurtz tried again. It didn't even click.

He got out of the car. "To hell with it. I'll go in the hospital and call someone to come get me."

"Can we give you a lift, Mr. Kurtz?" said Brian Kennedy.

"No, that's okay. I'll call."

"At least use my phone to call, old sport," said Kennedy, handing Kurtz a phone so modern that it looked like it could beam a person up to the Enterprise if you wanted it to. "I came to see Peg. Is that why you're here?"

"No," said Kurtz. He flipped the phone open and tried to decide who to call. Arlene, he guessed. He always called Arlene.

"Oh," said Brian Kennedy. "Tom here has a tool that might help."

Kurtz looked at Tom just as the big man smiled, pulled something metallic from his suit pocket, and stuck the ten thousand-volt taser against Kurtz's chest and pressed the button.

Kurtz's last sight was Kennedy catching his expensive cell phone as Kurtz fell backwards into blackness.

CHAPTER

FIFTY-ONE

Kurtz became aware of two things as he regained consciousness in the moving war wagon of an SUV. The first was the residual chest pain and over-all reaction to the taser blast—his entire body was twitching and tingling, hurting the way a leg or foot hurts after it falls asleep and has to come back to circulatory life. The second thing he noticed was that his headache was gone. Completely gone. For the first time since he'd been shot almost a week earlier.

I should call Dr. Singh at the hospital and tell him about this new therapy for concussion.

"Ah, Mr. Kurtz, I see you're joining us," said Brian Kennedy. "A brief nap for you, old sport, but a restful one, I trust."

Kurtz opened his eyes. He was in the back seat of the Laforza, wedged between Kennedy and the bodyguard who'd tasered him. His hands were handcuffed behind him—real, honest-to-God metal handcuffs this time—and the bodyguard had a semiautomatic pistol wedged in Kurtz's left ribs. One glance told him that they were on the Skyway, Highway 5, headed south past the Tifft Farm Preserve.

"Pierce Brosnan," managed Kurtz.

"I beg your pardon?"

"You look like that James Bond actor—Brosnan," said Kurtz. "I haven't been able to think of his name until now." The headache was *gone*.

Brian Kennedy showed his wry, curled little smile. "I hear that a lot."

"And you said you were Sean Michael O'Toole's younger brother, too," said Kurtz. "You were only, what? Twenty years old when you sprung him?"

"Just turned twenty-one, actually," said Kennedy with that artificial British accent of his.

"And who did you douse with gasoline and leave behind?"

"No one of any importance, old sport," said Kennedy. "Why don't you rest, Mr. Kurtz? We'll be at our destination in a few minutes. You can chat then if you like."

They exited the Skyway at Ridge Road and took it into downtown Lackawanna. *If Kennedy's working with Baby Doc, I could be in a spot of trouble,* thought Kurtz.

They continued east on Franklin Street past Curly's Restaurant, past the little downtown, and parked in an empty lot behind Our Lady of Victory Basilica, just across the street from Father Baker's former orphanage.

"What do you . . ." began Kurtz.

"Hush," said Kennedy. "We'll chat in a minute. Right now, Edward is going to drape my trench coat over your shoulders and the four of us are going to get out and walk into the basilica together. If you make an untoward move or speak a single word, Edward will put a bullet in your heart right here, on the sidewalk, and you'll miss out on the last five to ten precious minutes of your life. Walk normally and keep silent. Is that understood?"

Kurtz nodded.

They got out of the SUV and walked the fifty paces or so along the main avenue here, up the west side of the huge church. Kurtz remembered the hundreds of times his class from Father Baker's had walked from the orphanage school behind them to the basilica for eleven A.M. mass.

The man who'd been driving opened a side door. They came into the basilica under the west staircase where Kurtz and Rigby had climbed to the choir loft that night so many years ago. The small supply room under the staircase where they'd exited the catacombs that night was now chained and padlocked.

Brian Kennedy removed a key from his trouser pocket and unlocked the padlock. "You stay here," he whispered to the driver, who nodded. Someone was practicing the organ in the nave of the basilica.

The supply room's shelves were empty. It looked as if no one used this small space any longer. The stairway to the underground tunnels was behind some white paneling—Kennedy knew exactly where to press to let the wall open—and the old door here was also padlocked. Kennedy used a second key to open this padlock. The other bodyguard turned on a bare light and led the way down the spiral metal stairs. The man named Edward prodded Kurtz in the ribs with the pistol and followed him closely as they descended. Brian Kennedy came last.

There was a final door and a final padlock in the dank space at the bottom of the stairs. Kennedy had a key for this lock as well. All three of them went through into the musty, damp darkness beyond. The bodyguard pulled the heavy door shut behind them.

Kennedy and the first bodyguard pulled out small but powerful halogen flashlights. Concrete steps led several directions down into old tunnels and conduits.

"No one knows why Father Baker put these catacombs under his basilica, old sport," Brian Kennedy said in a conversational tone, words echoing back from the concrete walls and into the darkness. "Rumor was at the time that he wanted some secret passages between what was then the convent and his offices in the orphanage. I, of course, don't believe such scurrilous gossip." He nodded at the bodyguard with the flashlight and they took the left corridor into the darkness.

Kurtz tried to remember the way he and Rigby had come when they were kids. He couldn't.

"You may speak now, Mr. Kurtz," said Kennedy. "I guarantee no one will hear us. No one above could hear even a gunshot from these old tunnels."

"What next?" said Kurtz. There was a half-inch or so of water in this tunnel and the flashlight beams skittered crazily off it. Something scurried and squeaked ahead of the light.

"Oh, I think you know what comes next."

"Why here?"

Kennedy smiled. The smile looked more like a demonic grimace in the harsh glare of the reflected flashlight beam. "Shall we say sentiment? Or it will be perceived that way when they find Detective King's body in the ICU along with your farewell note. I rather enjoyed the discussion you and the detective had about your days at Father Baker's. Very erotic."

"You had the Pinto bugged," said Kurtz.

"Of course."

"And my office, too?" His heart was pounding.

"Ah, well, not quite, old sport," said Brian Kennedy. They came to some steps, went down them, and paused where the wide tunnel branched into two smaller ones. Kennedy pulled a streamlined Palm-type PDA from his suitcoat pocket, activated it, studied a map of blue and red lines, and gestured to the left. The bodyguard went that way and the three others followed.

"Not quite," continued Kennedy. "We knew that if the Gonzagas and your friend Ms. Ferrara joined you there, that they would sweep it for bugs. So we used a dish from a rooftop across Chippewa, bouncing microwaves off your office window, to pick up bits and pieces of conversation. We came late to your war planning session, I'm afraid, but we heard enough."

They came to another junction where steps went up to a small tunnel and down to a broader one. Kennedy studied his glowing PDA. "Down," he said.

Small things squealed and scurried ahead and behind them in the darkness. Their footsteps did not echo because of the water underfoot.

"Rats, don't you know," said Kennedy. "I'm afraid the old catacombs aren't up to the high standards of your youth, old sport. After Father Baker died, those in charge bricked up all entrances and exits in the girls' building, the school, and the main orphanage. I'm afraid that the way we came in is the only access and egress these days—just in case you're considering running."

"I'm not," said Kurtz.

They came into a wider area of the tunnel. "This should do nicely," said Kennedy. The bodyguard turned his flashlight back and pulled a pistol from his pocket. Edward stepped away a safe distance and leveled his Glock at Kurtz's chest.

Kennedy pulled his trenchcoat from Kurtz's shoulders and stepped back, draping it over his own shoulders. "It's very chilly down here," he said.

"Will you tell me why?" said Kurtz. He'd been fiddling with the handcuffs, but they were expensive and well made and very tight.

"Why what, old sport?"

"Why everything? Why save the Dodger from the asylum and sic him on the Gonzagas and Farinos so many years later? Why use me as an instrument to kill your friends the Major and Colonel Trinh? Why everything?"

Kennedy shook his head. "I'm afraid we don't have time. We have a busy day ahead of us. I have to visit your secretary at her sister-in-law's, and say hello to the girl—Aysha—as well. Edward and Theodore have to stop by the hospital to say hello to Detective King. Busy, busy, busy."

"At least tell me about Yasein Goba before you go," said Kurtz.

Kennedy shrugged. "What's to tell? He was very cooperative, but—as it turned out—a lousy shot. I had to finish the work there in the parking garage. I hated that wig I wore—I never looked good in long hair."

"The police records show you in the air in your private jet at the time O'Toole and I were shot," said Kurtz. "O'Toole's e-mail records show you responding to her e-mail just forty-five minutes before . . ." He stopped.

Kennedy smiled. "It's a poor corporation that doesn't own or lease more than one executive jet these days."

"You flew in on a second one, earlier," said Kurtz. "You even received and answered O'Toole's e-mail from the other Lear."

"Gulfstream V, actually," said Brian Kennedy. "But, yes. It's amazing how few formalities one has to go through at the private executive terminal out at Buffalo International."

"You shot us and drove out there to sign in as if you'd just arrived. Where did your real jet—Gulfstream—land?"

Kennedy shook his head. "Can it possibly matter now, Mr. Kurtz? You're simply stalling for time."

Kurtz shrugged. "Sure. Just one last question then."

"We searched you for a wire when you were unconscious, Mr. Kurtz. We know you're not broadcasting or recording. You're simply wasting your time and ours right now."

"The stud farm," said Kurtz. "Is that yours?"

"Bequeathed from my father," Brian Kennedy said softly. Rats scurried just around the bend in the tunnel. "In Virginia, actually."

"Poor Yasein Goba thought he was in the hands of Homeland Security and then the CIA, but it was just your Empire State Security and Executive Protection building in downtown Buffalo and then the farm, wasn't it?"

Kennedy said nothing. He was obviously tired of the conversation.

"You never worked for the CIA," said Kurtz. "But your old man did, didn't he? He was the third part of the triad back in Vietnam—with the Major and Trinh. They kept the drugs moving after the war ended."

"Of *course*," said Kennedy. "Are you just now figuring these things out, Mr. Kurtz? I must say, you're a very poor detective. But you're wrong—I did work for the CIA. For just under a year. It was incredibly boring, so I took my inheritance and started the security agency. Much more interesting. And lucrative."

"And you continued to shake down the Major and SEATCO after your old man died," said Kurtz. "Did they think you were still CIA? Still providing protection the way your daddy had in the 'seventies and 'eighties? And now you want it all? Is that it?"

"I'm afraid you've committed the cardinal sin, Mr. Kurtz. You've bored me." Kennedy took three steps back to the edge of the circle of light. "Edward. Theodore."

The two bodyguards made sure their field of fire was safe and raised their pistols, aiming at Kurtz's chest and head, bracing their weapons with both hands as if they could miss from eight feet away.

"You look like James Bond," Kurtz said to Kennedy, feeling his heart pounding wildly. "But you're making Dr. No's mistake."

Kennedy was no longer listening. "Time to feed the rats, old sport."

The tunnel echoed to the blast of six loud shots.

CHAPTER
FIFTY-TWO

Both flashlights dropped and rolled in the shallow water; both ended up with their beams shining opposite directions. The dank air smelled of cordite. Two of the bodies lay still, polished shoes pointing upward. The third body did not move but a strange, terrible whistling came from it.

Kurtz did not move.

The man came silently out of the darkness. He was a tall man, very thin, dressed in a wool suit and a tan raincoat that looked too short and slightly dated. He wore a small Bavarian-style hat with a small red feather in its band. The man had a narrow, strangely kind-looking face, framed by thick, black-rimmed glasses, and had a thin ginger mustache and a slightly prominent lower lip. His eyes looked sad but very alert. He was carrying an unsilenced Llama semiautomatic pistol.

He walked to the first bodyguard, Theodore, stared down at him a few seconds, and then checked the second one, Edward. Both were dead. The man picked up one of the flashlights.

"Three," Kurtz said shakily, mostly to see if he could still speak. "I'll be paying this off in installments for twenty years."

"Not three," said the Dane, turning the flashlight and pistol in Kurtz's direction. "Four."

Kurtz's head jerked up. He braced his feet. "All right," he said. "Four."

The Dane shook his head. "Oh, no, my no. I don't mean you, Mr. Kurtz. I'm speaking of the man Kennedy left at the first door."

Kurtz felt a sensation that would be hard to describe to someone who hadn't experienced it. Mostly it had to do with the bowels.

The Dane knelt by the first bodyguard, retrieved a small key from the man's coat pocket, and unlocked Kurtz's handcuffs. Kurtz let them drop in the water.

"I didn't hear anything behind us," said Kurtz, rubbing his wrists. "I was beginning to worry a little."

"It is best not to be heard," the Dane said in his very slight Northern European accent. He took some keys from Brian Kennedy's trouser pocket. The fallen man stirred very slightly.

Kurtz went to one knee next to Kennedy. The man's carefully blow-dried hair was tousled and soaked. His eyes were open and his mouth was moving. It was the two bullet wounds in his chest that were causing the whistling noise. The two bodyguards had been shot in the heart, but the Dane had placed one bullet in each of Kennedy's lungs.

"That's called a sucking chest wound," Kurtz said softly. "*Old sport.*"

Kurtz pulled the glowing Palm device from Kennedy's pocket and held it up. "Do we need this to find our way back?" he asked the Dane.

The man in the short raincoat shook his head.

Kurtz set the PDA on Kennedy's bloody chest. No air seemed to be coming from the handsome man's straining mouth, just from the two ragged holes in his chest. "Here you go," said Kurtz. "In case you're considering crawling, use this as your guide on the way back. But try to crawl fast—rats, don't you know."

Kurtz grabbed the second flashlight and he and the Dane began walking back through the catacombs.

"I didn't know if you'd get my message," said Kurtz when they'd taken the first turn and left the bodies behind.

The Dane made a motion with his shoulders. He'd tucked the pistol away under his raincoat. "My other work was done. I had the day off."

"Will I hear about your . . . other work?"

"Quite possibly," said the Dane. "At any rate, today's work will cost you and Countess Ferrara nothing. It is . . . what is the legal phrase . . . *pro bono.*"

"Countess Ferrara?" said Kurtz. They moved into the taller tunnel with the Dane a step ahead.

"You didn't know that the lovely, former Angelina Farino is married to one of the most famous thieves in Europe and a member of royalty?" said the Dane. "I accepted her request in order to honor the Count. He is not a man one wishes to insult."

"I thought the old Count was dead," said Kurtz.

The Dane smiled his wry smile. "Many people have thought that over the decades. I always work on the premise that it is safer to assume otherwise."

"So she's not a widow?" murmured Kurtz. "Well, dress me up and call me Sally."

They arrived at the last junction and the Dane paused a minute to catch his breath. Kurtz guessed that the man was in his late fifties or early sixties. "You interest me, Mr. Kurtz."

"Oh?"

"This is twice our paths have crossed. That is an unusual circumstance for me."

Kurtz had nothing to say to that.

"Are you old enough to remember the old American television commercials for Timex watches, Mr. Kurtz? Done by the newscaster John Cameron Swayze, if I remember correctly."

"No," said Kurtz.

"Pity," said the Dane. "You remind me sometimes of the product Mr. Swayze was advertising—'Takes a licking but keeps on ticking.' Catchy phrase." He led the way up steps and down the left tunnel. In a few minutes they came out in the first basement area. The bodyguard who'd been left outside the door upstairs was sitting on the damp floor against the far wall, his legs extended and his stare riveted on the dark tunnel opening. There was a bullet hole in the center of his forehead.

"I know now why you're called the Dane," said Kurtz.

"Oh?" The thin man paused again. He looked vaguely amused.

"I used to think it was because you were from Denmark, but I don't think that's right," said Kurtz. "Now I think it's because every time you're around, it looks like the last act of *Hamlet*."

"Very droll," said the Dane. "Tell me, what is Dr. No's mistake? I saw the film many years ago, but I do not really recall it."

"Dr. No's mistake?" said Kurtz. "In all the Bond films—in all those stupid movies—the bad guy gets Bond or whoever in his clutches and then just keeps talking at him. Yadda, yadda, yadda."

"As opposed to . . ." said the Dane with his small smile.

"As opposed to putting two in his head and getting it over with," said Kurtz. He led the way up the final stairs.

The Dane used the keys to lock both padlocks. Up in the basilica proper, the Dane stopped to look at the central nave under the huge dome. Only a few old women were in the huge space, kneeling and praying, one lighting a votive candle to the right of the altar. Someone was still practicing the organ. The air smelled of incense.

The Dane handed Kurtz Kennedy's keys, including the keys to the La-forza SUV. "Be careful of fingerprints . . . no, I do not have to tell you that."

"Can I drop you somewhere?" said Kurtz.

The Dane shook his head. He'd removed his natty hat and Kurtz noticed that his blond hair was very thin on top. "I believe I'll step in here and pray for a minute or two."

Kurtz nodded and watched him step away, but then called softly, "Wait, please."

"Yes?"

"Do you ever take assignments in the Mideast? Say, Iran?"

The Dane smiled. "I've not been to Iran since the Shah's downfall. It would be interesting to see how it has changed. You can reach me through the Countess if you need to. Good luck, Mr. Kurtz."

Kurtz waited until the Dane had found a pew, genuflected, and knelt to pray. Then Kurtz went outside into the surprisingly bright morning light.

CHAPTER
FIFTY-THREE

Kurtz took the afternoon off. He cleaned up his apartment area as best he could, stopped by Gail's place later to tell Arlene that she could go home and take Aysha with her if she wanted. He picked up his Browning and cell phone while he was there. He stopped by Blues Franklin and returned the Ray Charles sunglasses to Daddy Bruce. He turned in early that night.

The headache did not return. Kurtz wondered idly if he should have taken the taser off the bodyguard in the catacombs in case he needed more shock therapy to get rid of the headache if it ever did come back. Maybe he could write some sort of paper about it for the AMA Journal or something.

The next morning, he was driving the repaired Pinto to the hospital when he saw that he was being tailed by a Lincoln Town Car. Kurtz pulled to the curb on north Main, reached under the seat to get the Browning, and racked the slide. It had taken him an hour to find the bug in the Pinto the previous evening, and he was tired of all this surveillance crap.

Gonzaga's man, Bobby, got out of the Lincoln and walked up to the Pinto. Kurtz thought that the bodyguard didn't look his best in a dark suit—actually, he looked like a fireplug that had been poured into a suit. The black ninja outfit had been more becoming on him.

Bobby handed Kurtz a sealed envelope, said, "From Mr. Gonzaga," and walked back to his Town Car and drove off.

Kurtz waited until the black car was out of sight before tucking away the Browning and ripping open the envelope. Inside was a cashier's check for one hundred thousand dollars. Kurtz set the check and envelope under the seat next to the gun and drove the rest of the way to Erie County Medical Center.

Rigby King was alone and conscious when Kurtz came in. They'd moved her overnight from the ICU to a private room. There was a uniformed officer on guard, but Kurtz had waited for him to step down the hall to the men's room.

"Joe," said Rigby. There was an untouched breakfast on the swing tray near her. "Want some coffee? I don't want it."

"Sure," said Kurtz. He took the cup off the tray and sipped. It was almost as bad as the stuff he made for himself.

"I just got a call from Paul Kemper," said Rigby. "With some very surprising news that you might be interested in."

Kurtz waited.

"Someone wasted your mafia girlfriend's brother in a maximum security federal prison yesterday afternoon," said Rigby.

"Little Skag?" said Kurtz.

Rigby raised an eyebrow. "How many mafia girlfriends with brothers in maximum security prisons do you have, Joe?"

Kurtz let that go and tried the coffee again. It was as bad as the first sip, only colder. "Some sort of yard shank job?" he said, knowing it hadn't been.

Rigby shook her head. "I told you—Little Skag's been kept on ice at a *maximum security* federal hidey-hole. Up in the Adirondacks. No general population. He didn't see anyone except the guards and feebies, and even they got searched. But someone managed to get in there and put a bullet between his beady little eyes. Incredible."

"Wonders never cease," said Kurtz.

"Why do I think you're not totally surprised?" She struggled for a minute with the gizmo on a cable that raised the angle of her bed. Kurtz watched her struggle. When she had it the way she wanted it, she looked exhausted to Kurtz.

"Do I know who shot me yet, Joe?"

"Yeah," said Kurtz. "It was Brian Kennedy and some of his guys."

"Kennedy? The security snot? O'Toole's fiancé?"

"Right. You got suspicious on Sunday—realizing that Kennedy's alibi didn't really hold up . . ."

"It didn't?" said Rigby. Someone had brushed her short, dark hair and it looked nice against the pillow. "I thought Kennedy was on his private Lear when you and O'Toole were shot."

"Gulfstream," said Kurtz. "He had two planes."

"Ahh," said Rigby. And then, "*Had?*"

"I think Kennedy took off after shooting you. He may be found. Maybe not."

"Where did he shoot me?"

"In the leg?" suggested Kurtz. The coffee was not only bad, it was now totally cold.

"You know what the fuck I mean."

"Oh. Your call. I think they're going to find his fancy SUV in Delaware Park."

"Or what's left of it, if he was stupid enough to leave it there," said Rigby.

"Or what's left of it," agreed Kurtz. He set the coffee cup back on her tray. "I've got to go. Your guard cop is probably finished pissing by now."

"Joe?" said Rigby.

He turned back.

"Why did I suspect Kennedy of shooting his own fiancée? And if he shot me in Delaware Park, how'd I get to the hospital in the middle of the night? Inquiring minds will want to know."

"Jesus," said Kurtz. "Do I have to do all your thinking for you? Show some initiative. *You're* the goddamned detective here."

"Joe?" she called again just as he was about to shut her door.

He stuck his head back in.

"Thank you," said Rigby.

Kurtz went down the hall, around a corridor, and down another hall. No one was guarding Peg O'Toole's room and the nurse had just stepped out.

Kurtz went in and pulled the only visitor's chair closer to her bed.

Machines were keeping her alive. One breathed up and down for her. At least four visible tubes ran in and out of her body, which already looked pale and emaciated. The parole officer's auburn hair was stiff and pulled back off her face where it hadn't been shaved off near the bandage over her forehead and temples. She was unconscious, with a snorkel-like ventilator tube taped in her mouth. Her posture in coma, wrists cocked at a painful angle, knees drawn up, reminded Kurtz of a broken baby bird he'd found in his backyard one summer day when he was a kid.

"Ah, goddamn it," breathed Kurtz.

He walked over to the machines that were breathing for her and acting as her kidneys. There were various switches and dials and plugs and sensors. None of the readouts made any sense to him.

Kurtz looked at his parole officer's unconscious face for a long moment and then laid his hand on the top of the nearest machine. It had been one week exactly since the two of them had been shot together in the parking garage.

His cell phone vibrated in his sport coat pocket. Kurtz answered in a whisper. "Yeah?"

"Joe?" It was Arlene.

"Yeah."

"Joe, I didn't want to bother you, and I've hesitated to ask, but Gail needs to know about Friday . . ."

"Friday," said Kurtz.

"Yes . . . Friday evening," said Arlene. "It's . . ."

"It's Rachel's birthday party," said Kurtz. "She'll be fifteen. Yeah, I'll be there. Tell Gail that I wouldn't miss it."

He disconnected, not interested in hearing whatever Arlene was going to say next. Then he touched Peg O'Toole's shoulder under the thin hospital gown and went back to the uncomfortable chair, leaning forward so it didn't press against his bruised back.

Sitting that way, leaning forward, hands loosely clasped, speaking softly only to the nurse when she came in from time to time to check on her patient, Kurtz waited there with O'Toole the rest of the day.